↗68

66-13469

Rikhoff, Jean.
Rites of passage. New York, Viking Press ₁1966₁

I. Title.

PZ4.R573Ri

Rites of Passage

RITES OF PASSAGE

Jean Rikhoff

New York · The Viking Press

First published in 1966 by The Viking Press, Inc.
625 Madison Avenue, New York, N.Y. 10022

Published simultaneously in Canada by
The Macmillan Company of Canada Limited

Library of Congress catalog card number: 66-13469
Printed in U.S.A. by Vail-Ballou Press, Inc., Binghamton, N.Y.

The lines of verse on page 61 are from "Forgive Me" by
Dilys Laing, first published in *The Carleton Miscellany*.
Copyright 1963 by Carleton College and used by their per-
mission.

For

Mark and May 15, 1964

Jeffrey and June 5, 1965

It is not necessary to be blind to the tragic limitations of life to affirm the importance of as yet unrealized possibilities.

—Helen Merrell Lynd,
On Shame and the Search for Identity

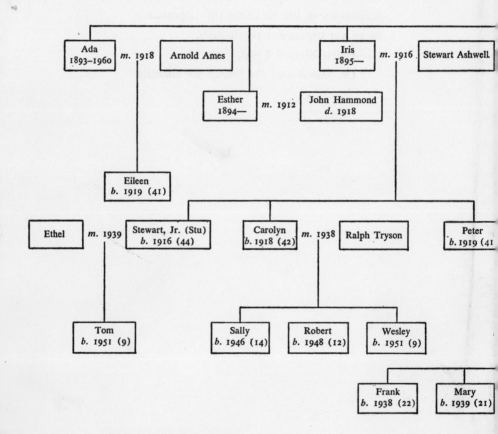

| Ada 1893–1960 | *m.* 1918 | Arnold Ames | | Iris 1895— | *m.* 1916 | Stewart Ashwell |

| Esther 1894— | *m.* 1912 | John Hammond *d.* 1918 |

| Eileen *b.* 1919 (41) |

| Ethel | *m.* 1939 | Stewart, Jr. (Stu) *b.* 1916 (44) | | Carolyn *b.* 1918 (42) | *m.* 1938 | Ralph Tryson | | Peter *b.* 1919 (41 |

| Tom *b.* 1951 (9) | | Sally *b.* 1946 (14) | Robert *b.* 1948 (12) | Wesley *b.* 1951 (9) |

| Frank *b.* 1938 (22) | Mary *b.* 1939 (21) |

NOTE: Ages of the descendants of the five Timble sisters are given in parentheses as of 1960, the year in which *Rites of Passage* opens.

TIMBLE FAMILY TREE

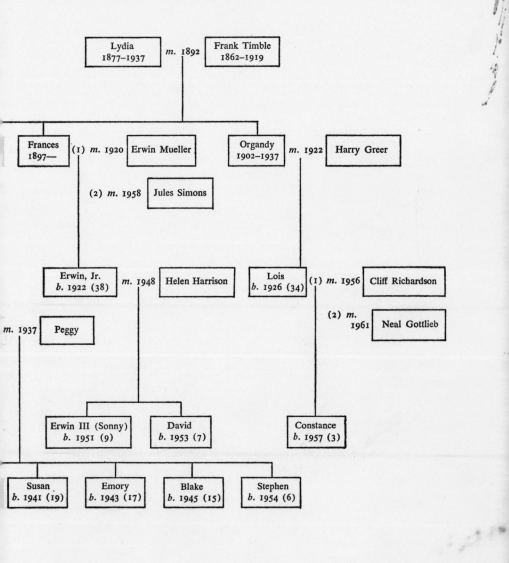

Lydia 1877–1937   *m.* 1892   Frank Timble 1862–1919

Frances 1897—   (1) *m.* 1920   Erwin Mueller   Organdy 1902–1937   *m.* 1922   Harry Greer

(2) *m.* 1958   Jules Simons

Erwin, Jr. *b.* 1922 (38)   *m.* 1948   Helen Harrison   Lois *b.* 1926 (34)   (1) *m.* 1956   Cliff Richardson

(2) *m.* 1961   Neal Gottlieb

m. 1937   Peggy

Erwin III (Sonny) *b.* 1951 (9)   David *b.* 1953 (7)   Constance *b.* 1957 (3)

Susan *b.* 1941 (19)   Emory *b.* 1943 (17)   Blake *b.* 1945 (15)   Stephen *b.* 1954 (6)

Rites of Passage

Chapter 1

THE MOMENT the hand rested on her shoulder, Lois knew. Though she hadn't seen him in ten years, she would have recognized his touch anywhere. "Neal," she said. A moment later she was in control; she held out her hand to give formal attestation to the encounter.

"For a moment I wasn't sure it was you. It's been such a long time." He kept hold of her hand as if he didn't know quite what to do with it; then he looked down, embarrassed, and released it.

Music had started, loud and tinny; the wooden horses were beginning to go up and down; Lois watched while her daughter gripped one of the poles tensely, the reins of her black horse hanging down around the animal's ankles. There should have been another child on that merry-go-round, an older child who might be on the big horse next to Constance's black one, smiling encouragement, hers and Neal's child. But of course the man beside her couldn't know that. She had never told him. Now, ten years later, he stood beside her, a man who had no idea he and she had once created life, and that he had helped to destroy it by his inability ever to commit himself completely.

Or at least she had thought he could not.

"Which is yours?" she asked.

"None. I just come to watch the other parents. My favorite Saturday sublimation, watching other people's children, other people's lives."

The carousel swung round them, a whirl of color and blurred children, grating noises and high shrill screams. Yet above all that thickening noise came one clear piercing call: from a little

3

blind girl whose parents had carefully strapped her upon her horse. Arms flung out to the air, sightless eyes upturned into an unknown sky, face transfixed by joy, she sent up exclamations so intense they drowned out those of the other children. As her wooden horse, bobbing faster and faster, undulated beneath her, her cries grew louder and louder. "Look, look, Mama! Look, oh look, Daddy!" But of course they could see.

The horses were working up and down furiously; tears stood out in Lois's daughter's eyes. "I wish they'd slow that thing down," Lois said. Just as he was about to signal the attendant, the motor stopped grinding, the machine began to lose power. In another instant the revolving dais had slowed enough for Lois to jump on. She was surprised to find Neal beside her.

"This is an old friend of Mother's," she said, unfastening the thick protective strap that had been holding her small daughter to the horse. "We used to know one another a long time ago. Before you were born, Constance."

The carousel was still going, slowly, in a soft peal of whistles and stiff steam sounds. The revolving circle, the moving horses, the shaky platform, the music, the blind child, meeting Neal again: Lois felt slightly sick.

Then the music broke off; with a jolt the merry-go-round came to a halt. Lois lifted her daughter down from the wooden horse, and Neal held out his hand to help her.

Constance looked away.

"It's the age," Lois said, taking her daughter's hand. "Three doesn't like strangers." She had been about to say "outsiders."

Lois lifted Constance down from the platform onto the ground. She saw the parents of the blind child putting another ticket in her hand. All about her children dodged in and out, screamed, scuffled, scurried over the gravel ground, under the dark park where the curled leaves were staring into the stillness with a thousand autumn-colored eyes. Constance ran toward the zoo and the high iron fence where, by their strong young legs, children were hanging head downward, arms flung out.

From the distance came the murmur of new voices, in back the music and steam of the calliope began again, on the path sun filtered through the trees, gold glistened everywhere—in the air, in the trees, on the path ahead, most of all in their sunstruck eyes.

"What's your name? Can you tell me your name? You do have a name, don't you?"

"Constance," Lois said, "Neal asked you a question. Tell him your name."

There was no answer.

Lois bent down. "Constance—"

The child looked at her. She had Cliff's face, Cliff's coloring, but she would *not* have Cliff's obstinacy. "Constance—"

The child mumbled; Lois accepted this as token defeat.

"I didn't know you'd married. I figured you would of course, but I just—just didn't hear."

"It was overseas, in Greece."

"Your husband worked overseas, he's an American?"

"We met over there and we got married over there and I had Constance over there, but it didn't work out, so now I'm back." That was, really, the sum of it. Except, of course, about how hard coming back on her own had been at the beginning—no money, having to find a job, having to leave Constance with someone else all those hours she was at work.

"Ten years," he said, "a long time. People *do* get married, have children. . . ." They had stopped, an unexpected intrusion of beauty had brought them both up abruptly. In front of them, in the heavy golden light, Constance was bent over, examining the red and gold leaves. She had plucked a blood-red one from the carpet around her feet and was looking at it intently. She held it up, she moved it close to her eyes; she transferred it nearer her nose, then she put it into her mouth.

Suddenly she spat. But now she knew what a leaf was.

"And you? What have you been doing?"

"The usual, everything and nothing. I went on working at the old job, got bored with it, quit, took off for Europe a while— yes, even stable old conservative me—but really it wasn't any big break, people are going back and forth across the Atlantic every day. I went thinking I'd spend five or six months, find out —oh, I don't know—what it was all about. But that kind of life wasn't for me, or maybe, to be more accurate, I wasn't for it. I got tired of the museums and the cathedrals, those awful seaside resorts, all the things you're supposed to see—even the crematoriums," he said in a strained voice. "So I decided to come back—"

They had stopped again, a squirrel scampering about Constance.

"—got another job, found another apartment, another girl, you know the story—settled down, got bored with the job, gave up the girl, repainted the apartment, began looking around for something I really wanted to do. Finally went back to school. Law, I'm a lawyer now."

Lovely cold logical Neal, all he needed was the proof of how messy other people's passion could be to reassure him his own life had order, symmetry, was sinless. He must be very satisfied now, seeing it all in such simple strictures in the briefs before him.

He was standing in a glaze of sunlight, a tall thinnish man with thick dark hair, in a very self-contained body that valued *control* above everything else.

My feelings always gave me away, Lois thought, rendered me defenseless to my enemies and foolish to those I loved. A dangerous way to live: exposed.

Leaving Cliff, Constance not even a year old, coming back to New York, finding an apartment she could afford, and job-hunting: a bitter experience, watching the small amount of money she had borrowed from her cousin Carolyn dwindling at a frightening rate, still faced with the major chores of the day when she got home: the apartment to be cleaned, meals to be made, bottles washed, sterilized, and filled with formula, laundry to be done (in the damp sinister basement where the washing machines leaked soapsuds and the dryers inexplicably turned themselves off and on without regard to the 'coins put in them). There were clothes to be mended, ironed, sorted, and all the while her mind ticked over and over, like a meter, measuring out the money she was spending in lights, soap powder, carfare, food, rent, babysitters, cigarettes, shoe leather, stamps, an endless exhaustion of funds, and where was she to find a job: just any job, she was beginning to think at that point—how would they live, just survive?

Lois always remembered that as the time she lay awake nights watching lights on the ceiling. Car lights came slowly, crept across the white expanse overhead; the bus lamps were big, bold, thrusting things that lighted up the whole room. In her crib Constance slept noisily, unaware of how close to the end their resources were.

It was a time of intense awareness, as all periods of trouble and change are. It seemed to Lois she had never seen her life more clearly—or in such brutal terms. She was young, she had intelligence (hence the scholarships in college, the honors degree), a certain amount of beauty (her husband, at the beginning in one of those odd flights of fancy men in love indulge in, had said she reminded him of what wine should taste like and didn't; in spite of the quantities of liquor he drank, he never developed what the women's magazine she finally got a job with described as a palate). It seemed to her she had wasted everything, the talent, the looks, the capacity to enjoy life; worse, the potential for a future that would offer for all that waste some justification, a stamp on her life, like the embossment on a coin, that marked it with a value all its own. Some women might find their value reflected in the lives of their husbands and children, but even if the marriage to Cliff had not gone wrong, Lois doubted this would have been enough for her. There was something in her that reached out; she wanted a distinction, a mintage, all her own. The breakup of the marriage had only accelerated, she felt, a longing that had been there all along.

Yes, a bad time, impossible to tell to Neal, under these trees soldered in gold and green and leaves colored the blood of the sun, how bad it had been. Instead she said, "When we came back, I had to have a job, of course"—how insignificant and common it sounded, as if one simply went out and selected work as one picked out peaches from the corner market—"and finally I found what I thought I was looking for." She named the women's magazine and saw his eyes raise in appreciation of its circulation, its sleekness, its occasionally avant-garde fiction. "They were going to let me do write-ups on books and the theater, new movies, art—you know, what they call 'The New York Scene.' Not at first, of course, I had to go through the break-in period, to see if I had the 'touch' "

—an ability, she might have qualified, to reduce the most complex problems to the absurdest simplifications, and of course to throw in the *bon mot,* wit with wisdom, as the older woman over her, being moved up, said with such awful sincerity. "So—" Her voice trailed off as they went down the steep stairs that led to the bears' cages, her heels knocking against the concrete, his hand faintly for a moment guiding her arm, all women on such stilts were in peril; those terrible hours trying to write short, snappy paragraphs about the celebrities rather than their work. "And I didn't—" breathless at the bottom, wondering how to say that she had failed, as she had—"didn't have the 'touch.' I read fiction now. Once in a while they let me take something I like. It's not too bad—and they pay well." Always *that* final vindication for all the grievances left unsaid. The results of all her battles, if she could have brought herself to state the truth, might be seen in exactly three stories in as many issues, and those spread over two years.

She paused, considering the man beside her, hardly handsome, a dark, brooding face (so much of him might be described in those giveaway terms—dark, brooding) but lovely hands. One was lifted now, offering her a cigarette, beautiful long tapered fingers; she could not at that moment imagine them turning briefs, yet she could very well picture them pointing at the members of a jury. Did he go before juries? What kind of law was it he practiced? She asked.

Corporate law, he said, beginning an explanation from which at its very opening, "Nowadays these big companies have to . . ." she found her mind disengaged, humming along to itself: Did your job, looked after your child, and when you occasionally went out, so careful to give the impression you were not to be touched *in any way,* least of all in your heart. No, not many of those men called back and those who did tired after one or two more attempts.

It was not love they were looking for, she thought in protest. Love would have altered their lives. They wanted—the picture presented itself and she rejected it.

Ladies like you, she told herself, who don't have children to turn to, buy Siamese cats. And examine themselves, thus sheltered, in front of the mitigating influence of animals. Tamer than these —they were at the bear cages—but nevertheless able to be viewed in anthropomorphic terms. My aunts would say I should never have left Springfield, Illinois and its salutary soil, where women were meant to be wives, mothers, and helpmates—and the men went to Chicago on conventions supposed to unburden them from more than the pressures of the mercantile world. They buried those black-laced episodes as dogs bury bones—sometimes remembering where to retrieve them, sometimes forgetting. The meat-packing capital of the world, why worry?

I am afraid of the sickness of sex, I long for an old outworn world where some of the kinder things still have use, she might have said.

In the first cage brown bears were standing on their hind legs, begging food. A middle-aged, tired, dyspeptic man was throwing peanuts, two children near him shrinking back, half-afraid but giggling. "Look, Daddy, look at his tongue," one said. Their father grunted and looked, uninterested. The children clung to him, bursting with the pride of his courage. In most instances cabbages must be made into kings.

Lois took Constance over near the big grizzly; he was sitting, patient and sleepy, staring out into the sunlight, his huge claws curled round his bosom, resting—but ready.

They moved on; ahead the bright umbrellas on the terrace of the cafeteria. For a man—she counted, Neal must be thirty-seven or -eight—to end up at that age alone was hardly a recommendation of reliability. Strong ties to the mother, too strong; sexual fears, but who didn't have them; basically infantile emotions, but weren't they all in the same boat; emotionally at the (oh, those lovely categorizing words) anal stage, unable ever to pass beyond to the adult genital one.

Wasn't it perhaps just possible he had never found the right girl?

When the right time came, the right girl presented herself. "I always thought you'd marry. I always pictured you with some nice"—she paused—"Jewish girl, quietly, *contentedly*—"

"I'm not the contented type," he said, as if reciting a statistic from one of those obscure academic journals that specialize in articles on alienation. "I never was." How, then, did he reconcile corporate law with his own image of the outrageous? It was impossible to imagine him trudging the streets of Europe searching for his soul, even less conceivable that he should turn to her, as he did now, and announce, "Very few are, unless forced."

"And law is the force?" she could not prevent herself from asking. "You've chosen the right game, then, haven't you, Neal? The others aren't exempt, but you are."

They were close to a quarrel. A contrary, impossible, ridiculous thing, the human heart, so many compartments where the disguises were donned and where, at the end, these were found to be not masquerades but costumes of choice from our own illusions of ourselves. The last thing in the world she wanted was to argue with him. Yet, as if over ten years had not passed, they were able still—and easily—to wound each other. But wasn't that, after all, what love was?

I belonged to Neal for years and years, she thought. The hand, the lovely hand curled around the cigarette, and the body, glowing with that radiant flesh, pressed close to mine, and the words, all those words I poured out to him, she thought, while he listened, silent, shut off, naked next to me, so naked no clothes would ever cover him, but it was I who was always talking. Wasn't that the real reason for my love, he let me open myself up?

Was it not also true that all along I wanted his child, that it was a drive I would not admit to myself, a desire of which I was afraid, hoping that somehow he would know, as he seemed to know so many things, without my telling him. Proud Beauty, he once said, and made me into one. So that in the end I could not force him to the final test of love, fearing that we should fail one another, that the purity would be gone forever. I never told him about the child but went and had it cut out.

You would not say the word love and I killed the child, and what is there left now? she might have asked him.

And answered, Only the regret, the endless, immutable regret, for what might have been. And wasn't.

Can we ever go back and redeem the wrongs of the past? she
asked herself and had no way of knowing. *Who did?*

They had been lucky to find a table along the edge of the open
porch of the cafeteria where, over the heads of the crowd, they
could see the seals. It was almost feeding time and people were
hurrying to finish, leaving the tables laden with crumpled paper
napkins, dirty dishes, cartons empty of milk and orange drink.
On most of the tables there stood two sentinels, the mustard and
ketchup. "I'd like some kind of salad. Constance, a hot dog. One
milk and one beer. The milk is for me and the beer for Constance,
in case you're wondering."

He was looking out over the crowd. "She'll be able to see them
fed from here." He looked at Constance, waiting for some sign
of recognition. The child stared down obstinately at the table. She
was not going to watch the seals fed.

Then he was gone, swallowed up by a stream of people flooding
through the swinging doors, large ladies laden with Bronx accents,
young lovers dazed by the dream, the disaffiliated in leather jackets
and strange shoes, odd old mumbling men, and young mothers
that two or three children had undone.

Who was it who had maintained that all passion founders on
reality? The habit of mind necessary for desire required a propor-
tionate kind of negation; otherwise it rapidly disintegrated into
servitude. One had only to look at the tired, scorched faces of
those mothers with dangling, whining children at the ends of their
hands; love had burned them with its brand—submission, sub-
jugation, spiritual emptiness.

I am an empty woman myself, she thought, closing her eyes.
A question of belief, she told herself, of *wanting* to believe.
I am not sure of this, she thought.
Nor of many things.

All about her, people went as if secure in the knowledge that
they had a place in the chain of being, whose reliable and recognizable and valuable place was like that medieval one somewhere
between the angels and the animals. Did they ever see, as she
saw so clearly at that moment, that the whole condition of life

might be tyrannized by the incessant demand for love? Could they not envy, all of them, the ephemera, born at dusk, dead at dawn, whose only purpose in life was to reproduce, so that they came into the world without mouths, and had neither need to eat nor drink nor look upon the sun?

She had been willing to have Neal refuse her the word love itself, if in some manner he could have shown he was capable of understanding its concept, but she had waited in an urgency of anticipation that was never consummated. Though he was often at pains to execute the act itself, his was a spasm which shook the body alone, left the heart untouched.

"Tuna-fish salad, hot dog, beer, milk, and—ice cream. One roast-beef sandwich, two Miller High Life. A piece of pie—for whoever wants it."

Constance did not look up. Instead she put out her small dirty hand and pushed first the hot dog, then the ice cream, away. "I have to go to the toilet," she said. "I have to go to the toilet Ihavetogotothetoilet—"

"Cigarette?" Neal asked.

Bending over, Lois took one from his pack and waited, head to one side, while he put a match to its end, seeing the seals at an off angle as they lifted themselves out of the water and begged in hoarse, impassioned voices for their meal. She had a momentary understanding of how sailors in other ages might have made the transformation from mundane mammal to mystical mermaid, as she knew all distortions of vision clouded the distinction between the real and the romantic.

"You never even called."

"No."

"Why not?"

"I went home—back to Springfield. For a while. To get away. But I came back. *You* could have called."

"I did, the first couple of weeks, but no one answered and after a while—well, I had my pride, too. Not a word, no explanation at all, you just disappeared."

"I didn't disappear, Neal, I just went away for a little while. Home. To Springfield."

"But why? What was it? Without any explanation at all."

She wanted to tell him, she knew she owed it to him to tell him all that had happened, but it was something she had never been able to tell anyone, not even the husband to whom, for at least a little while, she had been close.

Flesh of the same flesh, she thought, looking at her child. Husband and wife, we loved each other. In the beginning I never dreamed I would one day feel so much hate for Cliff that I only wished him dead; and in the end I could never understand how it was that I had loved him so much that I had measured out my life by him, but for a while it was true, I lived my whole life through him.

"I didn't think we were going to make it," she said to Neal. "And I didn't want a lot of scenes, I didn't—I don't know—I just thought it was the easiest way out, for both of us, to go away. We didn't—we didn't love each other the way—*you* were the one who could never use the word love, remember?"

"Mama?"

Lois lifted a napkin and began to make amends to the small stained face trying to get her attention.

"More, I want more ice cream."

"Later. You won't be able to eat it if you get it now. Wait until a little later."

Mercifully, Constance accepted the notion as part of the workings of her mother's world. She began to squeeze ketchup into her empty ice-cream dish. "Don't do that," Lois said automatically.

Constance set the plastic container back next to its yellow counterpart. "Let's go down let's go down let's go down and see the seals."

Lois put out her cigarette and, in one almost instantaneous and completely reflex action, picked up her purse, looked at the sky questioningly for clouds, for an increase in wind, decided Constance could do without her jacket, rose, and then—remembering Neal—paused, the steady chain of everyday behavior broken, and looked down, uncertain, in confusion, for, preoccupied as she had been with the child, she had not even noticed whether or not he had finished the pie.

"Now I'll never get an explanation out of you, I'll never know why you ran away—without a word."

No, he probably never would know.

She took Constance's hand, and against the beauty of the day they ran, the sun shining against the water ahead, the seals slipping slowly into the glittering pond, the last of the fallen leaves, the late ones, rising on a small stroke of wind. So long as there was sun there would be warmth; only at night came the cold, the dark, and the scenes you could not shut off. She knew them all well, segments from a cinema that ran over and over inside her mind, which she was forced to view against her will. They came at random and in their own time, as if crying out, Redeem the wrongs of the past, go back and make amends, make amends. . . .

Where did you start? You could not resuscitate the child. Then with the mother whose suicide seemed to imply, even though you were only ten, a failure? With the father who less than two years later stopped sending checks for support and left, with a new wife, for the West?

With Eileen? How could she ever make amends to her cousin Eileen, Eileen who had been mad these ten years, never let out of the house, loved too much by the mother who had nothing else to show for her affections and not enough by the father who fed his ego on alcohol? Eileen had loved a man for years and years, and you came back to Springfield, and he left Eileen, he came all the way to New York to claim you after you fled Springfield: *and then you didn't even want him.*

But I can explain, Lois wanted to cry out. If you just give me a chance, I can explain.

I was torn and afraid, having left Neal, with the child gone. I didn't even know who the man was when he phoned that day in Springfield. Just some man who wanted to talk about Eileen. I only knew later, when it was too late: he wanted to marry her and her mother hated him and wouldn't let Eileen go. I felt sorry for them. Why wouldn't I, after what had happened with Neal?

I was still weak from the operation. Operation? *The abortion.*

He took me to that bar, we drank brandy. He kissed me in the car. On the way out to my grandmother's. Came to New York after me. And I sent him back—I *tried* to send him back to Eileen.

But not before you had thought it all through, that relentless voice inside persisted, not before you had decided to take what you could. I know, oh I know, the voice said, I know *all* there is to know about you.

All right, love was something I wanted, like everyone else, something I supposed I had a right to. If Neal wouldn't give me love, there were others who would, Lois answered stubbornly. It wasn't as if I started out intentionally to—

We judge end acts on original intentions? the voice asked.

I do not know how we judge at all, Lois answered. Then, after a moment, she added, Maybe that is what it is all about, finding out how to judge.

And how do you judge yourself? Even though you did send him back, the fact remains—

The fact remains, I went up to the Planned Parenthood Center. I had to have something safe. After Neal I couldn't face—

Three times. The first time the place was closed. The second the nurse was there, but no doctor. Come back at five-forty-five, the girl said. I went. Afraid. They might look at the face (my face) and see: not married, an abortion, that. It had taken a lot of courage even to get to the point of lying the first time, and I had bought a Woolworth wedding ring, and then when I got to the door it was dark and locked; the second time I screwed up my courage the doctor wasn't there; the third time I just didn't care any more.

Your name? Your husband's name? the nurse asked after she had written mine.

Neal Jacobson, I said.

How long have you been married?

Three—no, three and a half years.

Any children?

No (shaking the head).

Preventatives?

We used—condoms, I said. It was true, but I didn't tell her about the failure. Now they have the pills, the perfect peach-colored pills that prevent you from producing the all-important ovum, but then . . . But then, too, she thought, you never think the bad things can happen to you.

Reasons for change?

(Thinking) I don't like it—psychologically, I said. (Taking out a cigarette, lighting it nervously), I don't think that's the way one loves, with those.

What?

I don't think that's how one loves.

We haven't space for that. And it doesn't really answer the question. (She looked at me expectantly.)

I just heard about—the diaphragms.

(Silence. Shuffling of papers.) Go to the bathroom. Remove your pants. Empty your bladder.

The nurse was odd, perhaps only distracted. I had some difficulty finding the room. One toilet was stopped up, the other okay —just. I bent over and stepped out of my pants. I took a tissue and tried to clean myself.

You can get through anything, I said to myself quietly, not to go through that other business.

Then it came to me: Is the gift of love, one I am making in uncertainty, not even sure it is love, worth this? I stood, pants in hand, looking up first at the harsh white light, then down at the tile floor patterned with footprints. Be very careful, the lights above said. Remember the last time you trusted, the prints on the floor spelled out.

I remember, I said, and went out into the office, smiling on all the frightened faces who looked up at me and seemed to ask, How can we ever be sure? How can we ever be safe?

And I looked back at them, thinking, We can never be sure
We can never be safe
Never

And the nurse said, You can go in now. And after I came out, she said, Ten dollars.

And it was paid.

Cheap, at any price—save the price of trust.

Having learned my lesson: Never count cost when you commit yourself.

It's already too late, I thought. Once begun, no cost counts, it's too late to count costs.

There was just one last question, in the elevator going down, that came to me: If you really loved, you wouldn't be here in the first place, would you?

Withdrawal. Condoms. Diaphragms.

Preventatives, whined the elevator.

And this, of course, was what I had found out.

We cannot love that to which we cannot give ourselves

Fully

And I knew that this was true, because that man my cousin Eileen loved, who had left her and come to New York for me, I knew I had no right to let him make love to me. I had wanted him badly enough to go for the diaphragm, but I did not want him enough to have a child with him.

He never made love to me, she thought. Most of that was not having the opportunity in Springfield, where I wanted to. Part was perhaps Eileen, something I owed to Eileen; but the major part was chance, she told herself, never mind what you knew later, going down in the elevator, that there would never be love, real love, between the two of you. It was being home in Springfield and a man who put his arms around you when you needed it.

I had made up what I thought might be love out of my need, nothing more, she thought, and so I sent him away. I never want you to come back, Stan, I said, while he watched my face to see if what I was saying was true.

Give me a chance, he said, just let me try, I know I can make you happy, just give me the chance. And I stood there unable to answer, I was still hurt, still huddling over the hurt that was the destruction of my child and the shame of betraying my cousin.

I looked at that man who should have been saying all the things he was saying to me to another woman, to my cousin Eileen, and I thought, In Springfield you held me in your arms. In Springfield you seemed someone I was able to love. But in New York none

of this is true. You are a stranger on whose lips the intimate words
of love seem all wrong.

But how could you say to a man who had left a woman—your
own cousin—to come to you, Go away and never come back?
I don't really love you, it was all a mistake, it was something
strange and indefinable that happened because you were unhappy
and I was unhappy and the time and place made it seem right,
but it was never really right, and now we must repair the wrongs
we have done.

"Go back, go back to Eileen and make it right," she had finally
cried out to him, while he stood with a face set as if in stone and
said, "I can never go back. It's too late now. It can never be made
right"—as, of course, it couldn't. You could never go back to anything and remake it, and that's what she knew and could not face.

"I want you to go back," she had cried, "and try to—"

He didn't even answer as he went out. He was too decent for
talk.

"Don't, *don't,*" the child cried, rigid with fright.

"What is it? What's the matter?" Lois asked, taking hold of
Constance's shoulders, gazing into a face stiff with suspicion. A
moment before her daughter had been hanging onto the railing,
delirious with delight. The seals were still gliding through the
opaque waters, bounding up unexpectedly to snatch a fish, to
dip down and disappear under the water again, yet the child was
shrill with grief. What had happened?

"Don't don't *don't* . . ."

"Constance—"

"Don't don't—don't let him—"

"What is it? Just tell Mama, what is it?"

"He wants to hold—to hold—to hold me *away.*"

"But honey, he was only trying to help, to lift you up so that
you could— Stop it, Constance, Neal was only trying to hold you
up to the railing so you could see better, he wasn't going to hurt
you."

Inconsolable, the child sobbed on. "Please don't cry," Lois
pleaded, half understanding that some kind of test was being put,

not to her, but to the man beside her. Angry and impatient at the absurdity of the whole situation, she smothered the child against her. What had Neal done to her daughter that *he* should be on trial?

He's not her father, Lois thought, that's what he's done. He's the father she should have and hasn't.

"I'm terribly sorry," she said over the tousled head buried close to her shoulder.

"It's a shame," he said in a matter-of-fact voice. "But I suppose she's just tired and ought to go home. And I was about to suggest we go over to the ponies and— I wonder if they still have those pony-cart rides. But, of course, if she's so tired—"

The sobs subsided. In a moment equilibrium would be restored, anger replaced by approbation. Constance still believed in prizes for which you did not pay. She did not see what might lie behind a gift. When you were older, Lois knew, no such strange and marvelous belief held. You went back to the old understanding that savage spirits ruled the world, that in some dark corner of the universe the accused—any one of them—stood while the judges waited for the telltale singing bone of the dead, the murdered man's hand, to speak. You did not buy your way out nor did anyone step forward in fief for you. Only the young—and perhaps the mad, like Eileen—believed in a bright world.

Was the house where Eileen lived still shut up, blinds pulled, the windows gray blank eyes like those Greek statues that look out on the world unable even to pretend they see what goes on there? Was it as carefully closed off from the world as it had been five years before when Lois had pulled the car up, not sure whether Ada or Arnold would answer the door and let her in to talk to Eileen?

What could she say to Eileen to undo what had been done? I never made love to him—I know you think I did and that he left you because you wouldn't, but it isn't true, Eileen, I never did. Here in Springfield I would have, but there wasn't the opportunity, and in New York everything was different, I couldn't. Going to bed for me has to mean something, Eileen. It's hard for me even when I care.

No one answered the bell, her pounding. Loyal, fierce in her protective motherliness, Eileen's mother had set herself against the world, against even Arnold, her husband. No one would ever have the chance to pity the child who was lost somewhere where even her mother couldn't reach her.

Lois knew someone had to be inside. Eileen never went out, Ada never went out, Arnold seldom—but Lois supposed the habit of years was ingrained; it was said tradesmen came only to find no one would answer for the things that had been ordered by phone. Sometimes Ada shouted from an upstairs window; occasionally she opened the door a crack; more often the men from the stores departed in disgust, leaving the things they had brought on the back step or taking them away again, refusing to bring them back.

Determined, Lois went around to the back door. "Aunt Ada, Uncle Arnold, it's me, Lois. Uncle Arnold," she hollered at the top of her lungs, "AUNT ADA, it's LOIS."

There was no response. The warmth of the week before had melted most of the snow; only a few patches of grainy remains pockmarked the open earth. The grass lay beaten, brown, inert. An ugly landscape.

No way to the sea, no way to the mountains: Illinois was a rich country that somehow, without any of the natural barriers, imprisoned the people who lived there. Made their minds flat like the land.

"Aunt Ada, Uncle Arnold—please, it's Lois. Won't you open the door?"

Was it her imagination or had she seen a blind move at the far window? "It's important. Please open the door—*please.*" She smiled brightly, trying to show how friendly she felt. The door had opened an inch. "Is that you, Aunt Ada? I came to see Eileen, won't you open the door? Please—Eileen—*Eileen*—"

"She's not here," Arnold said abruptly, opening the door a little wider.

"Not here—I mean, when will she be back? I'd like to—"

"She's not coming back—at least not if they keep her. They don't know if they'll keep her. She has to stay for observation.

Then if they think they can do anything with her, they'll let her stay. They don't keep the hopeless cases. I won't know until next Thursday, but even so she can't have visitors. That's what the doctor said. They have to have her a while before they let anyone come. Even me. Strictly no visitors, not even family, it agitates the patient too much. I'm sorry, but you've missed her. If you'd come sooner—well, it probably doesn't matter. She doesn't know people anyway. Not any more, just her mother and me. And then when her mother took sick—"

"Aunt Ada's sick?"

"Nothing much, just her ticker isn't what it should be. A complete rest, the doctor said. She's resting up—upstate. Near Eileen. I'd ask you in, but the house—well, you know what a house is like when a man's batching it."

"Can you tell me where they are? Iris will want to know. Even if she can't go see Eileen, she'll want to know where she is. And of course if Aunt Ada's—"

"She's at the sanitarium, Eileen's up north at the sanitarium."

"You mean the *state*—"

"Well, you pay some. I mean, it isn't all free. It's a very good place. I went up and looked at it myself. Real fine people who run it, a very high-class type personnel who work there. I can't stand here, Lois. I haven't been well. That long drive. All this sickness. I'm in a weakened condition myself. I stand around here in a draft this way, and I'll come down with a virus or something."

The door shut. She stood in Arnold's back yard and stared at the raw ground, rubbed clean of grass in spots like sores on the back of the earth; she looked at the scaly grass, the patches of dirty snow, and all she could think was, My god, oh my god, the state sanitarium.

She hadn't known then the worst of it: that Arnold had taken Eileen there while Ada was in the hospital and couldn't keep him from doing what he'd been threatening all along.

It was a long, tiring drive and the doctor had warned her on the phone that she probably wouldn't be able to see Eileen. "Then she's going to—to stay?" Lois had asked.

"It's a strong possibility," he said guardedly. "With shock treatment such cases sometimes respond. Of course there's no way of knowing for sure, but—"

"But you feel—encouraged?"

"We feel—encouraged."

"I don't know how much Mr. Ames told you," Lois began. "I mean, about how all this started." She paused, but he gave no encouragement; on the other end of the phone he waited, silent. "I mean, I know something about it because I was sort of involved." Did the quick intake of his breath show interest? "I was responsible," she said, confessing for the first time. "It was my fault."

"I'd like to talk to you," he had said.

She had been surprised at how uninstitutional the place looked, impressed by the air of authority the staff had, as if they really held some secret knowledge of what went on inside the mind. Medicine and magic—the priest-healers, she thought, and held out her hand to the doctor, who took it as if measuring how much treatment, how much therapy, she was in need of. She was as fearful going into his white bright office as she might have been at the solemn killing and eating of the totem animal, her own tribal Host. Did not the guilty who ate die? Even in the Christian doctrine of transubstantiation the old underground gods proved their power. What was the belief that he who eats his Lord in Sin shall die but the cannibalistic practice of homeopathic magic?

The doctor held out cigarettes and Lois took one. How could you say to this firm, disinterested man, I am afraid for us all, even you? We do not understand life, we do not know what death is, all we have is the constant compulsion to confess even the crimes we have not committed but have wanted done.

A manila folder lay in front of him, a stencil identified EILEEN AMES. There was in that thin folder what these men thought they knew of the workings of Eileen's mind, of the things that had made and destroyed her life.

"I don't know whether Uncle Arnold—Eileen's father—whether he told you about what really happened—at the end, I mean. She —Eileen—had a lot of problems from the beginning, but if it hadn't been for what happened at the end—" For a moment Lois closed her eyes, unable to go on.

Then she started again. "It was one of those families, a mother and father who never really got along. I guess Ada—Eileen's mother—wanted to leave Arnold lots of times, but—well, she didn't, she couldn't, because of my grandmother. My grandmother was an awfully strong Catholic and she had a lot of influence over all the girls. There were five of them. All girls, no son. Maybe that says something about the whole thing, I don't know. I always thought it did.

"And so she didn't leave, Eileen's mother, she stayed with him —with Arnold—and it couldn't have been easy," Lois said, looking away. Over the desk there was a picture of a happy good-natured man, smiling, supremely confident. He looked like the kind of man whose luck had held all his life. DWIGHT D. EISENHOWER, the script underneath read. "He drank—a lot—Eileen's father, and I guess he got pretty violent sometimes. Things weren't too pleasant. Anyway, Eileen and her mother were awfully close and then she started to go out with this man—I mean, years and years ago, when she was in high school, I think—"

Lois fumbled and he produced cigarettes again. After a moment she bent forward to accept his match from across the desk. "She went with him for years and years," she said to those almost colorless eyes across from her. "And they were always going to get married, only they never did, and then I came home to Springfield—on a visit—" Now, she thought, *now*. But the breath was gone from her. She waited, looking into the swatch of sunlight cutting across the doctor's desk. Now.

"And he called me, he wanted to talk about Eileen. I met him downtown." There was no need to tell about the fainting, the brandy afterward at the bar, but about the feeling—yes, she would have to explain about that. "And something happened between us. I don't think I can explain it, I've never really understood it myself, we just sort of—" The doctor was watching her. "We were terribly attracted to one another," she said painfully. "I guess that's the way you'd put it.

"There was a party, at one of my aunts'. Iris—the one who

brought me up." No, she didn't have to say anything about her mother's suicide. That didn't have anything to do with it. Or did it? "And he called me there. He called me and—and Eileen heard me talking to him and—and that was the beginning of her being —being the way she is now. But she wasn't really—you know— bad, until after he came to New York and I sent him back. It was as if my not wanting him made it worse."

The doctor picked up a pipe, fussed getting tobacco in; he was frowning, the tobacco not settling properly. That annoyance made him seem for the first time human, a man circled round by his own awkwardnesses. Finally he reached over and took the matches, struck a flame to the bowl, and sucked on the stem. "And that was when she started to—retreat?"

Lois bit her lip and nodded.

"And her parents—the Ameses—never had—any—any—professional advice?"

"I don't know. Didn't Uncle Arnold—"

"Her father says not, but I thought perhaps the mother—"

Lois shook her head. "She was an awfully proud woman—it's a proud family."

He worried his pipe. After a moment he said, "And you feel—"

"I feel it's my fault," Lois finished for him.

"You helped," he said, looking away from her, staring out the window. What did you see out through that thick protective wire mesh? "But it wasn't all of it. Not nearly all of it. If that's any comfort," he said, swinging around letting those light, lifeless eyes rest on her. "In my opinion it would have come anyway, you weren't really responsible; you were only a catalyst, not an innovator. She was disturbed for a long, long time before the eventual breakdown."

Did he really mean to take away her sin? *Could* he? No. He was only a scientist probing fact. But wasn't it perhaps possible that in the end God was the only truly scientific fact, the one they could all never know, no matter how much evidence they brought in?

He stood up. "I appreciate what you've told me. I hadn't heard your part of the story—just from her father that some man had jilted her." The word *jilted* sounded old-fashioned and forlorn, just right for Eileen, the forty-one-year-old woman who played with white mice and dressed dolls. "If they had done something right away . . ." His voice died, emotionless, without even sorrow. It was all out of his realm.

"But there's hope? You think there's hope?"

"There's always hope, or we have to believe it in this business. Otherwise what would be the point of going on?"

Eileen was in a ward, sitting at a table with seven or eight "adults," working with rushes. Busy, interested, talking only intermittently, all remarkably adept with their hands: damaged brains didn't prevent their bodies from operating adequately.

Lois stood in the doorway, waiting for instructions from the nurse who had been assigned to show her around. She might, the doctor said, see Eileen and speak to her. If Eileen got up and wanted to come with her, Lois could stay for a short visit; otherwise he would prefer her not to press the matter. In the early stages they tried to keep the patients as undisturbed as possible. A feeling of security often helped to . . .

The woman directing the activities looked up with a quick birdlike glance, smiled meaninglessly in their direction, then went back to showing her patients how to use their materials. "We'll wait until she looks up," the nurse at Lois's side said.

Two of the patients were talking; one had gray hair primly mitered in curls all over her head; the other was a shrunken old man with granulates on the lids of his eyes. Suddenly the two commenced to giggle; all around the table eyes came away from work and focused on the pair.

When Eileen looked up, she stared at Lois for a moment; then she leaned across the table and brought her face next to the gray-haired woman's. "Naughty," she said sternly. "Nurse says that's naughty—not to be serious about your work."

She hadn't known who Lois was at all.

But now at this golden moment of the day, in this far-away park when the sun lay almost in ruins all about them and a small smudge of darkness had begun to overpower the sky, it was not the pain of that moment that Lois thought of, but the pleasure of the pressure of warm, firm fingers on her arm—that touch she had never in all these years forgotten, Neal's special unmistakable touch, which, it seemed to her, she would never not know, even when she was old and barren and gone with age, a small insignificant figure waiting for the end—even then the warm live remembrance of this touch, Neal's special touch, would come and move her and make her, for a moment, happy, even as, after all that had happened and unbelievable as it seemed, she could be happy now. He had that power.

Chapter 2

IN SPRINGFIELD, Lois's cousin Carolyn sat in front of the vanity and brushed her hair, trying to stroke away tension inside her skull by the rhythmical pull of the brush. She was thinking of Lois, wondering what she was doing at this moment far away in New York. For once in her life she would have liked one of those long, indolent phone calls so many women she knew seemed to exist on. Other women saw the world as it was: diapers and dinners, sewing up stuffed animals, enduring whines and complaints, separating siblings and soothing rivalries, indulging husbands, braving the fact that the majority of couplings they began never finished for them in anything save fakery or failure; resigned to tomorrows that were endless repetitions of today, with nothing to look forward to but the impoverishment of their energy, a permanent nearly paralytic exhaustion that turned no wheel save the one that broke their butterfly beauty; wondering where the self that had once been the nucleus of a personality had vanished or been vanquished; yet growing old smiling, imperturbable, content with their toy houses and funny connubial games. They had been loved. That threw the veil of mystery over everything.

Odd that, though growing up in the same house, she and Lois had never been the least bit close then. The age difference: when you were young, eight years made a tremendous difference. Later you only looked for someone a little like yourself. Their not being close at that time no doubt had something to do with Sans Souci, too—her mother's house made of love an iron yoke; it was not a family, the Timbles, blessed by any belief in indulgence. Indulgence led to indigence. God forbid.

It took a great talent to know how to love, a greater one to show it successfully.

Carolyn considered—briefly—her mother. Her mother didn't drink tea because she said it made her liverish, didn't drink coffee because she believed it turned her teeth yellow, didn't touch milk because someone had told her it was terribly fattening (never mind the toffees and chocolates, the forbidden sweets in the secret places); good cold water sufficed, and if it was good enough for Iris Timble, it ought to be good enough for everyone. A Midwestern life of good, clear, cold water, and Lois had run off to foreign parts.

Carolyn brushed. She had (it was said) her grandmother's head of hair: thick, coarse (it held the curl), auburn. Not her grandmother's tiny hands and feet. Her mother was the only one who inherited those. A "good" woman, her mother: she had taken in Lois, her dead sister's child, and raised her, as the expression went, as one of her own. It came to Carolyn that in any objective view of things Lois would probably be considered a better child to her mother than the children of her own flesh. Lois had (god help her) an open heart.

Carolyn laid the brush aside; her mind settled on the old familiar image she always had of her cousin. Hot, perspiring, panting, she and Lois dropped down on the dust-gray grass, laughing, Lois flung the tennis racket beside the empty can of balls, reached over and plucked a long weed with a wheatlike end, and began to suck it. Behind her the blue sky was like a furnace, the trees flames of green. Somewhere a cardinal was calling insistently and, all about, the insects sent their song up to that incandescent sky. It was August, and Lois was getting ready to go back to college, fifteen years before, when Ralph was away at war.

It was the first time in my life I was free from all the worries about money, about belonging, Carolyn thought. Carolyn Ashwell, of the Green Lawn Boarding Home (née Sans Souci), the one all the girls looked at oddly because her mother took in roomers, the one the boys shied away from or got fresh with too soon. And then Ralph Tryson, rich Ralph Tryson, came along and married me and suddenly I was Carolyn Tryson, someone to be envied: charge accounts at all the best stores, member of the country club, the Junior League, going to conventions in Chicago and New York a couple of times a year, and some day, if Ralph could only get the time off for a trip to Europe, even that. Three lovely children, a nice big home, and always the indulgent husband. Lucky, lucky Carolyn Tryson. That's what people must have said.

Away from Sans Souci, the Green Lawn Boarding Home, Springfield, Illinois: the world, her mother's world—boarders, beds, faulty plumbing, the attrition of a lifetime of failures wearing away at everything. Complaining, overeating, her mother would crawl to her grave pulling behind her the shattered remnants of a bad marriage, the iniquities of endless ill-advised schemes, the inadequacies of her children, her house, her husband, herself.

Carolyn thought of her father out there, lying upstairs in bed like something broken and unfixable, left about in the hope that someday something could be done to repair him. He could not be thrown away, the Timbles never threw anything away; squirrels and savers all their lives, they hung on until death even to what they did not want.

Pity me, her father's eyes cried out, I have had such a miserable life. I have failed in everything, oh pity me, pity me.

He scarcely ever spoke, he only looked. His eyes were sad, his mouth slack; he folded his hands in remission of all his sins. Bless me, Father, for I have failed, his blue-veined, parchment-like hands prayed. A prayerbook of excuses: Iris never wanted him to do this, Iris never wanted him to do that, Iris thought they should . . .

While her father lay inert, immutable, her mother scurried. Life was an endless rushing—mending, measuring, cooking, planning, ordering, serving, washing. It was the boarders who badgered her mother night and day: when they were there, with their endless demands; when they were not, with their interminable needs. Panting, gasping, her mother flew up the stairs, made beds, gasped at the sight of the bathroom, raced down, found brush and polish, rags and powders, raced back, bent, and scrubbed. When she was upstairs, the floors groaned under her weight; when she was down, the halls echoed with the heavy sighs that were always on her lips. Life was heavy, aching, awful—duty—except for the stolen, secret moments at the drawer where she kept the forbidden candy, the exotic nuts, the rich creamy chocolates and stuffed dates, the fudges and caramels, the beautiful boxes of pralines and Russian mints.

Her mother, her father, the boarders—it was as if all the occupants of that house had been caught in an unbreakable bond, imprisoned together in their failures and shortcomings. Yet they felt no pity for one another; like people ashamed of their identities, they slunk in and out, avoiding conversation, ducking behind doors to avoid chance meetings. Only mornings was there a brief lifting of the pall that hung, drapelike, over everything. Risen recently from sleep, freshly washed, in clothes that had spent a night of freedom from the anxious odors of their owners, the boarders ringed the scarred old oak table downstairs, brooding over their watery coffee, slowly swallowing their cold cereal, momentarily bemused over the chewing of their overcooked toast, but giving off an air of anticipation. It was possible then, for an instant, to imagine them as other people, marrying, begetting children, buying a new house, getting a better job, owning a shining expensive motor car—having something to show for their lives. But by the end of the day, when they crept back from the petty chase of their wretched careers, they were again themselves; when they gathered at night round the table, dread battened down the house like an ancient curse. No one went out evenings, lights never burned late, the lives of those within were spent in the dark, generating fear.

Might I not have been a different person, Carolyn wondered, not one whose capacity for love seemed diminished or warped, if I had grown up in a place of love, not in a house where the man and woman first fed on one another, then on their children?

Still, it was a sorry excuse. It was not her mother who was to blame for what had happened, or her father, lying in his bed with someone constantly having to watch over him as if he were an infant, but herself; no one else had chosen the man she had married, or borne him three children, two in duty, and one, the youngest, in a brief belief in passion; a woman who had come to grasp at any straw, any chance, to prove there was still in her a spark of hope, the youthful belief that better things lay ahead. Like love.

It was as if now, after all these years, her body had suddenly rebelled, demanded the attention it deserved from those countless times of the past when her husband had made love to her and left her aroused, unfulfilled, on edge, and she had inwardly shrugged and said, *Well,* as if it didn't matter.

But it had. All those innumerable nights of frustration had finally piled up until now she was like an open invitation for debasement, as if all her senses cried out for satisfaction, all her openings for enjoyment.

It was Myers who had made her feel again, Myers with whom all secrecy, all sense of shame, had vanished. He knew things about her that not even pride had prevented her from revealing. She wanted him to degrade her. Without the refinements he brought to their illicit beddings, the capitulations would soon have ended. He held her by innovations and aberrations, by the coarseness of his desire and the brutality of his seductions. There was nothing he did not demand of her and nothing she refused him. It was as if some kind of sickness had taken possession of her, but one she reveled in after the long tedious couplings with Ralph, whose dry, joyless love-making settled over her like fine volcanic ash that threatened, after years of inundation, to bury her in boredom, in paralytic decay, in the fine silt of redundancy, Ralph throwing himself on top of her, making love as if he were straightening up his desk, sharpening his pencils, arranging his papers, changing the date in the calendar holder, getting out the files, opening up the dictaphone, blowing off the dust—clutching her and panting into her ear, frantic, "You ready? Can you?" What was she supposed to say—no? And then, more frantic, "You ready? You ready? *Now,*" and then falling down on top of her asking that unanswerable question, "Did you?"

What was she supposed to say for god's sake—no?

She pulled the hair stiffly back from her face and combed it full out on her shoulders. Eyes, large and wary, stared back from the whiteness of her face, eyes large and knowing, too knowing; they were almost laughing. In punishment she brought the brush up and began to pull it vigorously through the heavy auburn hair that, had it not been tinted, would have been streaked heavily with silver. Every five weeks (a statistic of some sort for Ralph, who loved figures if not always the facts they represented) she had it tended under the competent hands of Opal, whose own head glittered orange and whose fingers, tipped in purple, gave an impression of some aborigine let loose from a far-away exotic isle. When Opal turned her head, the hoops in her ears swayed; when she bent forward, the black lace of her slip showed. Opal was vulgar, Opal was loud—but Opal was, unaccountably, happy. What Carolyn felt, looking into those heavily mascaraed eyes, was an envy hard to hide, just as now, what she felt, looking into her own eyes, was an impatience she did not bother to conceal. She looked the woman she knew she was: baffled, cheated, in search of a meaning for her life. If Opal was happy, it was because she had made herself so.

I have blamed Ralph for so much, for the despair, the disappointment, for the fear itself, even in a way for Myers, as if my emptiness had been *his* fault—for if I had not been so afraid I would not have run to find something, anything, to pin my heart to, like a child who needs to be loved, who desires to be loved in place of having the desire to love. But illusion was what mattered, I was in the realm of illusion where all was possible, most of all love, when what I wanted was someone who wanted me. Myers found me beautiful and desirable, made me feel I was in possession of a body formed for pleasure, convinced me the devil should have his due. I stop sometimes to marvel—Carolyn Ashwell, happy.

She closed her eyes and for a moment sun struck inside her head. Under an open sky, she was running, she was laughing, Lois had brought her racket down on a small white ball and was racing toward the net, a challenge on her lips, and Carolyn saw herself reach up, up, in a dazzle of blue sky and tilting green leaves, heard from the field across the way the hoarse raucous sighs of the peacocks, and fell down onto the court, watching the ball drop behind her. We were happy then, or so we thought.

Why are we happy so little of the time and then only in some small unplanned moment? Why is it the things we set our hearts on are taken from us or held too high, like the ball, for us to reach?

The deepest wrongs of all, she thought—having given your life to the wrong things, knowing how inadequate you are.

But with Myers each instant was unbearably sharp, as if each were an unwarranted, a prohibited, pleasure to be tasted and tested, every moral and ethical means called into question, defied, violated, all the rules overrun, all the restraints broken; they were explorers of sensation, there was nothing, nothing they would not sink the senses in, so that flushed, panting, sweating, they fell on each other like enemies determined—destined—to shatter the structures that underlay their lives. Desires had driven them to debasement, and the uncertainty of the future had made the present even more impassioned, as if all else had fallen before the will to feel, as if they were emptied of all else except lust.

You ready for it? You want it? he asked, knowing she was always ready, she always wanted it, that all she lived for was those moments when they were locked flesh to flesh, fighting for pleasure in that internal combat which was an aptitude for love; time meant nothing except the cruelty of his arms, the affliction that was his embrace. She thought of the times he deliberately kept her from coming, impaled at the peak of desire by being cut off from fulfillment, and he bent over her, smiling—oh, that smile—*you want it, don't you? Well, you're not going to get it, not now,*

maybe in a little while, but not now, not now. The time he brought
the cigarette down on her stomach. The time he bit her breast
until the blood came. The time he . . .

Together they had gone beyond all the limits of experience,
they had found their proper place in a scale that included the ape,
the bat, the rat, the roach, and the reptile.

Across town he waited; in another hour, if all went well, she
would be in his arms.

"They haven't *arrested* Esther, have they, Mother?"

It would have been too perfect; life so seldom dispensed comeup-
pances where they were due that Carolyn could hardly believe the
chickens, as her mother was wont to say in her special way, had
come home to roost.

The thief (like Esther) prospered, the honest man remained
honest—and poor. In the land of prosperity who honored the
poor? (Only the people who died young and unfulfilled, like
Agee.) One of the things money bought was the right to your own
oddities. God knew, Esther had enough of those. She should have
been domiciled in the British Isles, where they understood the
excellences of eccentricity.

Yet it was said of Esther of the eyes like agates, the inevitable
brown bag in grubby hands, that terrible voice bent like a bandsaw
cutting off one cliché after another, that she had loved her husband
passionately, to the exclusion of all else. Such a thing seemed impossible, but Carolyn had learned (painfully) that people are often
more than they seem. Somewhere a part of Esther perhaps stayed
suspended in the fantasies left over from that love. Miracles did
matter; that was why they had to occur.

Her mother brought current matters to hand. "No, no, they
haven't," she said. "But—"

"Well, then, what are you getting so excited about?"

"But they're *holding* her, Carolyn, down there at that department store. They won't let her go until we come down and get her,
sign something."

Putting her signature on anything terrified her mother; she felt
she had committed herself for life and, worse, it might C-O-S-T.

Her mother's life had been a long series of charges which she had paid ungratefully, duties for which she had no devotion but which she executed to the letter of the moral law, payment—no more, no less—to what was expected of her. All her gifts were begrudging.

The telephone would ring until the day Iris died, and someone would be on the other end demanding something she would have to give. Niggardly in her assets, miserly in her acceptances, her poor fat foolish mother would be, in a sense, down on her knees polishing her floors and doing her duty when everyone else failed.

But Carolyn had gone past the point of caring. What occurred to her now was not the trouble and torment she would have to go through with her mother and her Aunt Esther, but that this was her afternoon with Myers.

"Carolyn—*Carolyn*?"

"I'm here, I'm just thinking."

"Well, what should I do? I can't go down to that store by myself, Carolyn, I just can't. The disgrace—" Her mother's voice went up an octave. "Everybody will know. Everybody. You can't hide a thing like this. I mean, it was decent of them not to have her put in jail—they caught Esther redhanded, Carolyn. Redhanded. She was stuffing wool gloves in one of those brown bags she always carries. She had seven pairs already, Carolyn, and— oh, I just can't face it, it isn't fair I should have to face it, not after all I've been through. I called Frances and do you know what she said, Carolyn? You won't believe it, I couldn't believe it myself. Frances said, 'I'm in the midst of my improvement hour, I can't go anywhere now.' "

Frances lived on flattery as most people exist on the oxygen in the air. The type—in the female of the species at least—was easy to identify: it went clanking about (as Frances did) in the tomfoolery of costume jewelry, made an assault of every glance, endlessly awaiting approbation, demanding it; and yet if you had cut your throat to show Frances how much you cared, she would only have complained of the mess you made on her floor.

Frances was one of the stalkers, but the hunt had taught her something, too, of the shyness in all creatures, even herself. Somewhere, long back in the past, she must have once been a young girl whose eyes dreamed out an asking of absolution. From long ago, when Carolyn used to have Ralph pick her up at Frances's, ashamed of her own home and the boarders, she remembered the odd ragged doll she had come upon dangling from the bedpost in the conjugal room and the expression, trapped for a moment unwittingly on Frances's face, as her aunt looked away, saying in a soft voice, "I have it there—you know—at my time of the month so . . ." So, Carolyn had finished for her, my husband won't make—you know—love. There was a delicacy in such an act Carolyn could not before have conceived of in Frances. She was a Timble, one of the girls.

The girls, Grandmother Timble's five: Iris; Esther; Ada; Frances; Organdy, Lois's mother, the youngest, the one who had committed suicide years before, leaving of the five four and of the four two in mortal conflict, Ada and Esther; for what love had once joined together, money had soon split asunder. You never really know the members of your family until you try to settle an estate.

Ada, the oldest, the ugliest, the unhappiest, could never forgive her mother's complicity in not making Esther give back the money she had taken from old Aunt Clara. Her grandmother had set great store by the dollar, why shouldn't her daughters?

It was a family with no sense of proportion, no ability to value things for what they were really worth. Afraid of what everyone else thought but callous to one another's demands, they acted grand and extravagant to outsiders, but were petty and parsimonious among themselves. They had all become spoilers of happiness, Ada perhaps more than the rest. But then she had better reason. She was the ugly one.

A homely face (hairy), ugly hands, thick wrists, lumpily veined legs, that quick nervous tic in her eyes—she fed on enmity and it ate at her. She went about communicating the anguish of abandonment, a desperate sense of desolation.

An unfair world, but the only one we have, Carolyn thought.

There was no way out of going with her mother to see what was to be done about Esther, and that meant she would lose her afternoon with Myers. She would have to call him at the office, something she hated to do, not because she had any apprehensions herself but because he did; it angered him, and his voice, when he acknowledged her call, was tinged with a barely controlled impatience that threw Carolyn into first confusion, then consternation, and finally fear; he was capable of being vindictive, Myers, and nobody knew better than he how to get back at her. The double edge of anger, the imperfect division of love—with a man like Myers a woman edged her way cautiously along the abyss of love.

"It's my sister, Carolyn, my own sister, you don't understand because you've only had brothers. Brothers can't be close to you the way sisters are. Esther's just like—like a part of me. Oh, I tell you I'm just glad Mama isn't here to see this. She had it hard enough with Organdy and then the way Ada and Esther carried on—"

"Listen, Mama, this isn't helping any, raking up the past. If we're going to try to do something, let's do it, only let's not sit around—" If she hurried, she might manage to salvage something, she might not have to give up the whole afternoon, she could see him later and if she was late coming home she always had the excuse for Ralph that she had been downtown with her mother. She could call Ralph, explain; she might even be able to get away for the evening. She and Myers could drive out to that restaurant outside of town where no one would see them, and afterward in the car—they had never made love in a car. An element of risk, the hazard of exposure, some dark deserted lane with the chance of a police car coming on them—just enough danger to give the evening piquancy but not enough to put them in real peril. She was sure the idea would appeal to Myers. He was the one who had taught her that the renewal of the senses rested on innovation, but she had a quicker mind for extremes than he.

"I'll meet you in front of the store—no, it's too cold, I'll meet you inside the front door, the *front* door, Mother, right by the umbrellas. In half an hour. All right?"

"All right, Carolyn. I'll call that man back. I'll tell him we're on our way. Oh, Carolyn, you don't know—"

"I know, Mother, I know. Please. I have to get dressed. Half an hour by the *front* door, next to the umbrellas."

She hung up, in despair. Myers might already have made other arrangements. Lately he had become touchy, was easily irritated, a different person from the man who had made the initial move of indiscretion. A party at the country club. Cocktails. She had on the Kelly green gown with the open back. They had got to talking. Danced. Drunk too much. Said things with their eyes.

Outwardly she supposed their behavior appeared no different than that of people all around them, a couple of compatible acquaintances letting themselves relax in the congenial atmosphere of the country club, but their eyes had sent messages over their cocktail glasses, on the dance floor their bodies had made exploratory motions against each other, when the music stopped they stayed up against each other for an imperceptible but meaningful moment.

He had not called her after that evening, though she had expected it. *Experienced,* she thought now, pausing, her hand on the phone ready to pick it up. Other men had made overtures before and she had always evaded them without offense, lightly brushed away the too familiar hand, adroitly outmaneuvered the determined drunk. So she had been expecting a phone call and debating whether or not this time she would venture as far as lunch. She was at the age for invitation, having passed through the disillusionment and despair of her marriage to the renewal of hope, that year she and Ralph had come together again in closeness, the year they bought the farm and she was pregnant with Wesley.

But the hope she felt that year had turned out to be another fabrication, a conscious and determined direction her mind had taken because if it had not selected an act of purpose at that point it could not have gone on. If she had not chosen to believe in Ralph then, she could not have believed in anything; everything had failed her, most of all herself, and the only thing that seemed admissible was the dark firm image that seemed to stand beside her—the final finishing with all the false illusions with which she had tried to support herself, the escaping of all pretense, an end, death, where no more was asked than the final dark peace of sleep.

It had come to a matter of selection—life or death; and in making as her payment the pledged flesh, Wesley, who had been named for that man who was Ralph's friend, long ago killed in a war no one remembered much any more, she had elected life.

What Myers must have known was what she had learned that first year after Wesley's birth: that all illusions emerge into the actual; in compromise one loses one's rectitude as well as one's righteousness; and there is no such thing as a final commitment; so that, patient, practiced, he had executed no such obtuse act as phoning, but stayed quiet, letting her imagination do his work for him. She had waited, wondering if, after all, her mind had made up what her body had wanted to believe until, almost a month later, she had run into him at the annual Easter ball.

Immediately he had come up to her and, as if everything was understood between them, as perhaps it was, moved her slowly and knowingly around the dance floor until, later, when they were alone, in the damp hall downstairs near the locker rooms, his hands had begun to do things that pre-empted forever her ability to abjure the ultimate. It did not even shame her to remember he had first had her the next afternoon in one of those cheap hotels downtown.

Her mother was standing in front of the umbrellas, nervously twisting her handbag, her fat little figure encircled with a nimbus of unfurled parasols pointing at the ceiling, where a gigantic display of Thanksgiving paraphernalia showed papier-mâché Pilgrims and Indians, plaster turkeys, and wax pumpkins. Next week this would all be gone, and the plastic Christmas carolers, the fake Santa, reindeer, and god knew what else would be cascading under these ceilings, trying to inspire the populace to spend.

"I hope you haven't been waiting long. I tried to hurry as fast as I could."

"Oh, Carolyn, I'm so glad to see you. I just—I don't know—

why is it, when anything happens, I'm always the one who has to see it through? Organdy—Mama—Ada and Esther—now Esther."

Yet her mother was like one, in long cold, who goes to the fire and spreads her hands gratefully against the warmth. If there was one thing she loved, it was the scent of the scuffle. Esther's apprehension had brought a youthful flush to her mother's face, a fine sparkle to her eyes as she pushed her way through the packed aisles. No doubt she was reconstructing (as Carolyn was) the central legend of thirty years or so before. Great-Aunt Clara had arrived on a "visit" at Carolyn's grandmother's, bringing a battered steamer trunk, a pile of wicker valises, and her pet hen Hetty. She had stayed until the day she died, a disagreeable odorous old woman. But wealthy. For this Grandmother Timble and the girls overlooked her faults. Clara eventually went, but the fortune—alas—seemed to be gone too.

Nothing ever *proved,* of course. But they all thought they knew that Esther, alone with Great-Aunt Clara when she died, had taken the money. Ada knew better than the rest; it was the kind of knowledge a woman like Ada would be less likely to dismiss than would her better-looking sisters.

Brooding, bitter, Ada would not let the matter rest, and the final quarrel had proved fatal. Ada said Esther had caused her mother's death because she had taken the money. Esther said it was Ada who was to blame because she had said those things over the after-dinner coffee; the family said—well, the money was gone, what was the point of compounding interest on a bad debt? And certainly, Carolyn considered, maneuvering her mother through Gloves and Purses, Bijoux and Beauty Aids, they were never going to get it back. Carolyn brought them to a stop in front of the elevator—her mother was afraid of the escalator, having, when it was first invented, seen a small child's fingers caught between the rubber band and the inlet. "Which floor is it? Business offices, I suppose."

"He didn't say, Carolyn, he just said they were holding her. Like a common criminal. Oh, I could just—"

"Don't," Carolyn said briskly and propelled her mother into

the elevator; the doors shut with a snap, the gears made a rattling noise. They ascended in a whir of machinery. A quotation Carolyn had read somewhere—where?—was in her mind.

. . . reality has nothing to do with the dream of a perfect love, as great and free as wind and—

She searched about for the ending, the part which at this moment, stranded in space between the floors of this gigantic warehouse of worldly goods, she needed, something to remind her of the world beyond this one, where a man she wanted waited. It seemed to her the inner time of her life was utterly different from that outside; the long hours of so many days, the senseless straining of week into week, months grinding by, were as nothing, like motionless shadows—the self—on the screen of existence. What we are, Carolyn told herself, is in sum the supreme sensations of our lives. And the rest of the quote came:

water. "We have loved each other," they say, but with the sadness one feels at the thought of never being alone.

Virginia Woolf: that strange, elongated, and oddly lovely woman who had believed life was a process of trying to join the broken, who had seen love as the only bridge that could be built across the great canyons that separated the cities of the self—or selves?

Her mother, gripping Carolyn's arm, moved closer. "Oh, I'm so nervous, Carolyn, you have no idea, I'm just—"

I am many people, Carolyn thought. When I am most identifiable—as at this moment—

"Third   Floor . . . Cafeteria . . . Business   Offices . . . Credit . . ."

—helping her mother out into the foyer—when I am most identifiable, as at this moment: Carolyn Ashwell Tryson, whose mother, Iris Timble Ashwell, stands at her side and whose husband, Ralph Joseph Tryson, has paid all those monthly bills for the twenty-some-odd years of their marriage, whose aunt, Esther Timble Hammond, sits in this store publicly accused of stealing;

saying, to identify myself unmistakably to this young woman strapped into earphones behind the desk and dealing with rubber ropes that connect this little inner world with the larger outer one, "I'm Mrs. Tryson, I believe my aunt's here, I believe there's been some trouble about my aunt, Mrs. Hammond," yet at this moment, when I am presumably the "I" I always am and will ever be, yet I am most in the act of becoming, for while I take on a role I often have to play, the respected wife of one of the better-known businessmen of the city, inside, oh inside, where the voice of the heart is heard, I lie back naked upon rented sheets and hold out shameless arms to a man who will, at the moment of making love, debase and defile me, knowing myself that the self is never the self but one of several selves warring and skirmishing, retreating and returning to attack that citadel of the body that seems the self, so that we are always in a state of siege, we constantly fall before a strong assault of the instincts or an impulse of abstraction of the intellect. It is not that we need to know our self but our selves . . .

"Sit down, Mrs. Tryson. Mr. Maynard will be right with you."

. . . and turned, seeing in her mother's face those signs of anxiety which had always seemed to Carolyn the central fact of her mother's existence, so that she said to herself, Mother is on the verge of hysterics, and then wondered what other sides of that self she recognized existed unknown inside her mother, shut up, imprisoned, and taken out only in the hours of darkness, where, in her own concealed eye, her mother was young and lovely with long lashes over velvet eyes and milk-white arms finding their way from the folds of a gossamer gown, she danced and laughed, she sipped punch and dangled a tasseled card before the imploring eyes of handsome young men. Might not, in the myriad ways of those mystic hours, her mother be young again? Might not one side alone grow old while another stayed lithe and gay and full of promise?

"Let's sit over here," Carolyn said, while her mother, pulling away, leaned over the counter that separated the receptionist from the rest of the room and brought her hand smartly against the wood so that the whole office resounded with her indignation.

"I want to see my sister," she cried. "I want to see my sister. *Right now*."

"Mr. Maynard will be with you—"

"That's not the name of the man who called. His name was— oh, I can't remember, but I'd know it if I heard it and it wasn't Maynard, I'd swear to that on a stack of Bibles."

"Mr. Tompkins?"

Her mother shook her head.

"Miller?"

No.

"Saybrook? Sargent? Bibly? Stircreast?"

None of them. Stricken, Carolyn's mother bent closer to the girl, watching her mouth for the magic word.

"Griswell? Carpenter? Nift? Wool—"

"That's it, Woolson, it's Woolson, isn't it?"

The receptionist plugged in one of the connecting cords; a light flashed, buzzing stopped. "Mr. Woolson? There's a—"

"Mrs. Ashwell, Mrs. Hammond's sister, he called—"

"There's a Mrs. Ashwell out here, Mrs. Hammond's sister, and she— Yes, sir, yes, I see. All right, sir, I'll tell her." She unplugged the cord, turned to Iris. "Mr. Maynard is handling the— the problem now. If you'll just be seated for a moment, Mr. Maynard will—" And she looked beseechingly over Iris's head; Carolyn moved forward and gently took the chubby arm.

"Carolyn," her mother said in a heartbroken voice, "they've been moving her from room to room."

"Well, we'll try to settle it soon. Why don't you sit down? There's nothing you can do standing and—"

"I couldn't sit down if my life depended on it, I'm just that unnerved. Why'd she do it, Carolyn? It isn't as if she couldn't afford them, she's got lots of money—"

A man was advancing toward them, the professional smile of the pacifier misrepresenting him. "Mrs. Ashwell?" he said, coming up to Carolyn and holding out a large ringed hand.

"I'm Mrs. Tryson, Mrs. Ashwell's daughter. This is Mrs. Ashwell, my mother—"

"Mrs. Ashwell?" he asked, fixing his hand now in front of the right person.

"Where is she? Oh, where is she? Is she all right? It's a kind of sickness." Carolyn's mother sobbed. "Something in the family, there was some Irish blood, way back, and it keeps cropping up. I suppose it's been there all these years and we just didn't see, we didn't want to see, we should have seen, only—"

"Now, now, Mrs. Ashwell," he said anxiously. "You mustn't upset yourself. Even in the best of families—"

"Why, my husband's grandfather was one of the most prominent men in the state. He ran for governor or something, people used to come for miles around to see our house. Teak floors. Real *teak*."

"Mrs. Ashwell, I'm sure—"

"She's sick. There's something organically the matter with her. She—"

The man turned to Carolyn. "Mrs.—?"

"Tryson."

"Mrs. Tryson, perhaps you—"

"You can't punish a sick person, they need help—"

"—we could settle this in the—"

"—medical attention, they're always talking about how it's a disease, well, Esther—"

"—other room. Your mother—"

"She didn't know what she was doing, that's all there is to it, she wasn't in her right—"

"—seems a little upset."

"—mind. Oh, another one, another house case, just like Eileen," her mother cried and broke down in sobs.

Carolyn took her mother by both arms and turned her around so that they were facing each other. She'd told Myers she'd meet him at five and it was after three now. Even if things went smoothly, it would be a tight squeeze. But if her mother insisted on throwing one of her emotional scenes, god knew how long it would take or where they would all end up. "Listen," Carolyn said fiercely, "just listen," and waited while her mother, sobbing and hiccuping, tried to bring her attention into focus. "You go sit down over there and stop this, you hear? You're only making matters—*Mother!*"

Her mother looked up, tears brimming over her eyes.

"Will you just go over there and sit down and let me handle this?"

"All right, Carolyn," she said, blowing her nose. "All right, if you think you can. I just don't have the strength—I'm a broken woman, this has just broken me into bits and pieces. After all I've been through with—"

"Mr. Maynard," Carolyn said coldly, turning her back on the noisy grief beside her, "if you're ready?"

He led the way through an aisle between desks where girls typing, filing, studying statistics, looked up curiously. Carolyn marched resolutely behind him, meeting each pair of eyes defiantly, head up, her beautiful sable scarves, a present from Ralph on her last birthday, the conspicuous statement of her status, the long white gloves dangling from the expensive alligator purse, conscious that the matching skin shoes on her feet, the beautifully cut suit on her body, the Liberty scarf at her neck, told an opposite story from the one of the not-quite-clean and grotesquely dressed woman sitting in Mr. Maynard's office clutching her brown paper bag, that receptacle in which she had tried to hide the stolen goods.

But Esther was not in his office.

Carolyn looked around, then turned, staring into the winking face before her; Mr. Maynard squinted.

"She's down the hall," he explained, screwing up his eyes, nervously extracting a pack of cigarettes, holding them out. "Smoke?" Carolyn shook her head. "We thought it would be better—I wanted to talk to someone in the family, in private, before—before I released her." He edged around his desk, dropped the used match in an oval ashtray, leaned forward, smiling, smoking, squinting. "Won't you sit down?"

Carolyn deposited herself in a leather chair.

"The thing is—ah, I hope you'll see our problem." He held up a sheaf of papers. "Our files. I've been going through them. Your family—you've been good customers of ours. Of course,"

he added, "your aunt didn't have a charge. But—well, I understand how these things are, some of the best families—" His eyes
narrowed until nothing seemed left but slits. "Yes, some of the
best families, but you must understand our position. We can't
afford to have our merchandise—well, taken without being paid
for. So—" He spread out his hands. "So—well—what we've done
in the past and it's worked out pretty well in other cases, I see
no reason why it wouldn't work in this, what we've done is insist
the person—the person who has this difficulty—stay out of the
store."

But how could he keep Esther out? If she decided she wanted
back in, she would come. "You explained this to her—to my
aunt?"

"Well, yes, I did, I tried to. But frankly—well, frankly, I don't
have the feeling she really understands, and that's where the
family comes in, Mrs. Ashwell—"

"Tryson. My mother is Mrs. Ashwell."

"Oh yes, excuse me. Well, that's where the family comes in,
Mrs. Tryson. If we don't prosecute this time, it's up to the family
to assure us they'll take the proper measures to see we aren't
bothered again."

"Well, we'll do the best we can," Carolyn began. "But—" He
had seen Esther, surely he must understand. "But—I don't know
—I mean we can't watch over her, Mr. Maynard, we can't keep
track of her every movement. She's got her own house, she comes
and goes the way she wants, I can't guarantee—"

"Well, then—well, then, that makes matters a little more difficult, doesn't it? I mean, if you can't assure us this won't recur,
we can't—can't—"

"Can't what?"

His eyes closing, he looked away. "Can't, I guess, pass over
the matter so lightly. I mean—you have to see our side of the
thing, Mrs.—Mrs.—"

"Tryson. I do see your side, I see it better than you know, and
we're—I'm willing to do everything I can but—let me talk to
her, Mr. Maynard, before I say anything more, will you let me
do that?"

"Of course," he said briskly, rising, pressing a button.

Carolyn stood up with him. The desk between them, they faced each other. "And if I can't get her to promise?"

"Let's cross that bridge when we come to it," he said with forced geniality as the door opened and a girl came in. "Will you take Mrs. *Tryson*," he said, smiling broadly, proudly, "down the hall to where—where that lady is, the one we had trouble with about the gloves."

"If you'll follow me," she said to Carolyn.

Esther was in an office two or three doors down, squatted on a couch, her legs apart, her hands hanging down, the paper bag dangling between them. Her hair was loose under an old hat Carolyn recognized as once having belonged to her mother, and there was a distinct line where the gray neck met the white face and she had neglected to wash.

"Carolyn," she said in her high breathless way. "Carolyn? I'm glad you came, oh I'm so glad you got here." She stood up, the paper sack clutched to her chest. "These people—*these people tried*—Carolyn, do you know what these people tried to say? Do you know, Carolyn, what these people tried to accuse me of, do you?"

"Yes, Aunt Esther, I know. I've just been having a talk with Mr. Maynard, he's the man—"

"You don't have to tell me who he is," she said scornfully. "I know who he is."

"Perhaps," Carolyn said, turning, "it might be better if we could talk alone."

"Oh yes, of course," the girl said. "Certainly. I'll be outside if you want me."

"I'm going to sue, that's what I'm going to do. I'm going to sue them for every last cent they've got. False arrest. Defamation of character. Public spectacle. They'll regret the day they ever tangled with me. I told that man with the funny eyes—you can't trust people with tics, Ada has one, Ada's had one all her life, oh I tell you it's a good thing she didn't see what happened. You won't tell her, will you? Oh, promise me you won't, Carolyn, you don't know what she's like, nothing's beneath her, nothing—like these people, sneaks, *spies*. If it's the last thing I ever do I'll make them regret the day they did this to me. They—they *grabbed* me," Esther said in a shocked voice, "right there in front of the gloves. This man *grabbed* me—" Plunged into recollection, overcome with humiliation, Esther sat down with a snap, tears gathered in her eyes. "Grabbed me . . . right there . . . right in front of everybody . . . he *grabbed* me . . ."

"Listen, Aunt Esther—"

"I'm a rich woman. I could write a check for two hundred thousand dollars right this minute. I'm a rich woman, you hear, a rich—"

"I'm sure you are, Aunt Esther, but the point is—"

"Where's your mother? Where's Iris? I told them to call your mother. I want your mother—"

"Please just let me talk to you for a minute. I just want—"

"I don't care what you want. You've never liked me, neither you nor your brother. I know that. *You* don't put anything over on me. Your brother Stu doesn't put anything over on me. *Nobody* puts anything over on me, not on Esther Timble, I haven't made my money by letting anyone put anything over on me, I'm suing, that's what I'm doing, and I want Iris as a witness. Where's Iris?" she demanded, standing up, outraged. "I want my sister. You go out and get her, right this minute, you hear?"

Glancing swiftly at her watch, which was moving toward four, Carolyn debated which would take less time, to argue on with her aunt or to get her mother. On the one hand, she was getting nowhere, but on the other the scene that would start when her mother and aunt were reunited . . . he didn't, he didn't *dare* . . . yes he did, Iris, right there in front of the glove department with everybody watching . . . he *didn't* . . . grabbed me, Iris, he *grabbed* me . . .

If ever there was a time for inspiration, this was it.

"Aunt Esther, you have a choice," Carolyn heard herself saying in a voice solid as stone. "You can either listen to me and do what I tell you or you can stay right here, in this room, until that man decides what he wants to do with you. I'm tired of all the talking.

I'm giving you three and then I'm walking right out that door and I don't care what happens to you and if you think mother's going to get you out of this predicament you're crazy. She's out there bawling and carrying on worse than a two-year-old child. You hear? THREE. One . . . *two* . . ."

Esther was at her side in an instant. "Don't go," she pleaded. "Don't leave me here. That man—oh, please don't leave me, Carolyn."

"Then you listen to me. Are you listening to me?"

"Yes, yes, what is it? What do you want to say?"

"You go out there and tell that man you'll never set foot in this store again, you hear? And you promise me right here and now you never will, you hear? And if—"

Esther's eyes were wide. "But why would I want to come back?" she asked. "After the way I've been treated, why would I ever want to come back? Wild horses couldn't drag me back. I won't even walk on the same side of the street. Because you know what, Carolyn? I wouldn't give them the satisfaction of ever getting any money out of me, that's what. I wouldn't spend one red nickel in here, not one. I'm going to live to see the day they come begging to me for my business, that's what. Come back? Ever come here again? Are you out of your mind?"

A quarter after five: hurrying, Carolyn plunged through the crowds, ready to make her assault against the night. The interior castles of the self were set to be beseiged, the bastions of pride waiting to crumble, the lonely fortress of the mind standing still, still and yet tense, waiting for the coming attack. In furs and flowers, begloved, ringed, scented, and powdered, she went to wage the war that would end in capture, the hardly reluctant captive in white expanses of sheets, the mind directing the final capitulation, the end of all her warfare not conquest but surrender.

She darted past dawdling pedestrians, pushed through the bunched salesgirls and tired businessmen waiting for the traffic light, pressed on past the throngs becalmed in front of the movie marquee, and turned left on Ninth Street, her breath coming in quick, shallow gasps, seeing ahead in the bludgeoning darkness the big black car, the dark shadowy figure of the driver hunched over the wheel. Along the street needle-stitchings of lights were sewing up a little path toward the outskirts of town; cars passed one another like stray dogs, lost and forlorn, determinedly setting out to find their way back home. Under the bright white light the black car humped and waited, its two head bulbs big cold eyes staring out sightlessly on Springfield.

Carolyn opened the door and waited, suspended in anticipation of his anger; then he bent over and took her arm, drew her in. "You're late," he said but he didn't sound too upset. A sense of relief began, slowly, to seep through Carolyn.

A moment later the big body of the car was nudging its way into traffic; the strong steady hands on the wheel spun it a little to right and left, weaving expertly in and out the rush-hour stream. Horns sounded, brakes screeched, but Myers, sure of himself, went right on.

"I hurried as fast as I could," she said. "But I got tied up." Shame prevented her from telling him how she had spent her afternoon. "Some family business, something I couldn't get out of. How are you? You look wonderful." Tentatively she put out a hand and touched him; in an instant his hand clamped over hers; in hard embrace he held it.

"Missed you—when you called—hell, I figured we'd have to put it off and as it is—"

"As it is what, Myers?"

"Let's wait and see, I've got to call Ginny later. Sandra's sick."

"Oh—I'm sorry."

"Sinus."

Then it couldn't be serious; Sandra was fourteen.

"You want to have dinner at the usual place?" he asked.

Carolyn sat quietly beside him; in his presence she could believe in the moment at hand, she was happy with what was, instead of what might be promised ahead. She felt, for a fact, a different person—less sure of herself, timid, even shy. She was afraid of not pleasing him, afraid of not being enough for him to keep on loving.

The city was sinking into a velvet gray dusk, and all about, for an instant unaware of the harsh well-lighted world, earth—lovely, lovely earth—included Carolyn in the circumscription that is belief. It seemed to her she had never loved before; love in her had been a demand, a sense of loss, a need, but never until now, at this moment when twilight touched the last edges of earth, had love been both a transference and an abridgment of joy, a poetry made up of the language of her own heart.

If they should live, she and Myers, a long time and continue loving, might they not learn how to live with life? What if they—

Resolutely she put the thought from her mind. He would never leave his wife and—and what? she asked herself. Something to do with Ralph and the children. Loyalty. Love, another kind of love. And we should keep the bargains we make.

The *bargains* we make? she asked herself and was confronted immediately by the image of herself in Myers' arms when she felt her body begin to come into its own, when the long tentacles of desire started up until, swollen, clutching, climbing, they caught her in one long squeeze of wanting, and Myers, suspended over her, looked down on the distorted face, the lust-lowered eyes, the open mouth and ready tongue, asking, as he always asked, "You want it? You ready for it? The business, you want the business?" and moved against her so that she felt him, large and hard, and cried out, then sank down into what should have been and never was a surfeit of sensation; he came closer and closer, using his hand to guide in and out, slowly in and out, the weapon with which he would desecrate her.

"What's the matter?" he said now, smiling because he knew.

"Nothing," Carolyn said in a hoarse voice. "I've just had a hard day."

"Why don't you break down, have a drink?"

She shook her head.

"It wouldn't hurt—relax you. I'd—" Keeping his eyes on the road, he said slowly, "I'd like to know what you'd be like with a little liquor in you. I'll bet you'd be—better. Even better," he amended.

"I don't drink any more."

"Couple of drinks never hurt anybody."

"With me they do. It's something I don't want to go back to, I know what it's like."

"You're a funny girl."

"It's the one thing I'm not. Not funny, not exactly a girl."

"No, I guess you're not." He laughed. "Been around the Horn, have you?"

"Something like that." There was something in his voice, something mocking, that disturbed her; he had never taken this tone before, superior, a little sardonic, as if he were edging up on her to do some violent and cruel deed he had just decided on.

"Put a lot of mileage on the speedometer?"

"Don't talk like that, Myers, I don't like it."

"Touchy?"

"Touchy."

Silent, she studied his face. It was handsome in a hard, outdoor, insensitive way, the mouth that of a man who made decisions without difficulty.

He swung off the main highway onto the blacktop that led down into a glen, almost the only real valley in the area, with woods and a stream, the restaurant on one side and a big white farm where the owners lived on the other. It was the kind of place where the prices gave you one surprise and the old men with their young girls at most of the other booths another. The house specialty was shrimp, steak, and salad, all not up to what was charged, but well worth the money when you recognized what you were paying for. At first Carolyn hadn't understood how a restaurant so remote, so expensive, with so little atmosphere, could do so well. But that was because she was in love and not looking. Now she understood: the proprieter was always only too glad to call down the road and reserve you a room, save you the embarrassment of that encounter without luggage or the look of the properly conjugal.

The couples in that restaurant all had an air of eagerness—even, she knew, herself, though the look on her face, she was sure, was far different from that of those handsome hard girls accepting with prepared delight the jewelry box with its opportune offering or the flat white envelope with the rent. There were always a few middle-aged couples in the darkened booths, local people "seeing." Myers called them voyeurs. He had an expression for everything—how are your bazookers? he would ask, cupping his hands around the breasts that had just been loosened from their brassière. Geetus, he called it. How's your geetus? putting one hand around her waist and running the other back and forth, back and forth, stroking.

The language of lovers, the private language of the lovers: all over the world men and women touched and made a language of their own.

"Here we are. God, I'm tired. I can use a drink. I just wish you'd break down and have one with me. If there's one thing I hate it's having to drink alone."

Carolyn shot him a measuring look. "You're making it hard, Myers."

"I want to," he said, and then she was in his arms, held close. He smelled of cigarettes and stale office air, expensive clothes and alcohol. He had been drinking at lunch. Maybe that accounted for the way he was acting.

Reaching over, he turned the switch for the headlights, and while she lay against him his hand began to move up her stockinged leg, reached the bare flesh, then slipped under the girdle's elastic covering, while she lay straight and motionless so that anyone passing might have thought they were merely embracing. Carolyn caught her breath.

She moved and the hand held her, so that, when she stilled, it went back to stroking, slowly, knowingly, first one finger, then two moved inside, he began to lift her up and down on those stiff fingers. "Tell me you want it. Say it," he said. "Say it."

"Please, Myers, please."

"Say it." He was moving her back and forth, up and down. A little shiver ran over her. Abruptly he pulled his hand away, bent, kissed her in a brisk gesture of dispatch, and, turning away, opened the car door, announcing, "I'm hungry."

Trembling, she looked out. He was standing in front of the car, waiting. Just waiting. He was not even going to come around and open her door for her. She opened the car door and climbed out while a small voice called out inside, You know what's the matter, don't you? You know very well what's the matter, don't you?

Straight, stiff, silent, she followed him up the steps, through the door, and into the booth in back, "their" booth. Lighting a cigarette, not looking at her, he said roughly, "You going to have a drink with me or not?"

"All right, Myers, I'll have a drink with you."

"That's better. Let's have a little fun. You're so goddam serious these days, you're not fun at all any more."

I am a serious person, Carolyn wanted to say to him. You knew that from the start. You always used to want us to be serious with one another. You said that was what you liked, you could *talk* to me, that and that we were good in bed together; you hadn't felt anything for Ginny, not in years, but you felt it with me.

"Whisky? Scotch?"

"A martini."

He pushed the cigarettes across the table, tore the empty matchbook in two, dropped it in the ashtray. She could take one if she wanted. He wasn't offering her any, but they were there for the taking. How many drinks had he had at lunch to make him like this?—an adversary, she thought, and looked away, afraid, while he said to the waitress, "One double Bourbon and water, don't mix it, and one dry—extra dry—martini. You got any Beefeater?

"Holy Jesus," he said, "You look like you've lost your last friend. Cheer up. Smile. Laugh. Let's have a little fun."

She tried to smile. The fingers toying with the cigarette pack felt frozen, the mouth widening under the impact of her will, gelid.

"That's better. That's more like it. How long's it been since we've had dinner together—a month, six weeks? We should celebrate. We should—"

The tall thin-stemmed glass being put in front of her contained in its oval that which, three years before, she had promised herself she would never touch. An offering of sorts. But was this not in the nature of an offering, too?

She put out her cigarette and lifted her glass.

"Cheers," he said, holding his Bourbon up, clicking glasses.

Carolyn drank. It was bitterer than she remembered and for a moment she thought it might not go down; her throat seemed to be closing up and renouncing what had been sent; then she felt the warmth, a little glow down in the midst of all that cold, and she knew it was going to be as she remembered; she lifted the glass and drank again, grateful that something could dissolve the ice inside.

He seemed to relax a little, too, leaning over, smiling in a way she knew and liked. "Cigarette?" he asked, genially now, holding up the pack.

Carolyn took one and their fingers touched. She looked up, ready to smile, to send a secret message, but he was intent on a drama across the room. A man had risen, white-faced, leaning across the table toward a frigid-faced girl. She was smoking a cigarette angrily, jerking it in and out of her mouth, not looking at the man speaking to her, turning her head first one way, then the other, ignoring the invective which had grown so loud it could be heard round the room.

Myers laughed. "No fool like an old fool," he said, thoroughly enjoying himself, while Carolyn turned away, sickened by the sight. The old man, abruptly, unexpectedly, had begun to weep.

"Another—what's the matter, Carolyn?"

"Nothing," she said, reaching for her purse and handkerchief. Seeing that old man's vulnerability, she had suddenly seen all their vulnerability. Like everyone else he had believed love would come and save him. Here in that gangling figure, collapsed back in its chair, pride crushed by its heart's hopeless longings, face crumpled, wet with tears, was the whole of her own pitiable illusion, saying, It is not what is outside, but what is here, in the heart, I must hold onto. It is love I must commit myself to. It is only love that can make me have a sense of myself.

"Well, if one martini's going to affect you like that—"

"It's not the drink, Myers."

"Good," he said, brisk and businesslike again, his interest on the booth cross the room apparently forgotten. "Let's live it up a little." He signaled the waitress with two fingers, mouthed the word *more,* then rose. "I have to phone Ginny," he said, and lumbered off, a big amiable handsome man with a glass in his hand. He looked for all the world as if everything went well with him, as if he liked life, the flow was strong, he would have what he wanted, to hell with the price.

Not at all like Ralph. Just the opposite. Maybe that was what had attracted her; she wanted a man who was ready to take what he wanted, not one who turned over every consideration in his mind and weighed, balanced, deliberated, evaluated, and still couldn't make up his mind.

But supposing she wasn't what Myers wanted any more: wouldn't he just as ruthlessly rid himself of her as he had relentlessly reached out for her?

And what will I do if I lose him? Carolyn asked herself, frightened. I can't lose him. It's not that I love him—not love as I understand it, not the kind Lois talks about, not the kind that transforms you. But it is a kind of love, she insisted to herself, the same kind that old man had—she glanced across to see him, half prostrate, now pleading, one hand gripping the girl's arm as if she might flee if he let go. And if you asked that man what he felt, he would call it love, just as, if you asked my mother what she felt for my father lying helpless up in bed, she would say, Love, it's love, I love your father, Carolyn. The mothers love their children, the husbands their wives, mistresses their lovers, lovers their ambitions, some love a house, and some money, and all these we call love. Esther, she thought, out in her house, counting coins; Frances looking in a mirror at her own reflection; my mother down on her hands and knees polishing her floors; Ralph with the children. So many soiled mouths playing with those words, Love O Love. I, too, oh I, too. More than the rest I have run after love, burned with desire and not been assuaged; the mouth I have turned upward in affection tastes only the stale smoke of cigarettes, the lukewarm stirrings of desire. Myers, she wanted to cry out, we have pressed our pale bodies together and felt only the husks of empty skins chafing against one another; soft, scaly whispers in the dense, dark night, our mouths called to one another the harsh ugly words, Lust it was we spoke. Love is a kind of poetry and we have only a dull hard prose from which no music is made. Where I have looked for tenderness, you gave back violence; when I have wanted comfort, cruelty. You have feasted on me as if I were dead meat, and I carry with me the taste of those lips that have pressed down in reluctance, the mouth that has devoured in distaste.

What if I lose him? she asked herself.

He was crossing the room, a worried look on his face. "I'm afraid we'll have to finish up," he said, "and get back. I'm sorry, Carolyn, but Sandy's having a bad time, and she wants me, Ginny wants me back." He put his empty glass down on the table.

Something in his face: he was glad to get out of the evening; Sandy was only an excuse. He didn't want to make love to her. He didn't want—but she had to be sure. "Yes, of course. But maybe—maybe—on the way home we could—"

"Could what, Carolyn?"

"Pull off, park somewhere for a little while," she said all in a rush.

Was it disgust she saw in his face?

"I mean," she went on hurriedly, "I mean—if you—I thought the idea might appeal to you—you know," she said, desperately trying to re-establish the old intimacy between them, "I mean, Myers, it might be fun to—"

The face he was turning away from her to look for the waitress was one etched in disbelief; to think, it seemed to say, of him making love in a car, was she crazy?

The children were in bed, Ralph in the big brown armchair by the fire. A book lay in his lap; he had been dozing. When she slipped into the room, hoping he too would be upstairs asleep, she was startled to find him, head tilted to one side, hands fluttering slightly over the open book in response to some dream down deep, his chest rising and falling rhythmically with the breath of sleep. She stood for a moment seeing him as if he were some stranger, perhaps through the sudden sharpness three mártinis had imparted to her world: the baldness, the glasses, the large head on the thick slab of neck, no, he was not a handsome man, but he was a good man, he had tried with all he had to make the life he wanted, and failed.

". . . is it too late, Carolyn? Tell me that, is it too late?" he had asked one night ten years before.

I don't know, she had said, and for a fact she hadn't. What she had wanted was not to know but to believe.

When they lay down that night and made love, she had. We'll have a new start, Ralph had said. We'll move out of this house and go somewhere and find a house we want, the right house, and we're going to make it the way we want it. You've got to believe me, you've got to trust me. It's going to be a whole new life . . . Carolyn, he had said, looking at her that night in the old house, just love me a little, won't you?

Faith had been strong inside her, strengthened by Ralph's conviction they had to change not only their attitudes toward each other but also the environment in which they lived. Changing their house, he had been certain, would change their lives.

They had begun looking for a house all that fall; it had seemed to them they would never find the house they had in their minds; what was available was mostly a duplicate of what they were trying to escape—the split-level levers against status, the fulcrum of which was how much the kitchen had cost. If it was not one of those modern misfortunes, it was some mishap left over from the nineties, exuding the brown gingerbreadish air of Emersonian evanescence. All they wanted—and it should have been simple, but simple things, she was finding, are the hardest to come by— was an old country farmhouse they could fix up.

Month after month Carolyn had been taken by spinsterish ladies —flat shoes, big bags, calcified smiles—or old-men relics of another age—flushed, happy, alcoholic—from one bad house to another. It had never occurred to her before how much bad building went on. Discouraged, she would report evenings to Ralph the latest broken porches, bent barns, cantilevered caprices or mock Stone screens she had viewed that day.

Then she discovered she was pregnant and her usually strong constitution broke; she spent most of her day lying in bed upstairs or downstairs supine on the couch. She was tired most of the time, and sick most of the time. She could no more face those trips in and out of the suburbs or over the back rutted roads of the peeling countryside, the car swept by raw winds, everything wet, rusty, and saturated with cold, than she could persuade herself that the sickness, the tiredness, would ever pass and she would be herself once again.

But it was the usual first three months of nausea and despair; by the middle of the fourth month she was not only robust but in possession of the place she wanted—a big rambling white rectangle with a country kitchen and three small front rooms where, once the walls had been removed, they had a long, low living room with fireplaces at both ends. Though the land around was the flat prairie fields of the plains, they looked toward trees and a windmill on the next farm, and down in a small indentation there was a stream which took enough bends and dips to give the land contour. It was a view of peace, of placidity, and Carolyn, standing on her back steps, big, awkward, unwieldly, often rested her hands on the unborn child inside and gave thanks. It was one of the few times in her life when she had been truly happy—not just with the sense of well-being that is often confused with happiness, but a feeling, fixed and indefinable, of being open to life, of having the whole future ahead. She had recaptured the capacity to transcend what is of now and today and to live for the mysterious future of tomorrow.

I have a son coming, she would say to herself, who will grow tall and strong and have a place of his own in this uncertain world. But she was no longer in fear of that world; it was a challenge to be met. The human condition was fear, the human distinction the courage to overcome it.

For almost a year she had believed in her own rebirth.

Remember back to that night, she told herself, when you lay close with your husband and loved him. Remember back to the days afterward when you went about cloaked in an excitement that robbed you of sleep, kept you in a constant state of agitation, your sensibilities raw to the smallest feeling.

Then gradually, incontestably, the paths of their lives rewound themselves in the old patterns—Ralph silent, withdrawn, staring out into the unknown, the child held on his lap in a trance of solitude, and Carolyn caught in the world of words, living her life in books where others, better equipped, had taken the trouble to write it all down, a life that was essentially learned instead of lived. By the time Wesley was walking, they were strangers once again.

Now Ralph, the stranger, slept in his chair.

His eyes were open. "Carolyn," he said sleepily. "You're late." "Yes, I got held up."

"Everything turn out all right? You get it fixed up about Esther?"

"It's a long story, but I think we got everything straightened out—at least for the time being. If she just doesn't—you know— get into it again."

Abruptly she sat down, loosening the furs at her throat, stripping from her hands the long and now slightly soiled gloves. If I raised my arms now, she thought, would he hear the rattle of invisible chains? If I look at him now, will he see in my eyes the emptiness in my heart?

She reached across and opened a leather box, lifted a cigarette from inside. "Ralph," she said slowly, "I'm kind of wound up, I think I'll make myself a drink." She saw the look of pain on his face, rose before he had a chance to say anything. With her back to him, she said, "One drink won't matter, and I need it after a day like this." For a moment she waited, then she went into the kitchen. She did not even trust herself to ask him if he wanted one. But clearly, sharply, like an indictment that she had been drawing up, unknown, in her mind, there came to her the weeks and weeks that had gone by since she had let her husband make love to her. And yet she could no more have spent the night in Ralph's arms than she could have done without the drink she was now in the process of pouring.

Chapter 3

SHE HAD no business getting involved with Neal again, and Lois knew it. One did not stay twenty-five all one's life. A convenient demarcation—after twenty-five didn't the cells start their deterioration? One might say that from that point on everything was in the process of wearing away. One was to start growing old, unfoolish, encumbered. Mistakes, foolishness, flight were fancies for the young.

Where was the wisdom she should have had in exchange for the destroyed child, the bad marriage, all the rootless running around she had done? One could hardly say wisdom lay in being happy (*happy!*) at the prospect of spending an evening with the man who had once torn her life in two, who had been responsible for sending her from New York to Springfield, from Springfield to Greece, who had set in motion the chain of events which had ended here in the long evenings alone, the deep feeling of failure, the guilt and anger and bitterness, in an inability to uncover some central core on which to base her beliefs.

She knew very well common sense, to say nothing of the sense of self-preservation, ought immediately to have warned her she was in danger (well, she did know that), then should have given her enough power over her unruly emotions to act as she should: a polite handshake in the park, some small conversation, a brave escape.

Unable to control the impulses of emotion: where was there wisdom in that?

Lois stood looking down at the child banging water with wet

fisted hands. The small soapy waves leaped against the sides of the tub and Constance cried out in delight. Toys were afloat on the water, the washcloth a sodden mess of soap on the floor, two strong sturdy legs flashed in and around the tub, and Constance, catching sight of her mother's dismayed face, laughed; her eyes brightened in mischief, she beat against the water with hands and feet until it mounted over the sides of the tub. There was such pride of power in Constance's eyes, such a feeling of reassurance at the sight of that sturdy little body, that Lois did not scold her daughter. She would have beautiful good firm flesh. It was only a beginning, but a good one.

She did not know, this lovely child, what terrible crimes could be committed in the name of love.

Let her never know, Lois thought.

> *Forgive me for neglecting to show you*
> *that the world is evil.*
> *I had hoped your innocence would find it good*
> *and teach me what I know to be untrue.*
>
> *Forgive me for leaving you open to persistent heartbreak*
> *instead of breaking your bright heart with medicinal blows*
> *I had hoped your eyes would be stars*
> *dispelling darkness wherever you looked.*
>
> *Forgive me for a love that has delivered you*
> *unwarned to treachery. Now I confess that the world,*
> *more beautiful for your presence, was not fine enough*
> *to warrant my summoning you into it. . . .*

Let her know it all, Lois thought, but arm her with courage, give her the guard of believing in herself. Let her love herself enough to face fear. To be able to love back, with belief. Not to be afraid of the future. To give to each day its due not in guilt but in grace. Teach her the reverence that can be life as well as its humilities.

And, struck by such a wave of love for her daughter that it threatened to inundate her, Lois reached across and touched one small hand lying atop the white enamel tub. Her daughter looked back, wary. Checked, Lois took her hand away, waited a moment until that sea of emotion inside subsided, then said, "No more now. Let the water out. You've got to be dressed and have dinner before Mrs. Collins comes."

"I don't want Mrs. Collins to come. I don't want Mrs. Collins to come. I want to go with you."

"You've had a nice day, it's time now to call it quits. Hurry up, out you go." Like the seals earlier in the afternoon, Constance slipped under the water, then reappeared, glistening, only to slip under again. Lois grabbed and pulled. Wet, slippery, protesting, her daughter was deposited on the damp bathmat; a cry went up.

Naked, dripping, Constance disappeared down the hall into the bedroom they shared. She was remarkably independent for her age, perhaps because she had to be. Lois's working at a job had made her accept her own responsibilities to herself from the start. What else could she accept without bitterness—not having a father?

Two years, Lois thought, and he's never really tried to get in touch with us. He didn't care how we got along, he didn't care what happened to his own daughter.

She could understand many things, but this, no. How could a father not care what happened to his own child?

She had followed Constance down the hall and now she stood in the doorway, looking into the face of the child for whom she would have denied herself everything, even the love of a man who might make her happy—a man like Neal, you mean, she said to herself.

During a recent visit to New York Carolyn had said, in that brittle, biting tone she brought to bear on things of which she did not approve, " 'The fulfillment of love in all its marvelous rarity!' I'll tell you what that marvelous rarity is: It's some foolish woman deluded, *deliberately* deluded, by her own helplessness and desire to have some dream that she's beautiful and desirable and has value. She doesn't put any value on herself. Some man has to come along and do it for her. That's what we call love, we women, thinking we're worth something to the world because we're of some slight value to some man. Who can accept that, Lois, just answer me that?" Carolyn had stopped, her eyes bright with anger, her cheeks inflamed by it. Then unexpectedly she smiled, showing what seemed like a thousand perfect white teeth. "Love never lasts, *name one love that's lasted*," Carolyn insisted, almost as if she were throwing the words in Lois's face.

But I don't want to believe that, I've never wanted to believe that, Lois thought. I believed—I still believe—the best of you comes out in love.

The insatiable need for love, she thought, the common cry in all our hearts. And yet when we find love, what do we do? Afraid of it, we abuse it; uncertain of it, we ask too much in proof.

She stood in front of the small wet unclothed child, who solemnly regarded her as if to say, We do bad things when we are desperate, and the more desperate we are the worse our acts are.

She must have inherited much from him that I do not admit, Lois thought, just as I do not remember the good things we had together, Cliff and I, when we were close. What I hold inside now are only the cruelties at the end.

He made me pay, she thought, again and again for every moment I tried to love him, for every moment he felt love for me. Because there was something in him that was afraid of love—something too perhaps in myself—we felt we had no right to it. We had married like unto like.

Still, I tried. I wanted to love him. To be loved. And in the beginning it was almost that, but of course in the end it was not love we felt for one another, but only the instinct for inflicting pain.

We lived in the cage of our humiliations, our bars broken promises, misused confidences, constant betrayals, uncountable failings. It was those very failures which kept us locked together; they were so complete they were like crimes. Yet we lived with the desperate deception that we might stop all the abuse, the endless arguments, the violent fights, and forgive each other, start over, make a decent and honorable life. It was the only thing that could right the wrongs of the past and the one thing in the whole world we were incapable of consummating.

Lois thought of the party that night in Greece when the Fays were down from Corfu, and all the talk had been bright and happy. People seemed to be laughing all the time, not the usual forced laughter of synthetic convivialty, but naturally, spontaneously, and then she had noticed how Cliff seemed outside it all, off by himself, brooding, drinking more than anyone else. That momentary glimpse into what was to be so bad later, to ruin their life together, had been blurred by her own pleasure at the moment. It wasn't until she saw, through the rest of their eyes, how badly he was behaving, drunk, swaying and stammering, telling off-color unfunny stories, showing a coarseness and brutality that shocked and shamed her, that she realized she was seeing him for the first time as if she were an outsider, and what she saw revolted her.

They had got home somehow. He had insisted on driving and, though her hands went white gripping the sides of the seat, she said nothing. She was afraid of him. He seemed like a person capable of great harm.

In the house he had gone at once to the liquor cabinet and poured himself another drink while, wordless, she went back to their bedroom and sat down on the bed, shaking, frightened at the intensity of her emotion. It was as if, suddenly, the realization of the terrible mistake she had made had come to her. And now she was married to him; she was going to have, in a few months, his child.

She went into the bathroom and took three sleeping pills. One was supposed to be strong enough to put her to sleep, but she needed something beyond what was normally called for to get her through this night. She lay down and closed her eyes, hearing him wandering about in the next room.

She did not know how long she lay awake, aware that he knew she was angry and outraged, and that his not coming to her was in the nature of rebellion—he would damn well do what he pleased. Her heart turned over, she felt the sickness of a sleep that would not come rising inside her, and she thought that if she could not turn off the clicking of her brain and shut out the knowledge that lay like a weight on her mind, all the buttresses she had built up as an adult would fall, there would be nothing left of the structure she had made of herself.

In the morning he reached over to make love to her, the way he always did after a night of heavy drinking. The moldy hangover of alcohol seemed to increase his sense of isolation and insecurity and he needed her, wanted arms around him to protect him from his fears, lips that murmured words of reassurance, turning to her with his sour breath and swollen eyes, saying, "Honey?"—it was a question—and always before she had comforted him, held him in her arms as if he were a child. But that morning she turned away, cold, withdrawn; smelling the strong rank odor of liquor on his breath, she shrank away, while he kept repeating, "Honey?" and then, finally, "What's wrong?" It struck her as reprehensible that he should try to pretend he didn't remember how he had behaved the night before, and she was unable, even as she tried, to stop the words that came, all in a rush, in hatred and humiliation, disgust and final rejection: "I'm ashamed of you, that's what's wrong. Ashamed of you and of myself."

She turned her face to the wall and let him go. She knew just where he would go anyway. First to the bar by the post office. Then over behind the Cathedral. And then on and on to all those little bars in back alleys until he passed out in his car, or was brought home by some kind friend.

Why was it she could not keep the love of the people who meant something to her—her mother, her father, Neal, now Cliff? What was it he needed from her that he was unable to get, that she was unable to give? It seemed to her there must be some vast lack that turned people away from her as soon as they knew her, really knew her.

Yet she had worked and worried with Cliff all through the months after that terrible night, trying to give him whatever it was he needed to keep himself whole, for when the moods of depression struck him he sank into despair and went out on those wild drinking sprees, or withdrew to such an extent that speaking to him was useless, he would not answer, perhaps did not even hear, drinking away his demons, all through the long weekend days, every night when he came home from work, trying to dissolve the devils that obsessed him. There was nothing she could do to help. He was lost to everyone, even himself.

The night Constance was born it had finally come home to her that nothing would ever help him. He had not been drinking for three or four weeks, trying to get control of himself for when the baby came. Then that night he had not come home from work at the usual time, and she knew, waiting hour after hour, smoking cigarettes, later sipping whisky, waiting there in that foreign land, the pains coming with more and more regularity, increasing in severity, he would not be coming home at all.

It had been a friend from the bureau who had driven her to the hospital and waited with her while she was admitted, a tall serious reporter whose kindness she would always remember, and whose eyes when they allowed themselves to fall on her, showed only too well that he understood. And why shouldn't he? He lived near them, he worked with Cliff, the whole story was perfectly clear.

Lois thought of how ashamed she had been when the doctor had asked her where her husband was and she had said, hesitantly, He's away—gone was really what she meant, but seeing the look on the doctor's face she had not been able to tell the truth. He's gone on a story up north, she had lied, and then, gripping the edge of the desk, she had said, For a day or two, he didn't think—and shame was stronger than the seizures, she had been sick with shame while they helped her down the hall.

In the center of pain, alone—the nurse had shaved her and given her the enema and then left—she had stared at the ceiling in amazement at the calm that had come over her. She remembered wondering again and again, Why don't I feel more? I'm alone in this hospital having his child while he's off some place getting drunk and I don't feel anything one way or the other except this strange calm.

Perhaps physical pain had dislodged consideration of everything else. It no longer seemed a matter of life and death if he broke his promises, behaved atrociously, disappeared for days, might even now be hurt and in need. She had understood at last that nothing could ever change what was—even his wanting to—and that she must live with that knowledge and act upon it. She could not depend on him, she could never trust him, she would always be, essentially, even if she stayed with him, alone.

Yet, oddly enough, it was herself she blamed. No one had ever promised her she would be happy. Happy? Why should she expect happiness? Love? A sense of being safe? What made her think she was exempt from what life gave back to everyone else?

Pride, perhaps. No, more likely, need.

Having forgotten, Lois thought, my Catholic background. One never really loses the imprint of the ashes on the forehead, the feel of the wooden benches on the knees. No matter how far one runs. It is the good Jesuit priests who sit inside me, the good Catholic fathers with their lovely long sticks for switching and their harsh hearts for telling a girl what a sinner she is. And why not? Which of the commandments have you not broken? There is not one. How many can say that?

Leaning into the mirror, Lois carefully applied red wax to her mouth, decreasing the contours at the corners. She believed her lips too large. In order to discourage embellishing at an early age, her Aunt Iris had told her that beetles were ground up in the pomade. The things women used to adorn themselves—if a man stopped to think before he embraced a woman of all those substances with which she had smeared and anointed herself, what would happen to the human race?

The drawing of the mouth done, Lois dampened a small brush, blackened it from a sticky matter made of god knew what, beaded eyelashes, smoothed down brows artificially shaped by steel tweezers. She sprayed her hair with a substance that solidified like glue, smoothed a cream said to contain the jelly of bees on her hands, and finished off by running a stick of green salve over the lids of her eyes. She was well camouflaged, it would be hard for anyone to tell what was inside.

Men had to manage other ways. Shut in silence, like Neal; withdrawn in alcohol, like Cliff. Yet, perversely, they all proclaimed they wanted to know one another.

They did; they didn't.

Either way—in isolation, in exposure—the ambushes lay in wait.

She wondered if at this moment, somewhere on the public transit system, Neal was also asking himself what could come from re-opening their past. But of course that past was not the same for him as it was for her. What he recalled could not include the most important part, the child.

She turned out the light in the bathroom, crossed the hall, and looked in on Constance, lying asleep amid a jumble of toys. Impossible to know what the other person made of the experiences in which you had both participated: what, for instance, was he remembering as he sat swaying in the subway?

Really a rather standardized New York affair, she thought, as she went into the living room and took up a cigarette. Drinks, dinner, bed; films, a museum now and then, parties at friends'; quarrels, reconciliations, reproaches, an abrupt end. Abstractions without individual issues, everything unsaid.

The Armenian restaurant, for instance. Surely he remembered that. How had that woman lasted as long as she had? Lois never remembered more than four or five people in the place. You brought your own wine and listened to scratchy records run on a machine that had to be cranked by hand. Nothing ever tasted the same twice. And the appliances were always wearing out or breaking down so that there were apt to be tears or tirades along with the rice and lamb. The coffee was thick and black and awful, there was no subway stop anywhere near, the street was going to hell, but they always went back. Lois even remembered the coat Neal wore that winter, a hound's-tooth check, and the way he carried the wine cradled against his arm in the long slender unmistakable brown bag. And the wind, there was always the worst wind anywhere in New York that last block.

If she made an inventory of the affair, it would most certainly start with the Armenian restaurant. But why should he remember that simply because she did? And after that? The esplanade along Riverside Drive. That nice Italian restaurant on Thompson Street where they had had their first quarrel and the waiter wanted to know what was wrong with the food; neither of them had been able to touch a thing. Odd, she could not recall in any detail the first night they made love—but there were other nights she remembered too well, the ones where something had gone wrong.

And of Neal himself, how much did she really know? He was

Jewish, he had read all of Marcel Proust, he left his hound's-tooth coat unbuttoned in the worst weather and never wore a hat; he had an aversion to small men who walked large dogs; and he knew terrible facts. It was he who had told her of the famous tenor who used to go to the zoo to watch the monkey and masturbate. From that seemed to spring a loathing of all opera. But he was passionate about concert music and people who rented Carnegie Hall for inauspicious debuts. They went that winter to see a lot of bad singers paying for their first performances before a New York public. He smoked too much, drank too many cups of coffee, wore shoes that usually needed a shine. Like most men, he was untidy, tardy, and untalkative about small events. He had lovely hands.

You won't find an answer in Neal, she told herself, just as you didn't find an answer with Cliff in Greece. She thought of her last days in Athens and she saw suddenly in her mind the contours of the house on the hill, that lovely house where she and Cliff had lived, the sun slanting down over the ribboned hills; you could have drawn it in straight thick shafts, that sunlight; it was easy to see how some had come to see God in a pillar of light.

She had hidden at a friend's house down the street, waiting through Sunday with Constance until the weekend was over and Cliff would have to go back to work. When Monday came, she went back to the house to get the things she needed in order to leave; then she stood looking out, stricken at the sight of those hills, those beautiful bone-dry, blood-red hills. She had turned and there was her cat looking out, crying to come with her: that was how love ended, with the animals you left behind and the hotels where you waited, alone and afraid, for the knock that never came.

And Cliff, wherever he was now, did he ever wonder about them? He had written only to tell her he was not going to be taken in by any lawyer she got. He never even asked how Constance was. A very unstable man, the lawyer had said, and that merely on the evidence of letters. He had looked at her oddly, the lawyer, wondering, no doubt, how she had come to marry a man who would not answer a letter about separation, about support, about divorce, about his own wife and child.

Neal, you couldn't love me the way I wanted that winter we

were together, and I tried to run away from you, I tried to substitute one set of feelings for another—I tried to love in one man what I hadn't found in another. And failed there, too, and ran away from that, to that man my cousin loved, who left her and—

Ran away into the arms of someone else, Cliff, and fled from him too—

Mistakes, foolishness, flight. Again and again.

And now, Neal, she wanted to ask, do you really believe it is within our power to go back and remake what we ruined? Do you really think we can reuse the past? Is that what you would call wisdom, Neal—going back to take up what was once your worst failure?

The doorbell and telephone rang at the same time. Even though the phone was on the table near the door, the cord was not quite long enough for Lois to reach the lock. She let the phone ring, fumbled with the bolt on the door, then rescued her ears from the insistent ringing. Mrs. Collins and her umbrella came in with Neal. Mrs. Collins always carried an umbrella. She wanted to be safe in the side streets.

"One moment please, long distance calling," a disembodied voice said to Lois from the receiver.

She covered the instrument with her hand and directed Neal toward the kitchen for a drink. He shook his head. Mrs. Collins began turning on lights; she was afraid of the dark. The *News* and *Journal-American* had imbued her with a violent view of life. Yet she had what Iris would have called a "good heart." Obliquely Lois was both grateful to and envious of her: she had all those hours alone with Constance. If I leave my daughter with a stranger, it is not because I want to, she thought, but because I must. Still, there will come a time when she's bound to resent my being gone. No father, a substitute mother during most of the day: *what right had I to bring her into the world?* Lois asked herself, as a voice on the other end of the phone, unmistakably Carolyn's, began, "Lois? It's Ada, Lois, Ada died this afternoon—a heart attack. Eileen found Ada and no one was home, god knows where Arnold had disappeared to, but anyway Eileen didn't know what to do, I guess, and so she just stayed there—with the body—for a while, and then, then she went running out—"

"Out?"

"I know. The neighbors caught her, some people who live next door. They saw her running around their back yard, acting odd, it must have seemed odd to them she was even out, without Ada, you know Ada never let her go anywhere, even in the yard, alone. Well, they went out and got her and called Mama because Ada didn't answer her phone. And of course Mama called me. I went over with her to get Eileen. We didn't even know Ada was dead until we tried to get Eileen to go back home. She wouldn't. She didn't want to go back because Ada was in the front room. On the floor. Mama asked me to call you. The funeral's going to be Wednesday. Mother made it Wednesday so you could come. I mean, *I* really don't see why you should have to come, but Mother—you know how she is, Lois. The family should all be together for the big events. It's not as if Ada would *know*."

Neal was prowling the apartment, scrutinizing the pictures on the walls, checking the names on the backs of the books, picking up the periodicals. He's finding out what I am now, Lois thought; all the clues are there if you know how to use them.

"With your job and all, I know it's hard to get away—"

"I guess it's the least I can do. The *least*."

Carolyn's voice was crisp. "It wasn't your fault, I don't know why you keep blaming yourself. No one can hold a man who doesn't want to be held. He'd have left Eileen anyway, he'd been waiting around too long as it was, he was worn out with waiting. And bored. Who can blame him? But I've missed you," she said abruptly. "You know I'd like you to come back. But I don't think you should feel you *have* to."

Neal's reappearance, Ada's death, how much of it all was really chance? An opportunity perhaps to pay back, to buy her way out? How could she ever know unless she did go back? "I'll take the first train I can get on Monday, Carolyn," she said in sudden decision. "I'll wire you the time I'm coming in."

"I don't want you to think I—"

"No, I'm glad you called. I *want* to come," Lois said in certainty.

He lifted his wineglass and looked at her as if reassessing her. "You know, Lois," he said after a moment, "you were the only one I ever really felt close to, really close to, and that wasn't enough, was it, not for you, you wanted more, that was what was wrong, wasn't it?"

"I couldn't get through to you—or at least I thought I couldn't. We seemed like two people very far away from one another who couldn't even call out, we could just wave, and what can you accomplish with such simple signals?"

"People have all kinds of signals—all kinds of communications —they send to one another without words."

"I know that, but I need the words, the words are awfully important to me. The power of words—God was supposed to have been able to create the world through the power of words, wasn't He?"

Neal turned his wineglass round in his hand. "It all goes back to that one word for you, though, doesn't it? That one powerful little word, love."

Lois reached for her own wine so that she wouldn't have to look at him. "Not just that one word, that is maybe the most important one, yes—but not just that one word, many many words, all the words that finally make up an explanation of what a person is, how he thinks, what he believes. But with you it seemed words weren't meant to communicate, they were used to conceal. You didn't tell me the things that really mattered. I'm sorry, Neal, but I—"

"It's the thing I always remember about you, how you were always saying you were sorry. You still do it, don't you?"

Unable to stop, Lois heard herself saying, "And do you remember when I said it most, Neal? It was in bed I used to say it, when —when—" But she could not finish, looking down, the tightness gathering inside.

"Why should you have felt that was your fault? Why shouldn't you have blamed me since I didn't make you feel enough, since I was so clumsy—"

Silent, they waited while the waiter replenished the butter dish, refilled their glasses. A nice restaurant, French, but she missed the Armenian place, the high wail of Oriental reeds, the louder complaints of the proprietress. Neal reached across the table and took her hand as the waiter moved away. "Did you ever—with anyone else?"

Lois looked away. "Once in a while," she said, "with my husband, at first—but never enough to make up for that private territory of terror that women have, that there's something the matter with them, that it's their fault they don't feel what they should," she said, taking her hand from his and picking up the freshly filled glass, "that they ask too much, they want love to be everything to them." She put down her glass, "What they can't be alone—fulfilled," she said. "I don't think you can ask that of anything, of anyone else—to make *you* feel fulfilled. But at one time or another I suppose it's what we all ask of something or someone, to make us feel whole, to make us feel unafraid."

All around, people looked happy and unafraid, forking in their food, leaning across cluttered tables to exchange intimacies.

"I suppose it all goes back a long time," Lois said, "to when I was young and felt—I don't know—that whatever I did was wrong, I could never please people, no matter what I did. I really didn't know how. I tried—I wanted so much to *show* the right reaction, but—but it never turned out right somehow. I felt I never came across with the love I had. Maybe I never have," she said slowly.

"Nobody feels adequate—whole—Lois, don't you know that? I don't, nobody does—not just you, but everyone, *everyone*." He was trying, she saw. "Like everyone else, I wanted to be something I wasn't too," he said, looking at her closely. "And what I wanted was not to be, god help me, a Jew. But I was and there was no escaping it, ever, and especially not in a small town. In a big city like this—hell, most of what happens here in New York happens because of the Jews, but in a place like Akron you just belong to one of the minorities, the eyeties, the niggers, the hunkies and the hebes," he said in an emotional voice. "People even call you up on the phone sometimes to shout obscenities at you, they tear your name off the mail box, write KIKE on the sidewalk in front of your house. Most of the time it's in chalk, you can wash it off, but during the war—*during the war*—when millions of Jews were dying for no other reason than that they were Jews, someone *painted* JUDE on our front walk, on the front walks all the way down our Jewish street. I knew from the time I was a kid there was something that made me different, made all of us different. No matter how hard you worked, someone would always say behind your back you'd gotten where you were because you were one of the Chosen Ones. No matter what you accomplished or how fine your mind was, there would always be someone saying, 'We don't want kikes in this country club,' there would be signs saying RESTRICTED and areas where you couldn't buy a house or ever fit in, *no matter what you were yourself*. And don't you think that leaves a mark? Don't you think that hardly makes you feel *whole, unafraid*? Love," he said in a bitter voice, "who can find love in things like that? No wonder I don't believe in love, don't believe in a Benevolent Being—Christian or Jewish—when all around what I see is hatred, brutality, barbarity, evil. I don't use the word love, Lois, because I don't believe it exists.

"I believe something happens between two people, something with chromosomes, maybe glandular secretions that excite the body, that stimulate the heart, but that's not love. After a time when the mutual demands of desire have been satisfied often enough, the lovers tire of each other, start looking around for someone new to stimulate them. How can you call that love?" he demanded.

"What I'm trying to tell you, Lois, is that I don't think anybody knows what this big word love is. It isn't universal good, how can you call it that when you look at what goes on around you? And if it's only physical attraction, we're giving it the wrong name.

"I know what people like me—the neurotic Jews—" he said bitingly, shushing her with a movement of his hand before she could interrupt in protest, "are supposed to be, in their cynicism, in their everlasting evangelism. We're just afraid that what we really want from others is compassion, not love; pity, not empathy;

indulgence, not involvement. Suffering and self-denial are stamped on every one of us, and what the Chosen One means really is the Chosen One to Be Martyred. We aren't allowed happiness as part of our heritage. Happiness—whatever that means. Freud said it was the fulfillment of childhood wishes, but I don't believe that because the man in me is repulsed by what I wanted as a child. Because what I wanted then was not to be a Jew. *Not to be a Jew.* And god help me, sometimes I think it's what I want now, too. What a thing to say, not to be what you were born, not to be what you were made."

He put down his glass and laid his hands on the table in a wooden way, a man she no longer knew. The Neal she had known would never have spoken like this, would never have told her what he was really feeling inside. That man had been incapable of communicating anything about which he cared or was ashamed. Was it their inadequacies, their imperfections, which people looking for love really wanted to share? Enjoined in unhappinesses: who could accept such a definition of love? Those who were looking for a place, she thought. The barrenness of such lives, which she understood only too well. Love is duty. A typical Catholic concept, a typical Timble one. Was it Jewish too?

I reject this, Lois thought.

He looked up, having retreated, she thought; in a moment he would commence speaking to her in the disciplined, remote voice of one who has once more put on an invisible mask, the male make-up.

"You've changed—a lot."

He made an abrupt, impatient gesture with his head.

"Don't be annoyed, I meant that as a compliment."

No doubt it was the lawyer in him which now said, "I hate people who feel compelled to share all their messy little anxieties with someone else."

"I don't."

He was looking down, disaffiliating himself from the confidences of a moment before. She would wait in vain for any further unfolding.

"We shall never get anywhere," Lois said wearily, "if we have to battle about this." He had lifted his head, as if he might have said, *And where are we going?*

She had no answer; how was she to know? Only her heart, earlier, had been—what? Filled with expectation. Now it felt drained, as if it had once again resumed the empty beat of the last two years.

"If you're finished," he said.

She nodded; he motioned the waiter to remove the plates.

"Dessert?"

"Just coffee."

"Two coffees. Brandy?" he asked.

"Chartreuse."

"One brandy and one chartreuse."

Silence between them, and all around voices from the other tables, people close and in communication.

Neal had bought her dinner and drinks; now he would take her home and what would he expect? Bed? That was the way one of these evenings went, wasn't it? Nothing to it, done all the time, why should she have this smothered sensation?

Politely take his hand at the door. Thank you so much for a lovely evening, but you see I haven't slept with anyone since I left my husband, and I'm afraid I can't make an exception tonight.

He would try persuasion, she evasion.

I don't want to ruin it, it's been such a lovely evening. You said things like this even if they weren't true. Being formal, being polite.

More argument, then, at last, the truth—or as much of it as she could bear to bring out.

It's been a lovely evening, thank you so much. I'm terribly sorry but I can't let you make love to me, you see it's been such a long time and I have such—such painful memories.

So you see, Neal—

But how could he ever see?

For her the act of love had to be more than the end of an evening. She valued her body's ability to make compact with her heart. Anything less remained for her profane. The good Catholic fathers, no doubt.

She was very busy with her key, making up her mind how to ask him in for a drink without indicating that any more was at stake, feeling old and tired and played out.

The white overhead light was burning with a glitter that raked the hallway, the lock was obdurate, her key unsure; then she was in her living room, Neal behind her, the yellow and white glads she had arranged yesterday in the tall green vase bent on cold stalks that disappeared into the open mouth of the vase, Mrs. Collins blinking from the chair over her knitting, the afghan she was making for her married daughter in Queens trailing onto the floor. An old patient woman, underpaid—husband dead, children scattered or ungrateful—but glad to be up this late. She understands I need her, Lois thought, she feels she's still of use. It's the game we all play, for what it's worth, feeling needed and of use. She began to explain to Mrs. Collins she would be away the next week, a death in the family. Mrs. Collins understood; she would come Monday, a week, she said, brandishing her umbrella. Lois walked her to the elevator, wishing the whole evening were over, Neal back in the bowels of the city, tunneling his way home. They had nothing more to say to each other. The evening had just been one of those unsuccessful experiments in trying to renew the unrenewable. For a moment there in the restaurant she had hoped—

But even if he had gone on, even if he had allowed himself to open up, what then would have been expected of her? And whatever it was, could she have given it?

The elevator doors opened; Mrs. Collins, preparing herself to descend, offered a final word on loss. It came to everyone, she said; then, just as the doors closed, I hope she wasn't someone you were real close to.

No, we weren't close, Lois thought, I haven't been close to anyone in a long time.

But she had Constance. Did Neal have anyone? Of course he must. In a city this size there were no end of lonely women who—

He had felt sorry for her, alone with a small child in New York, probably didn't get out much; that was the way he must have reasoned, and because of the past he had felt an obligation to take her out.

She stood in front of the elevator, sick with shame.

What is the matter with me that I grasp out for closeness so?
Why can't I accept the limitations of my life as they are? I have
Constance, I have a halfway decent job, the apartment's adequate
for New York, I am not afraid of being alone, I value the in-
dependence I've managed to make for myself, why must I ask for
more?

But I haven't, until this afternoon, she answered herself in
honesty.

"You all right?" He was standing at the door.

She pulled herself up, affixed a smile on the red wax mouth.
Be polite, be false, go in disguise so as to be safe. "Just seeing
Mrs. Collins off. Bourbon? Scotch? I'm sorry, there's no brandy."

"Bourbon."

"Water?"

"On the rocks."

Do not pause when you pass him. Do not try to talk about
anything important. Above all conceal what matters. After the
polite nightcap, he will go. You'll never see him again. A fortuitous
meeting in the park . . . you can think of it that way.

In the "efficiency" kitchen she bent down to the bottles. He
was in the doorway, watching. "You expect to be gone long?"

"Probably through next weekend." Be nice, be uncommitted,
show you understand the impulse that sent him to spend twenty-
some-odd dollars on such an unsuccessful evening.

"So that leaves tomorrow."

"Tomorrow?"

"That you'll be free."

She stood up, the bottle of Bourbon in hand, examining his
face, trying to trap some emotion she could identify and work
with. Not a flicker of feeling showed; he simply looked a man
waiting for his drink, tired and thirsty. She went for ice.

"Or maybe you'd rather not—go out. Packing and all."

They were like little children who didn't know how to act with
each other. The whole situation was hopeless, just hopeless.

"I ran away, Neal," Lois heard herself saying. "I ran away
from you because I was going to have a child, your child, Neal,

and I didn't want you to know. Of course I never did—have it. I couldn't face—everything after that. And certainly not you. I couldn't tell you—the way we were. I thought—I thought it would be like forcing you to some sort of decision. I felt that if I had to ask you to decide whether—*I was afraid if I told you,* YOU'*d ask me to get rid of it.*"

"Is that how you saw me? Is that what you thought I was like? What I would do?"

Why else would she have destroyed the child? He was a lawyer, the evidence was in, all he had to do was argue for a verdict.

Who wants to convict himself of such a crime? she asked herself, sorrier more now for Neal than for herself, than for the small life that had not been allowed to find its own chance. For the first time it occurred to her how final her judgment had been. If the truth was terrible, however, running away from it was worse.

And you take pride in thinking *that,* a voice inside said. A proud woman who wants no inadequacies from the man she loves, who cannot stand inadequacies *because they seem a reflection on you.* So you ran away from any test involving loss to yourself the moment you thought someone failed you, or that people might pity you, or when you pitied yourself. Pride, stubbornness, fear of failings in others: these are what have ruled your life. An empty, vain, imperious woman, the voice said, who deserves just what she has got because she has none of those virtues she always said she cared so much about. Love, my dear, is a state of believing.

"Lois, I asked you a question."

"I know you did, Neal."

"And you haven't an answer?"

"I don't have any answers, that's been my trouble all along."

He poured liquor into the glasses, handed her one. In order to be approved for love, one had to vacate hate. One had even, eventually, to forgive oneself: there was such a command in all religions, wasn't there, even the one that centered around the self? Solipsism, wasn't that what it was called?

He put down an empty glass. "It's late," he said, the ideal embodiment of evidence. The clock read one-twenty. His voice —his face—indicated nothing. She looked at his hands. They were pale and still at his sides, like balanced scales on which the justice of his case might be weighed. It was she who had destroyed the child. Where was the court that would free you on faith, not facts?

In her religion (abandoned), you confessed (as she had just done), you were truly repentant (as god knew she was), you did penance and were given absolution. Had not even Neal's god demanded the filial sacrifice? Yet Isaac was spared, to live of all the patriarchs the gentlest and longest life.

"About tomorrow," she began. What could she say to him— we have only ourselves and that is not enough? "About tomorrow, you could come for lunch . . ." she said just as if the voice had not warned her earlier in the evening, You have no business getting involved with this man again.

Some voices you had to learn not to listen to: they might be rational, they might be right, and they might just as easily ruin your life.

Chapter 4

SHE SAT on the train, gazing out at the elongated Illinois fields. After Europe and New York, the flat fields, the humped houses, the long glowing golden prairie seemed like something from another scheme of things. Yet it was a feeling of acknowledgment Lois was experiencing, not estrangement. Part of her was forever associated with these flat fields, these odd high boxlike houses.

Here the sun hung heavy, a glowing golden globe, its warmth shed prodigally over the excited earth; green things pulsed up against the light, truculent, tumescent, grasping, aware of their own power; orange flashes of autumn—gourds, pumpkins, the late flowers of fall—lay against the earth, fulfilled by the act of entity. In the city the sun had swung overhead like a bare bulb burning weakly through the thick gray pollution inaptly called sky; underneath, in ugly ovenlike warrens, the people of New York—she and Neal among them—lavishly gave up the littleness that rounded out their lives to what at that moment seemed to her all the wrong energies. Lusting after love does not insure its undertaking; the greed to live is often a guarantee to nothing more than profligacy.

Yesterday, for instance, what did they want to be to each other, to themselves, breaking bread with busy hands over her dining-room table while their eyes avoided each other? He ate with slow, serious concentration, spearing cheese, cold meats, debating over olives and onions, his mouth pursed in thought. She had spent all morning fussing over food, now had no appetite to eat. With thin nervous fingers she pulled the cigarette in and out of her mouth, wondering what she was supposed to say. I have lost somewhere (Greece?) the capacity for unpremeditated pleasure, I have lost the ability even to care about the things on which, for an instant, my heart sometimes seizes. What are we to do when what we want and get gives us no joy? Is it because we have asked, all of us, too much of love, Neal? Was that what she was to say over the mayonnaise, the mustard, the thin tubular jar of capers?

Moodily he forked up potato salad, emboldened for a moment to let his eyes rest on hers, as if he were about to say, we could have had so much, we could have had . . . But in the empty silence between them he looked away. What lay ahead for people who could not even speak to each other of the things they cared about? It takes a certain kind of piracy to live in any opulent world, even that of the mind. Cautious, miserly over the croquettes, they had not the courage to take what they wanted: a feverish afternoon of flesh. Instead they had walked Constance to the concrete park where the sad-eyed children were warned away from the squirrels (disease, infection, bites) and looked disconsolately on the trucked-in sand, the dangerous, heavy, metal swings, the slides that faced away from the trees. Even over cocktails the desire to destroy lust was stronger than the desire to learn from it. For some the act of love is an identification with life, for others a forecast of death. Yet she remembered: *We are in two worlds at once; it is the emotional involvement that matters, not the actual facts as they would look to outsiders.*

She glanced at the little girl beside her, mouth open, eyes closed. Constance had been all right the first part of the trip—they had not left until six, there was the intoxication of boarding the train, the novelty of settling into their seats (there was no question of taking a roomette, the expense; nor would Lois fly, the business about heights, her mother falling, it was all linked together in her mind), then dinner and nestling down as best they could for the night. Only when they got to Chicago and had to wait for the connection to Springfield had the hard time come. Though they had looked in shops, gazed at the candy bars at the service counters, had an orange drink and a hot dog, time did not pass.

Constance ran, she sat, she wiggled, she squirmed, she threw her legs over her head, she slipped down to the floor and was filthy before Lois could get her up; she fingered things, she started into the men's toilet, she sprang up first on one bench, then another; she picked her nose, she pulled up her dress, she snapped the elastic on her underpants, she played with the buttons on her dress, she whined and fretted and complained and at last, when it was time to go and they had, mercifully, got to the gate, she had to go to the bathroom and they had to go back into the station.

The Chicago station was the same one where Lois had seen her mother for the last time, and while she tried to cope with the restless child her mind was on that final meeting—her mother pale and nervous, withdrawn, Lois frightened and unsure, unable to speak. They stood together like two statues who would never be able to communicate, though they faced one another for all eternity; then her mother had bent down. "Be good," she had said. "Oh, be good. Behave with Iris. For me. I'll be down in a week or so to get you."

But of course she had never come. A week later she lay smashed on the inside cement court of some hotel out in Denver.

A protest? An assertion? A counteraction to shame? An affirmation of some belief Lois did not know?

And what was it she knew?

Nothing, nothing, she thought, remembering the moment with Neal, Sunday night, when after the walk in the park she had put together the soufflé for them in the apartment and they sat across from each other, the spiky stems of the salad glistening in the candlelight, he had begun again to open out, partially the wine no doubt, the flickering tapered lights, but something more, a definite effort on his part; and then later, with coffee, he had unexpectedly bent down and put his hand on her shoulder, and she had risen abruptly, deliberately keeping him from a beginning to which she feared the end, going to the window, feeling that there would never be any way to explain to him why she did not want him to make love to her, hearing the quiet voice behind her asking that question all people ask who have suddenly been shut out, "What is it? What have I done?"

She told him the truth. "Nothing, it's not you, it's me. I feel lost. Really lost," she said. There were lights going off in windows all around; below and above darkness passed swiftly from house to house. It reminded her of the story of the taking of the firstborn, as if, like this, death had gone quickly from house to house, putting out lights. "If it weren't for Constance," she said slowly, "sometimes I feel there wouldn't be any point in going on, I feel outside, really outside, with no way to get back in. My trouble is I can't bring myself to believe. I want to, but I can't."

"Don't try, let it come. If it comes, it comes. If it doesn't—" They had left it at that. She supposed one of the troubles was that they were both trying too hard, there was so much to make up for.

Things he doesn't even know, Lois thought: what happened in Springfield after I fled from him in New York, what I have done to Eileen.

Eileen. Lois rested her head against the seat, pressed her eyes closed. She tried to hold down the upsurge of culpability she experienced whenever that name rose in her mind. Like a little girl, Carolyn had said; maybe she's lucky, she lives and sees what she wants. But you wouldn't recognize her any more. Do you remember how pretty she used to be with those lovely blue eyes and that

long curly hair? Well, she looks like someone else, as if some other
child had been put in her place, like the changeling child in one of
those old fairy tales.

You mustn't blame yourself.

How could Carolyn say that?

They shared, she and Carolyn, the Timble family traits, above
all an excess of the wrong kind of loyalty: morbid preoccupation
with the idea that what one Timble did reflected irrevocably on
the rest. Lois wondered if some defective gene, a tendency toward
too much guilt for "the clan," might not have been passed on,
like the predominance of the Timble cheekbones (high, Indian-
like) or the Timble nose (long and sloping); some portion, too,
of this Midwest on which she now looked out: the flat fields, the
prison-like sky, the stubbled spears of corn and wheat in the field
which were like weapons to imprison the onlookers in the belief
that outsiders were interlopers, that it was only *the family* you
should care about.

She had tried to run away from geographical, genealogical nar-
rowness. I have been in far places, she thought, but I am still the
same girl, bigger and stronger and perhaps somewhat surer, but
the mainspring is still there. It winds and rewinds on the old
notion, Blood belongs to blood.

Watching Carolyn come toward her, Lois realized how much
Carolyn had changed in the few months since she had seen her
in New York. Lois remembered a woman whose clothes were the
latest style, face freshly made up, beautiful hair just so, a woman
sure of herself, but the Carolyn kneeling down to get a closer look
at Constance was like a tracing of that former self—the lines
were the same but the face seemed blurred. When Carolyn rose,
even though she smiled, she seemed like someone who served in
sadness.

Lois was encircled in an intense embrace. "God, it's good to see
you," Carolyn said while her pocketbook banged against Lois's
back. "Did you have any trouble—about getting away?"

"No, they gave me the time off. It's company policy—with
deaths."

In all the confusion Constance was quiet, properly impressed. Anyone would have been. The sable stole, the pin on the lapel of her suit a circle of sapphires, even the smile on the face, seemed something fabricated in a fancy shop.

What had happened to her? She was no more the long, leggy girl of the tennis court than she was the cool beauty of a few months before in New York, smashing out a cigarette, saying, I no longer believe in the lies, I can stand without believing there has to be something like love to hold me up, the base deceitful mendacious libel of love to hold me up. I believe now love is the lie on which, wrongly, we try to build our lives.

Lois picked up her cosmetic case and, holding Constance's hand, followed the porter across the platform. Something else slipped into place in her mind from Carolyn's last visit to New York. Carolyn had stopped drinking. But a moment before Lois had smelled alcohol.

The car was at the curb, Carolyn at the wheel leaning across to open the door. Constance climbed into the front seat and Lois helped the man with the two suitcases, gave him some money, and, pausing, tried to pin down what had altered about the scene. Then she saw. Ten years before all the trees had been cut back; now they had grown tall again, there were lanes of tall trunks, like pointers, to the center of the city. She got in, gratified.

"Mother would have come with me," Carolyn said, "but she didn't feel she could leave Dad. You know he's pretty bad." The car moved forward. "Completely bedridden." They were adrift in traffic. "And Frances—she was going to come, but"— Carolyn laughed—"but she says she's staying out of sight until this thing about Esther blows over and anyway this is her afternoon with the vibrator."

After New York, Springfield looked small and slightly out of style. There didn't seem to be enough people on the streets.

"What thing about Esther?" Lois asked after a moment.

"Honey, don't tell me you don't *know*?" Carolyn shook her head. "If only poor old Ada—Esther got caught lifting some—"

"Esther *what*?"

"Esther was caught shoplifting. *Gloves*. Seven pairs of *gloves*.

Stuffed in one of those brown paper bags of hers. I had to go down with Mother and— They smooth these things over nowadays," she said, shoving her foot down on the accelerator. "And you know, Esther must operate under some kind of special star, as Frances would say. Any other time there'd have been no end of talk, but with Ada—"

Carolyn forced the car in and out of traffic at a terrifying speed. "How's Eileen taking it?" Lois asked when they were once more in the clear.

"She's held up pretty well. You know, sometimes she seems so—so right. And then, just when you're convinced maybe she's going to come out of it, she has one of those spells. They had this big fight, the family, about whether she should come down to the funeral parlor or not. Personally, I was against it. I didn't see what good it could do and conceivably it might do a lot of harm. Well, first she was going to go"—Carolyn braked abruptly behind a big convertible—"and then she wasn't. Go, not go. Argue, all right she should go. No, she shouldn't. Finally someone said to call the doctor and ask what he thought and he said no, she shouldn't go, and that was the end of that." Carolyn swung out sharply, pressed the accelerator, the car roared past the convertible just at the edge of an intersection.

"I'm planning to go as soon as I get unpacked and washed up," Lois said between clenched teeth. If someone were coming around that corner—

"Tell you what, why don't you come out to the house and have a drink first, call Mother, tell her you're here, but you wanted to see the children. There's a lot to catch up on. Wesley will look after Constance, he's good with kids. Not like Sally or Bobby. Teenagers," Carolyn said in disgust. "We're going to send Sally away to school in January, I can't take it any longer. Wait till yours grows up. Dates. Arguments about hours all the time. And she's only fourteen. Bobby isn't so bad. He's always been quiet and twelve's an age of withdrawal anyway, but Sally—" Carolyn slammed on the brakes. They had almost gone through a light. "We hardly ever see her—which in some ways is sort of a break, but you worry where she is, and when she is home, she's hopeless.

I tell you, she's made my life miserable this last year. I can finally appreciate how I must have been with Mother, all she must have gone through with me, but—but all the same," she finished, "I hate to think there's a comparison that close." She ground gears, pushing the car to its maximum power, struggling with the wheel. "God, I could use a drink. Traffic drives me wild. And, hell, it doesn't make any difference whether you drop in on Ada this afternoon or tonight."

"A drink would probably go right to my head. We sat up all night."

"You sat up all night? With a three-year-old?"

"It was the only way I could make it, Carolyn. Things are kind of tight."

"He doesn't help at all?"

"No, I haven't heard from him in six or seven months. I don't know where he is. The last I heard he was in Ankara, working in the news bureau there." She might as well get it over with all at once. "That was when we were trying to reach some kind of agreement about—about at least a separation. Then it all broke down. And now—it's just the way it's always been."

"Can't you sue him for support or something?"

"You'd have to find him first. Anyway, I don't want any money out of him, I just want to be quit of him and get it all settled once and for all and not have to worry about his popping up and making trouble."

"You should have a little talk with Erwin, he'd appreciate some of your views. On money at least. Helen's got him by the b-a-l-l-s," Carolyn spelled. "He's not going to get out of that one. Every time they see each other, even if it's only in the lawyer's office," she said, starting to pass on a hill, while Lois held her breath, and then dropping back, "they get into a Thirty Years' War. So far as I can see, they enjoy it. Well, everyone to his own aberrations, I always say"—but Carolyn said it in a funny way.

"You and Erwin, you were always so close. We always thought he was your favorite in the family." Carolyn's voice trailed off in tact. She was waiting for an explanation, Lois supposed, for what Carolyn had said was true: of all the cousins she had loved

Erwin best. While she was growing up, he had been her god. From him she had first learned how men and women went at the act of love; from him she had first felt what it was like to admire a man; and from him, ten years before, she had finally learned how disillusioned a woman can get with a man she has loved. For an instant, as Carolyn ran a red light, Lois saw Erwin as he had been the night Helen had nearly lost her child—impatient with illness, unable to cope with inconvenience. He had drunk enough Scotch in the kitchen to pass out before he even got around to asking Helen how she was. Lois had had to shake him awake. But shared judgment of someone you loved had always struck her as disloyal. She had previously kept her own counsel; she kept it now.

"Well, most of us grow apart as we get older and more difficult, and god knows he's gotten more difficult," Carolyn said after the silence. "Erwin always reminds me of Mark Twain's American who blew out the lamp that had been burning a thousand years."

What was it? What had happened to her?

They made a turn off the main highway and started down a long dirt lane. "When it snows, this is impassable, but otherwise it's all right. A little bumpy after it rains, but the privacy's worth it. You ever think about what a treat silence is any more, that there's almost no place left where you can be quiet? There it is, that lovely house. Every time I see it I feel a little better, that a few people out here knew how to put up proportions like that."

A dog ran out to meet them.

"Booze," Carolyn explained, then, leaning over Constance, she said, "He won't hurt you, honey, but why don't you stay near me until he gets used to you. He just barks a lot."

Constance crouched closer to Lois. "The city," Lois said, "doesn't give them much experience with animals."

"No, I suppose not," Carolyn replied, climbing out. "How do you stand it, crushed in with all those crowds?"

"I have to, it's where I make my living."

"But couldn't you—no, I suppose not. They don't publish magazines in Springfield." Carolyn was going up the path. "I'll take Constance upstairs and see if I can't get a box of some of Wes's old toys down. The kids don't get home until later, it's a long bus ride, and Sally—well, she comes when she feels like it. Come on, honey, let's look for some nice toys." She opened the kitchen door and they filed in. Carolyn reached up and opened a cupboard, took down a glass and put it on an old cabinet. From the icebox she took milk and half a cake. "You want a piece of this?" she asked, and over her shoulder she called out her mother's telephone number. While Lois dialed, Carolyn was getting out glasses, bending down to open a cupboard where liquor was. On her knees Carolyn looked up, an appeal on her face; she was biting her lip getting ready to speak when Iris's high, piercing hello came over the wire.

"So," Carolyn said, rising, "that about fills you in."

She was finishing up the family history—Erwin and Helen's final quarrel ("He was drunk downtown at some damn sales thing and she was fed up and called her father and he came over and when Erwin finally got home they wouldn't let him in. The next day they had all the locks changed on the doors and I don't think he's been back inside since"); Esther's theft of the gloves ("She's been doing it for years, Lois, it's a wonder she hasn't been caught before"); the problems of her brother Pete and his wife Peggy ("Ralph gave—Ralph made—a job for Pete, Lois, you know that, and there's nothing much to it, but he can hardly hold it down. If it were anyone else—don't say I said so, though—but if it were anyone else, Ralph would have gotten rid of him a long time ago, and that's the truth, but we feel so sorry for them—god, wait until you see Peggy, she's just worn out"); Frances's remarriage ("Nobody can figure out how she got him, he's a nice man, sort of natty and old-fashioned, a period piece, but sweet"), and Frances's house.

"Wait until you see the house, Lois, she's got petrified dough in the bedroom."

"She's got what?"

"These figures of dolls in dough," Carolyn said, "all over the bedroom. Frances got these bread dolls from Ecuador and they started getting these funny pinpoint holes all over them. They had bugs. You should have seen her face. But she wouldn't throw them out.

Cost too much money. Anyway, never throw anything out, not this family. So she had them *sprayed,* can you imagine? All these bugs just poured out. Thousands and thousands of bugs came crawling out of her Ecuador dolls, she was fit to be tied." Carolyn stopped in the doorway, the martini pitcher hugged close to her. "Let's have another and then I promise to drive you home."

"I don't think I should, Carolyn. It's after five—"

"One more—" Carolyn did not wait for an answer; in a moment she was in the kitchen and Lois heard the sound of the refrigerator opening, she was getting out ice.

The pictures on the wall were big blocks of bold colors, save for two small Deleavantes around which the whole of the rest of the room seemed to revolve, two humorous, beautifully executed Brueghel-like scenes that held your attention no matter where you looked. On the couch, with a marker, lay a faded reddish book, *The Enormous Room;* newspapers, magazines, quarterlies, two paperbacks were piled next to an enormous brown chair. And in the kitchen, Carolyn making more martinis: the girl who held open her mind was trying to close off her heart.

Carolyn came through the doorway, shaker raised high like a battle standard. She went to the bottom of the stairwell. "Wes, come down and give Constance something to eat, will you? A banana, a cooky, something. She's probably hungry again. I have a theory," she said to Lois, "that the way to keep kids under eight out of trouble is to feed them every twenty minutes." She crossed the room. In back of her sounds came on the stairs. Constance, holding Wes's hand, passed through. "She's awfully pretty," Carolyn said.

"It'll be a nuisance later on, they get spoiled thinking their looks will carry them, and then—then they're left with having been pampered long after they're no longer pretty."

"I don't know. I don't think girls can be too pretty. Men, sure, but not girls. You don't care about that in a man, you're looking for something else." Carolyn's face had a funny, puzzled look. "You know what I mean?" she asked, leaning forward. "In a man you want something else—vitality, I guess that's it. What were the four Greek virtues? Courage—"

"I thought it was knowledge, knowledge of virtue they were always talking about. Areté, wasn't that what it was called, a sort of combination of courage and nobility—excellence, moral and physical and intellectual excellence."

"But you remember, there were four cardinal virtues—god, virtue, that's an out-of-date word, isn't it? An out-of-date idea," Carolyn said after a moment. "Lois," she said, "how did you ever have the guts to walk out?"

"There wasn't anything else I could do. At the end—at the end I was afraid for Constance. I could have stood it for myself, but I didn't want anything to happen to her." She wanted to tell Carolyn the whole truth, but she couldn't. She wondered if she would ever be able to tell anyone. Probably not. But until she could she would never be able to be free of him. Wherever he was, he held her still. Maybe that was why she hadn't been able to let Neal even take her in his arms.

"I'm sorry. I wouldn't have brought it up if—"

"It's all right. A long time's passed. It doesn't bother me the way it did. You get over anything in time—it just takes time. For years I thought I'd never be able to talk about my mother—to say she was a suicide. I'd just say she'd died when I was young, my father had remarried, and an aunt had brought me up. And then one day it came out, I said it quite easily and I was surprised. What had once had the power of life and death over me had only become another fact in the account of my life, and I could look at it without emotion, so that, presumably one day, maybe even sooner than I expect, I'll be able to make a simple little statement of fact about Cliff, too. But—but in the meantime you learn to live with it, you tell yourself that people make too much of the whole thing of falling in love. Other people in other ages didn't set such store by the whole experience, they took it in their stride, made practical—and perhaps better—marriages, concentrated on their ambitions, their potentialities, instead of wasting all their energy on emotion. Falling in love was even looked down on, a sign a man was a weakling, like a woman, interested only in emotion. But we've been brought up in an age that specializes in romance—everything around us is charged with the idea love moves mountains, love makes the world go round, love is the means to fulfillment, that's all we're to set our sights on any more.

"But maybe I only speak for myself. As a matter of fact *he* didn't care about it, not after a while, after the initial excitement died down, he wasn't really interested in love, he wasn't interested in any of it, not even the—the bed part, he drank too much. I suppose you shouldn't say something like that," Lois said. "It's too personal. Anyway it's the age of alcohol. The men drink and can't make love and the women drink because they aren't loved. I read the most awful statement the other day—awful because it struck me as so true—what some psychiatrist said, he said, 'The size of the erection is, so to speak, a measure of a woman's desirability.' Well, in the end you might say according to that standard I was a bust, a complete and utter bust, because he was no damn good in bed, and that's the real clue to how it's going, isn't it, how it is in bed."

"He's very good in bed—mine. Don't look like that, you guessed, didn't you? Wes," Carolyn called into the kitchen, "You about finished?"

"We're through," he called back. "Come on, kid, I'll show you my chemistry set."

"It's nothing to worry about," Carolyn assured Lois. "He just makes perfume and stuff like that. Nothing explosive."

She bent over and took a cigarette from the pack lying on the table. "You mind if I talk to you? I feel as if I have to talk to someone. I think if I could get some of it out I would feel so much better. I don't even know how it happened. I mean, I wasn't looking for an affair or anything. Oh, I was fed up, fed up with everything, the house, the children, Ralph, even myself—mostly myself. I felt that if something didn't change, I'd end up exactly as I was, as I had been, for years and years." She took up her drink. "Myers made me feel I could come alive. In that awful cliché,"—and her face was hard over the rim of the glass—"he made me feel again. But he did, oh god, he did." She had set her glass down and was opening and closing a box on the table. "I wish I could convince myself love was just one of those definitions like yours, one of those awful definitions that psychologists give you—a primary narcissism given secondary confirmation, an affair of the ego, a nervous disorder, something cold and objective like that, but I can't, I'm still hooked on the old idea, that love maybe does make a center to your life, does give it focus and meaning—and—and *warmth*."

Lois didn't have time to answer.

"But maybe I'm just trying to fool myself. One side looks at it from the glands, the other from the brain box. Has it ever struck you most of the philosophers never married? Plato, Heraclitus, Schopenhauer, Spinoza, Kant, Descartes—"

"Descartes never married?"

"Well, maybe Descartes. But Nietzsche never did, certainly not Nietzsche. Sartre," she said. "What about Santayana?"

"Sartre had Simone de Beauvoir," Lois said.

"It's not the same. It's a fine distinction, but a distinction nevertheless." Carolyn took a long puff on her cigarette. "Everything has one—like in our case, who seduced whom. I thought he had been attracted to me, he showed all the signs, and then he didn't call or anything and I started wondering, I found myself thinking about him all the time, so the next time I saw him—you know the rest. It had started, and once it had started, I couldn't stop it. Not that I tried very hard. Once in a while I'd think, This has got to stop, and I'd make up my mind I would break it off, and then I'd be with him—" She caught her breath, unable any longer to keep up the false chatter, the fake sophistication that covered, Lois supposed, the horror of her own emptiness.

"I tell you, I'm frantic, I don't know what to do. I keep trying to call him and he's busy. I thought of going to his office this morning, but I haven't the courage. You know, he always used to call, oh once a day at least, and then suddenly, nothing. I even called his home last night, but he was out. Do you suppose he's got someone else?" Her streaked face—eyes dilated through the tears, make-up running, mouth moist—looked at Lois desperately. "Oh no, he can't. I don't know what I've done—maybe been too demanding—but I'm willing to change, I'm willing to work at doing whatever he wants. But how can I explain this when he won't even talk to me? It was so sudden, without any warning. It just came out of a clear blue sky. Everything was fine one day, and then the next—" Carolyn struggled for composure. "I was supposed to meet him for lunch. We'd go some place and have lunch and then—then there's this hotel—you'd know the name if I told you, it takes afternoon couples. Myers—he'd call up ahead of time and they'd tell him the number of the room. They never gave you a key, you just went up and locked the door—and then, when you were finished, Myers went down and gave them the money at the desk, I went on ahead, we didn't come down together. It wasn't embarrassing that way." Her face looked like a mask. "I used to live for those afternoons. Nothing else mattered. I was dead the rest of the time, just dead.

"I couldn't meet him that day because I had to go down with Mother about Esther, so I called and he said all right, we'd go to dinner in this place he knows outside of town. There's a motel not far away—I thought, you know—I was so happy when I finally got through with all that mess downtown and got away, I remember getting in the car thinking that if I didn't have Myers, I didn't know how I could go on, he was all I had, I was so tired after everything I guess I wasn't thinking very clearly, I was just glad to be with him, but now I realize I should have known something was the matter when he kept trying to get me to take a drink, but I just thought he—I don't know, he wanted to do—something different, if you know what I mean." And she looked away.

Lois felt a little sick.

"And then, inside, at the restaurant"—tears were trembling in her eyes—"the way he talked, it was just awful, he'd never been so—so cold, and it was almost as if he were laughing at me, and I kept trying to make things go, and then suddenly he got up and left me—but I forgot, before that, something that happened." She brushed the tears away impatiently. "An old man, at the next table, this girl was treating him horribly and he started to cry and Myers *laughed*. I didn't know what to say, what to do, and when he came back from phoning—he said, real abrupt, almost as if he were glad, that he had to get home, his girl didn't feel well, but it wasn't anything serious, Lois, just some minor thing kids get, and she's not little any more—it was an excuse, and we got up and he just walked out ahead of me, without even looking to see if I was behind, and the way he acted, as if he were glad to get rid of me, I had this feeling, I *knew* right there, but I wouldn't let myself believe, I didn't want to believe, and I came in the house, and Ralph was sitting in this chair, he'd been reading and he'd fallen asleep. I'd had a lot to drink—well, not too much, just three martinis, but I wasn't used to it—and I stood in the door looking at him and he opened his eyes and looked at me, looked *through* me, and I went out to the kitchen and made myself a drink, Ralph was standing in the doorway, he had *that* look on his face, disapproving, you know, because I was drinking again, and something kind of snapped inside me. Damn you, I remember thinking. I picked up the glass and swallowed the whole drink right in front of him, just to show him, and he didn't say a word, he just stood there with that look on his face, so I told him, I couldn't stop myself."

"What did he say, Carolyn? How did he take it?"

"He didn't say anything. He just turned around and went upstairs."

"But I mean later, did he—"

"He hasn't said anything since, Lois. We haven't spoken to one another since."

"But what about the children, aren't they—"

"We sort of talk around them. I guess they know something's the matter—kids always know—but I don't suppose they know what. Or how serious it is. And now," she finished, looking up at the ceiling, "I can't even get hold of Myers. It's as if—as if he knew I'd said something to Ralph and he was angry and wanted to punish me. But of course that's nonsense, he's got no way of knowing—"

"Unless Ralph—"

"No, Ralph's not like that. When he decides what he's going to do, it's me he'll deal with. Myers is an outsider. In Ralph's world you don't let outsiders in, ever, not even after they've made love to your wife." She looked down, examining her hands, the one ringed with the big engagement diamond and the band of brilliant stones, the other holding the cigarette. "So there you have it, the

whole pretty story. Isn't that a pretty story?" She stood up.
"Ralph'll be home in a little while. I know you don't want to stay
around for that. I'll drive you home. I'm terribly sorry, Lois. I
don't know what's the matter with me. I've got to pull myself
together." She turned. "I felt as if I weren't anything before this
started, as if I had lost whatever individuality I had, but now it's
worse, now I know I had hold of something then, even if I didn't
know it, there was still a little left, but now—now—it's as if I've
stripped myself of everything, even any notion of decency. All I
think of are terrible terrible things, desperate things, like going
to his office and—oh god, I can't, I just can't, I couldn't, I just
couldn't, could I, Lois?"

"Where have you been? People have been calling every five
minutes wanting to know where you are—even long distance—
New York—some *man*—he called *three* times—and what could
I say? Oh, I was so humiliated! Your first day back, you get off the
train and just disappear. You and Carolyn were out drinking,
that's what you were. Let me smell your breath. With a small
child, Lois, oh Lois, with a little baby like that, how could you?
Oh, you poor child, you poor poor child."

Down on her knees, Iris hugged and squeezed the poor child.

Lois and Carolyn stood in the hallway of the old Civil War
house with the suitcases. Lois had a vision of her apartment, her
nice inviolate apartment back in New York, where, were she
home, just about this time Neal might be ringing the doorbell,
standing with a bottle of wine cradled in his arms, the meat was
in the oven, Constance in the tub, and the worst hour, from six to
seven, Lois's hour of hell where all the chores clamored at her
to pay attention, do something, take care, was over, she could
be a human being again. What had ever possessed her to leave?
But she knew. She wanted to believe in a future again.

"That poor child probably hasn't had a thing to eat," Iris said,
looking at them accusingly.

"How are you?" Lois bent over and bestowed a light kiss on
that puffed tearful cheek. She felt, in spite of what should have
been a sharp sense of guilt, light and carefree. Neal had called.

"Oh, you don't know, honey, you have no idea—oh, I've been so worried that I have, you know, the sugar—that terrible thing where you have injections."

"Now, mother—"

"Oh, I know what you think, Carolyn, that I *exaggerate,* but you don't know the pains I have. My heart," she said, "flutterings all the time. And now this new worry. Diabetes. And you know how I am about needles. Honey, where have you been? Oh, the phone's been ringing and ringing. That man in the East. Stu. Pete and Peggy. Even Dad. He's been driving me crazy with that bell. Ring ring ring, that's all it ever does. 'Where's Lois,' he says, 'Has Lois come yet?' And I have to run up and down those stairs, it doesn't ever seem to occur to him I'm human, I can wear out, just ring ring ring."

"It's only a little after six," Lois began—it was closer to seven—while Carolyn began backing out the door. She had to get home, she had her own supper to worry about, Ralph would be home, the children . . .

Cosmetic case in hand, Lois was left in the front hall, staring up the teak stairs to the bright bulb at the upper landing. She might have been ten or twelve again when, arms piled high with borrowed books after the long walk from the library, she had let herself in and started up the stairs, softly, so as not to disturb the boarders, and all along the hall faint noises from behind closed doors sounded mysteries strange and wonderful of the lives of Mr. Bertrini or Miss Scooton, those perennial plants in Iris's economic arbor. Miss Scooton, having wilted in her late fifties, had gone West to seek the sun, but Mr. Bertrini had been cut down two years before the retirement that would have taken him and his endless supply of peppermint lozenges, the aid, he called them, for acid indigestion, to wherever people like Mr. Bertrini went when they were old and no longer useful. Sarasota? Fort Lauderdale? Some place where the aged bloomed a little longer.

"It's for you, I know it's for you," Iris said dramatically, against the ringing of the phone in the background. Then she disappeared into the back hall under the stairs and Lois could remember her complaining in that same voice whenever Miss Scooton wanted ice or Mr. Bertrini had asked if someone would bring up a little hot lemon juice at nine. Would you do it, honey? Iris would ask. I'm just dead. I can't move another inch, and it's an imposition, they shouldn't ask for these things, but maybe you'll get a nickel. Lois never did, but she always went with hope.

"Yes, she *finally* got here. Yes, I'll call her. Lois, it's Stu." Iris handed, without a glance, the phone to Lois. "You come along with me, honey," she said to Constance. "Those girls," she said in despair. "They always were the death of me and they're no better now that they've grown up and have children of their own than they were when I had to plait their hair. No sense of—of responsibility," she said, bearing Constance by the hand out the door of the hall into what had once been the sewing room. When Lois was little, it had been the master bedroom. Now she supposed Iris slept there alone; her uncle was upstairs. A creature of small but infinite habits, Iris would rather move her husband than herself even if it meant running up and down stairs to wait on an invalid.

Lois picked up the phone. It seemed somehow right Stu should be on the other end. First Carolyn at the station, now Stu on the phone. The three of them who had grown up together in this house had a special bond. There had been one more son of Iris's, Pete, but too early a marriage and too many unwanted children had removed him from their worlds. She, Carolyn, and Stu somehow seemed the real brother and sisters, Pete the outsider. Poverty marked people in insupportable ways. Yet Lois had never been— or felt she had never been—a sentimentalist. Sentimentalists tried to make of people more than they could be; she accepted Pete for what he was. And was sorry. But being sorry did not change what was. How often, she wondered, did it help?

"Stu? How are you?"

"That's what I'm supposed to be asking you. You're the one who's been away," Stu said.

"I'm a little tired—the long train ride and all. Carolyn met me, and we went out to her place and had a couple of drinks and—I don't know, just being back. It's strange. You know who I thought of first? Mr. Bertrini and Miss Scooton."

"My god, I haven't thought of them in years."

"He had peppermint lozenges."

"That bad stomach. And died, poor old bastard, before he ever had a chance to get out and have any fun. You think you can get out, Lois? I'd like to see you. Tonight, if possible."

"I don't know. You know I want to get down to the funeral parlor—"

"I could take you by first," Stu said. "And then—then there's something I want you to do with me."

"All right, but—"

"I'll be by about eight." Then he hung up. It was something she had forgotten, how he hated to talk on phones. "Every time I hear one ring," he used to say back in New York when Stu lived there too and they had first come to know each other well, "I think it's Ethel on the other end, getting ready to hound me." He hadn't been living with Ethel then. A drifter. A man of moods, often dangerous ones. They came and went unaccountably, but whenever a call came from him in New York Lois always knew one was about to start. Sometimes, she had discovered, being with her helped; more often she suspected it didn't. Then he would disappear, drop out of her life completely; after a number of weeks another call would come, he was himself, they would resume without reference to the interruption their regular schedule of drinks and dinner at her place. She had the cut-up apartment on Riverside Drive then; it was the winter with Neal, the summer she and Stu had both come back to Springfield; he had stayed and she had gone back to New York and then eventually to Greece; he stayed because Ethel had gotten pregnant and he thought he should. He had been trying to do what he thought was right ever since. Unsuccessfully. Part of his trouble was that he had picked the wrong woman to try with. She wondered for the thousandth time what under the sun had ever prompted Stu to marry Ethel, but it was a question people always seemed to be asking about the married people she knew. What did she ever see in him? How can he stand her? Marriage—like the Army—more often than not brought out the worst in people.

She thought of the night ten years before when they had both stood on the porch upstairs here in Sans Souci, gazing down at the green growing night, August and the night sounds—insects, cars, murmurings from the rooms inside, their own soft voices coming from behind the bright ends of cigarettes. I'm glad you're not going back to New York, she had said. I think it's right—for you. But not for you? he had asked. No, not for me, she had said, and gone away, left him here in this house with the big bloated unloved wife who had his child growing inside.

She had not seen Stu for five years, and then only briefly on that three-day visit to Springfield. He was turning over some object in his hands, she'd forgotten what, seemingly concentrating all his attention; then, unexpectedly, he looked up and gave her that lopsided and (what she supposed he considered) cynical smile. "It didn't work out so well, my coming back and staying, did it? I mean, when you consider the things I've run through and the rate I've run through them, you can hardly call me a success, can you? I can't even," he said through the bitter mouth in the twisted face, "find it in my heart to love my wife, and that's just a beginning, isn't it?"

Lois shook her head, trying to stop him, but he would not be stopped. "But, christ, it isn't because I haven't tried. You're the only one that understands that, Lois, that I've tried. The others just think I'm a son of a bitch, that I *like* lousing up Ethel's life as well as mine."

Why couldn't he have had a little luck just once? Maybe because, like Saul, he just wasn't born to it. There would always be the Davids of the world who could do no wrong and there would always be the Sauls, the Stus, who could do no right. She wondered where in such a scheme of things her own place was.

Constance had gone almost immediately—and, blessedly, without too many protests—up to bed. Lois and Iris were in the kitchen finishing up what roast the boarders had left (Iris made them eat early, no matter how often they complained that they hardly had time to get from work to her table by five-thirty; it's my life, Iris said, and I can't spend *all* of it washing up), when Iris, pausing in the midst of an aphorism—"An even exchange's no robbery,

Lois, that's what Mama always used to say"—suddenly stood up, her paper napkin clutched to her breast. "The bell," she said as if the world were coming to an end. "Someone's at the front door" —and waited, mesmerized, for the next sound.

Lois got up. "It must be Stu," she said.

"I don't know why you have to go out again. Dad will wake up and he'll be so disappointed when he finds out you're gone *again*. Of course I don't like to interfere with your plans or anything—" The bell was audible again over her entreaties. "I'll get it, I'll get it," Iris cried and fled into the hall before Lois could stop her.

Lois sat down to finish the last mouthfuls of meat and mashed potatoes; the peas were impossible. They canned everything here in the land of the fresh and the green.

Then Stu was in the doorway, in an awful overcoat, a beige scarf hanging down from either side of his throat like one of those stoles that priests wore. He looked older and grayer and somehow stronger; he had put on weight. "You've let your hair grow. I'll bet that's the first thing Mother said to you, wasn't it?"

Iris drew herself up. "I never mentioned it. I said—what did I say?" she asked Lois.

You've been drinking, Lois thought, but aloud she said, "She must look like her father, she doesn't look like you."

"Well, the child doesn't, but are you sure that's what I said? It seems to me—no, I don't think that was the first thing I said, Lois, I think—surely I said I was glad to see you back?"

Stu was fumbling with a cigarette. "Don't let me rush you. I'll just sit down—"

"I'm almost finished," Lois said quickly. "But I want to give your mother a hand with the dishes."

"Oh, we have a machine now, honey. I gave it to myself for my birthday. With all the work with Dad and all I thought I deserved it. I don't know how I ever lived without one, I really don't. Only the repair bills are terrible. Last week something went wrong and a man came and blew down this tube and said thirteen eighty-five and I said, 'You mean to tell me it costs thirteen dollars and eighty-five cents to blow down a tube,' and you know what he had the nerve to say? He said, 'It's not how long it takes but what you know.' " She threw out the martyred arm which had been forced to sign the fatal check. "Lawyers, dishwasher men, watch repairmen, those men that work on the car, I don't trust—"

Stu cut her short by the neat expediency of kissing her on the mouth. Words were throttled in her throat. Startled, gurgling, she looked about with open eyes, waved her arms, then embraced him.

Lois moved swiftly up the stairs for her coat. Down the hall someone was crying. Small sobs shook the stillness, a voice was calling out plaintively, "Jesus . . . Joseph . . . Mary, oh Mary, help me . . . help me. Jesus . . . Joseph . . . oh Mary help me . . ."

Lois went to the open door. From the look of fright and panic on the face of the man lying on the bed, she knew he didn't recognize her. "Uncle Stewart?" she called softly.

"Oh . . . oh! Iris, *Iris*," he called frantically, his voice rising. "Iris!"

High heels sounded staccato from the stairs. "Coming, coming. What is it? What do you want? Are you wet?" Iris demanded, coming abreast of the door and pushing past Lois, confronting the frightened face on the pillow.

One emaciated arm raised itself and pointed.

"Oh Dad, it's Lois. Didn't you know Lois? Here you've been waiting all day for Lois and—" Leaning over the bed, she bent down and shouted in his ear. "It's Lois, Dad, *Lois*. See, he knows you," Iris said triumphantly. "He gets a little confused sometimes, but he's worse at night. It's the lights, the lights from the cars bother him—he watches them on the ceiling overhead," she explained. She leaned over and in a very loud voice she said slowly, "Doesn't she look fine, Dad? Don't you like *her hair*? She's let it grow."

The thin, almost translucent arm remained raised. It seemed to Lois she could see through the pale enveloping skin to the shell-like structure of bone, the pulse that was life in the wrist. The hand half raised itself. So slight a signal in another might have gone unnoticed, but he was beckoning—Lois moved closer, looking down into his eyes. The half-smile there was like his son's. "Uncle Stewart," she said.

He nodded, acknowledging what identity was left. The head moved negatively, twice, on the pillow. Then the eyes closed. The interview was at an end. She had come home and he had seen her; nothing more was needed; dying, he could cross one more name off his list, one more face he had seen as it made obeisance over the bed.

Stu, standing awkwardly in the doorway, bent forward, narrowed at the waist, like a bearer of solemn tidings, and said simply, "Dad."

His father opened his eyes. In the old days when she was growing up, Lois remembered how Stu and his father treated each other like new boarders encountering each other for the second or third time. The initial introduction was over, but the relationship had not given any promise of developing; they were two strangers of necessity polite but by preference aloof. Affection had at last, in illness, allowed itself to show. The father was dying, the old king's heart must be extracted and eaten by the firstborn.

Stu came in to stand by his father's bed. He did none of the things she might have expected, neither touching his father's hand nor straightening the bed covers; he stood intently, talking with his eyes. What was he saying to his father? Something to do with the unbreakable bond of blood? No matter what happened they were bound by blood. Wasn't that really why she had come home?

"The old man," Stu said, holding the car door open for Lois, "doesn't look much like himself any more, does he?"

"I knew he'd been sick, Stu, but I didn't know he was—when you look at his hands—"

"It's the hands that get you, the hands and eyes." He held the door open for her, stood staring at the big jars of wandering Jew, moribund; the leaves had been frozen in a frost the week before, but his mother always had slips in coffee cans saved for the next summer; she cut them in September, they were all over the kitchen all winter. Thrift motivated her almost as strongly as the need to make scenes.

"I should have made a phone call," Lois said.

"Make it in the bar, it's fairly quiet in one of those booths. You don't want to get back in there and start Mother going again, do you? All any of us has to do is pass through that front door and she's rewound, the record drops, the same old music starts." He laughed.

She had forgotten what a nice sound his laughter made. Something unforced about it, about all of him. Why couldn't he be happy? Why couldn't they all?

Not the point, that was why. There had to be more to life than just being *happy*.

"I want to go over to the funeral parlor first, get it over with, and—and I probably ought to stop by Pete and Peggy's."

"It wouldn't hurt," he conceded. "They're the ones that usually, one way or the other, get left out."

Stu turned the key in the ignition and pressed his foot to the accelerator. She felt tonguetied over the scene she'd made when she'd taken him up to see Constance, when they'd both stood at the side of the bed, looking down in the small slash of light from the hall on that fair head, that beautiful fair head. For a moment Constance had opened her eyes; then she had smiled, and Lois caught her breath. Stu turned and gave her a look of astonishment; had he seen then the tears in her eyes? She was ashamed, but couldn't help herself. Emotion—silly, feminine, idiotic emotion—had overcome her for a moment. She loved her daughter more than anything in the world.

He must have been remembering the Lois he had first known in New York. He'd been so sure she was "going to make it"—those had been his very words. Now he must have seen how changed she was—the lines, the eyes, the mouth, the way the whole of her held off.

"You want a drink to pick you up, make your call, and then go see Ada?"

"I had some martinis with Carolyn, Stu. The call's waited this long, it can wait a little longer. Anyway, I'd rather get it over with, you know. I'm an awful coward about these things."

"How well I do know. But even cowards occasionally have courage. Who'd have believed way back when that I'd get a grip on my-self, cut out all that drinking, those fights, the mess of things I made —still make," he amended. "Well, I didn't do it all on my own. That's what I wanted to talk to you about—but it can wait until later," he said hastily. "I never do anything all on my own," he said after a moment. "I even needed your help to come home, you had to make me come home."

"I didn't *make* you—"

"Well, the truth is I wouldn't have come if it hadn't been for you."

He pulled the car into the oval driveway and under the lacy wooden canopy; the funeral parlor was an old Victorian house, once Knitter Reilly's answer to the charge of Potato Irish. The place had lost Reilly's racy touches such as the painted iron Negro jockey in front where the Ould Sod friends used to tie up their quarterhorses, and the big rosy bulbs on either side of the front door that were in what was called "questionable taste." Trans-formed now to the mortician's taste, the house leaned toward them gloomily in the artificial light, much as old Reilly himself must have been at the end when the Little Depression, drink, and his thieving friends had done him in and he went back to the Church and the Ward for his faith.

"You go in, I'll park the car out back."

"If you don't mind, Stu, I'd just as soon stay with you, we can go in together."

"Suit yourself, it's your show." After a moment, maneuvering the car down the narrow drive to the parking lot, he said, "She won't be there—Eileen. The doctor told them to forget it, they'd be lucky to get her through the funeral."

"I know, Carolyn told me."

"Arnold, though, he might be around—not that he puts too much time in down here, but someone's always around. Mother thinks it isn't *nice* if there isn't a welcoming committee. Who's she think is going to come to see the old girl?" He pulled the car into a space marked VISITORS, braked, and waited a moment be-fore turning off the ignition. Sighing, he said, "Don't let it get through to you. It's nothing to get upset about, just a dead old dame. There isn't any of the energy left that made up Ada. That's what death is, isn't it, a kind of complete discharge, no more power to tune up the battery, to make the machine run." Wearily he got out; too much talking had always tired him.

They walked up to the side door, silent. She passed in front of him onto the thick carpet, into the still air that seemed heavy like something solid, the pearly light, the sacred music murmuring against a backdrop of velvet. Ada Timble Ames, a sign said, was down the hall, and their feet rose and fell without imprint, without sound, on the nap of that wall-to-wall carpeting.

"She looks—I don't know," he said, trying to help, "like somebody else, but then, come to think of it, I'm not really sure what she really did look like, it's been so long since any of us saw her. They made a mess of her before Frances got in there," he said, pausing, she thought, to give her a chance to collect herself. "Frances made them do something about her mouth. They had her mouth open. You could see every filling she had. Poor Ada, if she'd known they left her mouth open like that so Esther could come along and count all the cavities she had . . .

"My god," he said softly, on the threshold, "speak of the devil."

"Stu, Stu, *Stu Ashwell*," the harsh high voice screeched out. "Where's your mother? Where's the piano? That's what I want to know. We're entitled to a piano in this price room."

"Piano?" Lois asked. "Is there going to be singing, Aunt Esther?"

"There's always singing, isn't there?" But Esther sounded uncertain. "Where's that man—that undertaker gone? He was here a moment ago."

Almost instantly he appeared, full of condolences and commiseration. The rain . . . the damp . . . a terrible time for all of them . . . so near Thanksgiving . . . what could he do for them?

They were all standing in front of the coffin, but the undertaker, trying to placate Esther, had moved backward, gently guiding her away from the remains and out into the hall where any disputes could be settled in a more congenial atmosphere—there where the faint hymns were piped in and the lovely green carpet ran from wall to wall. As he glided backward, he leaned forward consolingly, talking about weather, radiation, atomic experiments, his eyes moistening, his hands tenderly anchored on Esther's arm, his feet firmly propelling them both backward, away from Ada, and the serene smile on his face seemed to say that the air in the void all around him was full of high-powered radioactive encouragements to his trade, in another year or so the hydrogen holocaust would come and he would be a rich, rich man, someone to reckon with.

Splendidly silenced, even her galoshes hushed by the maneuver, Esther stood beside him, gaping into his placid pale face, and behind her, soft and soothing, the sad voice of a soprano sang from the kingly shadows of the hall,

> *Come, Holy Spirit, come,*
> *With energy divine,*
> *And on the poor benighted soul*
> *With beams of mercy shine.*

"I just wish they wouldn't *display* them," Lois said. Ada didn't look like anyone she knew. Lying there, she was more like a big photograph of herself—flat, distorted, cut-rate. She made death seem a little silly.

Lord, forgive me, Lois thought, I see so much wrong everywhere.

"God, you look great, just great!"

She hadn't heard him come in. Turning, she looked into Erwin's blond, happy face. "You don't come back often enough," he said in that synthetically enthusiastic way he had. "I mean, it's great to have you back, why don't you do it more often, we need bucking up." Then he started to laugh. "I said *bucking* up."

The dead woman might just as well not have been in front of them.

What was she supposed to say? Numbed, she simply stood there, nodding, trying to tell herself that under that incredible exterior there was still a heart that understood the Pierian spring, the silvered birds, the long summer afternoons that seemed to last forever.

She had cared so much for this cousin once, and love ought not to diminish because it is called upon to give an account of itself.

"I say something wrong?"

"I'm just tired," Lois said. "It was a long trip and I didn't get much sleep."

Suddenly he bent over and brushed his lips against her cheek. "You're still my favorite cousin, you know that, don't you?" Then he was all smiles. "How about a night out, a real night out on the town? Just the two of us."

"Well, I don't know," Lois said uncertainly. "I mean, I don't know what Iris has got planned for me and with Constance—"

He wasn't paying attention, his eyes suddenly glued to the door.

"I thought you'd get something better, over there in Athens, Lois," Frances said, sweeping into the room in an ambience of Persian lamb, hooped earrings, silver and rhinestone pins, and Sortilège. Lois looked down at Ada; if she was interested in the dead woman, she was the only one. "You remember that time I read your cards?" Frances was saying. "Over at Erwin's? You were going to marry money, have a title—whatever happened, do you suppose? Well, don't let one disaster get you down," Frances said cheerfully. "Lemon Number One of mine was no pile of potatoes—nothing *personal* against the man who made you, Erwin —but in any objective analysis of things, he would have won low man on the totem pole. Not like good old Jules. Good old Jules has the nucleic acid. So when you swing for the second time, Lois, be sure there's a little jack to widen the way. You're Virgo and taken as a whole that's not bad, it's just that those born under Virgo, for all their internal purity, aren't too practical. The pure never are," she said with great finality. Then she turned to her son. "Down doing your little duty? Or flushing old Esther out, were you?"

Erwin regarded his mother glumly.

"You might as well count the cat out and on the town. And if Esther's having fun, why should you object? You're the one who's always been so hot on having fun, so if Esther's going to have some—" Frances stopped. "You mean you don't know, Lois? You haven't *heard*?" She looked from one to the other of them. "Oh, it's too rich, too rich for words. Why, old Esther was so thankful that Ada dropped dead before she heard about The Little Glove Episode, she's gone and joined some sect. They've been after her —or more accurately, her little pile of potatoes—for months, and now they've bagged her. You mean she didn't say anything about Harold and His Infernal Machine when she was in here? It's all she can talk about."

"She was worried about a piano, Aunt Fran—"

"I don't doubt it for a minute. What she really wants is to drag that machine in here and play some little song over Ada. Don't worry, Ada," Frances said, looking down on her dead sister, mascaraed eyes brimming with compassion, "I won't let her. It's bad," she conceded to the others, looking up, assuming her normal agitated manner, "but at least it isn't nude protest parades and pot shots at the Internal Revenue men like those nice people the Dukhobors."

"The Moscow subway," Esther said breathlessly, emerging from the doorway where Lois supposed the mortician had at last let her loose. "Harold's going to put it down in the Moscow subway, Frances, you know that, you just want to make fun of it, you make fun of everything, you always have. Well, you can't make fun of this because when the vibrations come through, those Russians will be *receptive,* then you'll see, then you'll thank your lucky stars there was someone like Harold doing something to bring the world to its senses while the rest of you were *devoured* by fritterings and frivolities. You're just like the State Department, you don't want peace, real peace, you're afraid it will upset the economy—a recession'll set in. It's the State Department that's holding us up," she said, turning to Lois. "They don't *want* to see how important The Instrument could be—"

Out of the department stores and into the subways—*What in the world was she talking about?*

". . . the harmonies of the hemisphere . . . *every* known natural and unnatural material known to man, that's what it's made of, Lois," she said breathlessly. "Harold's built it with every single natural and manufactured material in the universe. So of course it's *representative.*"

"It must be enormous," Lois said helplessly. She could not get over the notion that in a moment someone would come noiselessly sliding into the room to pass tea and cakes, that over the dead woman's coffin they would all begin to chat of the plays they had seen and the friends who were failing fast.

"Well, it's pretty big," Esther admitted, "but you can't expect to get heavenly harmonies out of a—"

"Harmonica," Frances finished for her.

Esther turned away. "*Some* people try to compare it to an organ —a *glorified* organ—but actually it's much more than that. The music isn't anything like organ music. It's a—a kind of celestial euphony."

"What?" Frances demanded, leaning over, all the costume jewelry she wore clanking together; for a moment she looked almost bowed beneath the weight.

"We sing, too," Esther was saying proudly. "We all wear white and hold these beautiful hand-blocked books that have words. Of course I'm just starting, a novitiate, as they say, I haven't performed in public yet, but the others, they even went as far west as Oregon," Esther said proudly. "It was their greatest triumph, Portland. Thousands came."

It was a little hard for Lois to imagine thousands of people in Portland, Oregon, flocking to a hall to hear Harold's heavenly harmonies, but in this room it was difficult to imagine, among these people, anything that was quiet and of song.

Then, gasping, Esther was talking about some petition, holding it up, a few forlorn names inscribed under a typewritten message, addressed no doubt to the President pleading with him to slash through the odious red tape of the Passport Department and send them all off, Harold, Esther, the Sisters, and the Instrument, properly visaed so they could mess up the Moscow transportation system. "Sign, I want you all to sign," she was screaming, waving her paper in the air. "It's for international understanding. It's practically our last chance to stop radiation and bone deterioration and the terrible things that happen to all those poor little fetuses—all the things they're trying to hide from us."

"Don't sign anything until you've read it line for line, word for word. You don't know what you're signing if you don't read it first. Let me see it," Frances said, grabbing. "But who can understand this?" she demanded. "What does this mean—'altruistic and autistic understanding'?"

"It means just what it says," Esther said with an attempt at icy dignity. "If you don't understand the meaning of *words*—"

"You've gone fiddy," Frances said. "Whoever heard of such a thing, playing music, *singing* in a subway? If you want to go and give a concert, that's all right, but hire a hall. Put it on in some auditorium. I don't blame the frooky State Department for putting you off. How would it look, a lot of Americans trooping down the stairs of a subway, lugging this great big instrument behind them, playing and singing while people are trying to catch their trains? What kind of unprofessional image is that, Esther? I just ask you, what kind of amateur image of our country is that?"

"But Frances," Esther protested, "that's the whole point—we want to get to the people. Not to the highbrows or the ones in power, not to the élite, but to the masses—and where do you find the masses? In subways, of course," she finished triumphantly.

"The point is there aren't any élite in Russia, everybody knows that. There's nothing but masses, that's the whole point of a place like that. Everybody's got to be a member of the masses, there aren't any upper classes, so if you took over some nice big hall and put on your show there—"

"It is NOT a show—"

"If you sing, it's a show, I don't care what you say."

"It is not a show," Esther repeated. "This is a serious effort to bring about the brotherhood of man. Harold says—"

"Harold Smarold, how much money has he got out of you?"

Esther drew herself up, the whites of her eyes widened in anger. "We don't have to put in anything if we don't want to, we contribute—what we can. From each his own."

"No wonder he's dragging you over to Russia," Frances said, shaking her head. "He's picked up a few notions from there himself. You'd better watch out, Esther, he's probably subversive as all hell. Have you had him checked?"

"Had him checked?"

"Yes, you know, looked him up in that list they're always talking about with all those unAmericans."

"You're going to be punished one of these days, Frances Timble," Esther said slowly, shaking her head from side to side. "Mark my word, the wrath of the Lord is going to fall full upon you."

"And just tell me one little thing, Light Fingers, when did it fall on you? Down there in the department store when—"

"Oh, for chrissake, mother," Erwin began.

Shrugging, Frances rearranged the fur collar of her coat, began buttoning up the front. "I withdraw. Don't say I gave up, just state I made a mild retreat, it all got too much for me in the winter weather, standing around this steamy place in this heavy coat and hearing all this mumbo-jumbo about heavenly harmonies and the ascension of the Virgin Mary—has he come to that yet, Esther, about how she's supposed to have gone up there *all in one piece*?"

"We are not interested in the bodily aspects of transcendence," said Esther with solemnity. "It is the spirit that commends the soul, not the flesh."

"Commends it all right on wings of silver—thou shalt not be crucified on a cross of gold, or something like that." And Frances, buttoned and furred, moved toward the door. "See you soon?" she called out to Lois. "I hear you and Erwin are to descend upon the town one of these eves to raise a little whoopee." Not waiting for an answer, her hand fell upon the front door; it seemed miraculously to open itself, and she stepped into a cacophony of sounds —wind, cars, a siren somewhere in the night—without so much as a backward glance at the dead woman lying among all those expensive, fading flowers.

"They still live in the same house," Stu said, maneuvering into the narrow entranceway to his brother's driveway. His headlights revealed in the open door of Pete's garage the old '51 Chevy and alongside and behind that a disarray of gardening tools, bicycles, laundry baskets, broken toys. When the car came to a halt, Lois was looking at a no-man's land that separated the house from the sidewalk, an expanse on which almost no grass grew and the small sign seemed to say DANGER instead of ASHWELL.

When they were at the front door, he said to her, "Brace yourself," then rang the bell. He was telling her to beware, Lois thought. In the short silence that followed, she felt she could hear the last of the leaves dropping, a star losing its life somewhere out in the firmament.

"Gee, Lois," Pete said at the open door, "it's good to see you, just great, come on in. Hey, Peg, look who's here, it's Lois, and she looks great. Mary—Sue—come on down. Lois is here. The boys are out," he explained, "except for Stevie. And I guess you know Frank's in the Army. In Oklahoma. Hey, Stevie, your Aunt Lois is here."

From all parts of that small, poorly constructed house footsteps sounded. Lois knew they lived bunched up, the three remaining boys in one room, Mary and Sue in a room almost as small as a closet. How was it possible to endure under such circumstances? —and then she thought, What an absurd question. People endured as they had to.

"Gee, Lois," Peggy said, and obviously meant it, "it's just swell to see you." Like most husbands and wives who have spent their marriage in penurious closeness, Pete and Peggy had come to talk—almost to look—alike.

There were too many people for the room, not enough chairs, not really enough space; shy Susan acknowledged an introduction, stubborn Stevie hung back. Only Mary came forward, a nice attractive girl, sure of herself, sure at least of one thing, it seemed to Lois, that she would not marry only to breed and feed a family; she wanted something else out of life; and those, Lois hoped, who wanted something strongly enough managed to wrest at least a part of it. Not the whole, nobody but a fool asked for all, just a part, some small part.

"For chrissake," Pete said irritably, "ask her to sit down. Can't you ask her to sit down?"

"Sit down," Peggy said to Lois. "Let me get you something. I think there's a beer in the icebox," she said uncertainly and then looked at Stu, stricken. "We could—*you* could share," she said hopefully. "Sue, will you look?"

"No, no, please don't go to any trouble," Lois said hastily. "I just had some drinks with Carolyn and anyway I can only stay for a minute, we can't stay long, can we, Stu, I just wanted to drop by and—please don't go to any trouble," she pleaded while Peggy ran from chair to chair lifting newspapers, straightening the room, then stopped, staring about as if seeing for the first time the strained sofa, rump-sprung chairs, frayed rug, the faded lampshade.

"Go on, sit down, make yourself comfortable," Pete urged, while Lois, standing next to Stu, suddenly found herself putting out a hand for support.

"Yes, please sit down," Peggy begged, and for an instant Lois had the sensation Peggy was about to break down, that she would fall before them, broken at last. "I mean, gee, Lois, we haven't seen you in—how long has it been?" she asked.

"A long time," Lois, low-voiced, said. "Almost five years."

"And, well, we want you to sit down, have a good visit," Pete said, "tell us what's happening in the big city, what's going on back East." Pete gave a laugh as if he had made a joke. "Yessir, we want to know what goes on in New York City." He said it sit-tee, and then laughed again. "Sue, see if there's that beer," he said, and Sue went, while Lois lowered her reluctant flesh into a chair, sat up against that worn upholstery.

"Hey, noghead," Pete said to his wife, as if he were making still another joke, but Lois saw he was really serious, that he was the kind of husband who would call his wife "idiot" and "stupid" in front of company as if in fun, while all the time people turned, as Lois was turning, uncomfortably on their chairs, well aware behind the thin veil of synthetic mockery the tall font of derision went pouring forth. "Noghead," he repeated while Peggy lifted her frail head and gazed at him, waiting. Such a face, Lois thought, belongs in a great painting instead of this faded living room.

"Honey?" she asked tentatively.

"Ashtrays," he said, snapping his fingers. "We need ashtrays."

Something—distaste, Lois thought—registered in Peggy's face, but she tried to put on a smile, she would make it go for the sake of the guests; she moved toward a table, picked up a ten-cent-store glass ashtray, and brought it over to Lois.

"How about Stu?"

"We can share," Stu said in what Lois recognized as shame.

"Nah, we got plenty of ashtrays. Stevie," he hollered, "bring us an ashtray, will you?"

In the pause while they all waited for the beer, the ashtray, Lois tried to concentrate on the notion that for each of us there must be some center of emotional life, and nowadays more often than not anger and violence were at the center of most people's lives. Something to do with the temper of the times, a frazzling of the nerve ends so complete that it shoved us all, she thought, into scenes we hate but cannot do without.

She watched Sue in the doorway vainly trying to signal her mother. "There's Coke," she said weakly while they all watched.

"I know there's a beer in there," Pete said stubbornly. "You just didn't look. Not that I blame you, not with all that junk your mother's got crammed in there, it's a wonder you can ever find anything. Why don't you clean that out once in a while?" he demanded, turning toward Peggy angrily, while Peggy, who had fallen into a stillness near death, suddenly started. "Why the hell can't you defrost the icebox once in a while?"

"Why can't you? Why am I the only one around here who's supposed to do anything? Or why can't one of the girls? They're older right now than I was when I was married and had two—three—children of my own. But do they help? Do you? I want some help once in a while. Is that too much to ask, just someone to help once in a while. I'm tired, I tell you, tired—"

"What the hell have you got to be tired about? Not from working, that's for sure—"

"Not from working? What do you know about working? If it weren't for the fact Ralph was decent enough to—"

"Mother, please—"

"Don't mother-please me. You'll see. You'll find out. You'll get yourself in trouble one of these days, the way I did, and then there won't be any way out, just the way there wasn't for me, you'll see then, you'll find out then. Oh Mary, be careful, please

be careful, I don't want you to end up the way I am, I don't want
you to—"

"Just like Mother," Pete said disgustedly, turning toward them,
as if for confirmation. "Christ almighty, you'd think the world
was coming to an end because someone asked her to defrost a
refrigerator. What's so almighty special about pulling out a plug
and letting some ice melt, will you just tell me that?"

"Because it isn't just pulling out a plug and letting some ice
melt," Peggy answered, her voice getting higher and higher. "Everything has to come out and you have to put trays of hot water
in and—"

"That's hard? That's impossible for you to do? Just filling some
trays with hot water? It's too much to heat a little water and—"

"If it's so easy, why don't you do it?"

"I'll tell you why I don't do it—because I work hard all day
and when I get home I want a little peace and quiet, *a little peace
and quiet,* I don't want to start doing the things you're supposed
to have done all day like—"

"Like endless washing and ironing, endless dishes and beds
and—"

"We've got company—COMPANY FOR CHRISSAKE—why can't
you act like you had some kind of bringing up instead of having
to get married because you got knocked up—"

"That's a nice way to talk, in front of the kids, in front of your
brother, in front of Lois—and who got me in trouble, that's what
I'd like to know, who was it that couldn't keep his hands off me,
can't ever keep his hands off me, who's—"

"Other women don't have kids the way you—"

"They're not Catholic. They had more sense—they had husbands who at least pulled themselves out!"

"Keep quiet," Pete said through clenched teeth. "Just keep
quiet."

"I won't keep quiet. Why should I keep quiet? Why should
I—"

"I'm warning you."

"You're warning *me*? You don't care what happens, not to any

of us, and you want to warn me? That's a good one, that is," and she gave a short, bitter laugh.

"Peggy, I'm warning you. We've got company—"

"Company—what do you care about company? Yes, I suppose you do care what other people think," she contradicted herself. "You care what outsiders think, but you don't care about your own wife and children. You want other people to think you're such a hot shot but your own family can go rot for all you care—"

"I'm warning you for the last time." He stood up, trembling. "I won't listen to this. You hear? I won't listen."

"You won't listen," she mocked him. "What makes you think you won't listen?" she demanded, standing up and facing him, her face rigid with hatred. "You'll listen. They'll listen. It's about time someone listened—"

"Get out of my way."

"Get out of your way for what? Why should I get out of your way?"

"Because I'm getting out—"

"Getting out?" she asked in disbelief. "Where are you going?"

"It doesn't make any difference. I'm not going to stay here and listen to this. I'm not going to stay here and be insulted. *Get out of my way.*"

On Peggy's face a look of alarm spread. "Pete, what are you doing? We've got company. Lois—"

"Sure we've got company, but did you care? Did that make any difference to you when you—"

"Please. Pete, I—"

Her husband stood uncertainly.

"Pete, *please*."

He shrugged his shoulders; suddenly he laughed. "Boy, what a temper she's got when she gets going," he said as if the whole thing had been some kind of joke. "A real hellion you are, you old bag." And the look he shot Peggy floundered somewhere between malevolence and make-believe.

"My phone call," Lois said in a pleading voice to Stu. "I forgot to make my phone call. It's long distance," she explained, turning to Pete and Peggy. They stared at her. "I mean," she went on in confusion, "I'd make it from here, only it's long distance—and sort of private." She rose, holding a smoldering cigarette with a long ash. "Oh," she cried as ashes scattered on the rug. "Oh, I'm so sorry. I didn't mean—oh dear," she said as she dropped to her hands and knees and beat at the rug.

"Don't bother," Pete said, springing, crouched, to her side. "Don't think anything about it. Nothing can hurt this old rag. Please don't think a thing about it, it's all right. See, you've got them all out. Please don't go."

Sentenced, Lois seated herself, looking at them bleakly. She was home: Pete and Peggy, Erwin, Carolyn, Stu. But not yet Eileen . . .

"You must—you must have had a hard trip," Peggy began in a hostessy voice.

"It wasn't too bad," Lois said painfully, slowly. "I mean, once Connie got used to it—settled down," she ended hopelessly.

"You ate in the diner?" Peggy prompted, while Lois nodded, unable to expand this cue.

"She liked that, I suppose," Peggy persisted in that bright, false voice, and Lois looked at her clear, determined face in amazement, wondering how she could continue to play the game in the midst of all this terrible furniture, with that terrible husband simply waiting to get at her. Practice, she decided, long, long practice. Scenes were second nature to Peggy; constant quarrels had equipped her with icy indifference; anger she allowed to flow when it was needed; when not, she turned it off. Something close to admiration came over Lois; Peggy seemed to her a perfect example of a creature who had made a complete adjustment to her environment. Surely out of everything, the squalor of her life, the remorseless draining of her energy, the empty specter of her future, she deserved at least some mention in an experiment on modern living.

With a smile luminescent and meaningless, she tried to tell some anecdote about the trip.

Fluttering, smiling, leaning forward, Peggy listened to her in rapt admiration, willing her, Lois felt, to go on; so long as Lois talked, she would not have to, Pete, too, would have to be still. How had they come this far? How had they ever even commenced such a journey, Lois wondered, and thought

Where there is no vision, the people perish,

permit me passage to a better place, let me make my voyage under different circumstances, send me out further than those who have come this way, trust in me, Lord—

Stu stood up, suddenly assertive, his face set. "We've got to be going," he said in a voice with which you could not argue. "We're supposed to be some place by nine and we're late now."

"I'm really tired," she said, walking close beside him into the darkness. "I don't think there's any more I could do tonight. What's happened to them, Stu? What happened to Pete and Peggy, to Erwin?"

"They bought all the wrong dreams," Stu said abruptly, as if he didn't want to talk about it.

They got into the car before he went on. "They bought the whole kit and kaboodle and now they're stuck with them and it's too late to back out, they're too deep in debt, the really bad debt you get Up There that there's no way of paying back. I know a pretty good bar where we can cut the taste of the past half-hour. You can't find any place that doesn't have television any more—look out on that side, Lois, will you, and see if I'm going to make it—"

"You're all right."

"—no place where people can just go and talk, but this has got a quiet place in back, away from the bar, and they don't water their drinks too much. It's just down the street. Two minutes maybe. And there's something I want to talk to you about. I wasn't kidding when I said we were suposed to be some place by nine. But we need a drink—at least I do. A good stiff drink first. It's okay," he said. "I don't—you know—get carried away, the way I used to. You don't have to worry."

"Well, I am dry," Lois admitted. "I feel as if I'd been licking a couple of thousand postage stamps. Carolyn got kind of carried away on the martinis."

"She say anything to you? She tell you what was bothering her?"

"A little," Lois said carefully.

"About this guy she's mixed up with?"

"Yes, and Ralph knowing."

"Ralph knows?" She heard the disbelief in his voice. "Holy mother of god, what next?" He paused. "She say anything about me?"

"Not much."

"But something."

"Something."

In a strained voice he said, "I've made up my mind. I'm getting out. I've got this girl—"

Silent, she waited.

"Only it's going to be tough on Betty—that's her name, Betty. Ethel knows."

"Women always know. Maybe your wife hasn't been too close to you for a long time and maybe you don't love one another any more, but you're used to one another, you're a habit to each other, and habits are the hardest things in the world to break, they're a lot harder to undo than just these—these—what is the word, Stu?"

"I don't know," he said, and let it go at that. "Here we are," he said, pulling the car toward the curb. "You cold?" he asked, coming up beside her and opening the door. He must have noticed the trembling.

"No, just shaky. The train—it wasn't exactly the Waldorf." She got out, pausing for a moment, trying to smile at him. Going up the path, she suddenly stopped. "I know this place," she said. "I came here the first time I ever met that boy Eileen was going with. He brought me here. We drank brandy." She felt she would never move. "We went in and the bartender was in back. It was hot, there were fans going—Stu, have you ever heard what happened to him? That man Eileen—"

She was standing, quite still, staring at the big sign BAR painted across the entranceway. "He came to New York. Did you know that, Stu, that he came to New York, for me? And—and I—"

Turning, she looked at him with a face she knew was suddenly converted to pain. "And I sent him back, or tried to. Did you understand, Stu, what really happened, how Eileen—"

"We all had an idea," he mumbled, "but it was never definite," he said in her defense. "Would you like to go some place else?"

With a shake of her head, she started determinedly up the path, came to the door, and opened it without hesitation just as he was saying, "You sure?"

"Beer," Lois said, pulling at her coat. "It's the only way I'll ever get rid of this thirst."

He was trying to help her, awkward and well-meaning. Then he smiled and suddenly it seemed to her things might be all right. After all, she was with Stu.

They found a booth in back and sat down, smiling at each other, but strained, silent. They both took out cigarettes at the same time, fussed with the business of getting them lighted. He held his match over toward her, exaggeratedly polite. Lois found herself unable to keep up the false front; her strength had gone for that kind of endeavor at Peggy's. "When we came here that time, he went up to the bar," she said, smoking, not looking at Stu. "To get the drinks. There wasn't anyone around to wait on us. We had the place to ourselves. It was hot and—I don't know how to explain it, Stu, it's just that there was something between us, it just sprang up, this feeling, it's the only time I ever had it really, taking you all of a sudden, as if someone had delivered a blow that knocked the breath out of you and you just sat there, stunned. I thought—I couldn't believe it but I thought—I was falling in love," she ended helplessly, while he hung over her, uncertain, it seemed, whether to leave her to get the beers or to stay and hear her out; she looked up at him and said, all in one breath, trying to get it out, "But-when-he-came-to-New-York, I-saw-what-it-really-was. Infatuation, I-think-that's-the-name-they-give-it-isn't-it? Infatuation."

He looked down on her with a face she scarcely recognized. What had she said to make him *smile*? "Oh, but I do know what you mean," he said. "I know only too well what you mean, that feeling you have when you first meet someone and—" He stopped, his face full of remembrance, as if he had a view of something only he could see, a look into his inner world, where the pulse of things, the principle of all his emotions, lay clear and blunt and easily able for him to see. But no one else.

"She came to buy some paint," he said, and Lois had difficulty following him; then she saw he was talking about a girl, some woman he cared for. "And my whole life got changed," he said, looking down. "And now—" He looked up again, something close to an appeal on his face. "And now it's like I have to make a choice between the woman I can really care about and the son I love." He looked at her. "Who can make such a choice?" he asked.

Odd; she might have said to him, Stu, if you love someone and you think it interferes, or might interfere, with the thing you and your child have, do you think—

Perhaps at the heart of all of them, each and every one of them, there was a cord that bound, the same things that mattered. If you tried to count them up, what would they be? Simple things they might seem if named, like love of a child, or the bond between a man and woman, or of people to the soil or a place, but the plain rough words could not convey the feelings, the mixed, anxious, bitter feelings that went with those bare unfurbished words. No image, she thought. That is the trouble, when you say, Love of a child, love of land, you don't really give an image; to have the image, to have the meaning, you must participate.

But money, she thought, a bare, unvarnished universal they all understood: I must have enough to pay my way. . . . What is in my pocket protects the images of my mind.

He had gone for the drinks and she watched the exchange: currency for liquor; thinking, Currency for everything. We cannot support love even without the necessary furnishings. It is an endless expense over which we must fight and cavil and eventually feel caught. The candles on the table, the wine in the glasses, the veal on the plate: all these must be paid for. But, my love, my child, do not think I have surrendered myself to a life of such servitude without choice. When I had you, I had also the end of what individual caprices I might once have been permitted; but, unlike Pete and Peggy, I chose that end.

But sometimes . . . yes, sometimes we all dream of being free, of beginning again.

But only for a little while, she thought. What calls us back are the self-imposed ties of love. The child, the house, even animals, she thought, remembering the cat at the window in Athens.

If you make mistakes, she told herself, at least learn to live with them.

She got up and went to the phone booth. During the whole day Neal had been with her and yet had escaped her; but at the moment he said *Lois?* she felt the marvelous power of this machine to bring him close. She hung onto the receiver, she wanted to move close to him, to touch him, to lie down with him for a little while, while a voice inside of her warned, *Of all things in life love is the quickest one to break your heart.* Yet there was poetry in the caveat of that cry. That was what was meant by love, hearing a voice but hardly hearing words. She could not remember, coming out of the booth, one sentence he had said except *When are you coming home?*

Why had he called it home? But that was the precise exact right meaning of the word.

She sat down, looking right through the bottles, the glasses, the faces affixed to the bodies crowded around the bar, as if they were not there. Stu put her beer down, lowered himself into the seat opposite, struggling with the smoke that came from the cigarette still anchored between his teeth. He set his glass on the formica, quickly yanked the cylinder from his mouth, gave an awful cough. He was essentially the same. The image in the mind, the obsessive need to speak of those we love, she thought, the obsessive need to keep them close to us, in words, in thoughts, in images. "You've probably guessed," he was saying, embarrassed, "that the reason I asked you to come tonight, was—well, you know—so you could meet her. You're the first one, Lois, the first one in the family I asked. Not even Carolyn."

Lois didn't quite know what to say.

"Betty—I know she'd get on with you. And then—then—" He tried again, his voice breaking down. "I mean," he said doggedly, "if she feels there's someone in the family who kind of backs her up, I mean, it isn't so hard—"

Impulsively Lois grasped the hand that lay next to the still smoking cigarette. "You mean you want me to take a stand, Stu?"

"Something like that," he said as if hating to admit it. "Not for me, for her. I guess what I really want is for you to back us up. Doesn't sound very strong on my part, does it? That I can't go it alone? But the truth is—hell, the truth is, Lois, I can't pull out on the kid, and that's what Ethel's made it, her and the kid or nothing and—hell, you might as well know the truth, she could cause trouble. I mean, about Betty and me. If she wanted to take it to court—" His face was all a frown. "The kid," he said, "or— Either way it doesn't seem like there's much of an out."

She wanted more than anything else to say the right thing, but what was the right thing? *The desires of the senses,* one who was wise had said, *draw you abroad; but when the hour has passed away, what do you bring back with you but a weight upon your conscience and a dissipated heart?*

"I want a place of my own," he said in the stubborn voice of one repeating something he has thought many times, "a piece of land all my own, and someone who loves me and whom I love and the rest of the world can go fuck itself for all I care. I've spent most of my life doing things I shouldn't and I've wasted a lot of time and I don't have any talent, so I don't have to worry about that, but what the christ is it all about," he demanded angrily, "if you can't even have a square of land to stand on and someone who won't cut you down to spend your life with? And yet that's just what it does seem to be about—look at all of us, at you, at me, at Carolyn. Look at Pete and Peggy. And what do you see? Just mistakes and waste and ugliness. It makes me sick, I tell you, just sick. It always has, but it's worse now because I can *see* something else, the possibility of something decent is right there in front of my eyes and they're trying to hold me back, they won't let me out, and this is the last chance I'm going to get, I'm lucky even to have it and yet—you know, when you went back to New York and I stayed, I wanted you to make it," he said, "I really did. More than anything else, I wanted you to have a little happiness. And you haven't, have you? Your life is as loused up as the rest of ours, isn't it?"

"I've got Constance and that makes up for a lot. But happiness—" She broke off, seeing the look on his face, shocked at her own insensitivity. Of course he must be thinking of his own son: her words had probably seemed to him like an indictment.

"It's all right, Lois," he said calmly, "I know you didn't mean that in—well—a *personal* way."

"No, Stu, I didn't. I was only trying to explain—"

"It's a swell world, isn't it? Where someone like you says, 'But happiness—' in *that* tone of voice, as if you didn't believe it existed, as if you—"

"It isn't a word I even think about much any more. It isn't something I care about enough to want it so much I think about it all the time." She tried to explain. "I want to feel that I haven't gone through what little life I have without giving something back. Do you know what I mean, Stu—*to have given?*"

"I always thought you were one of the givers," he said harshly.

"Well, right now I'm one of the ones who wants to be a getter. I'm tired of being a giver and not getting anything back. And if you think that's selfish and egocentric and all the rest, think it. But for once in my life, I'm asking, *I'm demanding*—" His face was angry and rebellious, filled with a fierce determination. She wanted him to have what he wanted—it seemed so little, really— but with the best will in the world she didn't know how to change what was. And what he had said was true: it was a new life, a new chance, but at the price of the son he loved. Who could make such a choice? Suppose, she asked herself, it came to a decision between Neal and Constance—

Then, she thought, there would be no choice.

"Stu," she said.

He looked up.

"Let's go and see Betty. I'll—" But what was left to say? I'll do what I can? And what was that?

Stu sat down heavily and from the pretty pattern on the plate in front of him selected a cooky, disturbing the entire arrangement. It was just like a man to do that, Lois thought, and tried to smile at the rather pretty woman across from her who was at this moment trying to pretend her heart wasn't half broken by the terrible sound of Stu's chewing. It orchestrated the entire room and the look on Betty's face seemed to say, Oh goodness, why can't he at least swallow and stop all that noise?

Stu paused, sitting in the thick silence, then, hastily, embarrassedly, did swallow, choked while Betty, while Lois looked at him with relief.

Then Betty stood up, looking disconsolately at her disarranged plate, leaned over, and smiled. "Coffee?" she asked and Lois saw the pleasure behind the smile she had put on was genuine; she was glad at last to have a chance to pronounce in public what she and Stu had been in private. She had the shining look of a woman showing off her prize Sèvres, only in this case the Sèvres was Stu. Women were always proud as peacocks when they showed off their men. Their faces all had the same conspiratorial look, as if they had captured the ancient enemy and now was the time for the triumphal procession with the once-proud prince crouched in his cage for all the populace to see. The whole institution of marriage, Lois reflected, nodding that yes she would have a cup, had probably come into being because women felt an overwhelming compulsion, like this one of Betty's, to publish to the world their idealistic—and hopelessly unrealistic—intention of loving and living with one man all their lives.

It was the illusion, of course, that one could break down the barriers of one's loneliness, could fuse with someone else, double identity was established. Or was it?

We are all so lonely, Lois thought, that is what makes the search so frantic. Perhaps what we are really looking for is the other side of ourselves, so that we can be put back together again, be made whole. If it weren't such a fragmented, loveless age, should we keep on insisting so adamantly that love is the most important thing we need in our lives?

Was this where the evolution, the escalation, of love had led, to their being afraid ever to stand on their own?

She took the cup Betty held out, waited while Betty held up the imperfect plate of sweets and cookies. Lois declined, then thought better of it and selected something with pineapple on top. Disaster seemed to wait in every corner of this blue room, ready to spring out at them: and what would this disaster have been? Merely to have to look one another in the eye, she thought, to *see*. Really seeing another person was one of the worst things that could happen; it opened up the world of vulnerability, it made each face his own isolation, his own lonely egoism, the inevitability of his own extinction. And of love they asked a way out of this.

She searched about for something to say. No sacrificial confabulation presented itself; she had not Peggy's knack for the trivial; mute, miserable, Lois clanked her coffee cup down into its saucer and stared at her candied pineapple cake, marveling that Betty was managing, between sips, to find anything at all to say.

She was talking about fabric, monk's cloth; and Lois, trying to play her part, began to explain how she had designed and stenciled her own apartment curtains. Aztec idols. Really? Betty asked. But what did you do about the border? And to all their amazements, Lois's most of all, Lois actually began a long, detailed description of the proper tools, the paints, the techniques of stenciling, the problems of laundering. It was as if, poised at opposite ends of a high tight wire, they had, she and Betty, begun to advance toward each other, one outstretched arm of each holding an offering, the other hovering overhead with a parasol to protect its owner's balance. Lightly, gingerly, but purposefully, they came toward each other, arch smiles affixed to their faces, their eyes glued straight ahead, their mouths moving as if they would never stop.

They had got, miraculously, from drapes to fruit. The uses of avocados had leaped into the discussion—it seemed they were Mexican fruit, and the tenuous relationship between Aztec idols, now stenciled on Lois's curtains, and the fruit which the Spaniards had taken back after the Mexican conquest had provided the link. Betty said the seeds, with some elaborate care, into which she went unflinchingly and thoroughly, could be planted to raise quite wonderful little trees—she was pointing at a green stalk in the corner—while Lois heard herself volunteer the invaluable information that there were male and female seeds, and the branching of the stalks suggested which was which. Stu simply stared unbelievingly as if these were not women he knew.

She adored guacamole, Betty declared, hanging for an instant on the perilous part of her wire, advancing toward a new subject and then drawing back at the last moment, surrendering the honor of ascendancy to Lois, who after all was a guest. Swinging nonchalantly back and forth, Lois parried. Did she think most people found avocados an *acquired* taste? Like olives, Betty said, and looked away from her. Then, as if taking a chance, Betty moved cautiously forward. Had Lois seen the new show all the magazines were talking about? Which show was that? Lois said, and then, finding no answer but a look of dumb misfortune on the face in front of her—Betty had obviously forgotten the name—she thrust into the gap adventurously, breathlessly, talking about *The Wall,* which she had just seen, about the intensity and vitality of the cast, the sheer force of the playwright's vision (she actually heard herself use the word *vision*); the theater, she went on, unable to stop, affected her the way the movies never did, that marvelous moment when the lights went down and . . . at any moment Lois felt she was going to plunge down, smashed on her own intensity, losing all sense of balance in the proclamation that the one thing she has missed most of all in Greece was the theater . . . then catching herself, moving quickly back and forth until she was in balance, stopped, seeing the look on Betty's face, Greece was apparently for some reason not a safe subject, and faltered, scraped her chair across the carpet as she leaned forward, Betty bowed her head, the act seemed to be running out, all was at an end, and in a panic Lois prayed they would go on, one of them would say something, anything, it didn't matter what, so long as they kept talking, so that the three of them would not just sit in silence, prayed as she seldom had, earnest, sure the end was near, breath caught in her throat, and heard, to her profound relief, a voice going on, picking up in assurance as it went, as if in the final lunge toward each other Betty had recognized this was the moment of all or nothing, and she was saying, "But then of course the movies . . ." and then, just at the moment Lois's faith had come back, Betty stopped. The moment was the worst that Lois could ever remember. The one that came after was even worse. Stu said, "Betty, let's cut out all this crap and—"

Betty's face went red, then white; she was sitting stricken, coffee cup in hand, staring through the plate of cakes and cookies into the floor. Lois felt she was looking right through the floor into her own personal version of hell and was horrified to discover it also included Stu. Didn't she know no one could make you tremble and suffer like the person to whom you had given all the hopes in your heart?

"Betty?"

She would not look at him. He had mortified her, he had— the worst thing a man could do to a woman—let her down in front of other people. Why had he to be so vulgar, so common? When she and Lois were trying to be so nice, to make it all go so well, he had said *crap*. Betty's face, so silent, so set now, seemed to say to them, These are the last moments I shall love this awful man.

"Lois was up all night, Betty," Stu was trying to explain. "I know she's probably done in." But something in her face stopped him. He quit even trying to explain.

"Stu," she said and Lois knew she was rebuking him. It wasn't *time* for the visit to end, no matter how tired Lois might be. "Stu," she said again, sadly, as if in saying his name she had a power of magic, she could put him under her control, and for one moment Lois had an image of all the women in the world who had tried to cast their spells, calling out names, hoping to put men forever under their thumbs, and failing.

"Listen," he said, as if all their lives depended on what he might say in the next few seconds. "I appreciate the efforts you girls are going through, but the point is, isn't it kind of silly—I mean, we're all tired, we're all nervous—at least I am—" He stopped.

The bewildering emotions of his own love showed on his face.

He saw he had done something wrong and Lois could see the question present itself to him for the first time—did they really want to talk about avocados and olives?—and for an instant he didn't know the answer, he was at sea in the sudden universal discovery of men that they know nothing at all about women.

Something irrational was going on before him and he had tried, logically, clearly, like a practical man, to set it right, but he had only succeeded in offending Betty's sensitivities. Hostile, she looked at him as if he were an intruder; he had come into woman's world, where of course they talked of avocados and olives, and he had said something crude and obscene. She was drawn up stiff, her face absolutely emblazoned with outrage.

Lois wanted to reach over and comfort him. She wanted to say, But Stu, when women are asked what they want out of life, they usually answer, To get married. What man would answer that? There is the whole difference, if you can only understand it.

"What's the matter for once in our lives in just looking at something square in the face instead of pussyfooting around it?" he asked doggedly, determined to have his say, come what may. "Supposing, for a change, we just said what we were thinking instead of trying to cover up. If there's one thing I'm sick and tired of, it's all this sashaying around, it's so goddam Timble—"

Lois put down her cup, she began to laugh. She couldn't help it: the look on Betty's face, as if saying, Every time you commit yourself, the commitment is deeper, you get hurt more, finally people learn not to want love; the look on Stu's face, as if answering, If you think love louses you up so much, then what *do* you want?

And there was no answer for either of them, of course. Nor, she thought, for her. Because what I want, she thought, no matter how I may deny it, is something close to the same—not the same, close—to what they both want. What Carolyn wants. But as always, she thought, I want a little more than everyone else. Not a little more, something just a little different. What was that?

They were both looking at her in a duality of anguish and disbelief. How could she laugh?

"It's all right," she managed to say. "It's just that what Stu said struck me as so absolutely true. No matter where we go, any of us in this family, we're so goddam Timble. Even if we went as far as—"

"Alaska," Stu said, and the laughter died in Lois's throat, he sounded so convinced.

"Alaska?"

"Why not?" he said to her. "There they let you have land, there the government will give you land."

Stu? In Alaska? Surely he wasn't serious. But he was.

Why not? she asked herself, why in the world not?

A thousand reasons: age, background, lack of experience . . .

But when she saw the sudden clearing of Betty's face, the radiance that had returned, she asked herself again, Why in the world not?

Chapter 5

CAROLYN pushed open the central portal of the church doors and stared into the rectory garden next door at the fallen dahlias, the clinging chrysanthemums, inhaled the odor of cut wild chives, listened to the steady soothing sounds of a machine, the lawnmower that was cutting back, perhaps for the last time, the swollen grass, the rumpled weeds, the autumn asters, looking out on rotting leaves and stained woods, choked by a sensation of culpability, as if she personally were responsible for all that was dying, perhaps even for death itself.

Was it not said—time and again—they were all fallen?

Because the land is full of adulterers, because the land hath mourned by reason of cursing, the fields of the desert are dried up: and their course is become evil, and their strength unlike.

Across the way the mortician was helping Frances from the low seat of her white sports car.

In a flurry of legs and twisted skirts, Frances unfolded; from the vantage point of half a head over her, the mortician was treated to a view of the pale cream slip and the top of her stockings as she heaved herself out. A moment later, with the unconcern of an empress, she made him a present of her hand.

He stood as if struck dumb. Bedazzled.

But it was all illusion, an illusion of youth and glamour fostered by the low moaning sports car and the bright glitter of the jewelry shining from the figure advancing toward the church steps. Then sunlight struck Frances full across the face. Circles, smudges, rimples, creases, folds, pouches, rucks, corrugations, colorings: she looked like some terrible experiment in plan-it, paint-it yourself.

"I'm early. It's this lousy weather. When it rains, Jules always thinks the roads are going to be closed, we have to start half an hour before we should. It has something to do with what happened to him in Saigon or one of those little Maylaysian places." Frances released the black arm of the little man beside her, not even giving him a nod. Taking the stone steps in a quick flash of veined but trim legs, she bounded to a stop beside Carolyn. "It was in the cards for one of us to go. Well," she conceded, "Ada was the oldest. It was her turn. No one can argue with that. That a new dress? I don't remember seeing it before."

"Chicago, when we went up to the convention."

"Marshall Field?" Using her bag as a shield, she hunched over, hiding a cigarette. "Stand in front of me, will you? I just want to get in a couple of drags. Just until Jules gets the car parked. That man! I don't think he's ever heard of second. Before six months is out, he's going to ruin whatever it is they put inside those things that makes them run. I'm sorry I ever showed it to him, we'd have been better off with just the Caddie, but all it does is sit in the garage nowadays. Your mother here?"

Carolyn shook her head.

"She's waiting for an audience," Frances said.

They stood in silence, watching Jules patter down the misty street. Wetness tangled the trees, the sidewalks looked like sluggish brown streams. Afloat in all that massive moisture, Jules looked like the oldest man in the world. That was why Frances had married him. She was sure he would pop off any minute and leave her—in her words—"well fixed." But appearances, even in old age, are deceiving. His happy, lighthearted step, maneuvering among the fallen leaves and broken branches, was that of a self-satisfied man. In the juvescence of the year, Carolyn thought, comes Christ the tiger. And in the auxabois?

"Peaches," he said lovingly to his wife, "you shouldn't be standing out in this precipitation, you might catch cold. And you don't want to miss Thursday bowling, do you?"

Instead of an answer, Frances gave him a look. She had married enthusiastically two years before, a cruise conquest, and now, Carolyn thought, she must be meditating on the old adage, Look before you leap. It turned out Frances was Number Five. The other four were expensively interred, cremated and consecrated in crocks, amidst a variety of odd, quaint corners of the world. Jules always had them turned to dust; it was so much more sanitary, he told you, because you never knew what they might have caught from the natives in those funny places.

Jules took Frances's arm gallantly as he made the top step, gave a stiff little bow to Carolyn, and then, shepherding his wife as if she were at the terminal stage of a mortal illness, helped her through the main door, which shut them from sight with a slight grunt. Carolyn wondered if Frances was slated to break the pattern and be expensively entombed in America, fallen before she had a chance to profit from the matrimonial alliance which she had been so confident was going to give her "a rich, ripe old age."

"Gone, she's gone for good," Carolyn's mother cried, throwing her black-gloved hands up to her fat, flabby cheeks. "We'll never have her with us again. Oh, I know we all have to go, it's only a matter of time, I know I'm going soon—don't try to comfort me, Carolyn, she's gone, my own sister's gone and I'll never see her again." Iris stood dramatically in the middle of the vestibule, with arms outstretched. Grief had given her stature and texture; she looked tall and as if she were set in stone.

Carolyn watched the performance coldly. "How many years has it been since she was out of that house, Mother?"

"Now, Carolyn—"

"At least ten."

"I talked to her every day of my life. Every single day of our lives we called one another up. Sometimes twice. And now she's gone and she can never phone again." Nervously her mother dropped her arms, twisted her hands together, looked beseechingly at Lois at her side. "Could I help it if she wouldn't go out? *Eileen*," Carolyn's mother said as if that explained everything, as it did.

After a moment her mother unfastened one glove, reluctantly dipped her hand into the icy holy water of the stoup. "Have people —come?"

Her mother knew perfectly well no one save the family was coming. Carolyn didn't answer.

"She used to have friends, lots of friends. I thought—" Her mother did not say what she thought, but Carolyn was pretty sure she knew. Her mother had hoped to fill at least half the pews by those mimeographed announcements she had taken it into her head to send out, and had sent over everyone's protests:

It is with deep regret that we advise you of the sudden and unexpected passing of Ada Timble Ames, wife of Arnold, mother of Eileen, beloved sister of Iris, Esther, and Frances, who for many years has been unable to reunion with friends due to family pressures.

Mrs. Ames is reposing at the Eastwood Chapel and can be viewed from 2–5 p.m. or 7–9 p.m. Sunday, Monday, and Tuesday. A requiem mass will be held Wednesday morning at 10 a.m. at St. Catharine's. Attendance invited.

"What if no one comes?" Her mother stopped in front of one of the swinging doors and gazed through the small wired glass window into the darkened interior. Only the altar light was burning, a small speck of flame reflected behind the reddish glass of the sanctuary lamp which was never allowed to go out. He is in the Presence of the Faithful, Carolyn thought, the Saved.

"She did not die NOT saved," her mother had insisted to the priest when they got into a tangle about the burial arrangements. "How do you know what was in her heart? How can anyone know that? How can anyone—even a priest—know? Just God," her mother said with a certainty even the priest could hardly refute.

But the priest's problem had seemed simple on the surface: Ada had died in a state of sin and those who died without expiation —without confessional, absolution, extreme unction—were not entitled to ecclesiastical burial. A cut-and-dried case, it would seem.

Certainly not, Iris had said in her high excited breathless way. "She fell over before she had a chance to get Unction. *She had a stroke, she didn't have any choice.* HOW CAN YOU TELL SHE WASN'T IN A STATE OF GRACE?"

Ada hadn't made her Easter duty, not for years, that was how it was no trouble to tell, the priest said.

How can anyone sin who doesn't *do* anything year after year? her mother had demanded. What sins could she commit, staying inside her house all the time the way she did?

But the technicality upon which the whole question of Catholic burial rested was not on Iris's concept of sin but the Church's, and the Church maintained specifically that since Ada had not made the prerequisite visits to confession or gone to communion or received absolution for years, she was in a state of sin—mortal, unforgivable, unburiable sin. She was a known sinner—

"What do you mean 'a known sinner'?" Iris had shrieked into the priest's alarmed face, while Carolyn tried to calm her down. After all, they were in the rectory and some sort of suitable behavior was expected. "Don't you say that about my own sister, don't you dare say that. Why, she didn't have a vice to her name —never drank or smoked—my mother never allowed any of us to smoke, and let me tell you something, my sister put up with a drunken husband and took care of a daughter who's not—well —quite right. A state of sin? Why, she was practically a saint!"

It would not have been Carolyn's definition of Ada, certainly not Esther's, but her mother was apt to get carried away in argument; Carolyn let the matter stand as it was, particularly since the priest seemed to be turning it over in his mind.

"I'm sorry," he said at last, "but so far as the Church is concerned, the remnant of sin was not removed." He looked down at the papers on his desk, pretending to read. "She was in a state of mortal sin, so—" It was obvious he wanted to be rid of them once and for all. It was nearly lunchtime and every once in a while, during that terrible fracas, his stomach would rumble and her mother would stop arguing and look at him as if he were the one who should be asking forgiveness. "And you know anyone who tries to force an improper burial on the Church can be brought under the penalty of excommunication."

"It's bad enough about Organdy." Iris had wept, standing up and beating her breast. "I can understand the Church's position on that," she conceded, the tears cascading down her pudgy cheeks and falling into the shimmering facets of a brooch that rode the huge heaving breasts—all, Carolyn thought, the priest could probably see from behind his desk. "I mean suicide, that's serious," her mother had gone on. "But just staying shut up in your house, that's—that's only *peculiar*. Ada's just got to be out there with Mama," she had cried out, loud as someone beating a bass drum. "I'll never be able to face Mama when I go to my Maker if I let Ada be buried any place else."

"If she was a responsible person," the pastor had maintained, "she cannot be given—"

"Oh," Iris had interrupted in relief, "responsible? Good heavens, no. Everyone knows she was queer as a three-dollar bill. Even if she was my own sister, I'd testify in a court of law she was odd from the start, a borderline case, I used to say, but of course she went way beyond the border long ago. And, you know, her daughter—she's been a house case for years. Plays with mice. Oh, they're pets and all—I mean, she doesn't just play with any old mice, these are some kind of special expensive white mice you buy, but still—still—I think it's—well—peculiar, don't you, to like mice? No, there was no question. Ada wasn't just odd, she was downright addled."

He had thrown up his hands, the priest, and given in, as well he might, as Carolyn could have told him from the start.

"And once more she's going to have a decent Spiritual Bouquet," Iris had finished, "just like everyone else. I want people to know it was under the Church auspices."

The lavender-tinted cards were lying right now on the pews, waiting to be plucked by penitent fingers and used, like a pressed nosegay from the past, to preside over the future. There were two black crosses at the top; and in between, in italics, *Jesus have Mercy on the Soul of*

MRS. ADA TIMBLE AMES

Arnold wanted it to be Ada T. Ames. Arnold had wanted a lot of things, like the economy coffin and the cut-rate cortege, but her mother had won out. She had worn him down by words, appealing to the most basic of the male instincts, vanity, telling him everyone would expect *a man in his position* to put out the best.

Carolyn pushed open the swinging door to the interior of the church and watched her mother go up the aisle. The few mourners already there clung precariously together in the front pews. They looked like stranded survivors of some major disaster, huddled in the first two center pews and hardly filling those out. Her mother, once centrally located, put her head down in her hands and, as if by cue, sobs shook her. Her shoulders heaved up and down, her whole body shook; to an outsider it might seem the heart had been wrenched out of her.

Each tribe conceives and constructs its own totem: The Timble tribe, Carolyn thought, looking at her mother—what would be the sign of their totem? The two-faced god Janus, the doors of whose temple were shut in times of peace. Then she turned to Lois, silent at her side. "You going to wait out here? I could use a little company."

"I don't think so," Lois said. "I just thought Iris would like to go in on her own."

They both stood watching. Frances had leaned over and was

tapping Iris on the shoulder, waiting while Carolyn's mother made
an effort to pull herself together. It was one of the Spiritual Bouquets Frances was waving; Jesus was holding his pierced heart
up right under her mother's eyes.

Iris turned and pressed her tear-stained face close to Frances's.
She moved her lips, asking, Carolyn supposed, what was wanted,
and Frances, instead of answering, shoved the little card at her
and pointed. What precisely she was pointing at, Carolyn did not
know, presumably the reassuring message that there was life everlasting and, in that other and unknown world, a peace that passeth
understanding. Whatever the consolation offered, Iris took it. The
weeping stopped, she straightened her face out and tucked her
handkerchief inside the sleeve of her old-fashioned and too long
coat.

Where there is hatred . . . let me sow love, Carolyn thought,
*Where there is injury . . . pardon. Where there is darkness . . .
light. Where there is sadness . . . joy. Where there is doubt . . .
faith. And where there is despair . . . hope.*

The door rasped open; a spate of wind and rain blew through
the cold corridor. Shaking her umbrella, Esther scattered drops
of water. She was clutching a fistful of flowers. "I'm not too late,
am I?" she demanded. "I brought flowers. My neighbor . . ." The
voice trailed off. Carolyn saw the absent neighbor, unsuspecting,
climb into her car, leave her house, go shopping, while Esther,
stealthily, purposefully moved over her garden, snipping flowers
where they would least be missed.

"Everyone here?" she asked, propping her umbrella against a
radiator, hanging onto her flowers. There were hairs standing out
from the nares of her nose, gray bristly ones in the auricles of
her ears; under her chin thick black hairs hung down like a miniature forest. Her hands were thick, the knuckles swollen and distended, the bones of the wrist large and knobby, and the veins
on the backs of her hands thick ropes that strained against the
yellow flesh that slipped back and forth over the bone. At the
back of her neck, where brittle hair was pinned into a knot, there
were freckles and wens, awards of old age; her mouth was thin

and almost lipless, a small brush of hair covered her upper lip.

Resolutely tapping an ancient and soiled brown bag against her flat chest, Esther sucked in a little of the cold, musty air, then moved forward, like Caesar off to part Gaul, and passed, almost without opening it, through the swinging door and into the church. Carolyn could hear, however, the flopping of her galoshes as she went down the aisle.

It was a sound she would forever after associate with Esther. She had heard it many times during the past three days in the corridors of the funeral parlor, squeaky, rubbery trumpets proclaiming her aunt's arrival. Slopping through the halls, her aunt moved on vulcanized boots to do battle against the barbaric hordes of Mammon. It was money she was bent on saving and she went about her rescue with a dedication and determination that would have graced the lives of saints and martyrs.

The family was being overcharged; Ada was being understaffed, not getting the service she should. Esther's voice echoed up and down the halls as she fought first with assistants, then with the comptroller, and finally with the funeral director himself. The cost of the casket was a disgrace—A DISGRACE, she shouted at the top of her lungs, and sloshed back and forth in nervous, anxious anger over the carpets whose long, thick nap, so efficient for subduing unseemly noise, could do nothing against the arrogant anger of Esther's galoshes; the sound carried, along with her voice, everywhere—they were being charged for first-class service, FIRST-CLASS SERVICE—and then, outraged beyond restraint, she began to berate the undertaker about the room in which they had put Ada. "WE PAID FOR A MEDIUM-SIZED PARLOR, YOU CALL THAT MEDIUM-SIZED?" And while he trailed after her, in orisons of explanation, his low voice murmuring of the mysteries of embalming and preserving, the gnosis of inhumation, over the sibilance of his pleadings came the harsher cries of her overshoes.

In one awful moment of silence when the galoshes ceased their accusations, Carolyn heard next to the room where Ada was laid out someone padding about, opening a cupboard, unscrewing a jar, running water, putting a lid on a pot, making, Carolyn supposed, coffee.

"SOMEONE'S COOKING RIGHT NEXT TO HER," Esther's outraged voice had shouted.

Anyone would have thought she cared about Ada.

"COOKING, THEY'RE COOKING IN THERE, CAN'T YOU HEAR? IF YOU CAN'T, THERE'S SOMETHING THE MATTER WITH YOUR EARS."

The mortician thought, Carolyn supposed, that he had come to aid and abet grief; he couldn't know it was avarice he was dealing with. Unaware of his mistake, he stumbled on, attempting to soothe spiritual wounds and infuse new faith in the wavering. He was talking about the rewards of a long and fruitful life, and as he said *fruitful* in his rich and throaty voice, Carolyn had a picture of soft, ripe pears dropping softly, slowly through heavy hot air onto a soft, warm earth, a vision from a poem written years before but whose image was fresher at this moment than when it was written on a hot summer day.

"YOU CAN'T COOK NEXT TO THE MEDIUM-PRICED ROOMS!" she shrieked over the placating voice, the sound of the electric coffee pot, the final obloquy of a dropped spoon.

Carolyn thought of the last look at the "remains" down at the mortuary, how the line had stopped, and Esther had been standing rock still in front of the casket, peering down. Her face had a heavy, concentrated look; then she reached out, as if to touch Ada, as if to make sure it was really she. "The brooch," Esther said, "we have to take the brooch off. It was Mama's." Then quickly she bent over and unfastened the pin, holding it up. "There," she said in satisfaction. "And what about her ring? She shouldn't wear her ring—shouldn't we take that too?"

Carolyn's mother had stepped forward angrily. "Move on," she whispered. "They do that at the end."

Carolyn put her hand in the holy water, brushed her forehead, chest, each shoulder, making the Latin sign of the cross; she could not resist raising her fingers to her mouth as she had as a child, to test the water. It tasted slightly salty. The priest added that salt when he blessed and exorcised the water. One of the sacramentals. She went back, trying to remember the significance. Why salt? The sweat of the brow. To conceive in sadness and bring forth in travail, to pass a life in labor and suffering. Something like that. She could not remember the exact quote, but the sense was there —suffering, grief, the tragedy of human life, always the tragedy of human life.

Ashes, she thought, it is all ashes.

Holy water, ashes, oil for the sanctuary lamp. Why did they smudge your head? In penance? In remembrance? In anticipation? Ashes . . . dust . . . death . . . the ashes of the dead, the sins of the dying . . . it must have something to do with that.

Was it true that without being baptized there was no salvation, without extreme unction no expiation? No, Ada had proved that like everything else religion flourished on compromise. In a few hundred years, Carolyn reflected, the whole sealed secret of Christ himself would be unearthed; some psychiatric phenomenon that would account for suspended animation or a theory of hypnotic hysteria. In the end, she supposed, there would be no secrets left at all, just indisputable evidence, unequivocal facts, the whole of human history traceable, and imagination, like the human appendix, an unnecessary appendage of the anatomy.

The hinges of the vestibule door gave a rusty cry of anguish, and a small gray, beautifully gloved hand materialized, seemingly severed, on one of the panels; a moment later a long black arm appeared attached to a body on which the knoblike head, as if nailed to the upper portion of the door, nervously blinked its eyes, nibbled its lips, the mortician himself stepping inside.

He stood for a moment alone, flashing on her the hot happy look of the man who has triumphed. Then, in a blast of wind and rain, with wet leaves behind them as backdrop, two figures moved onstage, stopped as if paralyzed until the prompter set them in motion, hanging in the open door like marionettes whose strings have tangled, while Carolyn watched with a strange feeling of heartbreak, wanting desperately to help them and yet unable to move, as if paralyzed herself. Blown by the wind, they moved toward the mortician; the door smacked shut, the mortician raised his hand and, as if in signal, animation began. Eileen moved forward, the smooth dead expanse of her face embedded with two little blue eyes like dried flowers, while Eileen's father fretted, shuffling his fat legs back and forth, swinging his hatted head sideways, not looking at her, as if if he did not look at her, he would not be responsible for anything she did. Clearing his throat, Arnold opened his mouth, struggling for speech, and the clear, sharp, unmistakable odor of alcohol wafted over Carolyn.

Eileen pulled away and began to pat her gloved hands together over the open mouth of the marble font.

"Stop it," her father said angrily. "Stop that. Don't do that."

"Take off one of her gloves," Carolyn suggested. "Maybe she wants to put her hand in the water."

"Put her hand in the water? What water?"

Carolyn bent over and removed one of Eileen's gloves. While that small dimpled hand splashed about in the font, playing with the holy water, pushing it back and forth to make miniature waves, Carolyn tried to explain, but Arnold was not listening. "Cut it out," he said to his daughter. "Don't play with the water that way. Stop it. *Leave that water alone.*" He brought his hand across her wrist with a smart crack. Eileen began to cry, the stricken sound echoing in the high vaulted vestibule. "Oh god, oh god, there she goes again," her father said despairingly.

Morticians were, apparently, better prepared against the possibilities of disaster than most mortal men. Briskly producing a lollipop, this one peeled off the paper, popped the candy into Eileen's mouth. Instantly the sobbing stopped. They would have to wait, Carolyn supposed, until she finished; Eileen could hardly go down the aisle to her mother's funeral licking a lollipop.

"Hurry up," Arnold, impatient, said gruffly. Beside him, his forty-one-year-old daughter licked on. "People will start coming. You don't want people to see you stand here with that, do you?"

Eileen made no reply. Licking her fingers, she looked around happily. Then, with a careless movement of her hand, the lollipop lay at her feet. The funeral director bent and picked it up; with a swift flick of his fingers it was deposited in his dark suit pocket. Nervous underneath it all, Carolyn thought, put it in his pocket without wrapping it in paper. *Sticky,* she thought. The other neat dark arm was at Eileen's side, a support against which she might establish herself, but with clear untroubled eyes, wide and shining, depthless, she was looking beyond him. Her father had opened the main door to the church and like an enraptured child she was staring through to all the flowers, to the tall sentinel candles, toward the high altar. "Pretty, oh pretty," she said. "Look at the flowers, Papa, aren't they pretty?"

As the door squeezed shut, Carolyn had a final view of Eileen's flat, patent-leathered feet plodding altarward, her black shiny purse bobbing back and forth against her side.

Outside, two big black cars had arrived, one bearing Ada, the other the pallbearers. When the men climbed out, they looked like a cluster of penguins against the peak of clouds that hung, like a distant mountain range, against the sky. Everyone who was going to come had arrived; the mimeographed sheet of summons had produced no appreciable results.

Carolyn entered the candlelighted nave and went down the aisle to the second pew. Her mother, Arnold, Eileen, Frances, and Esther—the "immediate" family—were in the first. Esther sat, her shoulders hunched over, the asters behind her, a fan of forgotten flowers. Head in hands, her aunt gave the appearance of praying. For what was she asking? Better rates of interest? An eternal dividend? Why had she brought the flowers? Flowers were the emblems of love. She had certainly not loved Ada. And yet—

It is in forgiving that we are pardoned. And it is in dying that we are born to Eternal Life.

But who, after all, understood what that meant?

Not she, not Esther; not, she doubted, any of them. No one believed in Eternal Life any more. WHAT was the soul?

Something I cannot see, something I cannot touch, something I cannot know, Carolyn thought. But the body—I am inside *this* flesh, she wanted to cry out to the plaster saint, larger than life, who looked down on them all with glass eyes and a hollow heart.

They were at communion, the priest receiving the Host. That meant it was all, thank god, almost over. Her mother wisely had decided against the congregation participating—too many embarrassing absences at the rail.

Let us pray. Grant, we beseech Thee, Almighty God, that the soul of Thy servant Ada, which as this day departed out of this world, may be cleansed by this sacrifice, and delivered from sins, and may receive forgiveness and everlasting rest. Through our Lord . . .

They had better pray for Ada. She would need it. Not that it would probably much matter. Carolyn could almost hear Ada's voice ringing in the hereafter. She took Aunt Clara's money, *You* know Esther did and *You* let her get away with it, how could *You* let her get away with it? that's what I want to know. Carolyn could picture God backing off, trying to get away from her, unable to fight her off, knowing He'd *never* get away from her—HE wasn't going to make an administrative mistake like that. All the prayer in the world wouldn't get her past the pearly gates.

AND THE WORD WAS MADE FLESH, *and dwelt among us. And we saw His glory—glory as of the only begotten of the Father—full of grace and truth.*

And they answered, *Deo gratias.* Thanks be to god.

And Carolyn said, *Deo gratias.*

Chapter 6

"A DOUBLE DRY MARTINI, with lemon peel," Frances instructed. "Have to get going while the going's good," she explained to Pete and Ralph on either side of her. "Iris'll be in here corraling us before we get a drink half down. Iris and Jules," she corrected herself. "Thanks," she said as the drink was put in front of her. "The notion that this was waiting for me was all that kept me going." She lifted her glass. "When lovely lady stoops to folly," she called out. "Ah, what folly! Tally ho!"

"Not tally ho, light of my dreary life—cheers. The cup, not the chase."

Something happened to Frances's face. She took the glass away from her mouth, set it down on the bar, and turned to her husband. "The man with the crumpled horn who kissed the maiden all forlorn, who chased the dog that bit the cat that killed the rat that ate the malt that lay in the house Jack built. I knew you'd find me. How are things in Glocca Morra?"

"Precious jewel?"

"Is Iris all excited?" Frances enunciated clearly, as if speaking to a small child. "Is Iris on our tracks? *Jules, is Iris looking for us?*"

"Oh yes, I see, sugar. Yes, she is. She said I should—"

"Another double martini on the double, bartender, the enemy is closing in."

"Now, love, you know how you get in the middle of the day when you—"

"Jules," she said patiently, changing the subject, "who do you suppose Carolyn is calling in that phone booth over there? She looks so intense."

They all turned. Carolyn was bent toward the wall phone, her mouth moving up and down rapidly.

Ralph moved forward, away from the rest of them, his Bourbon held midwaist in one hand, his head turned a little to one side. For a moment he hesitated, then he said slowly, "I'll go see. I hope it isn't anything about the children."

When he tapped on the glass of the door, Carolyn looked up, startled, so engrossed in what she had been saying that she had obviously not seen him coming. A look of annoyance fanned her face first into anger, then into resignation. Abruptly, she hung up. To Lois, she looked bitter and resigned the way she had been in New York, a woman who no longer loved her husband, who could barely tolerate him. Lois wanted to cry out, Don't look like that, Carolyn, please don't look like that.

Carolyn gathered up purse and gloves from the telephone table, opened the folding doors, and stepped out. In a clear, strong voice they could all hear she said, "Spying?"

Ralph's reply, a murmur as he stepped in front of her and blocked off the view from the bar, went unheard. What they all caught was the angry tattoo of Carolyn's high heels as she stamped across the lobby. A second later they saw her husband following after.

"Sir, *sir*," the bartender shouted. "You can't take that glass—"

Ralph turned, stepped back into the bar, and left his half-finished glass on a table, then went in pursuit of his wife.

"The good don't always go to heaven," Frances said. There was a moment's silence; then she said glumly, "Oh dear, I suppose I've started a scene, and all I meant to do was take the pressure off here at home. Skoal." She looked around. "Erwin," she said, "you're sure looking frooky. Have you been having it out again with Helen? Excuse me, Lois, but you're part of the family, you don't mind a little family scene under the circumstances, do you?" Her husband she ignored so completely that he might not, even for the others, have existed.

"I'm just tired," Erwin said, moving his shoulders as if he were trying to shake her. "It'll all get straightened out eventually," he said in a tired voice. "The lawyers are working on it," and Lois wondered if he was remembering that scene in the lawyer's office Carolyn told her had become public property he complained about it so often; according to Carolyn, he had lost control completely and called Helen a goddam broad and a lousy slut. "You should see the way that lousy slut kept the house when the maid wasn't around," he had screamed into the lawyer's smooth face, while the lawyer's well-cared-for hands reached out protectively to grasp the fluted edges of a silver frame, turning over his wife's picture so that she wouldn't be witness to such goings-on, and this action seemed to enrage Erwin more than anything else that had happened to him—his being locked out of his own house, his being cut off from his children, even his being dragged into lawyers' offices week after week about money.

"She's never wanted anything but a meal ticket and she wasn't even willing to put out for that. Ask her how many times we slept together the last year. Go ahead, ask her!" he had shouted while Helen apparently sat unmoved, looking out the window, pretending he was nothing to her, never had been, he was just some disagreeable stranger they would all have to put up with for a little while but after he left they could all tell the truth, that he had been *impossible* but THEY had all behaved so well, held their tempers and kept their poise. She *would* acknowledge him, he had told people, by god, or—he had grabbed her by the shoulders and had begun to shake her. "Look at me, you goddam broad, you know goddam well—"

"Mr. Mueller, Mr. Mueller," the lawyer had said, rising from behind his desk. "That's the mother of your children."

Well, the mother of his children was also capable, when the urge came over her, Erwin told them, of coming down to his office and pulling a schnugger of a scene, screaming and shouting to anyone who would listen that he didn't care whether his wife and children starved to death, that he cared more about money than he did his own children, that she had found contraceptives—go ahead, ask him, she had shrieked at his secretary, at the man who was his superior and for whose job Erwin was gunning, but not, thank god, to his boss, who was out of town, he said, but of course who had heard all about it the moment he got back, a family squabble in public, the customers, the customers—go ahead, ask him, he can't deny it, I pulled the package out of his pocket when I was going through things for the cleaner. It would not have surprised him, Erwin told everyone, if Helen sent poison-pen letters to the Bureau of Internal Revenue, the FBI, and even —he wouldn't put anything past her—the CIA.

"Another?" Erwin asked Lois, pointedly excluding his mother.

But nobody excluded Frances when she wanted to be in on something. "I don't like that lawyer you've got," she said. "I never have. He's got those small, sneaky eyes. He's not—not *simpático*," she brought out triumphantly from a few days in Spain. "Down the hatch."

"He's okay, he's doing all he can," Erwin answered doggedly. "It just isn't easy, that's all."

"It just isn't easy," Frances repeated scornfully. "Boy, that's the understatement of the year. Why, she's going to take you bags, balls, and barometric pressure, and you—"

"Lay off, will you, can't we talk about it some other time? This is hardly the time to—"

"Yes, dove," Jules said, "Erwin certainly has a point—considering the occasion that we are commemorating, I think it might be more seemly if we left money matters to more intimate—"

"You always take his part. A lot of lousy fascists, right in my own family," Frances said indignantly.

"Now Frances," her husband began placatingly.

"Not Frances, Francesca," she corrected him. "After I have a couple of drinks I'm Francesca. The way they do in Rome," she said, breathing down her nose like a horse on its way home. "Rome, Italy. That's what they called me in Rome, Italy. The—the—what was the name of that place, Jules?"

And her husband, understanding she had lost her way in the claptrap of places she thought were Rome, tried as he always tried to send her where she wanted to go. "The Baths?"

She shook her head.

"Tivoli Fountain? Catacombs? St. Peter's?"

The despair on her face was truly awful. "You know, where they had those fights. Those big battles to entertain the public." In exasperation, seeing that he still did not follow, she finished, "Where the lions ate those Christians."

"Oh, you mean the Colosseum, lamb chop."

"Yes, the Colosseum, the moonlight on the Colosseum. We went there by horse—in a carriage. That was where we went in that carriage, wasn't it, Jules, and the driver overcharged us so and you said, 'Five thousand lire, that would buy the whole horse'? Lovely, just lovely, all that moonlight on those old stones. The guide there," she said briskly, dropping her ethereal tone, tapping Lois sharply on the wrist with one long, crimson, dictatorial finger to be sure she was listening, "said I was called Francesca in Italian, after a beautiful lady in a poem."

Lois thought better than to tell her that that Francesca had also been an adulteress who had been given, by a great poet, a most suitable and unhappy punishment to match her sin.

"So," once more girlish, Frances announced, "after two drinks I always say, I'm not Frances any more, I'm Francesca." There was no answer to be made to this; apparently she expected none. "You'd think," she began and then stopped. "Well, look who's frooking about, the little gray wren, straight from the nest, right off the incubator—hello, Peg, join us in a little loving cup? One for the road?" she asked around, holding up her nearly empty glass and regarding it balefully. "Chin chin," she said, finishing it off.

"Dear heart, please. Iris is going to—"

"Iris is always going to something," Frances said philosophically. "And we're all that's left—Always-Going-to-Do-Something Iris, Old-Money-Bags Esther, and me." She looked tired and unhappy. "How's come it was you never went over like Ada, Jules, how's come it was always your wives?"

"Mother—"

"No, I mean it," she said seriously. "Doesn't it strike you as odds all wrong that *four*—"

"Listen, Mother, if you think that's funny—"

"Okay, *olé*. I'm just depressed. Death always depresses me. Frooks up what sense of humor I have left. I join the fids in out-field. Anyway, Peggy hasn't had a little lifter, have you, hon?"

"I was looking for Pete. His mother asked me if—it seems to me I'm always looking for Pete," Peggy said, as if to an audience that had assembled especially to hear her grievances. "I'm always the one that's being left—first with the kids, now with his mother. And it's not fair," she went on passionately. "I like a drink as well as the next one, I like—"

"Aw, honey," Pete said, "we didn't mean to leave you out, I didn't deliberately—"

"You never *deliberately* do anything. You never think at all. That's what's worse—you don't even know I exist—you just—"

"Once more round the rosy," Frances called to the bartender, "and put it on *his* bill." And she jabbed a vicious finger over her shoulder at her husband. He didn't drink, he didn't smoke, he fornicated infrequently. What he went in for was sports. Hence the bar bells, the bowling, the tri-weekly workouts at the Athletic Club. One thing you could say about Jules, though, and once in a while when she was feeling good even Frances said it: he took care of himself.

He took such good care of himself that he would live forever. She watched him angrily now as he leaned across the bar and added, "And one V-Eight juice."

"Tomato's all we've got, sir."

"Then put a little lemon and Worcestershire in it."

"*Yes, sir.*" The bartender knew a big tipper when he saw one. It was the tie pin, a shining diamond big as a sucking stone. Jules didn't believe, as he so often said, in going halfway. For a moment Lois turned away, unable to bear his pained, wrinkled, but smiling face. He was like some awful footnote to the whole history of youth.

"Five of us," Frances said, taking up her new drink. "And then there were four and now there are three. And soon two—"

"Now, dove, please don't talk that way—"

"What do you care? You're not the one that's going to go. You're never the one that goes."

"Doll baby—"

"Don't doll-baby me. Don't tell me they all died naturally, all four of them," she said in a voice that showed she had spent a long time brooding over the matter. "Not four, not without a helping hand. Far away where no one would know what went on. How dumb do you think I am? Those odds just don't add up, not in my book."

"My god, Mother—" Erwin began.

She was not to be stilled, not Frances Timble. She knew her own mind and her own mind had told her, Not all by themselves in those far-away places.

Jules took her hand, on his face an expression of absolute supplication. "Francesca," he begged.

"Francesca," she said contemptuously. And that, Lois thought, is the end of that name.

"Oh, to hell with it. Here's to our frail old human hides. It doesn't take much to tan them and let them lie out in the sun. Lampshades," she said suddenly. "They made lampshades out of those people's skins."

But some depart with flowers, Lois thought, remembering the moment at the grave when Esther, holding the wilted crescent of chrysanthemums, ragged sleepy heads that drooped and nodded in the late morning light as if, at this hour, even the flowers identified with the deep sleep of the dead, had paused at the yaw in the earth and stared down, looking into emptiness. The casket had not yet been brought up.

Most of the sprays lay at the open aperture, big baskets, wreaths of white and palest yellow, the lovely buds and carefully selected blossoms carelessly heaped together. Dark clouds were colliding in the sky, but rain had not yet begun to fall.

The big box began its journey uphill. When it came to rest at the side of the open hole, the benediction began. They had sent a young priest to the grave; it was too wet and risky for old Father O'Shannahan who had said mass; and as that high, almost adolescent voice began the centuries-old words, *I am the Resurrection and the Life, he who believes in me, even if he dies, shall live,* it rose in conviction, it almost inspired confidence; they all bowed their heads; a small fine wind, a thin cold rain, came down the valley and fell upon them.

They were asked to pray, to repeat an Our Father for the departed, and a mumble of voices began to stumble along the familiar words.

Lois lifted her head and looked across the open hole at Esther, who was repeating blindly, like the rest of them, the words learned in childhood . . . *Thy will be done, on earth as it is* . . . and the look on Esther's face seemed to say, Someone pursues me, O someone pursues. And is it myself?

The prayer was finished. In the quiet, through that small but steady spray, amidst the silently, smoothly moving wind, the family watched the big box as it was lowered into the grave, a loud purring accompanying the pulley's automation, while Lois thought, If every crime must be expiated, who shall cry out against death? Though all about—the deepened sky, the dense clouds, the wet still earth, the cluster of black mourners—clamored for an explanation, a revelation, of what they all faced, the only answer seemer to be, *We have failed.* . . . Others . . . ourselves . . . the dead woman.

A whir of machinery, hysterical, out of control, a hideous grating sound, a click, almost inaudible, then the awkwardness again of silence, the priest stepping forward, and as the earth was cast over the coffin, as the priest intoned the last rites of the dead, there came a flash of color, a broken cry, Esther flinging her flowers down, Esther crying out over the open orifice of the grave. "Ada—oh, Ada—good-by."

"Oh, here you are," Iris said, coming up to Lois as she emerged from the ladies' room. "I've been looking all over for you. Are those men in the bar?" her aunt demanded. "Is that where they are? Everything's ready and we're waiting. I don't think that's considerate at all, I really don't, going off to *drink* on the day—and Frances is with them, I just know she's with them, my own sister drinking in a public bar on the day her oldest sister is laid to rest. Oh, it just breaks your heart, the way people act. I won't go in and get them, I won't be seen in a public place where liquor is served on the day my oldest sister—Lois, will you? Will you just— Oh, dear god, look." Iris sprang toward the door of the bar. "Frances, Frances Timble, YOU'VE BEEN DRINKING!"

The waiter went around and filled glasses. It was a nonalcoholic "wine" Iris had selected for the occasion, thick as syrup and almost as sweet, but held up to the light it had a beautiful color, deep and heavy as the dark heart of the garnet. They were drinking to Ada, though no one had proposed a toast. In the embarrassed silence, someone coughed; here and there about the long table people began to raise their glasses, surreptitiously sip. It was as if, Lois thought, silently, they were saying, To Ada, to Ada, while lithely, swiftly, the waiter went round the long oblong table of the private room with its gleaming linen, its shining silver, its inconspicuous flowers of pearly white, only the centers palely tinged with pink.

Who in this room identified the transcendent and the immanent with the Almighty? Who asked of the dead woman, Whither hast thou gone and why? And what hast thou found, out there in the silent reaches of space, where God stands against man?

The waiters were passing a fruit cocktail in thin fragile crystal bowls sunk in a silver-rimmed circle of crushed ice, not fresh fruit but canned cubes of pineapple, the small sad off-green grapes, the quartered ends of cherries sticking up through white cubes of diced canned pear and apple. A sprig of fresh mint had been propped atop to give an illusion of elegance, an illusion, Lois knew, that would lead into the creamed chicken in the thick pastry shell, the ubiquitous Midwestern canned peas, a salad in the shape of a candle, with a slice of pineapple forming the base, a banana jutting up as the candle, a cherry (whole this time) atop as flame, and creamed cheese with chopped nuts at the base in the form of a handle. Ice cream and cake would indisputably come as dessert, and then a glass plate of multi-colored mints would be passed. It was the $2.35 special Iris had chosen, the one used for ladies' literary luncheons, bridge parties, and the more economy-minded bridal buffets. But though it was the cheapest package Iris had chosen, it was the best hotel. With Iris it was not the food you ate that counted but where you were seen eating it.

Eileen, eyes enormous with disbelief, sat across and down from her, picking the pimento centers out of green olives. She looked up and stared at Lois, unblinking, her eyes as still and sightless as the socket of the inanimate olive in her hand. Is it for me the banquet begins? she seemed to ask. No, they would have to answer, it is for another, the mother who all these years stayed sealed up in that house because—

As if she understood, Eileen choked, and for a moment, while everyone waited, she leaned forward, face crimsoning, eyes bulging; then the mortician got up hastily, clumsily, the chair sounding rupturous in that still room, and slapped her on the back until she bent forward across the table over the flaming cherry that topped her salad. The eyes that looked out at them were clear and untroubled, or so they seemed. But to Lois what those eyes were saying was, I am afraid, O I am most awfully afraid. There are so many people, so many faces, all those mouths opening and closing, the waiters like birds gliding in and out, in their hands they hold white napkins like signals, what do they signal to one another, gliding in and out between the tables, in between the people with their opening and closing mouths, between the long table of food that is smoking and heaving under the hot bright lights overhead?

O I am so afraid, so terribly afraid. All around me there are things of which I am afraid, and no one to help me. I'm all alone, all alone, where—

"Dear, you must try to eat, just a little. It'll make you feel so much better." The fat face suspended over concaves of crushed ice belonged, of course, to Iris. For a moment no one said anything. Frances—tee i gee aitch tee, as she would have said of herself and often did, Oh, I'm tee i gee aitch tee, and it's grand, grand—leaned forward and shook her head. A characteristic Timble gesture, they all did it; it meant, I wash my hands of the whole thing, I have from the start.

"They shouldn't have brought her," Frances said to Lois. "I told Iris Eileen shouldn't come, but Iris wouldn't listen. She said she had to come, and once she says something, there's no getting her to back down. Rather be right than President, they wrote those words about Iris, even though they didn't know it. Who did they write them about anyway, Lois?" she asked curiously.

"Al Smith, Winterbottom, somebody like that." Lois wasn't really paying attention.

"Winterbottom? Did he ever run for President? I can't remember anyone of that name—"

"Frances, Frances," Iris called, leaning across the table and pointing a fork like a prompter at Frances. "I want to know if you and Jules are coming back to the house. I told Dad I was going to bring some people back. He needs company, Frances, he's lonely. And you know I'm always the one anyway who has people in—"

"If I don't know it now I never will." Frances shook her head. "You *like* confusion. It's beyond me, simply beyond the powers of my imagination to envision how *anyone*—even you, Iris—can go on year after year, decade after decade, millennium after millennium, doing the same old thing over and over again, shut up in that same old house. Never go out on the town. Never take a trip. Never get out and see what's around you. And pretty soon it'll be too late. Like Ada—she's never going to get out and around any more and neither are you one of these days."

"I *like* my life—"

"You must, to keep repeating it over and over. Doesn't it ever bother you that for you nothing ever changes, that there's never anything to look forward to?"

"You don't seem to understand," Iris said between a tightness of lips meant to reprove her frivolous sister. "I love my house, why should I want to leave it? My children all grew up there—"

"And those boarders," Frances interrupted, waving aside with vermilion-tipped fingers any merit of Iris's argument. "Year after year of those impossible old men and ugly young girls shuffling up and down the stairs. No help, down on your hands and knees—"

"I have a girl who comes in once a week—"

"I should think so. Look at the size of that house. What you need is a full-time couple."

"I don't want someone always around underfoot—"

"Why don't you get rid of that Civil War monstrosity? All those fiddy boarders? You've filled your little pot of gold by now—"

"I only keep the steadies—"

"Work yourself to death, never do anything interesting, never get away—romance, Iris, there are places all over the world, ports of romance—"

"You came back here, Frances Timble, so that shows—"

"Jules wanted to do something about his roots," Frances said, shrugging her shoulders again, abrogating *all* responsibility for the return. "He didn't have any family of his own so he was tickled to death, poor boob, at the prospect of annexing mine. I think that was one of the reasons he married me, there were so many family figures lurking about. At me day and night to come trundling back to this shitty city and put down his goddam roots. Why couldn't he have put them down in Chicago or San Francisco, some place interesting like that? No, he's got to cultivate where, as he says, 'there's a feeling of permanence.' Well, he got it all right, this family has been set in stone for generations." Angrily she unsnapped her purse and scrambled inside for cigarettes. "We could have dug down in any number of fascinating places, but he wants to grow his little garden of Eden here in the bread basket of the West. If all those wives hadn't died in foreign ports before they *bore,* and his mother and father hadn't popped off at an early age, we might be living it up in Beverly Hills."

"I just want you to come for a visit, Frances, I'm not asking you to *stay*."

"I wish he wouldn't keep smelling his hands like that," Frances said. "At least not at the table."

Jules, helping himself to celery and olives, looked up. "Who, dumpling, who's smelling his hands?"

"That man, the mortician," Frances said, looking across at him.

"Does he do it all the time?" Jules asked. "You make it sound like he does it all the time."

"Every time I look at him he's doing it. I don't mind so much some place else, like—well—where he *works,* but here, where we're all eating—"

"Chicken—are there seconds on chicken, Iris?" Esther had methodically eaten through everything on her plate and now, item by item, she was refurbishing—first the rolls, then the butter, relishes, radishes, olives, and even the small green scallions. But she wanted the substantials. She ate irregularly out there in her big barn of a house, with all its old-fashioned appliances that scarcely functioned, the early-thirties gas stove, the refrigerator with its motor on top that made inordinate amounts of noise.

Lois knew she opened boxes of cold cereals, nibbled at dried-out cheeses, munched on old apples and flabby crackers. No wonder she wanted seconds.

"Of course not," Iris said angrily. "It's a luncheon, a sit-down luncheon, not a smorgasbord."

Esther looked around, as if asking, Was it true? Yes, it was true. The waiters were already hovering about, waiting to clear when the first, the fast, were through. Then she saw Arnold being given another plate. In order to save a scene, Iris had ordered two dinners for him. "Look at Arnold," Esther said in outrage. "He's getting a second serving."

"Well, he's one of the bereaved," Iris said. "He—"

"What do you mean he's one of the bereaved? *I'm* one of the bereaved. That was my own sister we buried out there today. What do you mean he's one of the bereaved, we're all bereaved."

"Yes, but some are more bereaved than others."

"What makes you think he's more bereaved than I am?"

"He's the husband." And Iris smiled and cast a beneficent nod upon him, as if conferring a distinction.

There was a pause. Then, oblivious to the dispute, the maître d'hôtel moved forward. "Does madame wish the wine passed round again?" he inquired, his voice pausing archly on the word *wine*.

Stu leaned across the table, one hand on his almost full glass of wine. "Mother, he wants to know if you want him to go round with that stuff again?"

"Go around with what again?" She looked up and down the table. "Well, I suppose he can if he wants."

Stu nodded imperceptibly and the man moved on, the bottle came from behind his back, and, proceeding on a tour of pouring, though almost no one had touched a glass, he bent solicitously over each place. Frances had rolled her eyes at the first sip, but the others had been more polite in ignoring their glasses without comment, concentrating instead on the food, the lesser of two evils. The pastry shells, sticky, limp, lay in the middle of most of their plates like a rebuke; the candles, fallen, had lost their lights, the bananas were browned, the cream cheese uneaten. Plate after plate went back to the kitchen almost untouched, but Arnold ate on.

While he forked up his food, his mouth hung open, ready; the fat, not quite clean hands cut hastily—stabbed, speared, shoved; his little eyes blinked with pleasure, he patted his hard, knotty stomach now and then in satisfaction.

"It was a very nice service," Peggy said, an offering Lois had been expecting, one in which Peggy had been coached again and again by her mother-in-law. "Now, Peggy, when dinner's over," Iris had said, "you start off the remembrances by saying something nice, something like, Well, I thought it was a very nice service. Or, It was impressive, don't you think, the way Father O'Shannahan conducted mass?"

"A *very* nice service," Peggy said desperately.

No one answered, not even Iris, watching the chocolate ice cream being put in place. Coffee cups rattled as they were refilled. In the pause Lois looked from face to face, on each an expression of petulance, the petulance of children who had been thwarted. Was that what death meant to them, being thwarted?

Over the fallen candle of her salad, Eileen's eyes were blank and blue, the face she held up to Lois white, unlined—beautiful. While she looked at Eileen and Eileen looked back, a multitude of emotions passed over that old but unaged face—confusion, bafflement, and finally resignation. She had no more idea now of who Lois was than she had had five years back at the institution.

It was necessary she know. But not now, Lois said to herself, now is not the time. Later . . . you will have to go out to that shut-up house later and—

Neal back in New York, Stu the night before at the bar, Carolyn out at her own house, suspended over the rim of her martini, Eileen here with her blank uncomprehending eyes: it is all part of a pattern. And what is being asked of you, she thought, is what all these interwoven intricacies mean.

Napkins lay in various agonies on the table. The plate of mints was almost empty, people were stirring and rearranging their wraps. "It's all over," Iris said sadly. "Not one single thing went wrong. I just can't believe it. There wasn't one real quarrel or fight. Somehow it doesn't seem like a real get-together when nothing goes wrong. Of course it was funny Ethel wasn't here—but other than that it went well, don't you think so, Lois?" she asked anxiously.

"Very well."

"But don't you think it was funny about Ethel? I mean, she never said she wasn't going to come and Stu never said she wasn't —of course, they, well, they don't always—see eye to eye," she finished. "But for a family funeral, she should have come." And before Lois could compose some innocuous answer, Iris went on breathlessly in what Lois recognized instantly as her alarm voice. "And, Carolyn—"

Alerted, Carolyn looked up.

"—the man says gratuities aren't included. They give you the room," Iris explained, looking around, "But you have to tip. I'm afraid—oh, Carolyn, I'm so afraid Arnold won't give them enough.

I'm going with him, to sort—sort of help settle things. How much should he give, Carolyn? You know about things like this. How much should they get?"

"Fifteen per cent at least."

"Fifteen? I thought it was ten and then if you liked the way things were done, a little more. I'll never be able to talk him into fifteen, Carolyn, you know that. Even ten—he'll probably think even ten is steep, you know how Arnold is. Oh," she cried, and grabbed Lois by the arm, hanging on, her eyes bright with half-shed tears, her mouth quivering. "She's gone, Lois, Ada's gone—"

"Stop it," Carolyn said sharply, "just stop it. We've been through all that before. And Eileen's behaved so well this far, you don't want—"

"She was good, wasn't she?" The tears evaporated. "I mean, she didn't spill too much of her food and she only started acting—funny—that one time, and then that waiter, it was like he understood, that waiter went and got her another ice cream. Maybe you are right, Carolyn, maybe they do deserve fifteen, everything went so well—but I'll tell you both one thing, for the life of me I'll never be able to figure out why Esther threw those flowers, why she even brought them in the first place. She knew we were all going in on the spray—even though we'll never get her share out of her. I mean, if she wanted to send a special basket, I suppose that would have been all right," Iris said doubtfully, "even though we all agreed to go in on the spray. But to go and bring flowers to the church, to throw them on the grave that way," Iris said decisively, "that wasn't right. Doesn't that seem strange to you?"

"Why don't you ask her?"

"Ask her? Why, Carolyn, what do you mean, ask her? I don't want to make her mad, Carolyn. She's got all that money. All that money—and somehow it doesn't seem fair that Ada, who had so little, should have—have passed on—without knowing about Esther and the gloves. It would have meant so much to Ada to have known about the gloves. It's one thing I'll blame myself for the rest of my life, that she never knew, but Mama, she wanted us to be loyal, so I didn't think I should say anything, at least not right away. And now Ada's dead and she'll never know. It would have

been some kind of vindication for Ada if she had only known."
Iris seemed genuinely sad; then she turned her attention to Lois.

"Honey, you aren't serious about this boy that keeps calling
you up all the way from New York, are you? Oh, I can appreciate
your need for male companionship and all, but he's not the man
for you, not with what you've told me, all the problems there'd
be—you know, different *faiths*. Oh, don't look like that, I'm not
going to ask you if you go to mass and all, I know you young
people have all fallen away, but you'll come back, wait and see,
when you get as old as I am, you'll want the comfort. I know,
I've been through it. But, honey, just remember what I told you,
it doesn't do to mix blood. You know how it was when you
married that—I can never remember, was he Italian or Greek?
Just promise me you won't—won't do anything *hasty*, anything
spur of the moment, just promise me you'll give yourself some
time. Will you do that for me, will you just do that for me? There's
a lot of your mother in you, God rest her soul."

Hasty? Lois asked herself.

But of course Iris was right. Not for her the well-deliberated,
carefully thought-through plan; rather the rush from one unwise
action to another with, as Iris had said, much of her mother in
her.

"But—but if you do *decide*, there's one thing I want you to
promise me. I want you to promise me here and now you'll come
back here to get married, that you'll have the ceremony at Sans
Souci," she said, looking up at Lois with eyes brimming with
hope. "You know how I've always wanted a wedding in the house,
that that was the one thing in my life I really wanted and never
had."

She turned with an agonized expression and regarded the drink
that Carolyn had quietly ordered and which was now being put in
front of her. Speechless for a moment—a moment only—Iris
gaped, while Carolyn, her fingers stiff, fumbled with the bottle of
soda beside the half-full whisky glass.

"You're not going to drink now—*in the middle of the day*—AT
ADA'S—"

With a voice completely under control, Carolyn said, "Yes, I have a drink about this time every day. If I didn't, I don't think I'd make it. With you it's candy, but there are some times when chocolates just don't do the job."

With dignity, her mother said, "I don't think you ought to talk to me that way, Carolyn, I really don't, not when we've just been through an—*an event* of this kind."

Proud, if tired, Iris sat in the center of the old-fashioned hotel dining room, commander of the forces that remained, Eileen and Arnold having finally found a cab in which, at the last minute, Esther had also left. She was going downtown to do her Thanksgiving duties with Harold and the Sisters, carols infused with timely references to The Cold War and The Bomb, and since the cab had to pass across Ninth, she would just hop out there and avail herself of a free trip—if they didn't mind, of course. Not that they had much choice. It was raining hard now; they were lucky to get one cab, let alone think of two, so the three of them had gone, united in Ada's death the way they had never been in her life.

It was the end of the day. A mauve light hung over the room, humming; Lois could almost hear night pour in, gravid with the sweet breath of roses. The room, sinking down in shadows, closed round her like a clamp, making memory for the moment more real than what was going on about her, this room with its slowly shifting waiters, its occupants at the table, their faces showing white teeth and livid eyes, figures whose gestures blurred, ran together as if the flesh had turned to warm wax, their voices like water flowing back and forth on some distant shore. But what was inside was a forest sheathed in silver, the cry of a bird circling in a stand of pine, and a house, an old-fashioned, badly built house which had seemed, in all its marred imperfection, such a thing of value that she longed to insure it as the landscape of her life, a place from which perpetually to take bearing. There had been, of course, a man against that landscape; that was what always gave her landscape any significance, the presence of someone loved. Married, they had given to the world a child. She had kept a part of him, nurtured it and let it grow until it made an entity of its own. For love of him she had been a part of creation.

Greece is a thing of the past, she reminded herself, where all the idols crumbled.

She rose; her legs suddenly unsteady. She hung for an instant on the edge of the table, the faces around it now excessively clear, an eye extended here, a nose there; mouths moved, arms extended themselves into sinister semaphors, the bodies bulged and swelled, all that flesh rising up in a great undulation of accusation. She did not love them. She did not love, really love, anyone. She knew nothing at all about love.

"Why, it's Lois," Arnold said in a rich, folksy voice she did not recognize. "Imagine that—Lois." He's been in the basement, Lois thought, having a little libation in honor of the day, sitting down there on his Army cot helping himself from the bottle in the brown bag. He always hid his liquor when he brought it into the house, respecting the neighbors. "Well, how are you, Lois?" His voice was so pleasant that who would have dreamed he had just returned from the interment of his wife?

"I'm pretty well, Uncle Arnold. I just thought—"

"Yes, yes," he said, raising his hand to put an end to any condolences she might be about to utter. "A very sad event, but her time had come. You living in New York now, Lois? Myself, I wouldn't like it, too much time indoors, I always like to get out, be with people. Gregarious," he announced, his eyes vague and watery. "Ada, now, she didn't *like* to go out. *Always* in the house. 'Get out more, Ada,' I used to say, '*mix*,' but you couldn't budge her. Well, each to his own, I always say." He leaned forward, opening the door a little wider. Lois felt the air around her escape in what sounded like a hiss; it was filled with the strong scent of Scotch. Then she realized the sound had come from Arnold's false teeth; his plate was slipping and he had to suck in to put it back in place.

At her wit's end, Lois decided on all or nothing. She stepped forward. "I wonder if I might come in, if I might see Eileen? I hate to bother you at a time like this, but—" She grasped the doorknob in a surprise maneuver, catching him unaware. Before he could regroup his forces, she stepped inside. Through what seemed a solid wall of alcohol, she bent and kissed him on the cheek. "I'm so sorry about everything," she said, moving back, breathing, "and I'd like to see Eileen, if I could."

"Well, I don't know, I mean you know—a day like this. She's been—well, you know, *down* . . ."

"I'd like to see her, Uncle Arnold. I came to see her and tell her how sorry I am about—about everything."

"Well, that's nice of you, Lois, awfully nice of you. I'll see. . . . You don't know what I've been through these past few days, nobody ever will," he said in a voice full of self-pity. "Eileen—*Eileen*."

He was plowing his way through furniture, pushing aside old newspapers, making his way toward the stairs. "Eileen, *Eileen* . . . oh." He gasped. "Oh, there you are. For chrissake, why didn't you answer?"

Eileen moved forward, her pink mouth in a moue; she was making a face at her father.

"Stop it," Arnold said angrily. "Stop that. Don't act like that. Cut it out," he said to his daughter. He brought his hand across her wrist with a smart crack. But she simply stood looking at him, seemingly unaware he had struck her.

"I'm not going to put up with any more nonsense," he said. "You come here right this minute—right this minute or—or out go those mice, you hear? Out those mice go, I'll turn them right out in the street, you hear? Goddammit anyway, why me? Why do I have to get stuck with this? Listen to me, are you listening to me? If you don't behave like a human being right this minute—" He closed his eyes, shook his big head. When at last he could look on the world again, he said, "She's all yours, Lois. I'll be down cellar if you need me. What I've had to put up with these past ten years, God alone knows."

"You remember me, Eileen? Lois—"

"Oh yes, Lois. *Lois*," she said again, this time sharp and precise. Now the eyes that looked at Lois were full of icy anger. "Yes, *Lois*," she said again.

We are ready to forgive only after we have had some kind of revenge, Lois thought. If I told her what happened with Cliff, would she consider that revenge enough? If I gave her in return for what happened to her with Stan what happened to me with Cliff, might not that help?

"Did you know I went to Greece, Eileen? That I got married and had a little girl?"

Eileen, a grown-up Eileen, a woman with a woman's anger showing on her face, turned her head stiffly away.

"She's three now—three, and—listen, Eileen, I feel—I feel so responsible, and—and I want you to know I realize I *am* responsible, and I'm sorry. But what is so terrible is that I don't know what to do. I don't know how I can help, and that's what I want more than anything in the world, to help."

"He never loved you—my mother, my mother didn't want me to marry him and he knew, but he sent me these messages, she never knew he sent me these messages, she never knew, not in her whole lifetime." She stared at Lois with an intensity that seemed as if it would go on forever. "I've been kept away from him all these years. *All these years*—but he sends messages, they come every day, he doesn't have to write letters the way other people do, he has these *rays*—" The eyes glittered, the mouth was moist, the hands held themselves up as if the rays were right there in the air if only Lois could see them. "Now that Mama's dead, you could bring him back."

For a moment Lois let herself believe. Bring him back, start all over again.

Eileen took hold of her arm. "Mama isn't here any more," she said. "Bring him back. *You can bring him back*."

"I don't even know if he's still in Springfield—"

"You could go *see*." The eyes glittered. "Or if I could get out—"

Chapter 7

"I LOST HER," Arnold said disgruntledly, "somewhere in the weeds." He looked around hopelessly. "She just got away." Something was changed in him. Then Stu saw: he had a false plate now; Stu could see it move up and down in the street light which had just gone on, making little ripples of Arnold's mouth. "The first thing I knew she was gone. I had her all ready for bed, and she gets out on me in a nightgown. She'll catch her death of cold in that outfit. So of course I called your mother."

Of course, Stu thought, but instead he said, "It probably has something to do with—you know—the day." Arnold cast him a cold look. "Her mother and all," Stu said inadequately.

They were standing in the middle of an alleyway, one of the old-fashioned cut-throughs between two streets that used to serve as an entrance to garages. Across the alley were two vacant lots overgrown with sycamores, ailanthus, thorny bushes, a tangle or brush suggesting a picture from one of those detective or true-romance magazines, the site of a sadistic crime or a senseless drunken stabbing. Stu could see Eileen, nightgown blown back by the wind, escaping before the outstretched hands of a mad murderer or a deranged rapist. Crazy, of course. It was only her father she was fleeing.

The day lay in ruins all about him. That business with his brother's wife—he had been struggling into his coat at the hotel after dinner when Peggy came up beside him. "Why do you always try to avoid me?" she had asked, and then he felt a gentle tug at his arm. He shoved his arms through the sleeves, turned, and faced her. "I mean," she went on, flustered, "I don't know, you never seem to—how are you, Stu?"

"I'm fine, Peggy, just fine. How are you?" Over the years he had learned to be gentle with her. She was a very frail little girl underneath, easily hurt, waiting, it seemed to him, for rebuke. He did not understand her, he had never understood her, but what he had come to understand was that in some shy, secret way she cared for him. She made him nervous, she never said anything that interested him, she had a facility for catching him (as she had now) at the wrong time and trying to talk to him, but the very fact of her caring put him in commitment to her. We must always honor the act of love. In whatever form it comes.

"Tired," she said and stood uncertainly in front of him, twisting her hands together. "Of course it's easier now that the big ones are out working, but—but they still have to eat," she said. "When they come home, they're all so hungry. And in the morning—but—" She faltered. "It's always the same, Stu, that's what's begun to bother me. I thought it would be different when they grew up, but you just have bigger problems, that's all. You think all the time they're little that when they grow up they'll be able to help, but they don't, they just go off on their own."

He tried to think of something to say.

"You take Mary," she said, it seemed to him almost desperately. "I mean, she's old enough to get married, I know that. Most girls are married by twenty-three, and she's got this nice boy, he comes from a good family, Stu, he really does, and you'd think she'd want to settle down with a home of her own, but, Stu, would you believe it, she says she doesn't want to get married, she *never* wants to get married, it's nothing but cooking and cleaning and having babies—and that's true, but, Stu, all girls get married, what else is there for them to do, especially when they don't have a college education?"

He didn't know.

"I'm so afraid she's going to get in trouble," she said and waited.

Stu searched his head for some shred of encouragement. "They're pretty smart, the girls nowadays," he said at last lamely.

"I wouldn't worry if I were you, Peggy." She had put her hand on his arm and it lay there, thin, fragile, helpless. "Well," he said, trying to smile. "Well."

"You're leaving now?" But she left her hand where it was.

"I was just going."

She was uncomfortably close, peering up into his face as if she were scanning for some sign only she would recognize. He tried to look pleasant and brother-in-lawish, however the hell that was. But the whole thing was beginning to unnerve him; she had a way of bringing on this feeling of bafflement and annoyance. "Well," he said. "Well——"

"Stu?"

"Yes?"

"I mean, how is it——" She turned away from him, her thin veined hand grasped his arm; for chrissake she was grabbing onto him, as if trying to prevent him from leaving; the pressure of her fingers was insistent, she was sending him some kind of message, and he couldn't interrupt it; he had no idea in the world what she wanted, but he just wished to hell she'd let go.

"How is it—why don't you like me, Stu? What's the matter? Why do you always try to avoid me?"

"I don't try to avoid you," he said, knowing he was lying.

"Yes, you do, Stu. You never—never look for me. You don't go and try to find me—to talk to me."

What the hell could he say?

"And whenever I come up to you," she went on, relentlessly, "you always make some excuse, you try to get away from me as fast as you can."

"Well, I'm sorry you feel that way, but——" He had started to sweat.

"There isn't much to me, I know that," she said unhappily, gripping his arm more forcefully. "I mean I never really had a chance to develop, I know that. It was—was like I never really had any good times, I was never a girl, going to parties and dances and things, I was just a child and then we had the baby——"

He felt desperately sorry for her, but what was he supposed to say?

"—and then, I don't know, how can you figure out what you are when every minute of the day is taken up with something, when at night you just want to fall into bed and forget you're anything at all, when you just want to sleep and sleep and—" She broke off. "There's something I've got to tell you, Stu, something I've just got to say. I've been holding it in for years and years, and now I know I've got to tell you or—my life will just go on the same, in this same horrible awful impossible way, and I can't stand it any more, I really can't, I've come to the end of my rope—"

Good Christ, she had started to cry. "Here," he said helplessly, trying to get free of her arm, but she only clutched harder, as if she were afraid to let him go. "Let me get you a handkerchief. You're just upset. The funeral—"

"I don't want a handkerchief," she declared passionately. "I'm not just all upset. It hasn't got anything to do with the funeral. What do I care about Ada? I haven't seen her in years. She's just a name to me—just a name," she repeated, her voice slowing down from its restless recital to pause in wonderment over that phrase. "That's what I'll turn out to be," she said, as if she were speaking to herself, as if she had forgotten about him, and, for a fact, her grip loosened. "Just a name. There's nothing there but a name. Peggy, do this. Peggy, do that—all they ever call me for is to do something, but they don't care about *me*. And maybe they shouldn't, maybe there isn't really a me at all, I'm just somebody who fetches and carries for other people. Stu," she implored, "tell me the truth, is that what I am, somebody who only exists to wait on others?"

"Nonsense," he said, trying to sound strong and sure when all the time he was frantic to be rid of her. Where was her husband, for god's sake, why didn't he come and take her away? Did she carry on like this all the time? And he had just never realized it before? Loony like the rest of them.

Looking down into the imploring face pressed up toward his he heard her saying, all in a rush, "I love you, I've always loved you, you've got to listen. I've wanted to tell you so many times and I never could. It was like I just couldn't bring myself to say the words, I was afraid, and now you know, now I've told you, and I'm glad, oh Stu, I'm so glad, I've wanted you to know for so long, ever since you came back, ten years, ten whole years of wanting to tell you, but I couldn't say anything, not with—with the way things were. Ethel—"

Christ, he had to do something. He couldn't just let her stand here ranting on. "Peggy," he said, while she looked at him in adoration and anguish, and he thought, Jesus H. Christ, this is the end, the ee-en-dee. "Peggy, you don't even know me," he said feebly, while she hung onto him and cried out, "I know you, Stu, oh, I know you better than anyone else in the world, you don't know how well I know you, I—"

She was clinging to him like death. He took hold and pushed them both toward the lounge, where, thank god, there were people, clamorous, insistent, gesturing throngs.

Where were those quiet, simple people who went to church and gathered with relatives for the funeral feast, then went home to lie in chairs dreaming in front of the fire? There must still be such people, people who expected and loved the simple things in life. But he was not among them.

"I'll never never NEVER let you out," Ethel had screamed at him that morning while she was getting dressed for the funeral. She had been fussing with her hair, couldn't get it right; the brittle broken-off dyed yellow ends were curling the wrong way, breaking off on the brush, standing out from her head as if she were some strange aborigine preparing herself for the puberty rites.

Ethel's hair, woman's crowning glory, lay on her head like some shattered crown that could never be soldered together again. Tears streamed down her bleached white face; Ethel had thrown down the brush in a fit of rage. "Don't look at me like that. You hear me? Don't you dare look at me like that! You think you're so goddam smart. Goddam superior!" she had screeched, the tears splashing out of inflamed eyes. "Lose one business after another, always in debt, and now—now"—completely out of control, screaming at the top of her lungs—"It isn't enough you've ruined my life, you got to—you got another woman. I'm not going to that goddam funeral, you hear? Not you, not nobody in this world can make me."

Stu trudged after Arnold down a small, swampy path. Cold, disheartened, almost angry, he knew he was going to have one hell of an evening. There wasn't much time, they had to hurry before it got dark.

Christ, all these women were just too much—Ethel at the house, Peggy in the hotel, his mother and Carolyn on the phone. "You have to go over, it's a man's job." (A man's job, there was one for you.)

Arnold stopped. Puffing, pulling on his pants (trouble with that big belly keeping them up, Stu decided), he planted his feet firmly in two holes of mud. Stu hoped he stuck to the earth. "She went that way," Arnold said, pointing left.

An obvious impossibility: the undergrowth was so thick that she would have had to cut her way through, yet not a twig was turned back. "What makes you think that, Arnold?" You had to be polite.

"Saw her."

"But there's no trace of anyone—look, not one branch is broken, no footprints." Eileen might be mad but she still couldn't walk on air.

"I saw her," Arnold said stubbornly.

"But why would she go through there?"

Arnold shrugged. He reminded Stu of all the family. Shrug shrug shrug. Or if they weren't shrugging, shouting. Arnold drank down cellar and Ethel ate chocolates, reading *True Story* on the john. "The loo," he reminded himself. "The trots," that's what bothered her so often. And after he cleared out? He could just hear her saying, "Stu's off on—a little vacation, he needs a rest, the doc said." Never call a spade a spade—and also always bring authority to bear. Might be the whole doctrine of middle-class Midwestern morality. Gold the god, Having an Endowment the Hereafter, and all god's liddle chil'ren got bosoms and bazookers. To tell the difference, you know. Christ, what a myth sex was. It turned out to be the one really unimportant thing in life and you spent all those young years jammed up over it. Just the smell of some woman sometimes—but as you got older—

"Who knows?" said Arnold. "And of course I couldn't get through myself, so I went around and looked over there, on the next street. Vanished, into thin air."

Years really since he'd cared much about it, since it was the prime mystery that moved his mind, since he had organized his life around it. Then Betty's blue slip on the bed, a momentary flare-up, I used to pant for it all day, but of course that didn't last long either. Like dogs we tire of canned food, we want fresh meat. Christ, what a mean thing man is.

But I love Betty, it has nothing to do with screwing; it's almost as if I don't care about the screwing any more. Is that bad?

"She's got to be some place. Most likely in somebody's house. Out in this weather in a nightgown, somebody sees her, takes her in, that only makes sense."

"Takes her in? But what would they do with her—I mean, the way she is."

"Call someone, I guess."

The SPCA? The Humane Society? Who could you call?

The creases in Arnold's neck, long ropes of old-age flesh, suddenly inflated; he looked like some tropical fish whose equipment for fecundation was located near his head. *"What if she . . ."* He was unable to finish.

She was—how old? Forty-something-or-other. Just at the time of life when the rage of sex seems to pass, when age begins to bank the passionate impulses, but in those who have lived a life of denial the fire rages up to consume the flesh. That was why she had gone out in her nightgown.

"Does she know anyone around the neighborhood?"

"She never goes out." Arnold's synthetic teeth chattered; did the false feel as strongly as the true? He must remember to ask himself that question at those moments he was so "kind" to Ethel. "But then, I mean, the people next door," Arnold said, "she knows them, of course."

"How old are they?"

"How old are they?" Arnold repeated. Obviously he couldn't understand a simple question.

"Forty? Fifty? Sixty?"

"Oh, you mean, how *old* are they? She's in her forties, maybe early fifties, he's about fifty, fifty-five."

"That's where she is." Stu started to turn around.

Arnold stayed obstinately planted in his two holes of mud. "I mean, that's just next door, why should she come all this way, in this weather, just to go next door?"

"Because you were running after her."

Arnold considered. "You mean she didn't want me to know?"

"Something like that, but more likely she just wanted to be free, to be out on her own for a while, and she knew you'd take her back. So she decided to get away from you and—"

Arnold shook his head. "Well, I suppose it's worth a try. Anything is, at this point, I'm frozen to the bone."

Stu would have bet his bottom dollar Eileen was making one hell of a scene with that man next door.

"She's here all right," the man said, taking out a handkerchief and mopping his brow. "I tried to call but—"

"I guess we were out, looking for her."

"—I couldn't've got through anyway, she was at me that bad on the phone. Maybe if the wife hadda been home—but then, I don't know, these things, you can't tell, I mean she might have— the wife mighta upset her. That was a bad storm we had this afternoon, wasn't it?"

Stu looked around the living room.

"She's upstairs," the man explained. "We kinda had a scuffle on the stairs, she's strong, they say they are when they're like that, and of course being drunk besides—there's not much I could do with her, she'd made up her mind."

"Drunk?" Stu turned to Arnold, but Arnold obviously didn't know. He was shrugging again. A world of shruggers.

But the stuff was in the house all the time, why wouldn't she eventually help herself? The mother gone, the father such a boozer himself—it all figured, oh it all figured all right, and they were in for plenty of trouble.

"She's drunk all right, you can smell it a mile away. And she's —well, she's in a *nightgown,* or at least she was, I wouldn't swear to it now, being the way she was." He led them to the bottom of the stairs. "Might be best if you went up, you know, alone, I'm not—" He shook his head, a nice middle-aged man, one of those simple folk who had gone through the day, settled in front of the fire, only to find the real flame at his front door. A nice-looking guy, not heavy, just spread, still had his own head of hair, big hands on him, probably worked outdoors: he was perfect for the role, simple, big, and available. Stu wondered if the man had any idea that this was just a start.

"Why don't you go up?" he said to Arnold.

Arnold wasn't enthusiastic. "I don't know," he said. "I mean— well, she don't always *take* to me. But"—he turned to Stu with expressive eyes, his new teeth gleamed—"she's—she's always been real fond of you."

What was the use of arguing? It was all fated. Resigned, he went up the steps.

Odd how the insides of these houses, regardless of shape and size, were all alike. Why not? he asked himself. The people who live in them are all the same. Going past the knobby-legged table with the awful lamp, the picture of "The Gleaners" over it, he thought of his own house, the groaning plumbing in the bathroom, inadequate closets in the kitchen, badly placed window in the bedroom, the long rectangular living room with its *moderne* furniture that creaked when you sat down, the plastic cracking at the seams, the legs of the sofa obscene in the way they sprouted, fat and dumpy, from the underside, and the two matching chairs, mohair and maple (imitation) $144.95 SALE LASTS ONE DAY ONLY.

He took what shredded courage was left in his hands and advanced toward the open door, past the high-backed Victorian chair with the little knitted things on it. "The wife" also kept crocks of aspidistra. He looked around for the fake flowers—they were on a crocheted runner at the end of the bureau over which, framed, Sir Galahad disappeared into the mist in search of his grail. A very pure house.

Eileen was sitting up in bed with the sheet pulled up to her throat. Stu was surprised, really surprised, at how beautiful she looked. She had soft dimpled shoulders, like something done in silk. Her hair was wild, her eyes were wild, but her face looked young and flushed, the face of an excited woman wanting to have love made to her.

The best thing was not to go too near her, to talk to her, calm her down, get her for chrissake to put some clothes on, get her out of that man's bed and home. All he needed now was for "the wife" to appear.

What did you say in a situation like this, you had to say something and it wasn't Happy Hanukkah. "It's me"—I, you cluck—"it's me, Eileen—Stu." She just looked at him, her big wide blue eyes ransacking his face as if in search of her fate. "Your father—he's worried about you. We're all worried about you." She looked away from him. "You—you about finished here, you about ready to go home?"

"I'm not going home." She sounded very sure. "I'm staying here."

"But this isn't your house—I mean, these people, this man—*and his wife*—it's their house, and they want—"

"I'm not going back, I'm staying here."

"But have you ever figured—I mean—whether they want you to stay?"

She shook her head; she meant it as a general *no* to the whole conversation, she wasn't going to talk to him any more, she had made up her mind, she was staying, and that was that.

The thing to remember was not to excite her, not to excite her more than she already was. He took out a pack of cigarettes. "You smoke?" She shook her head, not looking at him. He took his time lighting up, getting the first drag, trying to think out some plan to make her move; but all he seemed to see was a slide of Ethel in her old age very much like this—not crazy, of course, but running after men, an old washed-up woman haunting bad bars with the worst kind of drifters, because those were the only kind that would have her; a big beefy woman drinking cheap beer that would make her even broader, her breasts hiked by straps and cunningly-cut cloth so that they gave an impression of firmness and, hell, by the time some poor son of a bitch got around to letting them loose he would be in no condition to compare what seemed to be with what was.

She had always liked it, she made no bones about that. It was one of the things that had turned him off. Sweating inside his coat, he saw Ethel's fat, short-nailed, not-quite-clean hands, those hands that pawed him. No wonder he felt the way he did; she had long ago made a quick-sale bargain-basement thing for him of desire. And now on those days—the best—when there was the stiff silence, he thanked his lucky (?) stars he wouldn't have to fend her off. On others the vituperation and squalid scenes saved him. Ethel raged, she ragged him, she found words so obscene he had forgotten them, she flew at him with arm upraised, she struck, she spat, she yelled, she screamed, and then in the end she cried. Broken in battle, her big bloated body collapsed in a chair and heaved out heartrending sobs so that, for a moment, he was tempted to try to comfort her, until he remembered that there are times when pity is useless; to be strong—merely even to save yourself—you must turn your back on the weak. It was the hardest lesson to learn, Stu knew; it cut part of the heart out of you, but it permitted you to survive and try again.

And Betty—well, the hell of it was, and it would be hard to explain but god, it was true, the more you thought of a girl, the less you wanted to—well, have her. If you really cared for her, that dampened your desire; the admiring seemed somehow to work depressively on the sexual. Perhaps the two emotions were in direct conflict, incompatible; you could not adore what you debased. But why did the sex act seem a debasement to him? He didn't know, it just did. Some of those things with Ethel in the beginning . . .

Eileen's fleshed burned under the lamplight, her hands glowed on the sheet; she was quite mad, there was nothing you could reason with in her mind, and yet she was beautiful and she wanted a man, maybe she even wanted love. He felt hot and sick and inadequate.

"You have to go home," he said roughly. "You want to put your things on yourself or—or you want me to call your Dad?"

No answer.

He crossed the room and took hold of her shoulders. She turned her glittering agate eyes up at him. "'Stu—Stu Ashwell," she said, "can't you have a little Christian charity?"

She was home, enticed back by the most basic of promises, another drink. It had suddenly come to him, bending over the naked shoulders, resigned to using force, and then smelling the raw acrid odor of Scotch, that of course she was probably thirsty. "Let's get dressed," he had said quietly, "and go home and have a drink."

Now, easing the car away from the curb, pausing for a moment to let settle the stiff drink Eileen had insisted he have with her, he looked at the single light upstairs; she was up there with her tumbler of whisky, too far gone now to care about the other; in a little while she would slip down into a drunken sleep.

An age of alcohol—they all seemed to need it to keep going. Carolyn; he himself would no doubt lose what little control he had gained one of these days; even Lois needed it now and then. She hadn't been exactly what you'd call stone-cold sober in that bar, leaning across the table, her face flushed, her eyes burning too intensely, saying in an anguished voice, "It's a family that's never learned how to love."

He wondered how anyone ever knew what love was, how anyone held onto whatever it was people felt for one another. He had been telling himself he loved Lois more than anyone, perhaps even more than Betty, because he was disinterested, and that had been true. But it was also true that at the moment Lois started to open her heart to him, he was no longer bystander but participant, involved, asked to take a stand, and at that moment something went out of him, he yielded up a part of his admiration, his immeasurable affection, because she asked of him entanglement and that meant energy and time and trouble and commitment, so that he could no longer love her wholly; he was a part of her, and his imperfection marred what an instant before had been her beautiful inviolability, because he saw her as she was—someone, like the rest of them, *in need*. He knew there was no such thing, ever, as perfectability, and though he had known and believed this, he had allowed himself the hope that somewhere in this rotten, defective world there existed an object for adoration; she had given him that illusion, and he had loved her for it.

Then she had made him face what he did not want to see, that they were all, each and every one of them, even she, a reflection of imperfection, pawns in a world over which they had no control and whose prime purpose was to smash and destroy them—that's what she had shown him and he hated her for it. But was not hate the other side of love?

But isn't what we're all looking for, who we are? Lois had said. *More even than love, we want to know who we are. . . .* She had been formulating some reason to go on—but it struck him now she had also been formulating his, perhaps all their, hopes, the answer to the impossible question, What is the point? And Lois had said, *maybe to give.*

Have it out with Ethel. Fight for the boy. Marry Betty. Have children. Stand up and fight for what you want. It's the trying that matters. What you see, what you *do,* he thought, not necessarily where you go, as Lois said.

But Christ, he couldn't give up his son. And the courts always gave the mother custody. If there was a fight, Ethel would drag Betty into it. The price of a new life, of the dream, was his son. What about the boy—didn't he have any rights? Why should he be ransomed for his father's freedom?

He thought of Ethel, the house, what little life went on there, and one picture came through clear and sharp: the bathroom with powder spilled all over the top of the toilet, bobby pins scattered about, a lipstick left open, and on the floor movie magazines, wrappers from Hershey bars, the newspaper open to Hedda Hopper, a shoe abandoned in one corner, soiled underwear in another, and hairs, broken off from the helmet of Ethel's dyed head, in the sink. How could he abandon his boy to a life symbolized by that?

And if he wanted a new life, what about Ethel, where was her second chance coming from? How was she going to get another time round?

He cursed what it was in him that always made him look at the opposite side of a thing, envying those lucky bastards who made a plan of action for escape, then went out with a free conscience, an untroubled heart, and took what they wanted. His trouble was that he saw her side, he felt her right.

Through the leafless trees a wild wind was blowing, black clouds were bunched in a blacker sky. A long way away a sickle moon skimmed in and out. A harvest moon in the making. Thanksgiving. The season of rejoicing. A year of great hardship after which the Pilgrims and Indians gathered together to render thanks for the harvest of the summer. The colonists—what had sent them here in the first place? Lots of reasons given—economic opportunity, religious freedom, political asylum—but why bother? Cross an ocean, come to a strange land. What did they think to get out of it?

Still there was something. Something you were ashamed to talk about, he supposed: the belief in a life of one's own. Alaska. Yes, he was willing, too, to try to take. He hadn't made all those inquiries for nothing.

He saw a wood with a good strong creek running through, and past the woods, which ended at a little incline, a long sloping meadow; it was spring and there were anemones and bluebells, thick strong grass, the kind an animal could grow fat and sleek on, and down past the meadow more woods, running as far as the eye could see. Here, on the edge of this knoll, so that the front door opened out on the meadow, he would construct his house, a big room, longer than it was wide, with a stone fireplace at one end, not so big that it was impractical but big enough so that it would help heat the room, so that you could cook on it, big arms of iron and good strong hooks inset in the stone; and windows looking out on the meadow and on the side facing south so that the sun streaming in also helped heat the house; at one wall a long ledge

with a basin for washing next to a wood stove and a good smoothed
surface, hard and strong, on which to slice and pound and mold.
Meals would be simple, everything would be simple; anything that
became too complicated or caused too much trouble would defeat
him. Each thing would have to be elementary to be possible within
the imposed limitations of a new life, the largest of which was his
own ignorance, his own inadequate abilities.

It seemed perfectly feasible for him and Betty, so long as they
kept it very simple—one big room to begin with, and very basic
meals and the earth being turned up bit by bit, some of the woods
left; he felt very strongly they would need to leave part of the
woods, a place to walk in, to rest, there in the far north.

Who, that first day over two years before, when she had come
in the hardware store for help about paint, could have foreseen
what would come after?—certainly not Stu. She had seemed an
ordinary distraught housewife confronted with problems beyond
her ken. His trying to explain water, rubber, and plastic bases to
her was out of the question, the basic idea never seemed to seep
through; then, in a moment of misguided philanthropy, he had
offered to go over to her place, if it wasn't too far, and see what
the problem was.

He had looked at the bedroom she wanted to paint, conscious
of the slip that lay across the bed, palely blue and laced, and she
had tried to retrieve it and put it away before he noticed; then back
in the living room, she had offered him coffee, something stronger
if he wanted it, and even though he knew he had no right to leave
the store untended on a Saturday afternoon, he tried to rationalize,
to tell himself it was locked, wasn't it? who would break in? Fifteen minutes more wouldn't make that much difference, not with
business the way it was, to hell with it, and he elected the stronger
stuff, even though he knew—he knew damn well—he had no business drinking whisky in the middle of the afternoon with a woman
he didn't know, not when, from the moment of seeing her slip
lying on the bed, something had come over him which must have
communicated itself to her, for certainly there was something in
the air, a feeling strong, swift, unmistakable, of their doing wrong.
It was "wrong"—not bad, but certainly not right—to be drinking

together when he should have gone back to work, she should have got on with her painting; yet one drink had passed to two, two to three, until with a noticeable dissension in his head, he stood up and said he must go. He was afraid that if he stayed longer he would do something really wrong, the idea was already with him, and he couldn't understand himself, he hadn't been this way in so long he couldn't remember, he hadn't even thought about women, they had, for a fact, lost interest for him, embroiled as he was in trying to make some business of his own catch on and always failing, he didn't have time to do more than work and worry, mostly worry, and when you were consumed with doubts and dread, the last thing in the world you were going to worry about was going out and screwing some girl.

It came back to him anew, making the turn into the street toward his house, that moment of clarity he had experienced that first afternoon in Betty's flat when he had seen how little Ethel was involved even in the periphery of his life; he hadn't slept with her in months, and then only under pressure when, beefed up on beer, she came at him with that easily recognizable I-want-a-little-of-it look on her face and there was no way out short of the shrillest scene, which somehow always seemed to include Tom, and so he gave in, got through as best he could, it was only an animal act after all, at least under these circumstances. Yet he was always afraid that when he was put to the test he would fail, he found her that distasteful, so that, as he stood at the door to Betty's apartment, his inner life had suddenly relived that last time, months before, when Ethel had thrown her arms around him; her wet, sticky tongue was up against his mouth, she was grinding herself all over him, trying to get him excited, when all he felt was a shiver of repugnance, and she, taking that perhaps for some sign of his willingness, had reached down and put her hand on him, and he was scared to death he would never be able to make the necessary effort toward the act which now conclusively had to be got through.

Absurdly, he had held out his hand to Betty, that idiotic gesture which seemed to make itself when he felt he was in the presence of "a lady"; he hated himself and tried, abruptly, at the last moment, to move his arm away, but already her warm, firm fingers were pressed against his, their hands were interlocked, and Stu had suddenly felt sick with sensation.

She was not the kind of girl you grabbed and kissed—god, no —though she had been married and divorced, now lived alone, supported herself, all of which quite naturally suggested a picture a man got quite clearly: he could make himself at home without incurring too many costs or responsibilities. He would be expected to pay for liquor and some food, a present now and then, maybe help out on a new fall coat or see some of the spring bills through, but nothing that committed him. It was an arrangement for mutual benefit: in exchange for companionship and attention on one side there was to be companionship of a sort and attention of a sort on the other.

Yet Stu had seen that no such circumstance was involved here, for with the openness of the revelations of her past life, there had also been a kind of innocence. Betty had seemed more in need of protection than possession. Her honesty, her simplicity could so easily be turned against her. She would be hurt, and the last thing Stu wanted, standing at the door, still holding onto her hand, was to hurt her.

"Well," she said, "I certainly want to thank you."

All he wanted to do was to take her in his arms, lift her up and carry her into the next room, where, on that bed where the blue slip had lain, he could undo the pressure inside. "That's all right, I'm glad I could be of help." And then it had come to him he didn't even know her name. "Mrs.—Mrs.—"

"Bergen—Betty." She looked down at her hand and he let go of it. She was laughing. "I'll have to drive you back. We forgot the paint."

The blessed, blessed paint. That hardware store, which four months later was taken away by creditors, had saved him. Driving back, sitting next to her, he had been able to collect himself, formulate what he could do next. Not *should*—no ethical consideration was involved. That moment at the door had bound him, as though he might, in taking her hand, have sworn an eternal vow to love, honor, and protect her.

It seemed to him she needed him and, oh god, she would never know how much he needed her, but how was he to convey this—that they had been seemingly sent to each other? She was not alone in the poorness of her life, the broken marriage, the perfunctory divorce, the long days of working in an uninteresting job, of trying, as she had said, to make a life for herself. When she spoke, it was to relate facts—the bare, destitute bones of what was left of a life that had started out in promise and pleasure; she did not pause in pity or regret, nor did she distort; she had endured what she had passed through, miraculously untouched by bitterness; there was sorrow, yes, and some sadness, but of vindictiveness, vengeance, none; she was a woman able to look at her life with clear eyes, see its deficiencies and work against its mistakes, and say with a smile, "But I'm working it out pretty well. I've managed to buy some things"—looking around—"that I like and I read and—and I have friends. You find friends are often better to you than the people who are supposed to love you."

My god, didn't she see how vulnerable she was?

At the hardware store, Stu made up his mind. As he took down the cans of paint, he rehearsed how he would say it. Betty . . . Mrs. Bergen . . . no, Betty was better . . . Betty, I want you to know something, I . . . No, it was all wrong. How could you blurt out that you were married but didn't love your wife; that, as a matter of fact, on the evidence of one afternoon you thought you had fallen in love. It was crazy, people didn't just fall in love in an hour; they were attracted, yes, but that wasn't love, not what he wanted out of the word, that word for him meant a world, and yet, handing down the paint, how could he turn and say to her, I want a world with you, but that was what now he knew he did want.

He wrapped two gallons of cerulean, a gallon of white, and one large paintbrush for the walls, one small one for edging. On a pad of paper he started to figure up costs, and then in a moment he knew there was nothing he could ever say that would be right, she would pick up her package and walk out, and that would be the last he would ever see of her. He never finished those figures. He just lifted his eyes and looked at her, and she looked at him, and somehow it had all been understood. He took the paint and walked with her to the front door and locked it. They went back to the apartment and never even turned down the spread on the bed.

"You're not fooling me, I know where you been."

He unbuttoned his coat.

"You think you're so smart, you think you can do what you want, any goddam thing you want and get away with it, what do you care about anyone else, what do you care about your family, out running around, tomcatting. I know, you're not putting nothing over on me."

He slid out of his coat and started to hang it up. She was at him. "I hate you, I tell you, I hate you, run around, leave us alone—"

He tried to shake her off.

"—come in here after you been with another woman, what do you care, you go and have yourself a good time—"

She couldn't really hurt him, but she was working herself into hysteria and he'd never be able to talk with her. He hadn't planned on reasoning with her—he never did, that was asking too much—but he wanted to settle it once and for all.

"—out screwing some no-good—"

"Cut it out, Ethel, don't talk that way."

"I'll talk any way I want, *out screwing some no-good*—"

"Stop it, Ethel."

"I won't stop it. I won't. You hear, I won't—*out screwing some no-good*—"

He brought his hand over her mouth.

Her face seemed to fall into bits and pieces, make-up washed down her cheeks, her mouth bubbled, she made funny sounds.

"Tom," she shrieked, muffled, from behind his hand. "Tom, oh Tom, come help. Your father's—"

Christ, he had forgotten about the boy. He had forgotten about everything except her endless accusations. He just wanted to talk it out but she wanted vindication.

His son was standing in the door.

"Tom, oh Tom," she blubbered while Stu saw a look of disgust pass over the boy's face and he let go of her.

"Look at him," she shrieked. "That's the kind of father you got, runs around with other women, that's where he was tonight, out with another woman, I want you to know, I want you to know the kind of father you got, I want you to know what I have to put up with, running around with another woman—"

Stu took hold of her shoulders.

"You let go, you take your dirty hands off me. Don't you never touch me so long as you live. Running around with—you come from that whore, don't you touch me, you hear?"

"Go upstairs, Tom."

"Don't you listen to him. You stay here. You protect your mother." She turned on him with a fierceness Stu had never seen before. "You think you can run around on me, I'll show you, oh I'll show you. Call the police, Tom," she shrieked. "Go call the police, I said. Right this minute. You'll see, you'll see," she screamed. "They'll *make* you do what you should, I'm your wife," she screamed. "You hear? I'm your wife and you'll *never* get rid of me. And you can tell your two-bit whore I said so. I'll never let you go. Never never never."

Chapter 8

LOIS had her coat on. "You're an angel to look after Constance," she said to Iris. "Of course I don't think she'll wake up— she almost never does—but if she should, I know she won't feel strange with you there." She leaned over lightly and kissed Iris on the forehead. "We won't be *too* late."

"Oh, stay out as long as you like. With Erwin I don't worry, it's family."

"You ready?" he asked and Lois nodded. "I told Mom I'd bring you by. She's got some newfangled contraption she wants you to see. She wouldn't say what. It's a surprise." After a moment he said, "I'll bet."

Lois stepped out into the November night—the warm weather, the false spring, was definitely over, but it was a beautiful night. Stars were sprinkled like salt against the black sky.

At her side Erwin stamped his feet against the frozen path and slapped his arms against his sides, trying to get warm, not looking at the sky, flapping his arms back and forth and giving off grunts of displeasure at the cold. Yet all about him—

"Look," she cried.

He raised his head to those stars, his hands fell to his sides, he stood staring up, silent, solemn, seemingly *seeing*.

Then something happened to his face, as if he were in the center of a seizure. He grabbed Lois's arm and held on, seemingly too frightened to move.

"What is it, Erwin? What's the matter?" Lois had hold of him, gripping him in genuine concern, saying over and over, "What is it? Tell me what it is?"

For a moment he clung to her, eyes terrified, as if suddenly he had seen into a huge mouth and had discovered all the bodies it had devoured. He would be eaten too. They all would, one day. Had he just found out about death, here under this star-studded sky?

Then the spasm seemed to pass. Weakly, he tried to smile. "Gas, I guess," he said. "Kinda got through to me for a minute, but I'm okay now."

"Let's not go. If you're not feeling well—"

"No," he said stubbornly, "I'm all right. I don't get to see you very often, I want to go out."

"But if you're—"

"I'm all right," he insisted, but she couldn't help noticing that his hands were trembling. "What I need is a drink," he said shakily. "Never let the well run dry. Don't worry about me. I know how to look after Number One." Then he gave another grunt, grabbed her arm, and they were pacing off the path. He helped her into her side of the car, went around and opened the door to his, paused a moment, looking out, as if asking something of the dark night, then got in and began fussing with the ignition. In a moment the motor caught; they moved away from the lights on the signs, and he said, "You hear the one about this Scotchman who was on his deathbed . . ."

There was something sad in his voice, something she could almost touch in the false brogue, the steady rhythmic telling of the joke. "And the friend said, 'Hoot, mon, you mind if I strain it through me kidneys fur-st?' "

She heard what she supposed he would take for laughter coming from her mouth. He had been so wonderful to her once and now wasn't he trying to be wonderful again? And failing. Oh, god, failing, the way they all did.

He took the driveway to his mother's too fast and had to slam on the brakes. Lois gripped the door handle. So many men were bad drivers; it seemed to have something to do with their pride.

Without waiting for him, she got out, then they started up the path to Frances's. Jules must have heard the car because he was at the door, smiling and beckoning from inside.

"Ah, the fair and fetching Lois," he said. "Nymph, in thy orisons be all my sins remembered. Enter, enter, *entrez dans*—love, oh love-dear, look who's here, the heir apparent and the lovely Lois. Have we not libations for our guests?"

"You know where the hooch is as well as I do," Frances shouted from somewhere within. "I'll be right out. This machine's only got another five minutes to run and I'm trying to recondition my scalp. Tell Lois I can't wait for her to see what I've got. If it looks good on me, it'll make her look like a million dollars."

"Have you noted the large orb the heavens have presented us with this evening?" Jules asked Lois and stepped out into the night air, arms hugging himself for warmth. "An astounding sight. We were favored with the first showing of its magnificence just as Walter Cronkite came on the air—an odd coincidence, since he was reporting another air disaster. If men will go up in their infernal machines, they must expect to fly too close to the sun, singe their wings, and be cast down. Still, it gives one pause to consider eighty-four poor souls who might have been in bed tonight now lying in bits and unidentifiable pieces because they decided those fools who said they were safer flying about the sky in airplanes than riding on earth in their own cars were right. A pity, yes, a pity, but not past authorization. So, dear boy," he said, turning to Erwin, "you are to witness another transformation as it were—when your mother dons her headpiece and emerges some woodland sprite to the maenadic rites newly come. A remarkable woman, your mother, Erwin. I believe she lives in the wrong age. She should have been Mayan."

"Mayan!" Erwin exclaimed.

"Well, perhaps Toltec," Jules conceded. "One of those hot, steamy, barbarous peoples. Human sacrifices. Violent. Insoluble mystery, something for the mind to work with, like your mother, an endless puzzle for which most of the pieces are missing. A good way for a man to go out, still interested in the game. The game of life," he said slowly, "with all its unpredictable stakes, its unopposable odds. Yes, a good way to go out, still matching one's wits with the unfeasible, the impractical—the impossible. Shadows on the silver screen," he said, "who don't know—or have forgotten— their lines. Where has the Great Director gone?" he asked dramatically. Then, coming back to himself, he laughed. "A little wettener for your whistles?" he inquired.

"Never turn down a free drink," Erwin said and they went into the house.

They came upon Frances on the sun porch (now glassed in) lying like some artifact on which the management had spared neither time, trouble, nor expense, stretched out on a couch with her face masked. Holes marked the eyes, nose, and mouth; from out of the mouth a cigarette stood up, giving off smoke, and when Lois bent down, unsure, to peer into the two ocular holes that were the eyes, Frances looked back, alert, on guard, her pupils distended, her corneas somehow displaced: it was like looking into long unused wells.

One of her hands flew up, the bloody tips enclosed in plastic traps: she had just done her nails; to keep them from smearing she had on what Lois recognized as her guards. She had her podiatric sandals on too, the ones that had small slats between the toes so that, when freshly lacquered, her nails would not touch and smear.

Unexpectedly, she rose; and, taken off guard, they all jumped.

The cigarette came out of her mask, she let out some kind of speech, but her voice, behind the cloth, was unintelligible, a series of strangled groans. Then, using her free hand, she jerked up the cloth over her face impatiently and while they watched in horror the black mud shield over her skin began to move and at last spoke, her attention on Erwin. "Another of those perfect days in the park with the wee ones? The children in the poison ivy, Helen on the phone to the police, and the dog loose and in heat, oh one of those oh so ideal days."

Pulling her mask over the mud, she sat down, for a moment stilled, regarding her son with that dead cloth face from which the bottomless eyes stared; then she sagged back, lowering her body into a straight horizontal position, folding the encaged hands over the upheaval that was her breasts. She looked more dead to Lois than Ada had ever been, and she stared down on her aunt, marveling. It came to Lois that in all probability Frances *would* outlast good old Jules, who at this moment advanced across the moss-green rug like a warrior on his way to pay homage to the queen, in his hand not the ceremonial lance but the ubiquitous chalice of gin— martinis were Frances's favorite drink, she claimed they hit the bloodstream faster—and why not offer, at its proper age and place, alcohol instead of armor?

"I'll have to take these off," Frances said, raising her hands aloft and rattling the plastic protectors.

Jules put down the pitcher. The ice made a clinking sound against the sides.

"Music to my ears," she said, sitting up, freeing herself of the cloth covering so that her face, emerging out at them again in its covering offered up the cracked parody of a smile. Against the hills of black that were cheeks and the tenebrous hole of her nose where the terrain gave way, Lois viewed her teeth. She was paying tribute to them with a regal and official smile. Freeing first one hand and then the other of their encumbrances, she leaned over and seized a glass, held it out to her husband, who bent toward her, letting liquid run in an arch from the pitcher. Had men come up from the mud for this?

"Lois," she said in the midst of a sip, "you look positively gorgeous. I still say you got the best legs in the family."

Frances leaned over and grabbed a pamphlet off the top of a sideboard. Lois saw a flash of stars and a turbaned woman bent over a bubble-shaped glass. It was Madame Zolar stalking all their fates again and pulling in the pennies with her little pamphlets. "The root of character," her aunt announced, "is balanced in Libra, but the green leaves of personality are nourished in Cancer. Pity poor Peggy, who was born under neither. The only thing she should have done was grab her douche bag, the trading stamps, and run. But of course," Frances reflected, "I expect she doesn't have a douche bag, that's been the trouble all along. Converts," she said sadly.

"Look, mother," Erwin began, "do we have to start that again?"

"Dustbins," Frances said with fervor. "That's what most people's lives are, dustbins. If only people could learn to push themselves beyond the actual, to undertand the mind is only a servant, never a master. The Soul, that's what I'm talking about," she said, tapping Erwin sharply on the arm to be sure he was paying attention, and while he took a step back she rose and advanced on him with all the conviction of those who have seen salvation in one form or another.

"Into your hands with the help of the stars comes knowledge, but how will you use it?" she demanded of him. "You who turn your back on the temple. Pass in—pass in—through the silence of the soul, and there in humbleness recognize the ceaseless wheel of fate turns not just for you but for all of us." Suddenly she brightened. "Gin, anyone?" she asked. "Jules, lover, where *is* the gin?" She threw her long lacquered hands up in excitement. "Oh, lover, I'm just dying for a little of the nectar of the gods." She leaned forward, glittering. It was as if out of her cocoon she had emerged, not a butterfly but a dragon. Her teeth gleamed, her newly painted nails sparkled, her eyes were polished bright. "Nothing like a little glow in the early evening, I always say." And she opened wide her jaws and swallowed between sharp, carnivorous teeth the last of the pale offering in the stemmed glass.

Whoever had said that time diminished the passions and left the aged wiser and more content with their lot had never run into Frances.

Suddenly Lois stiffened. She felt her stomach leap, and for a moment she thought she was going to be sick. Someone had been scalped, there was human hair lying on the couch.

Her aunt reached over and lifted the hair. She popped it over a fisted hand and, as she moved it back and forth, the hair swung about as if—

"Put it on, go on, put it on," her aunt urged. "Of course it isn't your color, Lois, but you can get an idea—I think you'd look terribly *femme fatale* with hair like that. I mean, I like your hair the way it is and all, but don't you think it's a little *severe,* pulled back like that?"

Suddenly she plucked the wig off her hand and plunked it down on Lois's head; Lois went under, out from sight, then recovered and came up. She must look awful, just godawful. Even Jules gasped.

"Well," Frances said dubiously, acknowledging the undeniable, "I don't think, to be perfectly honest, it does a lot for you. To tell you the truth, honey, I wouldn't look in the mirror," she said, holding onto Lois. "To be perfectly honest, you look—well—kind of done in."

An instant later she had the hair back on her hand, swinging it back and forth, fluffing it out; then, hoisting the wig to her own head, she expertly fitted it over her hair. "But on me," she conceded, "it's nothing short of divine." She turned to them with a radiant smile. "I can just see myself in Mexico City, poisoning all the other women's good times—oh, we didn't tell you, did we? Come April, we're off on another honeymoon.

> *Spring is here, I know, I know,"*

she sang,

"Robin redbreast told me so.
Spring is here, I know, I know,
Pussy willow told me so.

And now to the gaming tables and the beakers of booze. It's that time of the evening. Oh, how I long for the twilight hour and my little glass of tilty water when all the world looks warm and even good old Jules seems like something out of the Orient—opulent, dearie," she said, throwing mock love-stricken eyes on him, "and potentatish." She turned to Lois. "What bad luck you've had, honey, but with your looks and those legs something good's going to come along yet, you wait and see. Just stay away from Springfield and the suburbs, set your sites on BIG game. None of this frooky local stuff."

With a bang that seemed to nail it to the table, she set her glass down and rose like some naiad new to the meadows come, and in a golden flow of grace—if you did not let your eyes wander to her face—she was gliding away from them, out of the room and toward the phone in the hall with its hoarse ring.

Lois watched her go, feeling as if something significant had happened, but nothing had passed, save that she had looked at the stars, drunk some gin, watched Frances put on one of her performances; yet inside her head Lois had a vision of all of them as predictable parts of a tableau, seasoned players who had gone through their lines without a hitch, giving the audience—themselves—a sense of security; it was all such old-hat stuff, but emotion—yes, there was emotion present, too; it was in Erwin's strained face, in the fast-fading flesh of Jules, who, hoisting his ginger ale, smiled at them with the painful knowledge of stiff joints and hardening arteries, it was in the remembrance of Erwin stopping on Iris's path, as if a terrible tidal wave were about to inundate him, as if he were at the end of his chances and knew it, so that now, standing in the midst of this room trying to hang onto himself, he couldn't, and that was what made the look on his face so terrible to contemplate, there was nothing he could grasp, not even a pale shade on which the thick fingers might fumble, nothing of substance he could point to that would come and save him from himself, as if some mighty voice had called out, "Burn, baby, burn," and he had felt the fire, in a moment he would be consumed, nothing but a pile of unidentifiable ashes on the floor, and he was frightened, oh god he was scared, he wanted to cry out for help, Help oh help, I am so frightened, something terrible is about to happen and I—but no call came. There was this Scotchman who . . .

From the doorway, face split in a smile, hands upraised and moving parallel in concentric circles, as if she were doing some dance from the twenties, her aunt tapped out a little step. "Oh, I've got some news," she sang out. "Oh, I've got some news that'll knock your hats off," and she whirled her hands faster and faster, she shuffled her feet round and round. "Oh, you'll never guess, you'll never in a million years guess," and Frances's laugh, her rich throaty laugh, rang out. "Never never in a million years"—and the tempo picked up, she was going round and round faster and faster, her hands a blur as they whirled in frantic little circles. "It was Iris, dear old Iris, and you know what? I'll tell you what. Eileen's out again. Eileen's out on the town again in a diaphanous nightgown. That's what."

It could no longer be put off. Tomorrow she would have to try to hunt him up, see what might be done. *What might be done:* the absurdity of the whole statement struck her as possibly a summation of all their ills. Instead of doing, they would see "what might be done." She closed her eyes a moment against that sky which earlier had made her cry out for all its beauty. The simple truth was that she could not go back to New York, New York and Neal, until she had settled with Stan and Eileen. I'll call him, she thought . . . go to that sporting-goods store and—

Erwin could take her to a phone booth, she could call right now and—

"Erwin," she said urgently.

They were standing at the car. He turned and looked at her, petulant. A moment before she had been telling him she wanted to go home. "I know this bar you'd *love,*" he insisted, his voice sulky, his face pouting.

A bar would have a phone. "All right," she said.

Smiling, he opened the car door. "Now you're talking sense," he said. "Now you're acting like the old Lois I knew."

This bar he knew Lois would like—it wasn't tony or anything, he said, helping her into the car, real people hung out there, good joes you could talk to, not like that fancy place they'd put up at the hotel with one wall of old barn boards, one all of glass, in front of which the girl "stylist" sat playing the piano and trying to pretend she was a young Judy Garland, rolling her eyes and belting out those half-hoarse renditions of "A Good Man Is Hard to Find" and "Bill Bailey, Won't You Please Come Home."

This bar, the one he was taking Lois to, was what he considered a real good bar. There were bad ones, dirty dark holes where people you didn't want to know hung out, gaping at the television and not even sure what they were seeing; and there were the okay places where the drinks weren't watered, the television wasn't too loud, the guy who ran the place was on the up-and-up, but the people who hung out there were kind of frooky, the women got soused too easily and you had to watch it their men didn't try to start a fight. But the good places, the bars Erwin liked, he said, driving more cautiously now, were not big, the drinks were maybe not so good as at the okay places, but the guys who hung out there were real good spuds, men who liked a good laugh, who were good for a drink any time you felt low, they didn't run out on you just because it was late and they should be home, guys whose screw-their-wives attitude, we-wear-the-pants-in-the-family-don't-we? was healthy.

He had pulled the car to the curb and shut off the ignition.

"Good heavens," she said. "Not again."

"You know this place?" he asked in surprise.

"I've been here a couple of times before," she said, trying to sound noncommittal.

He was piqued, she could tell, but he got out and opened her door. Wordless, they went up the walk like people on an important mission. Just before they got to the door, he stopped. "Say, Lois, do me a favor, will you? Don't say you're my cousin."

She couldn't help being pleased. Did he really think she looked that well? She smoothed her hair as he opened the door.

But walking to a booth, she felt suddenly detached, critical. It was such an ugly room, like most rooms where people went to drink too much and pretend they were having a good time. What was there about bars that depressed her so, even the fancy New York places you would have insulted calling them that? Maybe it was just drinking itself as a pastime that brought on the depression: it seemed such a waste of time. An age, she thought, which has impressed on us our need to put our time to advantage; we must always show profit for our efforts or feel guilty. Even in the pursuit of pleasure, we demand gain. True, too, of Erwin, saying now restlessly, "There's this new place they got a combo, you can dance; maybe we shoulda gone out there."

He was trying to breathe life into the present from their performances of the past. They used to do some very tricky steps together, twirls, dips, outmoded operations like that. In the era of the big bands, Glen Miller, the Dorseys, Jimmy Lunceford, that girl who used to sing Betty Boop. Gone like so many other things that had made their growing up. He had even at one point wanted to be a priest. All religious for six months or so, one of those prepuberty stages which most Catholic boys went through between baseball and girls. Frances had bought him a clarinet "to get him interested in something else," then snatched that away from him when she was sure it was making his teeth protrude. He practiced in the kitchen propped up on an old metal stool; the only pieces Lois ever remembered him playing were "Old Dog Tray" and "The Monkey Wrapped His Tail around the Flagpole."

The child, the adolescent, incipient in this man had been the purveyor of many enviable skills: with beanshooter, with bow and arrow, a dead shot at conkers. Now he proved his prowess in obsolete dance. Surely somewhere inside her compassion lodged for such wasted acts. They cried out for understanding, as did his eyes. Any inclination toward love Helen apparently had dismantled. What could she, Lois, give back to him to show she still prized the old Erwin who had had such a steady hand, such a true if untried heart?

"You going to stick with the gin or—"

"No, no more gin. Scotch maybe."

"Two Scotches and water," he said to the waitress.

"Mixed?"

"No—and no ice," Lois said. The waitress and Erwin looked at her. People out here apparently did not drink like that. "It kills the taste, the ice," she said.

One of the men, short, stocky, with something of an outsider look, detached himself from the crowd at the bar. "Hello, Lois," he said. "It's been a long time."

Too much of a coincidence to be chance, she decided in the instant he bent down and took hold of the hand she held out. An unfamiliar touch: nothing recognizable, definable in it. She might have asked him, quite without irony, Who are you? He had meaning now only so far, she supposed, as Eileen was concerned. All of it was coincidence; she had known this, really, right from the start, with that sort of knowledge you should always listen to, the intuitive. Discursive wisdom might suffice for some, but those who went in deep went with the heart.

"Erwin," she said, "this is Stan, Walt Stankiewicz. Stan, my cousin, Erwin Mueller." In her startlement at having come upon him at the moment she was about to search for him in the telephone book, she had forgotten to sustain Erwin's little charade. At the word *cousin,* Erwin looked at her in a pained way. "I've seen you around," he said to Stan.

"Yeah, now and then."

There was a silence.

Finally the man towering over them said, "I buy you two a drink?"

"We just ordered," Erwin answered curtly, rising, hoping, Lois supposed, to make it clear they didn't want a fifth wheel moving in to try to turn their evening. There was an uncomfortable pause, both men standing over the table; then Erwin moved away with an excuse about cigars. Lois wondered if he had connected the name with its significance. He was watching them out of the corner of his eye as he moved away from the table; what was he waiting to see? How they reacted to each other, she supposed.

"I wrote you," she said. "But you—you never answered."

He nodded his head; the gesture meant, yes, he had received the letter; his look said, But after all . . .

"I wanted—I don't know," she conceded. "Anyway what I was going to ask of you then, five years back, that's all changed now. Funny, I was just on my way to call you—Eileen, she wanted me to —look you up. Her mother's dead," Lois said, "and she thought— Eileen thought—that might make a difference."

He was horribly embarrassed; it was painful to see such embarrassment on a man's face. "I'm married," she heard him say, a stammer hobbling the word. "I got married . . . just after—"

Of course, yes, she should have known. It was what any of them would most likely have done, what she herself had done—run from one unfortunate affair into another, one that seemed to promise safety, stability. And marriage was meant to be the final reassurance, wasn't it?

Erwin, on the edge of the crowd at the bar, was buying his cigars. Big, bulky, handsome, he hung over the counter waiting for change. ". . . two boys and a girl," the man standing at her side was saying. "The girl's in the middle. . . ."

Go back to Eileen and say, He's married now, Eileen, with three children. The blank blue baby eyes would look at her as if she were lying; in Eileen's world people didn't marry, in Eileen's world people just fell in love forever. Out again on the town in a diaphanous nightgown . . .

What kind of mating had he made, this man hanging over the table waiting for her own history? "I suppose you got married yourself?" he had just asked.

"A little girl . . . three . . ." she was saying, not, What one captures and carries home as a trophy loses its value once it is hung on one's walls. To covet, to care, one had to continue craving. What we are granted, we automatically devaluate. In her unreal world Eileen, of all of them, might be the only one who clung to love. *Name one love that's lasted,* Carolyn had demanded, and Lois might have answered her, she realized now, Eileen's, because she can't have it.

"She's still—" Tactfully he left the sentence unfinished. *Odd* was what Lois supposed he would have defined had he finished. Polite, you did not say mad. Polite, you did not recall your own part in the persuasion toward such insanity. Polite, you remained outside involvement. How could he stand there so lenient with himself? Didn't he realize—no, he did not; most men wouldn't, she supposed. Something to do with their whole part in the biological pattern: the impregnator could run; she who carried the child carried it wherever she went. No matter how you tried to talk about equality of the sexes, that basic fact refuted any argument. One had to be responsible, the other might run.

Even Stu wants to run, she thought. Alaska. His new start with another woman, another vessel for his seed. Back at Sans Souci Constance slept, her father far away, fled. Erwin at the bar, too, would one day begin again. And now, Lois thought, I want to look to Neal, Neal, whose seed . . .

They all believed in their secret hearts they had a right "to start over again." Stu's very words: but they might have been her own, all of theirs—except Eileen's. Eileen didn't want a new life, she wanted her old one back. Was that some sort of reverse definition of sanity, to stay satisfied with the past?

The duplicity of the human heart: she had been so sure seeing him would make matters better.

"She's still the same," she said to him, wondering how she could have deluded herself into thinking that after all this time . . . He shook his head, sorry. Here in this bar, shrouded in smoke, he went scot free; back in New York, if she so chose, she might in her own way abrogate the responsibility too. It all depended, Lois supposed, on what kind of images you carried inside your head.

He was saying something—vague—about how nice it had been to see her again. She found it impossible to answer. He bent down and touched her lightly, unfamiliarly, on the shoulder. And then he was gone, someone who had stopped at their table a moment, someone who had loved and run, and had no need now to go back.

"There's something about that joker," Erwin said, lowering himself into the booth opposite her, "that just doesn't add up to nine."

It was not exactly the way Lois would have put it, but—"I wouldn't play pool with him if you paid me. How'd you ever get mixed up with a schnook like that?"

"Reasons reason knows not." Lois said, and began to explain, watching Erwin's face change.

"*He's* the one all the fuss was about?" he asked disbelievingly. Then he dismissed the whole thing. "He's the kind that always loses by one point," he said.

She remembered the old adage, It takes one to know one. No one had ever struck ever as more of a loser than this cousin across from her—not even, it occurred to her with something close to optimism, Stu. He and Betty in impossible Alaska homesteading in some dreadful remote place—and happy. But Erwin . . . he was attempting to amuse himself by building some occult pattern from the discarded matches in the ashtray, arranging them in rows of varying mathematical panelings. "We used to be—you know, so close," he said, head bent over the burnt-out twigs. "You remember the old Dodge Mother had, the way we used to go looking for those goddam salt dips with her? Well, hell, I mean we were practically like—like brother and sister," he plunged on, as if determined to have a hearing. "And you remember that time I came out to the college and gave you the hundred clams? And the time you came over and stayed with me that night Helen almost lost Sonny? Well, what is it with you that—you know—we aren't close any more? You're closer to Stu now than you are to me—to Stu and Carolyn, but every time I turn up on the scene—what is it?" he demanded. "Christ, if you cared anything about me—"

"I do care about you, Erwin—"

"But you care more for Stu. That's the truth, isn't it? You like him better?" She didn't answer. How could she?

"That's the truth, why don't you admit it," he was saying. "Why try to gloss it over? I can take the truth as well as the next guy. You like Carolyn and Stu better than me, and that's that. Tell me something," he went on insistently, "do you think we can ever make things the way they were before?"

"I don't know, Erwin," she answered, so tired it seemed impossible even to attempt an explanation. It was as if, in making the additions and subtractions of her reasons for coming back, she had suddenly been bound by a balance that made no sense at all. The figures were there, but all the sums came out minuses and all of what should have been subtractions seemed to add up to something—something she did not understand. The common denominator was missing. And what was that?

The common denominator in any human relationship is its lowest divisible component, she thought. You must go back to the root. Way back to the root. The root was not that man her cousin had been in love with, but further back: the man her mother . . .

"I've made a balls of so many things," Erwin persisted. "Helen is just one in a long line of things that have gone wrong—most of them my fault. She—she found these things in my pocket," he said, "and she blew her stack, but why shouldn't she have? I mean, you don't carry those things unless you're going to use them so I suppose she had a right to get rid of me. And you know what's so awful, Lois? What's so awful is that I was almost glad—at first, at least. I was tired of her, that's the real truth, I was sick and tired of her —I mean, *ten* years . . . The truth is, I was glad to get out, I could breathe again, I felt free, I had more energy than I'd had in years—but it didn't last. After a week I was down in the dumps, really down in the dumps. I missed hell out of her and the kids, so I called, I tried to patch it up. Hell, I even sent flowers. But it was too late, it didn't do any good, she couldn't have cared less.

"And now—now I'm just sort of stranded. I can't go forward, and I can't go back. Even with you I can't go back, we can't be what we were."

In his own way he was asking her to help, to make his values anew. Helen wouldn't have him back; she herself couldn't take him back into her old adoration; something in his face said even he himself had no inclination to embrace what he found left inside: he was a man who had discovered the limitations he had imposed upon his own life, a life he didn't want in which he had imprisoned himself, and all she could do was look on helplessly while he went about arranging and rearranging burnt-out matchsticks. She didn't understand what game it was he was playing, she was not even sure he did. Who among them did? That was the question.

"But all of us, Erwin, we all feel something of the same—we think we've made such messes of our lives. Look at me—"

He did not let her go on. Abruptly—almost angrily—he raised his head. "You're all right," he said shortly. "It's written all over you. You'll come out ahead." Impatiently he swept his hand over the sticks in front of him; they flew across the table and onto the floor. "Okay, so you messed up a little here, a little there. That's allowed. What isn't allowed," he said, "is to make the big mess."

He moved his drink squarely in front of him and stared down into it. "You don't know anything at all about the big messes," he said. It was an indictment. You never knew, in these moments of rancor, when the truth was brushing too close to allow yourself comfort or escape. "You just let yourself get taken in by the little skirmishes, but when it came to a big fight you'd make the move that was right." He picked up his drink and stared into the bottom where the ice was rapidly dissolving. "It's—its like—you got different eyes, you don't see the way I do." There was no mistaking the tone of his voice: he disliked her for whatever it was he thought of as her "different eyes," disliked and envied—and forgave, she saw that the next instant. "It's probably got something to do with the stars. Mother loused me up but good when she forgot to have her horoscope checked before she looked to see what time of the month it was. Still"—and he leaned across, lifting his drink to her in mock toast—"I don't begrudge it, just remember that, I don't begrudge you any of whatever it is you've got. If there was anyone I'd like to see with the old bizazz, it's you. Esther will never leave you any of her money, Lois," he said quite seriously, "I'd bet my bottom dollar on that." And she saw that to him Esther's money was terribly important, that he was commiserating with her, he was truly sorry. "But you don't need it," he decided, cheering himself a little. "You've got all kinds of other incomes." He smiled, he was making a joke. "Me, I'm always in debt."

What could you say? My god, what in the world could you say? When you didn't have any of the answers yourself, when you looked at him and thought, But, Erwin, it's all in the way you see yourself. You have to *believe* you have a chance.

The last thing in the world she could say to him—to anyone—

was something like, You have to believe you have a chance. And yet, for a fact, if she had had to sum up all of what at that moment she did believe, she would have said, What we do have the right to in our lives is the choice to see things as we want. We cannot change many things, but we can look at them in such light as we will. And that is something, no matter how small, that makes us free.

Chapter 9

HER LAST DAY in Springfield, and still so much unsettled. To go back to New York and Neal incapacitated by the same sense of uncertainty was an admission—a confession—of not only an inability to act but also perhaps a disinclination to do so. Either you settled with the past and smashed what fettered you to it or you allowed yourself to live in its irons. At times in everyone's life there came confrontation, when the unknown awaited, for better or worse. It was easier, less disconcerting to stay with what one knew. But those avaricious of life asked of it the unexpected. A certain surrender to pain is perhaps a prerequisite of the brave. And who in the end wanted to be counted with the cowards?

Lois put her daughter onto a chair, ordered and paid for an ice-cream cone, made sure she had more than the amount of change she thought she would need, then went into the phone booth.

I must go back to the beginning, she thought, right back to the very beginning. I must put it all in place, piece by piece. Matt Baxter, she thought, that was the start—the start if you didn't count her father. If her father had been a different sort of man—but there was no point in even wondering about that. Given her father and her mother, their life together, there had eventually to be another man.

Lois unhooked the phone and dropped a coin in. *Matthew Baxter,* she said distinctly into the receiver, *in Denver,* remembering a tall tan athletic man, his hand clasped round a racket, easy-going, indulgent, but moving suddenly, swiftly, precisely, over the courts, placing a shot so well that even his opponent had to smile. And that summer, the long hot summer of the drought, when her mother and that man—

Inside her mind he held a racket and ran across the clay courts, a beautifully made piece of muscular machinery, with an indistinct face but strong, powerful hands, a man forever disassociated from her father's world of business, the tall smoking stacks of the big red-brick plant, her father's dingy little office inside, the sweating men with their streaked faces lounging with strange, almost sarcastic smiles against the outside of the building, and the prim, stiff, carefully dressed executives inside. Matt Baxter's world was sunlight and green grass and men in open flannel shirts drinking long cool drinks at the outdoor portable bar by the tack house. *Frivolous,* her father said of them in that militant voice he donated to anything not connected with the making of money. And Lois supposed it was true. *A tennis instructor,* her father said, condemning him once and for all to that class of men whom he considered "soft."

It was the "hard workers" who forced the world to turn faster, "elbow grease" oiling the axis. That he was one of the most lubricative went without saying, though her father said it often, wanting, no doubt, to make sure credit went where credit was due. Lois had not seen him since she was fifteen. He had stopped, unannounced, one summer day at Sans Souci, driving into the open alley in back by the tomatoes in a long blue Buick; Iris, indignant, thinking it was one of the boarders' relatives taking liberties, rushing to the back porch to open fire, then stopping, stunned, saying, "Why, it's Harry, it's your father, Lois"—standing there open-mouthed while he advanced across the gravel drive holding a gray felt hat. He seemed to experience no uneasiness over the fact they had had neither words nor funds from him in two years; he came across the yard unequivocally, circling the soft felt hat in his hands, a slight frown frozen on his face. He had stayed less than an hour and even that short time had been a strain; they had nothing to say to each other—why he had even come in the first place remained a mystery. Iris did all the talking; she told him what a good student Lois was, how neat she kept her room, what a *nice* girl she was growing into. Harry Greer sat in one of her mohair chairs, fingering his hat, and made no comment, but just before he went he handed Lois five dollars "to spend on something you want, but make it *worth while*. Not candy or trash like that." It was the last money they ever had out of him but he gave it, she remembered, with a flourish as he opened the big Buick's door and prepared to drive back West, where he still lived, though she never heard from him, not even in response to the Christmas and birthday presents she still, feeling filial obligation, sent. She could not cure herself of the idea that fathers and daughters ought to be close.

She supposed it had probably taken her mother a long time to get over the idea husbands and wives ought to be too. But in time almost everyone learns. Her mother had learned rather late, but she had learned, she had run away; and now she, Lois, was in this tight telephone booth waiting for the operator to trace the man to whom her mother had fled, that man who might give her some answer to the problem that seemed central in her life—that from the two poles of sacrifice with which she looked on love, there seemed no balance between sacrifice and mutilation. In Eileen she had seen the sacrifice, in her mother the mutilation.

Her beautiful, beautiful mother—with hair so dark it seemed unnatural, and that strange slash of white near the widow's peak; tall, with fine, firm legs and beautiful hands, made for caressing, made for caring. Why should she have deliberately destroyed such radiance?

"On your call to Denver, we have a party by that name listed at . . ." The ringing on the other end suddenly stopped; a cool feminine voice answered. Lois heard the operator talking, there was a pause, a name was called out in that beautifully modulated woman's voice, then a baritone voice came on.

"Mr. Baxter?" she asked.

"Yes?"

Lois took a deep breath. "Are you the Matt Baxter that used to work in Winnetka? The one who taught tennis at the country club —a long time ago."

"Yes," he said guardedly. "I was at the club in Winnetka—about twenty years ago."

"Well, I'm Lois Greer. My mother, she was Organdy—Organdy Greer."

He made no answer. She could picture them, hundreds of miles apart, holding their phones and waiting. Go on, she told herself, *go on.*

"I know it must seem odd for me to be calling after all this time."

He said nothing, waiting.

"Actually, I thought about calling a lot of times, but I—"

I what? I was afraid, she thought.

"But somehow I couldn't bring myself to—"

He gave her no help, silent on his end of the phone.

"The reason I'm calling—I mean I know it's been a long time, but I wondered—I've been wondering all these years, do you know why she—she might have done it?"

Lois hadn't expected him to answer right away; it would take anyone some time to marshal an answer to such a question. She could detect, she thought, the breathing of someone in deep exertion, physical or mental, on the other end of the phone, but no words passed down the line. "Mr. Baxter?" she began again. "I probably had no right to call but—"

"No," he said slowly, "you had every right—every right in the world." After a pause he said, "I always knew you would sometime. At first I used to try to think what I'd say to you, but then—then the years went by and I—I guess I sort of let things slip, the things I had decided to say to you—" He took a breath. "And maybe I didn't really know what I would say, I only knew what I thought, and after a while you don't forget, but you change your mind.

"At first I thought she—she did it because she couldn't face what she'd done, face it freely and accept it. I didn't realize—I mean, she tried to talk to me"—Lois thought of Neal—"and I didn't understand, not the way I should. I just thought she was sorry for what had happened—the way she had run off and all, the way she'd let you down, sending you to stay with her sister in Springfield that way. She was upset about that, but I thought we'd work it out, that I could—you know—make her see that maybe it was the only way until we could work something out ourselves. I didn't understand that what she needed was something quite different—something I didn't have. And that's what I'm not sure I know, what it was she needed.

"Maybe," he said a second later, "it was the way she looked at things that I didn't really understand. It seemed to me she felt guilty about—about *everything*. I couldn't see that. And to tell you the truth, I still don't. It was all right for her to feel bad about leaving her husband and sending you down to her sister's and all, but how could she keep claiming she was responsible for all the other things?"

" 'The other things'?"

"I don't quite know how to put it, but you know, *everything*," he repeated. "She couldn't keep evil—well—individual. She kept projecting it out, for everyone, for the whole world." He paused. "As if she blamed herself for the existence of evil itself," he said at last. "She was in need of a lot of help and I didn't understand. I couldn't because I didn't see things the way she did. In some ways I still don't, much as I've thought about it all. I can see what *we* did was wrong but she felt she was responsible—for everything that went on. And I think she felt that, in running away with me as she did, she, well *contributed*. I've had a long time to think it over," he said, "and that's the only explanation that makes sense to me. She couldn't stand the idea that she had brought evil, more evil, into the world, so she—

"I often wondered what had happened to you," he said finally. "She cared for you so much. Maybe really that was all she cared about, and how she had—well—let you down. And of course I remembered you, from the country club—"

"I stayed with my aunt."

"The one in that big house?"

"Yes, the one in the big brick Civil War house."

"And I suppose you're married now?"

There was no need to tell the whole truth. "And have a little girl of my own," Lois said. "I want to thank you. What you've said has been a big help. And I'm sorry if I disturbed you, if I brought this all up again. After all these years."

"I'm retired now and, as I say, I've thought about it a lot. I've often thought about you, too, and wondered what happened to you and it's—it's good to know." Just before he hung up, he said, "Your mother, she cared for you—more than anyone else in the world, I hope you know that, don't you?"

Then why did she desert me? Lois wanted to cry out.

A mental check list of items to cross off one at a time: Matt Baxter, slash; that man her cousin cared for, slash; Eileen—no place to take a child. She ought to have left Constance with Iris, but Iris had more than enough to do with her days without having the added burden of keeping her eyes on a small child, and she had been more than generous about babysitting nights.

Peggy, Lois thought; I ought to stop and see her anyway, an obligation—even if it entailed advantage—that filled her with apprehension. The dreariness of that poverty—the worst part of debt was that it drained your energy to the point where you didn't care. The poor lived inch by inch, maimed by too many demands.

Resolutely, she turned Iris's car, which had an odd knocking in its motor, toward Carolyn's. Just something that happened when I ran into the old berry bush out back, Iris had explained about the motor. But I don't think it's very important, she had gone on, it can't be or the car wouldn't run, would it? she had asked Lois in utter sincerity.

Now, lame and groaning, the car lurched down the road. Tappets, Lois thought, nothing at all to do with berry bushes. She would tell Iris when she got back—not that the information would be any help. If Iris thought berry bushes were eating at the insides of her car, nothing would persuade her otherwise. Her kind of faith in things might be awful, but it was intense; you had to admire the tenacity of one who held on in the midst of all odds, all information to the contrary. She really believes, Lois thought, that she got Ada into heaven. And who, after all, knew? If Iris had got her sister buried from the Church and that was the passport it took, then Ada might at this moment be somewhere up there (Lois peered through the windshield) strumming out her grievances on a celestial guitar. A Timble no matter where she went, she would never forget what was given or gone. She thought abruptly of Frances. A strange family of contradictions: Frances on the one hand, Ada on the other. From the same system of genes and yet—

She saw Frances's masked face, her currant-like eyes; she saw, too, the perfect clarity of Carolyn's chiseled classical features, turned away from the light, the bitter mouth, the cold but calm eyes. Sympathy was something rooted in Carolyn's heart whether she had tried to eject it or not.

Was she on the wrong road? No, that big silo looked familiar. She made, in relief, the turn up Carolyn's road. Perhaps she ought to have called first, there was no reason why Carolyn might not be out, but—

Carolyn, in old clothes, was sweeping up leaves with a rattan rake. She waved, dropped her fork, and came toward the car. "I hate doing this," she said, "and it's too windy to burn today, but if I don't get a start, it's going to be too late, and then I'll have to face the winter with *that* hanging over my head." She allowed Lois to fill in what *that* would be added to. From a bulky wool pocket affixed to the side of her heavy sweater, she extracted a cigarette, stuck it in her mouth. She looked drawn and tired, had the sharp, set look of malcontent so many women get at a certain age, the age, Lois thought, when the future seems to hold nothing that will awaken and excite them.

For the first time her lips were a tense line, wrinkles flowed from her eyes, her nose seemed in need of flesh.

A feeling of desolation so severe it severed speech swept over Lois. From behind a cloud of cigarette smoke, Carolyn's face seemed to say, I envy everyone else because there is nothing in myself I can care for. Then she turned on Lois one of her warm smiles —or so it appeared for a moment—until Lois saw the frozen, frightened eyes.

He hasn't called her, Lois thought.

She opened the car door and stepped out into the midst of a landscape burrowing down in browns, winterbound, yet full still of splendor, the glades below scooping out a slice of the strong violent

November sky, the high wind-nude trees demanding of her an affirmation of the permanence they evolved. In cities one forgot how much the land meant; out here, in the open, it seemed impossible not to believe in continuity—land, house, animals, children, the rock basis of life from which they had all strayed so far. Carolyn had come here for sanctuary—and look at the land, the house, the husband, the children: what has it brought me? Carolyn's face asked.

Were all their lives so contentless they could not even understand what it was they made in demand?

Impulsively she reached out to touch Carolyn: surely some warmth would pass through her fingers to reasure that cold face she cared.

But what Carolyn needed, she saw, was not the consolation of a cousin; what Carolyn's heart cried out for was some justification for that female flesh that imprisoned her. If the husband, the house, the children were not enough, what was?

Yet, stepping back, Lois said, as if that were all that was on her mind, "I thought maybe I could drop Connie off—"

"I'd love to have her," Carolyn said. "They're so nice at this age. Isn't it a shame they have to grow up and find out what fraudulent lives we all have?"

The word *fraudulent* was very carefully chosen, Lois knew, but what Carolyn really meant, she thought, was *unfulfilled*.

Arnold didn't seem surprised to see her again. He kept the door carefully secured, however, in one fat puffy hand, no doubt remembering how she had outmaneuvered him the last time she was here, had forced her way in. He looked better than Lois ever remembered; grief apparently agreed with him.

". . . so I thought I'd just drop in," she was trying to explain, "seeing it's my last day in Springfield before I go back to New York. And of course I don't know when I'm liable to get back . . . so naturally I wanted to say good-by . . ."

He held the door, uncommitted.

". . . to Eileen," she specified. "If that's all right with you."

He wasn't keen on the idea, but she could see he was having a hard time marshaling arguments. He had never been a very verbal man—violent, unreliable, selfish, and sure of his own ideas, but handicapped by a certain reticence of speech which left his angers and irritations unarticulated. He moved aside reluctantly and let her enter.

Dishes were piled at the sink. Dishes, dirty, lay smothered in grease, with the curling ends of uneaten food, on the tables. There were crusted pots stacked on the stove, on the floor by the refrigerator, on top of the hissing radiator. The doors of the cupboards hung open, drawers had been pulled out and left that way, the broom leaned crazily against the stove.

"It's nearly noon, she *should* be up," he said.

Lois tried to picture how they lived now that Ada was no longer with them, but she could not imagine them engaged in any of the normal things people do—not even making observations to each other over the effort of eating together. Perhaps they did not eat together, but picked up food when they felt like it, scooped out a place on the oilcloth, ate silently, swiftly, alone.

In the living room the television was running but no one was there to watch it. "She likes to listen to it even if she isn't looking," Arnold explained, flapping his way in old felt carpet slippers over to the stairs.

Suddenly Arnold stopped; a wave of red rose from his neck over his face, crimsoning it. With one sudden jerk he turned. "WHAT WERE YOU DOING DOWN THERE? YOU WERE IN MY THINGS."

Eileen, mute, caught, stood at the head of the cellar stairs.

"YOU'RE NOT TO GO DOWN THERE. HOW MANY TIMES DO I HAVE TO TELL YOU YOU'RE NOT TO GO DOWN THERE?" Anger had set his passions free, he knew she had been in his liquor. His hands rattled her shoulders; a shock of filmy material fell away from her nightdress under his angry fists.

Feet encased in gold, body wrapped in jonquil-colored tulle, Eileen was impossible to look on as someone *serious*. She was sick, she was insane, but Lois found herself incapable of real sympathy. It seemed to her there was an inadequacy so great that it forbade complete compassion. How much complicity, she was forced to demand of herself, is there in madness? in guilt? even in growing old?

Did it not perhaps come back to the image, to the complex image in which depth you saw yourself, and from what vantage point of perspective?

It seemed to her a question of culpability—that the mother who had thrown herself to the courtyard, the cousin who stood by the mound of leaves, the one in this filmy nightdress, were all at least partially responsible for what they were. Life had only small corners for the selfish, the spoiled.

Ten years ago she herself had made a mistake, but it was not perhaps the crime she had thought. Indulgence, overdramatization: *that* was what she should hold herself most accountable for. "Eileen," she said, and waited while Eileen bent toward her with eager eyes.

Not telling the truth would not change it; at any rate and whatever the conquences, it had to be said because it was so and nothing could ever change it. Eileen had to know.

"He's married now, Eileen. He has been for a long time. They've got three children—"

Eileen turned her back, tossed her hair, and put her hands to her ears. "Liar," she said. "*Liar.* You want him for yourself."

What she wanted to believe was, after all, Eileen's own choice, her own right, and Lois let her make it without one ounce of feeling that she would have to make amends this time for the delusion.

The afternoon seemed all of a preordained pattern as she and Stu got out of the car and stood on the grass, a carpet spread out to take them into the dark distant woods, her bright three-quarter-length russet coat an angry outcry against the bare woods, the dove-colored sky. For an instant, as she stood in the midst of all that stillness, a feeling of isolation came over her. The landscape made her aware of how insignificant she was, a drab meaningless cipher dressed in an outlandishly bright coat in the midst of something infinite and terrible that would go on and on long after she and Stu and all they cared about was destroyed.

A flock of birds rose in alarm over the far forest, stranded in space, and Stu, walking beside her, hands jammed in coat pockets, head hunched over, trampling forward as if going to the sentence of death, intensified the sensation that they all, even the birds, had been abandoned, spavinated against the greenish-gold sky.

Another freezing rain had fallen early in the morning; the bare architectural sculpture of the trees was filigreed in silver, the bushes bowed by weight; eyes of light sparkled up at them from the frozen path on which, slipping, they advanced toward the woods beyond. The whole earth looked as if it had been given a coating of white; all about them the heavy trees were motionless, only the tips of their young branches clattering; like enchained arms they rattled their bracelets of ice against the sunless, threatening sky.

"A real bitch of a day," Stu said.

She did not look at him, her eyes on the ground to direct her hesitant feet, hair blown back by a wind that had risen from the far hollow, a wind that gripped the branches in rage, loosening them from their joints. She felt as if everything about her were being truncated in primordial angers she could not understand, and she and Stu isolated in the midst of all this waste.

She stopped at the entrance to the woods to light a cigarette, her eyes on the mulch of leaves underfoot, rotten roots and broken limbs that lay like mutilations under the trees from which they had been disjointed; in patches where the water-soaked ferns lay fallen on their sides and the dark bog of earth protruded through, some moisture persisted, like filthy foam, a scum on the surface of the earth.

It was colder at the woods, ice sealed on the limbs of trees clanking in the wet wind that had come up. Fog would follow, it was that kind of a day.

She started into the woods. Under the soles of her shoes the earth made wet sucking sounds, around her head the thin limbs encased in ice sent up chimes. They were in the heart of the forest now. Wet, dank, it threw dark arms around them. Like two statues they stood, silent, in the dark forest, held to the noise of the trees, the voice of the wind. They might be hardened for all eternity in the center of this darkness, two people, troubled, who cared for one another, but both held it was the good who stayed silent. She was going to break an unspoken pact between them and tell him something he wouldn't want to hear. Wings were vibrating in the silence, wings of things unsaid, things he did not want her to say; *Lois,* she could feel he wanted to cry out, *don't tell me.* But already she had started to speak.

"I've got someone, too, Stu, a man I knew before. I was in love with him and it didn't work out. Something bad, really bad, happened and that was why I came back here, to Springfield, that first time we both came home ten years ago. Stu, did you ever think maybe there just comes a time when you have to have love, and so that's the time you find it. And you don't know, Stu, nobody knows —how alone I've felt. Oh, I had Constance, I was working, I tried to keep busy—you know, the way you tell yourself so long as you have your work you'll be all right—and I'd come home at night and make dinner for us, that was all right, but then Constance would go to bed, it was only seven and the whole night was ahead. Night after night of sitting and thinking—"

"We've both made messes of our lives," he said shortly. "Sometimes I wonder if everyone doesn't. First you try to blame other people or 'Life' and then of course you blame yourself. At first I thought it was Ethel's fault things were the way they were, but now I know that's not true. Her fault, my fault, just the whole loused-up life I lead. I tried, I really tried, but I don't know what's the matter with me, maybe I ask too much. I'm still asking too much. Another chance," he said bitterly. "If that doesn't take the cake. At my age, I want another chance, I want a new life for myself."

"But maybe that's what we all keep looking for, Stu. And I feel somehow we have the right to that chance. Only—only, well, it isn't going to be easy, not for either of us—Ethel," she said. "Cliff off god knows where, and Constance, and the fact that Neal's Jewish. Not," she said quickly, "that it matters so far as we're concerned, but with the family—it's so *closed*—and more, the way Neal feels himself, that there has to be a reason, it's got to be meaningful he was born into it, he has to find out why a man is chosen for something, even his faith. He holds off from me, I'm the outsider, maybe even the person to whom he's trying to prove to himself that he belongs. But doesn't he know that's the problem of all of us, that we can't find a place where we belong, where we can find our identity translated into some sort of substance, our actions into purpose, that the whole of our existence has a place in the scheme of things?

"I think we have a chance," she said. "So long as we believe we do have some kind of chance—haven't we maybe got one?—so long as we see the future as being ahead, it still is, we aren't old and done for, beaten. We still have the power to make new lives."

He took a cigarette between his lips and drew in, cheeks hollowed; shadows were all over his face, a feather of smoke rose, he looked like someone in great peril.

The fog was beginning to rise a little on the other side of them, as if under all that wetness something smoldered. Even the glowing end of his cigarette seemed some kind of warning. "I'm going to marry him, I think, Stu. That's one of the reasons I came back. It's going to take some time—we'll have to trace Cliff and we'll have to settle things between ourselves, but the important thing is that I feel there *is* a chance."

He looked at her.

"And what I'm trying to say about Neal, I feel is true with you, too, I really do, that you and Betty have a chance, that we can both look ahead, we—we can both go ahead and make new lives for ourselves. And I've never had this feeling before, Stu, that my life was able to be remade." She turned away, leaving him her back in its russet coat against the fierce icy arms of the trees, the tall black trunks. But she had not stopped speaking; it was only that, it seemed, she couldn't look at him as she brought out the words. "I've got to think of it, this marriage, like one of those ancient rituals where you break a bowl or eat from a basket, you go through some kind of initiation of being bound, that this is permanent."

Courage had many faces, she knew, not the least of which was tenderness. He stepped forward and touched her gently with his arms in embrace, a very brave man. Turning, she looked up at him. "Stu," she cried, "I want it to be right. How can I make it right? What can I do to make it right?"

"Just by being what you are."

It was the wrong season of the year for violets, her mother's favorite flower, and in the uncertain temperatures that came at this time of year unwise to offer real flowers, they would freeze and die, but Lois had brought them anyway, brought them for both her mother and Ella, chrysanthemums that could stand some cold, and the small carnations that had looked so lovely next to them.

She knelt, brushed clear the markers, and laid her offerings on the stones, obliterating the names. An odd idea, to offer flowers to those who can neither see nor smell.

This outcast grave, the debasement of being spoken of as one who had sinned beyond divine redemption, outside of human understanding—that was all that was left of the beautiful woman who had brought her into the world.

Her mother and Ella were buried next to each other. The rest of the Timbles were all huddled together on the other side of town. On consecrated ground. Her mother's burial had been prohibited in the Catholic cemetery because she had taken her own life, and Ella had been put there because she was black. Nobody said *that*— "Ella's a Protestant, Lois," Iris always said of the old family maid, "so of course she couldn't be buried with the family." That was how it had been put. Lois wondered what would have happened if her grandmother—that small, stern woman with a will of iron—had succeeded with her militant Romanism in converting Ella to Catholicism, but she had proselytized Ella's soul in vain. What kept Ella from conversion was the difference in Bibles; the Douay never moved her the way the King James did; she stuck to her own religion out of literary loyalty. So she had come to keep Lois's lonely mother company, the two stones inset in the ground side by side, as if the two bodies beneath were close in death as they had been in life.

Both of them outsiders, her mother and Ella. But together at the end. The two she cared most about.

She gazed down at the simple slab in front of her,

ORGANDY TIMBLE GREER

1902–1937

thinking, she was only a little older than I am now when she took her life. How could she consciously, deliberately, determinedly end her life at thirty-five?

I do not understand, Lois said to the stone in front of her. I know
I have made many mistakes, but I still believe in the future.

She *took* her own life.

She felt responsible for *everything,* Matt Baxter had said. I think
she felt that in running away she contributed to what she saw as evil.
The deception of self-projection, of seeing the whole world in terms
of one's own weaknesses, an inability to be objective, the fatal flaw
of always projecting one's own unhappinesses into a universal ethic.

But being a part of the world, weren't you then *liable* for it?

I don't know, she thought. Who really does? We are all so limited.
The mere fact of death—

Clouds crowded down on her, she seemed suddenly to be thrown
straight against a hard gray, slatelike slab of sky; then unexpectedly
the sun poured through an opening in that vast dove-colored dome
and struck, like a finger, one far corner of the earth. There came to
Lois an image, the old sundial in Iris's back yard

COUNT NONE BUT THE HAPPY HOURS

Iris had bought that sundial the year she embarked on her pro-
gram of "nature participation": they were going to have flowers
and learn all the names of the trees. Make scrapbooks. Go on nature
walks. Buy binoculars. Press specimens.

She had been so enthusiastic. They were going to equip themselves with a knowledge of the world around them.

A bird-feeding station of sorts had been erected. Crumbs were to
be saved and distributed. Iris bought bird books, a bird bath, the
sundial. But nobody read the books, crumbs from the boarders'
table were few and far between, the bird house had fallen in the first
storm. The bird bath was still there, waterless, visitorless, unsightly
and scarred, a memorial to her aunt's vanished hopes: none of them
knew a single species of the various sparrows that were their only
permanent avicular residents.

Iris had gravestones of her failures all over Sans Souci: flower-
beds that fostered nothing but weeds, hammock hooks on which
nothing had ever swung, the tattered remains of an "arbor" under
which no one had ever read: the half-finished "patio" in which they

were going to barbecue outdoors "together" and of course never did, the three broken slat-chairs down by the end of the lawn where, in summer, she thought she would have tea "with people." What people was enigmatical. Like the rest of her sisters, she eschewed friends in favor of family, and of the four sisters who might have shared sandwiches and passed about cups of mild Salada, one was a suicide, one shut up in a house with a defective daughter, one a thief barred and bolted inside her house, and one preferred gin and wouldn't have drunk the tea anyway because it would have made (she thought) her eyes puff.

Iris tried, Lois thought, looking down at her mother's grave, she really tried, Mama. I am grateful to her and I love her for all she has done, I owe her much, but she was not my mother. It is more gratitude for what she has done than for what she is. And I care for Carolyn and Stu—and, yes, even Erwin—but they do not make up the fabric of my life, I do not exist on their affection. And that is what I have wanted and never found, someone who is so much a part of my life that the whole of it is bound up in that person. A merging—that is what I have been looking for and never found.

Why can't I have the involvement with others that I feel for Constance, the deep and permanent commitment for all my life? I know I am not a world in my own, that there are many worlds outside; each person in his own skin is his own notion of what a world is. But the point is, in order to participate, no one can stand alone. We need the presence of others to give dimensions to ourselves. How am I to find the basis of this interchange with others? Is that what love is? An answer? An affirmation? An ability to be what I cannot be by myself?

For a moment she thought it possible that hundreds of miles away Neal paused and turned, as if he had understood; he came close and there was the sense of warmth, as if he held her, they were together and at last understood.

And then, in the next instant, she was shut out, separate, alone. He seemed a stranger, far away, in another town, a man who knew as little about love as she.

Lois stood looking down on the fallen flowers. But I feel I have suffered enough to permit myself a little peace, Mama, that's what

I think I came to tell you, that there is a man I can care for, that I believe I wish to marry and one day make a child with, and that's what people who love one another want, isn't it, to create something together? Because the essential of love is that it is rooted in life, it *is* life. And you, Mama, did you find out you didn't feel that way, that it wasn't really love you felt, and that drove you to destroy yourself because though you were beautiful you were proud, and pride never permits us to say how badly we have deluded ourselves.

But I've always cared for you, Mama—and honored you. And perhaps why I have come now is to try to tell you that and at the same time to let you know I am all right. I have learned how to come back to life, Mama. I have the desire to help it go on, and that is the largest act of faith I can make, to help perpetuate life, a life we believe in despite all that works against it.

The last time I was home while Ella was still alive, Mama, she gave me a blessing. But this time I have come back to ask it from you. I have done the best I could to redeem what was done in error in the past. I cannot undo the harm that has been done, but I am truly sorry for it and so far as I am able will do what penance I can for it. I do not know whether there is anything beyond this life except our beliefs and it doesn't matter; those beliefs are enough to make me weigh what I have done and mete out my own punishment, be my own judge and sentencer, they are enough to sustain me.

They say that when you can see things for what they are, when you can be what you are and accept yourself with some sort of grace, when you can go ahead to do what you should do, be able to enjoy the possible and confront what is not, use suffering to serve, stand on your own values and invest in tomorrow in relation to others, then you have made the steps necessary toward adulthood. I cannot say I have come this far, but I *see* where I should go, and when we accept, are we not ready to act?

I do not know, I say, Mama, whether it is possible that you can be aware of me standing here or not, but I have come anyway because I have always loved you and to come is an act of that love, and because Ella said there was singing at the end. She heard singing, that's what she said, and so in the infinite remoteness of the possibility you can look into my heart and see what is there, can understand why I have come, I ask you to give me your blessing, for the two of us, Neal and me, to tell me I am right when I believe in the continuance and perpetuation of life, in the belief we can go on to be better. Will you do that, Mama, though you took your own life, will you do that? Wherever you are, will you wish me well and a new life? Will you send me back to New York and a new beginning? Because I feel now I can go back and begin again.

Chapter 10

CAROLYN held up a sweater for Sally, fluffed it out, folded it, laid it down preparatory to wrapping it. If he had something for her for Christmas, Myers would have phoned long before: an afternoon would have been set aside. Since he hadn't called by now, Carolyn knew he wasn't going to call at all. Christmas was going to come and go without—New Year's Eve, she thought, her heart rising in hope, he'll be at the club, we'll—

He doesn't care, a voice said in certainty, and you know it. On the other side of town he went about his business, he never phoned, somewhere he might even be holding another woman in his arms. *You want it? You ready for it? You . . .*

Plunged in despair, Carolyn dropped the ribbon she had just begun to wind round the packaged sweater, and sank in a chair. She stared about like someone who had suddenly been struck down, her whole sense of orientation dislodged.

If only she could blank off the steady bell of despair that tolled inside her head, like the sound of a church bell in a doomed port

the plague had swept away—for was love not like some fatal disease
that had overrun the body?

The room grew large and strange, all the packages on the table
shimmered, as if to accost her in the rosy light of day, the ribbon
ran toward her and the presents, piled up, seemed to balance precariously close; in a moment they would all come crashing down,
she would be mercifully covered and cut off from sight. For that was
what she wanted, to hide away until the pain passed and her face
looked like itself, her hands moved without shaking, her eyes
weren't filled with fright.

She closed her eyes and saw her husband when he looked at her
in that odd way, as he had been doing all the past month, pained,
so that she almost loved him. He had that slow, sorrowing smile on
his face, and, while she watched, it faded and fell into nothingness;
pain came swiftly in its place; for the first time Carolyn realized
how much Ralph was suffering. What's the matter with you . . .
he's a good man . . . why can't you . . . what is the matter
with you . . . try . . . no, I can't . . . I don't want to, I've tried
and I just can't.

In his anguish he had been forced to speech; their silence was
broken by his agony.

"Why are you doing this to me?" Those eyes.

"I don't know, Ralph, I don't want to."

"You don't want to—if you don't want to, why do you do it,
then?"

"I don't know. Look around you. Where do you see any sense—
any rationality—in anything? Where do you see any reason in the
way people act or don't act?"

"Then why do you let me love you?"

"Let you love me?"

"Yes, let me go on loving when you—Carolyn, when you know
you don't love me, why do you let me go on?"

When she opened her eyes, she saw the table piled high with
presents, the glistening wrappings, fluted bows, satiny stickers, and
she knew that nothing she had bought would ever make up for what
she could not give them—I have bought them all gifts to make up
for what I couldn't buy and can't give.

She had seen inside herself and she was sickened by the sight. Nowhere had she been able to find anything except the frightened woman waiting for the telephone to ring. There had been neither love of husband nor devotion to children, not one single value to which she could cling. What she had seen was surely and simply outlined; she was a woman who had given herself to something that threatened to destroy her; she knew this and yet was unable to struggle against it. For a moment, in all the stripped illusions and all the plain and clear outlines of what had happened and was happening, she saw that she *must* fight, and yet, she knew that if the phone had rung at this moment, she would have gone anywhere and done anything he asked. Because she cared for him, she truly truly cared for him—perhaps because he had made her so unhappy. Pain is the major part of most of our commitments.

Carolyn loved the kitchen with its large windows through which the sun leapt toward the copper pots hanging on one wall and reflected in the open shelves of china and pottery on another. Outside, the bird-feeding station tempted the cheeky jays with their little flat black beards, the fluttery juncos, the busy chickadees, and the richly robed cardinals. Occasionally, at the suet, the red-dotted downy woodpecker paused, solemn and laborious, while the rest of the birds regarded him as if he were an odious outsider. There was something about the birds that gave Carolyn pause; the jays, imperious, no sooner fluttered to the side of the station than all the other birds rose in flight. The juncos were timid, the chickadees cheerful; as if each and every one of the species fulfilled some kind of preordained role—but wasn't it true that animals, birds, insects had no notion of any of their kind having come before or any feeling that any would follow? There was no past, no future, only the here and now, something Carolyn sometimes envied them. What would it be like to be free of the history of men who had gone before and the obligation to the men that were to come after? One would have no duty at all save to keep one's body going, to eat and survive.

It was not enough.

She could not have formulated a theory why, nor could she have upheld a position of any moral authority or responsibility, but she knew that it was not enough, and knowing that was what mattered; she felt that the deepest instincts sometimes could not be put into words, that those things one fell back on at the worst moments of need were the things the race had perhaps after all engendered as instincts: was that how some saw God?

God (a word to be used in many ways—the sacred and profane: God, as a prayer; God as a curse), God, if there was one job she hated, it was roasting and peeling the chestnuts, and with a turkey this size she could expect the process to last forever. Sally—if Sally was ever to be found—might have given her a hand, but Sally was out somewhere—another worry—with one of her young men; she had tried to corral Bobbie earlier, but he had disappeared; only Wes, standing at her side, looking dismally down on the mound of nutmeats, was around to help, and she felt guilty about asking him; he was always the one, it seemed, who ended up helping. Cheerfully, confidently, he came to service. Perhaps it was true that the child consciously created in a moment of love was more blessed than the one that merely came.

"Why is a candy cane like a horse?" he asked. He was at the riddle age.

"A candy cane like a horse? I don't know. Why is it?"

"Because the harder you lick it, the faster it goes," Wes said and burst out laughing, dropping an inaccurately peeled chestnut into the pot. Carolyn picked it up, peeled back the brown hairy skin that he had left on, and said "N.C.," the family code for jobs badly done. No Comment.

Perhaps it was the angle—so vulnerable as to be beautiful—of his head, but she suddenly understood anew how much she cared for him, and how quickly he would slip away from her. After twelve you never knew your children. When he was gone, where would she be then?

You have no future at all, she thought. I must, she told herself, putting down the knife as her heart began that terrible constriction that was beyond pain, a whole pulling in of herself; and Wes looked up, startled, he was saying something to her while she gripped the table with her hands and tried to hold on; it had come over her with the swiftness of certainty she might actually be coming to pieces, in another moment lying shattered across the table, calling for someone, anyone, to come help, she could no longer hold herself together.

She gripped the table and held on, conscious only that one small shattered fragment of her mind was holding out against everything else that was in collapse, that there was one infinitesimal link left with what she had thought of as strength, as the ability to endure, as the power of will over instinct: and that part of her said, *You have yourself.*

"Mother"—he had his arms about her and she was looking into his face, his mouth was moving, he must be saying something, but she could not hear, she could scarcely see, the violence of her heart beat so dimmingly, her head was filled with such pain, her eyes ached with it, her whole body beat up with it, and starkly, unalterably, on her mind those words, *You have yourself. Nothing more. That is how it is. That is how it has always been. It just* seemed *otherwise. You are all alone. Everyone is. All alone, you will always be. Always. Always. Everyone is. Everyone. Always.*

And she thought: I have come to the crisis of my life.

Mary Mother of God, Carolyn's heart cried out for her, help me.

The room tilted, revolved, righted itself, and unexpectedly Carolyn felt herself take hold. It was the boy's frightened face that had touched something responsive inside. "I'm all right," she said in a voice frozen in its despair. "Just a little dizzy. Must be all the excitement. Don't worry—you're not to worry. I'm all right, I really am," she said and managed a smile, but he was still looking at her with that terrible white face, those anguished eyes. She forced herself to stand up, brought up one trembling hand, and grasped the knife, and held it a moment, trying to fit it to her stiff fingers. "Let's finish these damn nuts," she said and took one up in lifeless fingers and tried to cut into it with the knife. It dropped to the floor and Carolyn, seeing outside a collision of clouds as if the world too were in disintegration, knelt down and, for the first time in thirty years, offered up a real prayer. *Help me,* she prayed, *O God help me,* and closed her fingers over the itinerant chestnut and, holding it, like some sacred scapular, repeated her prayer.

If ever God were going to answer, He would do so on this day. At this season of the year, as her mother would say.

Wes was working in great haste. He was afraid of her, wanted to get away from her. And she didn't blame him. But why should his Christmas be ruined by her sins?

"You don't have to do any more, I'll finish up."

He looked up, anxious.

"There are still an awful lot."

"Well, don't worry, I'll make out. Why don't you go out? Maybe take a walk, go down by the barn."

He hesitated.

"You can dress warmly. Go on, it'll do you good."

"You sure you don't want me to help?"

"You've been a big help, there aren't that many more, and I haven't really got much to do, the packages are all wrapped, the tree stand is up, the bulbs and lights out, I even remembered the tinsel." She tried to laugh. "Remember last year when you and your father had to run out everywhere looking for tinsel and everything was closed? It's our own fault, of course, we get in these predicaments, waiting until Christmas Eve to trim the tree, but we always have, I guess we always will. One of our few family traditions. You want a piece of fruitcake? The pralines are all gone—your grandmother."

Fastening his overshoes, he grunted, and she took it that he did. At the refrigerator she asked him, her back turned, if he would wear his scarf, though she knew he hated it, considered it sissy stuff. So long as she nagged or bullied him, he would think things were normal; he might forget the face she had shown him, that face of fear. Reassured, he would be given back a world he should have, or seemed to have—not the real one around him.

The ringing of the front doorbell in early afternoon was one of those little irritations that overwhelmed Carolyn, making her feel as if she were engaged in major conflicts that would change her whole way of life. She was always tired around two o'clock—something about her metabolism; it collapsed after lunch and did not rewind until three. After years of hopeless struggle against a recalcitrant body, a stupefied brain, Carolyn had given up; every day she rested for an hour and let the machine slow its purposeless engine so that lying down, eyes closed, it was as if she could hear the slow *tick tick* of the wheels as they tried to turn.

It was bad enough to have to open the door—the season precluded, after all, pretending you were out—but to stand face to face with your brother, wobbly, gloveless, hatless, and, Carolyn saw, drunk, was something beyond the call of holiday duty. *He's left Peg* was the first thing she thought, and the second, *I'm just like Mother, expecting the worst.*

"Carolyn?" Pete saluted her, smiling lopsidedly, wagging his head.

"Carolyn," she said, reaffirming the fact as she moved aside and he jerked through the door. In the hall Pete stopped, directionless; he and Peggy had been out to this house only once that Carolyn could remember, right after they'd moved, before Wes was born. He came to call, it occurred to her, only in an emergency, like the day he had been fired from his last job. So, if he was here, he must want her help again—he probably *had* left Peggy.

And god, he would want a drink and that would mean she'd have one with him—one? she asked herself. No, not today, she said to herself firmly, and knew that of course she would drink with him. She knew it and was afraid of it, but there seemed no way to flee from it. You went toward what you wanted and what she wanted more than anything at this moment was a good stiff drink. It was as if the god to whom she had prayed in the kitchen had not even been listening.

Was He ever?

His coat removed, her brother stood before her in an old blue suit, shiny, dandruff-drenched, the shoulders too wide, the pants too full. He looked like something left over from the fifties, a sad anachronism in a world where men were readying themselves for the moon by scrunching down inside cubicles of rocket capsules the size of skyscrapers. But what after all would the conquest of space mean to someone who had never been able to set his own small house in order?

Pete floundered over the room, looking for some place to put that

outdated relic that was himself and Carolyn asked the obvious.
"Drink?" Sure of the affirmative, she was already on her way for
the whisky.

Carrying two glasses and the liquor, and aware in her heart that
she was blaming Pete for the same lack of control that she would
not blame herself for, Carolyn came into the living room, determined to try to understand. "Noël, Noël," she said, handing him his
libation.

"Merry Christmas," he said, lifting his glass awkwardly. One of
the things that exasperated her most was that he never did anything
gracefully.

"You look as if you had been at the Christmas spirits already.
There an office party this year? I thought—"

"I didn't go to work." He lifted his glass and drained a third of
it. "I decided I was going to have one day off, one day to myself,
even if it did get me fired—not that Ralph, well, you know, he's a
good guy, he'd understand how it was—if I could ever explain.
Don't know that I could. Really—you know—*explain*." Pete looked
down at his shoes. "Carolyn," he said, sloshing the drink around
in his glass, "I've just come to the end of my rope. I don't think I
can go on. Not another day. Not in that house. Not with Peggy. Not
with the kids. I've had it."

Clouds were crashing against the window. Somewhere outside,
Ralph went, Myers walked, Peggy waited. "It's not that easy," she
said.

"Why not? There's nothing more they can get out of me."

Tired with that two-o'clock tiredness, Carolyn started to say,
There's always something more they can get out of you—and then
decided against it. "It's not that easy, Pete, you—"

"How much farther down can a guy go before he gives up?" her
brother demanded in an angry voice.

"I'm no Delphic oracle."

"What?"

"I haven't got the powers of the occult. If you want the eternal
mysteries unraveled, Frances is your woman. Or at least that woman
of hers—what's her name, Estrella, Zolar, something—is. You have
to put your faith in something, I suppose—medicine, astrology, re-

ligion, the carrot cure. It doesn't much matter so long as you're sure it'll save you. One swindle after another. Isn't it odd, if Christ was supposed to be the Son of God, he was born with a tube, the sign of sin, the proof of the flesh. Well, if Christ was the Son of God, He wouldn't have had that, would He? That would have been the final proof, wouldn't it, that he had a smooth stomach? Never mind. *The* birthday, you know," she said, rising, refilling his glass. If you drank enough you could drown out all the unanswerables—why Christ had a bellybutton, why God never answered your supplications, why Myers didn't call, what Pete was supposed to do, what was going to happen to all of them, those children who were supposed to be suffered to come unto Him, and who wandered about, helpless, seeking, the rest of their lives.

Pete reminded her of her father, something about the way he sat, the way he held his hands, the tilt of his head. One could forgive outsiders their inadequacies, but how could one forgive one's family? She was suddenly filled with rage at all of them—brother, father, husband, lover—who had caused her so much anxiety, so much grief and pain. She would have liked to strike out all of her former life, her father lying upstairs at Sans Souci (the Green Lawn Boarding Home, a voice called out to her) on that bed which was a symbol of life and death, the place to lie down in desire and make life, the narrow board on which disease played out its part and took you into death.

For an instant, her consciousness was divided, one part of her here in the living room looking down at the drink she had just poured into Pete's glass, the other off in that area of the past where one lived again and again the shameful moments of one's life, and she knew for the hundredth time the humiliations of her child- and girlhood.

"There, in that big box over on the piano," she said.

Embarrassed, Pete fumbled with the empty box he had open in his hands, trying to return it to the table from which he had taken it, but having trouble with his coordination. "I keep my cigarettes in that," she said, "and I guess I forgot to refill it. Ralph's are on the piano—he uses the big box, he's always got some in stock. Help yourself."

"I ran out—on the way over and—"

"They're filter-tip. To keep the illusion cancer can be kept away. Give me one, will you? I'll leave the bottle here. If you want more ice, sing out." To his bent back, opening the other box, she said, "You want to leave Peg, is that it?"

Turning, he looked at her. "When you make the kind of money I do, you don't walk out on your wife, you just go out and get drunk —once a year if you can scrape together the dough." He opened the box and held it out to her. "You blow off steam, you don't ever *do* anything. Once—it's so long ago I've almost forgotten what it felt like—I used to think maybe there might be a way to get out, start over, but of course I was just kidding myself. I was just one of those guys who got in trouble and went on getting in trouble. Hell, even if old Esther left me her dough, I don't think I'd get out, I'm trapped now *inside,* everything's been grabbed right out of me, I just don't give a damn any more. So this morning when I got up and I said to myself, Tomorrow's Christmas, another Christmas, and then New Year's, another year gone down the drain, another year, kiddo, coming up, and where did the last one go, what have you got to show for it, and the house was the way it always is, just all fu—fouled up, Peggy screaming and the kids all over, in each other's way, and I just stood there and said to myself, To hell with it. I got dressed and put on my coat and walked out without eating breakfast or anything and I went to the nearest bar and I said to myself, This is one day of my own, one day I'm going to have to myself, and then"—he looked away sheepishly—"then I ran out of money and—and I came here."

"Do you want me to give you some money, Pete?"

"Hell no, I came for a drink. You don't begrudge me that, do you, Carolyn? I can't take your money, can I, but it's all right to drink your liquor, isn't it?" He lifted his glass and took a long draft. "You come to the point where that's all you've got, those little distinctions. You'll let me keep those, won't you?" He was looking at her as if to see how far he could go. "You'll allow me my little distinctions, won't you, Carolyn? Oh, I know you've got all kinds of your own, *real* ones, but my poor little ones, you'll let me have those, won't you? You know, people like me don't ask too much. We're not like you, we wouldn't dream of wanting the kind of things you have. All we want is a little liquor now and then. So you won't begrudge me that, will you, Carolyn, a little of your—of *Ralph's*—nice expensive liquor. The boss's booze."

"I don't mind how much you drink, but let's keep it light, shall we, Pete?"

"Oh, by all means, Carolyn, by all means. We wouldn't want the big old unpleasant world outside to intrude in here, would we? We wouldn't want to ruin the nice atmosphere in this house with all the mean fucking things that happen outside, would we? We've got to be careful to keep everything nice, don't we, Carolyn? Carolyn likes things to be nice, everything right, we don't want to upset Carolyn, do we? That why you never ask us here, Carolyn, because you don't want to upset everything nice, is that it, Carolyn, you're afraid we'd upset everything nice, Peggy and me? Or is it because Ralph's embarrassed, working for him the way I do, it wouldn't look right, the boss and the hired hand, even if the hired hand is your brother, that it, is it, Carolyn?"

"You've said about enough, Pete."

"About enough? All these years I've been quiet, don't you think it's about time I told you what I think?"

"I know what you think, you don't have to go into detail."

"Oh, but I want to go into detail. I want you to know what I think for a change and"—he held up his glass—"how about a little drink? It isn't enough I take your husband's money, I'm drinking up his liquor, too. Ungrateful, is that what you'd call it? Not *nice,* is that what you'd say?"

She stood up. "You can have a drink any time you want—so long as you act civilized. But I don't want you in my front room talking like that about Ralph."

"Oh, isn't it nice to be rich? Isn't it nice to have a husband who's got money, isn't it—"

"Whatever it is, you have no right to talk about Ralph like that. I can take what you have to say about me, because it's probably true, but if you put the two of us together, you wouldn't strain enough guts through a sieve to make one of Ralph. So saying, I'm asking you to go. To get out."

"I'm going, don't worry, I'm on my way," he said, standing, swaying. "But before I go, there's just one little thing I'd like to say. You don't mind that, Carolyn, do you, just listening to one more little thing I have to say? And you know what that is, Carolyn, you know what I want to say? That you're no fucking good, Carolyn, that's what I want to say, no damn fucking good, and I know it, and no matter who you think you're kidding, you're not getting away with anything with me. You're no damn fucking good."

"Everything all right? You got everything under control?" He was trying to be cheerful, pretending, she supposed, that they had scarcely spoken all these days, that he did not know his wife went to another man's bed, that he had not seen the house as something that sheltered a wife who no longer wanted to live with him; for Christmas Eve, for the sake of the children, for God knows what else, Ralph was going to try to make things go.

Making an effort in return, Carolyn fixed on a smile. From over the punchbowl, she stared at Ralph's face, trying to bring it in focus; until he had come in, she hadn't realized how that last drink had hit her. She had been sure she was pacing herself, but now suddenly his features were blending and melting, as if she were seeing him under water.

"What's that you're making, Carolyn, some kind of punch?" he said in such a falsely hearty voice that she was sure he had recognized from her eyes what was wrong with her.

"It's a wassail bowl. I've decided to treat the season the way we should. So I'm making wassail. Wine, spices, roast apples," she enumerated, "nutmeg, ginger, cinnamon, and we'll all be sick, but *trink heil, was-haile,* and all that." It had come out wrong, she could tell from the look on his face. "We're going to light a Yule log," she went on, smiling in what she hoped was a winning way, "and trim the tree, light the Christmas candles. We might even all go to Mass."

"Like that, you want to turn up in church like that?"

"What do you mean 'like that'?"

"You know very well what I mean, Carolyn. Where are the kids? I hope they haven't—"

"Haven't *what*?"

"Why do you do it, Carolyn? If you don't care anything about me, what about the kids?" He stood patiently waiting for an answer, his coat open, his gloves on, hat in his hands. But what answer could she give him—that Myers hadn't called, that Pete had been here?

"I'm sorry, Ralph. I didn't mean—is it as bad as all that?"

"Why don't you go up and take a shower, lie down a little while?"

"All right, if you think that's best, I—I guess you're right, it's not very—very *nice*, Christmas Eve and all." She looked down at the big bowl in front of her. "You know what they say, no neurotic can stand the holidays. What I mean is," she hastened to explain, seeing the expression on his face, "what I mean is—I don't know," she said, letting her arms drop to her sides. "Maybe I don't know what I mean. The apples are in the oven," she said dully. "I'll just wait until they're done and—you can't have a wassail bowl without roast apples," she ended feebly, while they stood across from each other, gazing into each other's eyes in a kind of mutual despair. Once long ago they had shared a bed, slept in each other's arms, warmed flesh against flesh, safe through the long night; and then the quarrels had commenced; bitter and silent, each hugged his own side of the bed so that their bodies wouldn't touch, rose in the morning trying to pretend everything was normal, their faces fixed in falsity, the words on their lips a lie; and had at last come to separate beds, and then to different rooms; and now, looking in his face, she wondered how long it would be until they ceased to share the same house, when the only time they saw each other, like Erwin and Helen, was in a lawyer's office, and everything ended in viciousness and vituperation.

"Carolyn," he said, and she turned her head, unable to bear the look on his face. "Carolyn," he repeated, and she turned back and tried to pretend she did not know what was going on in his heart, forcing herself to face him. "Please," he said, "go upstairs and lie down, I'll look after the apples."

"A little walk," she said. "Just take a little walk. I'll be fine."

"It's awfully cold out."

"Won't go far, just down to the creek and back. A little fresh air—" She had pushed past him so as not to be caught and condemned to the room upstairs to lie on the bed and stare at the ceiling, feel the walls go round, the floor rise; outside, in the crisp, cold air, she might regain her equilibrium; in a quarter of an hour no one would know she'd had six—or was it seven?—whiskies during the afternoon. And dinner—it was early, she saw by the kitchen clock. Ralph must have come home early for Christmas Eve. There was still plenty of time to put some potatoes in, fix a vegetable and salad, fry the meat. A simple supper—nothing to worry about like, say, the look on Ralph's face.

She bent over, stepped out of her shoes and into her boots. Although it was only a little after four, the sky was already the color of crows' wings. The winter solstice had just passed, they were at the black night of the year. Cold, hard, cracked, the earth lay dazed under that sky, even the trees stunned. Still, she loved to walk out on that flat earth under the open sky; stamping over the icy ground, her feet seemed to feel the patient seeds waiting down in the frozen soil; she was filled with a certainty of spring.

She loved this land, the disorderly clump of trees down by the creek, the alluvial fields, smooth-surfaced, supine, couchant in their coming power: under their cover of fallen grass and hay lay the rich dirt of the plains.

She covered the distance between the house and the first sprouting of second growth near the small woods in two or three minutes, stood looking down at a fallen nest—the wind had no doubt dislodged it. It was a terrible wind, the tears on her face testimony to its power.

Moving hesitantly, Carolyn passed into the leafless grove, making her way to the bank by the stream. Her head had cleared; she was quite sure that when she went back inside she would be herself. Myself, she wondered, what is that? And knew that she had had an answer, or a partial answer, earlier when she had thought, *You have yourself. Everyone has.* It was that aloneness, that solitary thing you recognized, the thing within you that cut you off from others but made you distinct too, that diminished and enhanced you at the same time, the paradox that was the self: the aloneness that meant you lived inside your head and at some of the instances of your heart. You felt: perhaps that was it. You felt, you thought: and what *you* felt and thought was distinct from what anyone else felt or thought.

Over the frozen earth a girl had ridden, young and frightened, taken by an old husband who had got it in his mind they must go home to be counted, no matter how young, frightened, or frail his wife was, and so through the long cold day they went and came at last to a small town, seeking shelter. On a night much like this, black, dense, freezing, on straw, the child came into the world . . . the worship of the shepherds . . . the lamentations in Rama . . . Rachel weeping over the murder of the innocents . . . the flight into Egypt . . . His rejection, His betrayal—yet what we feel, Carolyn thought, is a sense of triumph, of great deliverance; what we remember, we remember in tenderness · and joy. . . . A child is born this day . . . Glory to God in the Highest and on earth peace among men of good will. . . .

She thought of the pale, high-voiced priest at Ada's grave. She saw Esther throwing the flowers and, an instant later, the image changed to an old woman with a brown paper bag in the office of a department store; then Myers looking across the room at the old man crying, Myers laughing. And finally there came to her the vision of her husband a few moments before, standing in the kitchen, his face sad, his eyes a rebuke. Why do you do it, Carolyn?

Why had Myers wanted her to drink?

She would never know. Some will to destruction she did not understand, perhaps sharing with Kierkegaard the belief that the highest pitch of passion was its will to destroy, or perhaps to test her, to see how far she would go with him; and then, having the proof, he lost interest. She hadn't even held out long enough to make it any real contest. They had passed through all the sensual experiments, the individual debasements, and come quickly to the end, her complete surrender. It was the collapse of her will he had been interested in, and that had happened, she realized now, early. He had seen all there was to see, gone round the sights with mild curiosity, and traveled on to new terrains where, though the diversions might be the same, their locale would be changed, he would have an illusion of difference. And wasn't that all that mattered, that you be able to reach beyond the everyday realm of reality into that zone of the imagination where it was possible for love to take place? For Myers, love was mystery. Why should he remain where there was no more mystery?

And then, like some dark large omen, a shadow passed over her, a hand held her arm.

Ralph was saying something in the darkness.

". . . I don't know, I thought we'd—you'd—licked it, and then just as I got my confidence back, just as I began to believe in you again, you—I don't know, Carolyn, I wish I could explain to you what it's like to be in my place, when you're like this—constantly—constantly—" His voice groped for the word. "Afraid," he said at last. "You spend your whole life afraid. Every time I go out, I wonder what you'll be like when I get home. Every time you go out, I wait and wait, wondering how you'll be when you come through the door. Your eyes," he said. "That's what I always look at first, your eyes. I can always tell by your eyes—and then the way you talk, repeating, slurring—the way you walk, the stumbling, the indecision. *I never know*—I'm always waiting. And then," he went on, his voice sounding cheated, "you quit, really quit drinking. I couldn't believe it at first, but weeks went by and you stuck to it. I told myself maybe it was going to be all right, I started to believe again, the fear went away. A year went, two, and then I *really* believed, and what happened? It all started over again, and I don't think I can go through it again, Carolyn, I just don't see how I can stand day in, day out living in uncertainty, never knowing how you'll be when I come home—if you are home—knowing every day I have to get up wondering how bad it's going to be today. And the days when you're not drunk, when I come home and everything's all right, I'm still on edge, watching—always watching and waiting. Are you going to go out in the kitchen and sneak a drink? Can we make it through the evening, always tense, never able to relax, constantly watching and waiting—what kind of life is that, Carolyn? Who wants to live like that? Why should your

drinking be the only thing I think about? I want to think about
something else, but it's come to the point it's the only thing I can
think about, it's on my mind day and night. Do you think I want
to live like that, afraid all the time, living with nothing but fear,
watching and waiting, with liquor the only thing I can think about?"

"No, of course not," Carolyn said numbly.

"The point is, I can't go through it again, I just haven't got it
in me."

"I know, I don't blame you." The wind rustled through the
creek, dead leaves rose. "I don't want to be like this either, I
really don't, Ralph, only—only it just seems as if I can't help
myself, as if—once I start—I just can't stop."

"Why do you start? You were doing so well, why did you go
back to it again? Why can't you drink like other people, have a
couple of drinks, let it go at that? Why must you go on and on, why
must you always end up drunk, why do you always have to have
three—*four*—more than anyone else?"

"I don't know. A feeling comes over me. Depression. Despair. I
need a drink. And I think, One won't do any harm, I'll just have
one and then—"

"But, Carolyn, you went for such a long time, it looked like you
had it licked. What happened? What made you go back, what made
you start again?"

"It was—something that happened."

His voice was full of pain. "Something to do with—"

Neither of them could go on. Finally Carolyn said, "Can you
give me a little time, Ralph, let me try to work it out?"

"I'll give you a reasonable amount of time, Carolyn, but I can't
wait indefinitely from day to day living with this endless anxiety.
And neither can the children. It isn't fair to them to come home and
find you like this. Hasn't it ever occurred to you that after finding
you like this a couple of times, they'll understand, they'll know
enough not to bring their friends home, but even more they'll stay
away from you? Drunks aren't very nice people, Carolyn. They
may think they're charming and people love them, but the truth of
the matter is that at best, Carolyn, a drunk is a nuisance and most

of the time just plain disgusting. A man has got to know there's a point where something is decided one way or the other, he can't live suspended indefinitely in indecision."

"I know that. And I know how patient you've been, Ralph, I really do. I don't know what to say—it's as if something's snapped in me and I can't get myself back together."

The wind was running hard down the hollow between the trees. Its voice, like Ralph's a moment before, sounded distressed, despairing, but now her husband was simply a still figure standing at her side, silent in the emptiness of her explanation. If she reached out and touched him, would he be as wooden as the trunks of these trees?

Then he was gone and for an instant she wondered whether he had been there or not, whether perhaps her mind hadn't made up the scene. In the rush of wind, the clear cold of night, the world was unreal, a formless void through which she was falling, and would never find a place to rest. And then, suddenly, she was still, poised, listening, and it came to her that of course what she needed was another drink. Another drink would make the nameless terrors go away.

If you started a Yule log this year and saved a piece for next, to rekindle the Christmas fire, the Christmas spirit, then there *would* be a next, Carolyn thought, they would all be together. A poem about it she had seen recently—Herrick. *With the last year's brand . . . Light the new block . . .* something, something *spending . . .* something, something, she couldn't remember . . . *That sweet luck may . . . Come while the log is tending.*

Unwrapping bulbs, arranging lights, attaching fasteners to the angels and miniature trees, the silver horns and tiny deer, her children avoided her. When their eyes nervously rested on her for an instant, they condemned; when, more often, they rigidly watched their father or one another, refusing to look at her, their faces were empty, as if a thief had robbed them of all expression. But she was the thief; she had taken away what was rightfully theirs this night.

When the fire was laid, the tree trimmed, Carolyn stood back a moment, gazing abstractly about the room. What had to be done next? The presents—she had to bring the presents down.

Every year after the tree was trimmed, they all stood back admiringly and someone said, "I think it's the prettiest tree we've ever had." And someone else said, "It's *much* prettier than last year. Fuller." Then the presents were put under the tree and the ritual continued. "I've never seen so many presents."

"I don't think we've ever had so many presents, it's almost criminal."

"Last year I thought we had more presents that we'd ever had, but this year—"

Now they all stood silent, looking at the finished tree. The colored balls shimmered, the spun snow glazed the green, tinsel fell like frost from branch to branch, and all the little figures Carolyn had collected over the years danced at the ends of their cords. It was lovely, a lovely, lovely tree.

"Shall I plug it in?" Ralph asked, and Carolyn nodded, unable to speak. She was waiting for one of them to say, This is—the prettiest—the fullest—tree we've ever had.

The lights flickered for a moment, then took hold. "Only one out," Ralph said. "That's a pretty good percentage." He unscrewed the slacker. "I'm sure glad we changed to those lights where if one goes off they all don't go off." It was what he said every year.

Carolyn waited. Now, surely now, one of her children would say —but Sally was busily putting tops back on the boxes the bulbs had been in, the two boys had sunk into chairs and were staring. I should say it, Carolyn thought, but something held her back: she was not the one who was supposed to begin the litany; one of the children should, otherwise it didn't have meaning.

Sally carried the boxes out to the kitchen and Ralph, standing back and surveying the lights, said in satisfaction, "They're all on now. Looks pretty good, doesn't it, Bob?"

Bob grunted. Carolyn waited for Wesley to say the magic words, but he sat mute, he would not look at her.

Carolyn put her glass down on the table. She was drinking

whisky. The large bowl of wassail was almost untouched in the other room; Ralph had had one glass. Still it was early in the evening; people might drop in—*people might drop in,* she said to herself. Who? Their friends were not the kind who "dropped in." Her family never came unless—a picture presented itself of Pete earlier that afternoon. Oh, isn't it nice to be rich? Isn't it nice to have a husband who's got money? Oh, isn't it, Carolyn said to herself, isn't it, though? Yet she knew, too, that something close to self-pity, accentuated by the alcohol, was what she was experiencing, but while there was a coldness in her house this Christmas Eve, an unspoken condemnation, what was transpiring at Pete's was undoubtedly a thousand times worse: arguments, loud bitter battles, *Drunk, drunk, you're drunk,* Carolyn heard Peggy cry out. That cramped house with its endless untidiness would be even worse as they struggled to create some kind of Christmas scene—did they bother any more with a tree, Carolyn wondered. And what kind of presents were there, behind in their bills as they always were, hard-pressed from week to week to meet even the basic expenses, though Ralph gave Pete more than he was worth.

Going into the kitchen, passing her daughter—cold, closed off—Carolyn felt it was bad enough to be herself, but what if you were Peggy, what chance at all would there be, what chance had there ever been? Simply, Carolyn thought, because she won't use a diaphragm. One small circle of rubber would have made all the difference in her life and she was prevented—prohibited, her mind corrected—from using it because the Church, celibates all in their eternal unholiness, took a positive position against it. Some kind of revenge on women . . . Saint Paul, she thought, that implacable misogynist. Someone, she thought, ought to make those men responsible for the suffering they had brought on people like Peggy. She pictured a judgment scene in which on all sides worn-out women cheered and raised angry fists against the heavens. The picture pleased her and, smiling, she went to the window and gazed out. It had started to snow.

I'll try to make it up to them a little, she told herself. No more drinks for another hour. In an hour it'll have worn off.

Leaving the whisky where it was, she went into the other room. "Look," she cried out to them, "empty-handed."

Their faces stared back at her, immobile.

"Empty-handed," she repeated, throwing her hands out for them to see.

"Please, Carolyn," her husband said.

"Please, Carolyn, *what?*"

In answer he turned his back and fiddled with something under the tree—the socket probably, he liked poking around in electrical outlets. Perhaps he would be electrocuted.

"Daddy's going to light up for us," she heard herself saying. "As a special Christmas treat, he's going to plug himself in and *ascend.*"

Not one of them laughed.

"To see if it's all true," she persisted. "And when he comes back, he's going to spread the word in handy little newly decorated packages. They'll be inspirational messages for the devout who must be nudged into disbelief—Don't despair, nihilism—"

"Carolyn!"

"Aren't you going to ascend, Ralph? Oh, I'm so disappointed. I'd been counting on that as one of my Christmas Eve treats."

The children were in the doorway. Their faces were frigid with disapproval. Ralphlike, Carolyn thought; they'll grow up just like Ralph's mother, that woman whose face always reminded Carolyn of a prune and whose sentiments—they could never be called opinions—were expressed in the words of Walter Winchell and Westbrook Pegler. *James*—her husband—had left her, like so many ladies in her set, well provided for, thank god. It was American Express and Banker's Trust who had the trouble with her, relieving Carolyn of the burden of making good the lack of Sanka in Paris and the absence of root beer in the Levant. She traveled.

Give up, Carolyn told herself. Go get your drink. The enemies outside—like her mother, like Ralph's mother—were easy to recognize. But what about the ones inside, the ones that had made her what she was, that had brought her to this Christmas Eve, drunk, faithless, and afraid?

Well, she would remove herself, leave them the tree. Still, something was missing, something had been forgotten. The presents. She had their presents to put under the tree. Ever since Thanksgiving she had been buying things for them—as if she really loved them and wanted to make them happy by choosing something special. Now, alienated, isolated, she left them, no more than an accumulation of accusations, and went upstairs where, in her room, the pile of presents lay. In the end, when you came right down to it, maybe her mother was right: Duties are ours, events God's.

Whose duty had it been for that frightened and frail young girl bleeding on straw, bringing her strange son into the world?

Downstairs Ralph had turned the radio on. "Hark the Herald Angels Sing . . ." a choir proclaimed, and in a fleeting evanescent instance, it was almost possible to believe in a Newborn King.

The eyes encountered in the mirror were first stark in accusation, then unwavering as they stared at the whisky glass in her hand. She had seen them all that month, the eyes of a pained unhappy man who does not know which way to turn. He was still dressed, a heavy middle-aged man, bald, bespectacled, spent—and what had he to show for all his years? A war in which he'd lost his best and only real friend, a wife who went to another man for her fulfillment, children growing away from him into absurd worlds of their own. It seemed to her for a moment that Ralph's face in the mirror knew it all. If they were all doomed to learn the lesson of how unintelligible and insignificant life is, was there not, after all, a bond? She cried out.

The drink fell to the floor, she was in his arms, his voice a pain of pleading against her ear. "Carolyn, oh Carolyn, I love you so much. . . ." Immobile under his hands, her flesh unable to respond, she yet felt that his desire might be met if only her mind went out to it; but the differences of feelings between them were so enormous that every caress of his hands only heightened the disparities, made her more conscious that her body was growing stiffer and colder under his ardor, the hot breath, blazing eyes, plucking fingers, until, in a moment over which she had no control, she felt herself recoil, and his hands were instantly stopped, and their faces confronted each other in the mirror, divested of all pretense;

cold, calculating, her eyes accused him, *You do not know how to love,* and his answer back, *It is you, you, who won't let me.*

Her breath came slowly, painfully; yet she felt something close to relief. It was all finished. Nothing more could happen—they had done all they could to each other. Not one remembrance of happiness or tenderness or pleasure was left, only bitterness and acrimony, an incredible desire for revenge and retaliation. In that instant she put down forever the hope that anything could ever be repaired between them.

She knew that the same murderous desire filled his heart, that his hands could have gone round her neck and crushed the slender bones without hesitation. She waited—and almost hoped. It would be an end. But a man, she saw, who once loved a woman could never hate the way a woman who had loved a man could. Because women built their lives around the men they loved, the loss of that love was deeper than anything else that happened to them. But men were able to turn away; they had other things around which to order their lives. To a man, contempt could come, while in a woman, only everlasting enmity. She could never forgive, but he could forget.

So it was, she saw, that he could turn, as he turned in the mirror, and walk away without one word, without one gesture, without even a glance that would show how deeply she had driven her hatred inside him. Later, alone, she even imagined him closing the wound, cauterizing it, consigning it to oblivion, the one thing she did not want. What she wanted was that for every minute of his life he would be conscious of how much he had lost in losing her, that for every second his heart pounded, it pounded the reminder that he had not been man enough to hold her, that for every breath he drew, he drew it to the knowledge that she had refused to let him make love to her because in her eyes he was inadequate. That was what she wanted him to remember until the day he died. Not man enough . . . inadequate . . . her mind beat at that retreating back, you weren't man enough, and don't ever forget it.

"Merry Christmas, Carolyn," he said at the door.

Chapter 11

IN THE living room the turkey, missing half its breast and thigh, lay in golden submission upon its side; Haut Brion was still gleaming in the long-stemmed glasses, Neal's head was haloed in a nimbus of cigar smoke. Lois rose with a slight nod toward the bedroom, went in, and looked down on the child who lay half asleep under a pale green blanket. For a moment Constance stiffened; back and forth went Lois's hand, kneading the small back, then gradually Constance began to relax. The child slept, body boneless, hands flat, eyelashes faintly fluttering over the soft cheeks.

Christmas Day had begun with the eight-o'clock bells from the church down the street and Constance, to whom all the myths still had meaning, all the people a special brand of belonging, the world waited for her and only her, had opened her eyes and looked up blankly, not yet quite awake.

An instant later she had pushed aside the bedcovers, scrambled out of her crib, and slipperless, robeless, was on her way to the front room where the night before her stocking had been hung and her mother's Christmas bouquet of roses, sent by special instructions from that nice shop on Madison Avenue, opened tight buds to expose black-tonsiled throats.

Carrying slippers and robe, Lois gave chase, came to a stop beside the child as the full magnificence of the tree struck her and Constance stood in opened-mouth awe. Lois seized the opportunity to project the child's arms into the sleeves of her robe, bent to put slippers on the small feet. When she looked into the child's face it was alight with instantaneous wonder, utter disbelief. Then, without another word, Constance turned and fled back to their bedroom, the sight of all that mysterious munificence too much for her. But then, too, it had been a taxing week. With her father back.

Holding the vacuum-cleaner attachment in one hand, Lois had listened to the doorbell. Who in the world could it be at nine o'clock at night? Not Neal—she had talked to him earlier on the telephone. A nuisance, this interruption; she wanted to get the cleaning finished; these night scourings and scrubbings—but what could you do when you worked all day and were trying to get ready for Christmas? And Mrs. Collins was too old to go down on her hands and knees chasing lint, to stand on a stool brooming down cobwebs from the corners of the ceilings.

Resignedly, Lois put down the brush she had been attaching for the books, knelt over the humming machine, and silenced its motor. Whoever was at the door was adamant, the bell sent up an insistent summons. If it was that woman with *The Watchtower* again—

Lois opened the door and stood for a moment transfixed, her whole head an empty blackness. She clutched the doorknob and clung to it while a voice she hardly recognized as her own said, "How did you ever find us?" All communications to him had gone out through the lawyer's office; she had taken the precaution of having an unlisted telephone.

"It isn't hard—if you know how," he said. He had gained a lot of weight, looked thicker and broader, off balance. It was the jacket, the wrong cut, the shoulders too padded, and he had the puffy, unhealthy look of the man who drinks too much. It was false weight he had put on, that was what gave his face such a bloated look.

He did not wait for her to ask him in, but brushed past her as if he had every right in the world to walk in any time he wanted. She saw that for a fact he felt he had. He was her husband, whether he supported her or their child or not. When he came back, he could come back to her. If he felt like it. And if he didn't—well . . .

She closed the door, shocked to find her whole body trembling.

"Nice place you've got here," he said from the middle of the living room, where he had taken a stance like a boxer's. After a pause when she didn't answer he added, "Must set you back a pretty penny. The kid back there?" He jerked his head in the direction of the hall. "I'd like to take a look at her."

Every instinct in Lois rebelled against his even looking at Constance, but this was hardly the time for a scene. He had come at an hour when it was almost impossible to summon help. The best thing would be to try to get rid of him without arguments that might escalate themselves into bad scenes.

She went past him, preceding him into the bedroom where the child lay asleep, too large for her crib.

He looked down into the sleeping face, silent. It was difficult to tell what he was feeling. Certainly his expression didn't give him away. After a moment he started prowling about the room. When he came to her dresser, he fingered the blue leather jewel case, casually turned back the top. Her wedding ring lay amidst the earrings and pins. "So you're not wearing that any more," he said, turning to examine her. He spread out his own hand, looked at the thick gold band, then suddenly slipped it off and threw it into the box. "Now you've got a pair," he said and snapped the case shut.

Lois waited for him to go back to the living room, away from the intimacy of this room, but he had begun a small circuitous tour, touching an object here and there, opening a bureau drawer, looking into the closet, standing at last next to her bed.

"You might at least say you're glad to see me," he said, and she was astonished to see he was absolutely serious; he thought she ought to be glad he was back.

Unable to answer, unsure of how much control she had, she turned and left him there by the bed. Back in the living room, she found her breathing heavy and hard in the midst of a murderous demand for violence that was flooding through her. For the first time she understood the uncontrollable impulse that made ordinary people into the bold black headlines of the tabloids.

With the rage mounting higher and higher, she knew there would come a point when her body would no longer be able to contain its anger, and then what would happen?

She didn't know. She could only grip her hands together, suffused with a terrible dark throbbing. It seemed to her she had never known what hatred was before.

He was back there in *her* bedroom—

She went into the kitchen and ran water, drank down first one glass, then another. Emotion had given her a thirst that was almost as engulfing as the feeling of bitterness inside. She would give him five minutes, five minutes and no more. . . .

The second hand moved slowly from three to four, four to five. It seemed to her impossible that one minute, twelve turns on the dial of that red hand, would ever pass. She ran the water and drank another glass. She looked around for her cigarettes. *What was he doing back there in* HER *bedroom?*

Then he was at the door, looking at her as he had looked at Constance, mildly curious. "Aren't you even going to offer me a drink?" he asked.

She opened the refrigerator and took out one beer—she would not drink with him—and went for a glass. "No whisky?" he asked in the same flat, unemotional voice. She shook her head, wondering if he would start opening cupboards to prove her the liar she was.

She set the glass and can down on the small table where the toaster and clock-radio rested. He gave a little grimace of acceptance and poured uncarefully, letting the beer foam. He lifted the glass and drank, then picked up the can and moved back toward the living room.

I've got to get through it, Lois told herself. There's no way out. I've got to sit down and talk to him, try to be reasonable, *unexcited*. She turned off the kitchen light and went into the living room. The vacuum line lay like a snake in the midst of the rug, the dirty dusting cloth like a fouled nest on the end table. He was sitting on the couch, hunched forward, pouring beer. She extinguished the overhead light, leaving the lamp in the hall alone to light the room. Somehow it seemed easier and safer to face him in partial darkness.

Her cigarettes were on the coffee table. She would rather not smoke than go near him.

"So," he said, not looking up, "here I am."

The air was like an apparatus of breathing between them. She could feel the room go in and out, in and out, the oxygen being used up; she felt herself fighting for breath.

"I take it you're not exactly overjoyed to see me."

The room inhaled, hung for a moment in its own laboring, exhaled; weight came down on her, crushing her.

"Well—I suppose I can hardly blame you. But still—" He picked up her cigarettes and took one. Putting a match to the cylinder in his mouth, he made contact; fire burned from the ends of tobacco, around the little white paper. He let out a plume of smoke, satisfied, dropped the smoldering match in the ashtray. "Still I suppose it would have been silly to expect you would." She stared at him, a man she hardly knew, partially obscured by smoke. "Not," he continued, giving an impatient shake of his head, "that I thought you would. But it never hurts to ask, as they say." It was, it occurred to her, a speech he must have prepared; else how could he deliver it without exposing one nerve? "So what I came about—outside of seeing the kid, of course—was to find out where we stood. What's to be done," he explained, "you know, to straighten out the mess."

He paused, refreshing himself from his beer. "There another one of these in the icebox?"

Mechanically she got up and went into the kitchen. It infuriated her beyond reason that he, who had never sent her a cent, should be drinking her beer, smoking her cigarettes, sitting on her furniture, moving freely around her rooms as if he owned them.

"I could probably get the goods on you here," he said from the doorway in that voice she remembered, the one of challenge and hatred and male triumph. "But it'd take time and it'd cost dough, so—" She waited, a pulse trembling all over her body, the room sucking her in and out in its breathing. "So I thought if we could work it out, you know, as they say, in a civilized way, we'd be better off.

"I got this lawyer," he said, "and he tells me it's no trouble at all—down in Alabama—if the parties agree, if they don't want to cause one another any trouble. Two, three days," he said, "that's all it takes if we work it out *amicably* up here first."

Then he started toward her. A terrible premonition filled her. "But, of course, if you said the word—" And then he had hold of her shoulders, he was raising her up, pulling her toward him, and one word—she was not even sure it was ever uttered—"*No*" came from her, but he was holding her to him, his pride in ruins. "I came here—I took all this trouble to track you down—because—because I wanted to try again. And that's the truth, Lois. Only I just don't know how to say it. God, you don't know how I missed you. I wanted to write—I did but, I don't know, something wouldn't let me send the letters. I thought you probably wouldn't want to hear from me.

"And it's funny, I missed the kid, too, even though I didn't really know what she looked like, I missed her. I missed hell out of both of you," he said, pressing her close to him, trying to make contact. "Take me back," he said, "give me another chance."

This collapse was far worse than anything she could have imagined. Anger, hostility, sarcasm, the desire for revenge, yes, but complete capitulation—that she had no way to deal with. It touched her, pled with her, the way bluster never could.

"I've been so lonely, so goddam lonely," he said, "you'll never know."

He was a human being in need, a person in pain, someone whose rights she had to recognize even if they were over her, and she felt a feeling of responsibility for him so strong that it seemed to her almost like love. She felt as if she were being asked to make a choice between decency and bravery and it was an impossible one to make. She was choked with pity, and that spoiled her hatred of him.

She pushed away from him, so stricken that even the ordinary act of ambulation seemed a labor too immense to undertake.

He stood before her, contrition surrounding him like an aura. They were two people, she and Cliff, who had wanted to love each other but couldn't, and this inadequacy had led to guilt, to hatred, and now to despair. It wasn't love they felt for each other at this moment, but the old demand to make amends. And she knew where that led. He who repents and repents and repents must eventually go back to repeat what he repents of.

She had committed crimes against herself—but who hadn't? The question was, Was she ever going to absolve herself of making mistakes, committing sins, augmenting evil?

I am not my mother, Lois thought. I refuse to recognize suffering as our only end. I have atoned, she thought, all I can.

I will not take him back.

Lois looked out at the lighted windows of Manhattan, staring at her with a thousand eyes like imputations from the rooms in back of them. Carolers were making their way unsteadily out of the corner bar, their arms upraised, their voices tipsily out of tune but raised in praise of The Birth.

She and Neal had been very wary of each other since her return over a month before. There were many things still to be said and their hesitancy to go ahead came from their knowledge of just how final those words might be. Yet the words would have to be said, or the gesture made, silent; it was merely a matter of time, or timing.

I can't go through with it, she thought, not the awful awkwardness of getting out of clothes—ugly, ugly—pulling things over my head, the hideous noises of zippers and cloth, buttons that won't come unstuck, and then the nakedness, that terrible moment when you consent to be gazed on and judged, the danger of being looked at, the fear of being seen and touched and judged. (Yet why else had she put on the black lace slip, new, the matching pants and bra?)

Love is the absence of anxiety, a probing mind had suggested— one that ought to know, having spent a lifetime listening to the sick, the anxious, the unloved.

Yet it was as if her heart were saying with every stroke, I can't, I just can't. *How am I to know it will be all right this time?*

How does anyone know anything? she asked herself.

In the past, she thought, I have sometimes made myself do things out of guilt, out of a misplaced sense of responsibility. Yet you gain nothing by trying *not* to carry your responsibilty to others as far as it should go; even I know that. Love is demonstration as well as demand. Perhaps it is a mistake to trust love as the passport to life, but if one does so give one's faith, one must act as if the law were so. Nothing is ever proved or disproved, after all, without *some* initial assumption. Since I have chosen to live my life as if love were its prime source, I cannot now turn my back on the obligations it chooses to thrust forth. Self-immolation is, after all, only one side of that service. There is the other—about which I know little.

But that does not mean I cannot learn.

What Neal must understand was that, for her, mind and flesh were one. She could not separate the longings and comforts of the flesh from the longings and comforts of the mind; they were bound together in a common pact to protect and aid each other; so long as one was unfulfilled, the other cried out in anger; when the body protested its needs, the mind took them and used them as fuel for all the reasons one should not love, and when the mind was restless and dissatisfied, all the impulses it sent out upset the equilibrium of the body. She needed a sated body and a full mind not to rebel against the limitations that were the compromises and sacrifices people must make against the loss of individuality that meant marriage. All I have ever become I owe to love, someone had said, and it struck her he might have added, And all that I can hope to become.

Unnoticed, Neal had taken his place at her side. Together they looked down on the small sleeping child. It had been a lovely day, a lovely dinner; in a moment they should move of one accord toward that act which might begin to create for them a life together of their own. Nothing now really stood in their way except themselves, he with his eternal feeling of being outside, *unloved,* Lois thought; that is what his Jewishness means to him, that he can't, mustn't be, loved, and I with my endless dread that I can't feel enough or that I feel too much, my inability to rely on myself as a center of belief, never ever allowing myself a little peace. We are so much afraid of the intensity of our desires, we turn our backs on them, Neal and I. We say to ourselves, Beware of entanglement, eschew involvement, don't trust anything that asks a price. But she also believed: only those who feel free to run up enormous debts, who are unafraid of what prices must be paid, are at liberty to live.

She turned and looked at Neal. He was here, safe; he had not been a member of the cattle cars, one of those, naked, thrust into the crematoriums, whose teeth (and gums) had been yanked out, whose body was thrown in the trenches and flamed into fertilizer; he had escaped by the lucky stroke of having been born in the land of the green—but still loveless—passport. Though they painted JUDE on his sidewalk, they did not issue him the yellow star; though he might be excluded from country clubs, no one cordoned him off in ghettos from which, in a matter of months, he would be "resettled"; though there were places that would be restricted from his presence and clubs he could not join, one place he would never be sent was the crematoriums, one club he would never belong to was the line leading to the room where the injection of phenol stopped the heart instantly and economically.

As a Jew it was somehow his duty to have been there: that was what Neal could never forgive himself. And yet in his heart he was glad he had escaped. All his life guilt would enclose him in a covering of the accident of his birth; all his life he would see that the only way out of liability would have been never to be born a Jew.

It was not bitterness that bowed Neal but self-blame. Too heavy a mantle of guilt. It had bound her and made her afraid, impoverished her ability to give, broken down her belief in the unforeseen, chained her to an unproductive past.

No one could bring back Neal's dead. One could mourn them, could care for them, could make, perhaps, living pledges in their name, but one could never ever resurrect even one of those six million dead. The cruelty of the truth again—she touched his untattooed arm, ashamed, but it was Neal she loved, not some symbol of suffering for which they should all atone. One gave up guilt, one grew out of the habit of it, when one saw it was useless and no longer of any help. She wanted to say, So then shall we two band together, Neal, you and I, to make a jest? Shall we deny what we know, decry the idea that each in his own life is prisoner of an eternal, solitary, and ill-conceived confinement? *Have we not been given mouths for music and arms to embrace, minds for making myths and marvelous brains to scheme and create?*

Shall we not say?

Why, having what no other creature claims, no other mind knows, no other heart condones, should we be afraid of being all alone?

Should we not instead laugh and say:

I shall love and live my life no matter what barriers have been put in the way.

The bus time had come. You never heard the agonies of those engines during the day; their suffering had too many other anguishes to compete with. All over Manhattan during the daylight hours the cries of pain canceled one another out, but late at night each individual plea—a pair of high heels ricocheting on concrete, an angry argument unconcealed behind tender walls, a child's stricken cry, the ceaseless groans of the big buses—came clear, isolated, complete. It was no longer possible to close off one's heart then against the knowledge of helplessness all about. Nothing was ever final, nothing ever completely understood. There was no way to know the finished facts so that one could strike out a segment of one's life. The buses came and went, grinding out their endless pain, and somewhere, Lois was sure, another girl lay frightened, unsure, sleepless on her bed watching overhead lights on the ceiling, hearing the sound of those bitter buses carrying their burdens back and forth through the night, and wondering how she would pay the rent, raise a fatherless child, make something of her life.

Outside, now that sound of suffering rose; she and Neal, silent, listened over the darkened dining table, drinking their after-dinner coffee, the last light of the candles hissing against the pools of melted wax in the bottoms of the silver candlesticks (one of the few of her wedding presents she had kept). In a moment the wicks would be extinguished in that hot wax; they would be left only in the forty-watt light from the hall, the fainter flicker of cigarette ends as they glittered against their mute mouths, in the flush at the windows of a Manhattan sky never fully extinguished. It was a city afraid to leave its people in the dark.

The dirty dishes (rinsed, guilt—duty—carried over even into the kitchen) were stacked in the sink, the child (crossly spoken to at the end, ersatz patience put-upon soon turns upon itself) thinly asleep down the hall: somewhere someone turned the pages of Eliot's thin black book and read

The time is now propitious, as he guesses,

but not, Lois knew, lowering her head, eyes closed for an instant in response to the hollowness at the center of her heart, propitious enough. Perhaps it would never again be. She had learned her lessons too well.

She saw still the cat at the window; its cries were a part forever of her look at life. What she had seen had taught her to shrink back.

If I give, I shall be hurt . . . each time worse than the last because each time takes more of an act of endeavor. In the beginning we rush for an embrace, but at the end—

I have not the courage to be held and hurt again.

Something must be said (something must *always* be said, the silences are too terrible); he was handing her words. They came across the table like gifts of great import whose wrappings she was unable to undo; she would never know what was inside, fumbling to open what was unknowable. She bent forward as if in the act of listening, but the sounds were like stakes driven through her heart: he was saying something about leaving. He rose as if to go, stood suspended in the altar light from the table, a tall dark figure whose hand held a cigarette now being smashed against the bottom of the glass ashtray under the open-throated roses.

"I have not the courage to be held and hurt again," she said.

"I know that. That's why I'm going." A finality of sorts, she supposed. His eyes did not tell, nor his hands. There was no way of knowing. This, or anything. Even what she herself really wanted. Somewhere the secret might be hidden (in her mother's bending back in that tanned man's arms? in her father's twisting his gray felt hat in assured hands? somewhere—where?), but she had no way now of ever going into the recesses of the heart and mind and finding out. She was like one who knew the history of her past but not what to make of it, because there was no one thing that held it together and gave it shape. It came to her for an instant that this one thing might be the terrible truth that no one had suffered for any of these things that had hurt her except herself. She hated still because she had had no revenge. She had let her life be obsessed by the worst in it. And it was this unacknowledged desire that had eaten away the best of her instincts and left her with only those that were low and mean and that made her afraid.

We must furnish our futures with something besides hate: grant me the grace once again of giving, she implored, rose, and went, still unsure, but armed with a kind of false courage in all their futures—hers, Neal's, even Constance's—toward him, unable, even as he took her in his arms, to believe the words faltering in her ears, Lois, oh Lois, touch me. . . . Oh Lois, I love you, *touch me . . .*

Chapter 12

THE LAST STROKE of the drum sounded, the band struck up a militant "Auld Lang Syne," people were blowing horns, snapping noise-makers, confetti streamed, balloons burst, couples embraced, the air resounded with cries for the New Year. Ralph stood beside her, hands at his side; a moment later he vanished. Men she scarcely knew gave her wet whisky kisses, a circle formed, hand over hand, and people, some tearful, some smiling, began to sing.

> *Should auld acquaintance be forgot,*
> *And days of auld lang syne,*
> SHOULD *auld acquaintance be forgot . . .*

"Carolyn," he said and bent, lightly brushing her cheek with dry, insensitive lips.

"Myers—"

> *Should auld acquaintance* BE *forgot*

Then he was gone. A woman Carolyn remembered seeing at the bar earlier grabbed her and shouted into her face, released her, laughed, and, carrying a large lemon-colored balloon, rose up into the arms of the first passing man and was loudly bussed. All about, bodies pressed up against one another, the strain of that throat-choking song pierced the air, men and women were lifting glasses and laughing. In some far-away place at this magic hour did people still unmask and weep and wish each other well?

Carolyn fought her way through the throngs, avoided being embraced by a man she intensely disliked, submitted to another she did not mind, caught her dress on the end of a couch, bent to release it, and rose to find herself clasped about the waist, staring into the mindless eyes of the club drunk, who, holding onto her, was trying desperately to say something and while she waited, standing still as a statue, he blurted it out. "Happy—happy *new* year," he cried.

"Happy New Year," Carolyn answered, pulling away from him and moving onto the landing where, a few feet away, stairs descended to the lower level and the ladies' room. People were kissing one another extravagantly on the landing; at the bottom of the stairs a man was fumbling over the body of a woman not his wife and when he looked up briefly, as Carolyn passed, he leered into her face, his eyes magnified with drink, his lips rolled back in greed.

Farther down Carolyn saw two bodies in back of the coats groping at each other and near the end of the hall a couple disappearing, coatless, outdoors toward the cars.

Carolyn opened the door to the ladies' room, stepped inside, quickly closed the door behind her. Here all was quiet save for a steady dripping from a faucet in the lavatory, the incessant hum of a fan somewhere overhead.

She sat down and stared into the mirror in front of her. Her make-up was intact, her hair hardly needed straightening, the folds of her dress were in place, even her eyes were all right. She hadn't had a drink all night. What she had come to see was whether anything showed—in her face, in the way she held her head, most of all in her eyes. But the image on the quicksilver in front of her looked ordinary and urbane. There were no telltale marks of anger, no signs of the cast-aside woman fraught for revenge, not one single trace of the savagery she felt inside.

She opened her evening bag and took out the gold compact Ralph had given her for Christmas; it opened with a small clip set in semi-precious stones which, when Carolyn touched it, flew up to expose a shallow well of powder, a miniature mirror, and, along one gold side, her initials, C. A. T. Carolyn Ashwell Tryson. Cat. It had been a nickname, an intimacy, of Ralph's around the time Wesley was born, but he hadn't used it in months. She wondered whether he had been conscious of that when he'd ordered her present and asked on purpose for the initials to be put there or if he had automatically used the nickname without remembering the weeks of silence before Christmas, the estrangement, the confession. Even that drunken Christmas Eve he seemed to have put out of his mind when, handing her the present Christmas morning, he had smiled.

There was no way of telling. He was a quiet man who kept to himself and if, as tonight, he saw her drink soda or quinine, a glass of ginger ale, he had said nothing, though she imagined she saw in back of his eyes a small stirring, as if he were ingesting new material for the machine that was his mind, that file of odd facts and uninteresting statistics that he used to fill in ordinary conversation. "Did you know the leading country for pianos is not the U. S. but Japan—not Steinway or Wurlitzer but some company called Nippon Gakki?" "Practically no tin at all is mined in the United States." "It is not Mohicans actually, but Mahicans."

Percentages were a passion with him; graphs and charts caused strange sensations to overcome him; he was held enthralled by numerical averages. Somewhere inside him an enormous computer must be ticking away, and tonight when he looked at her he fed it new data: *December 31–January 1 Carolyn Ashwell Tryson my wife not drinking,* and the gears moved, buttons flashed, cards went through, and he came out with some kind of answer, though what it might be she had no idea. Over all his emotions he threw a smoke screen; behind his eyes he camouflaged the currents of his mind; whatever moved his heart was cunningly concealed by intricate devices.

If you lived with a man year after year you were supposed to know him, and there was, of course, an infinite amount of information she had accumulated. She knew his favorite foods, his quirks about clothes, the temperature he liked his bedclothing, the way he arranged his drawers. But of the larger issues—what held his life together, which values made up his beliefs, even about his god—she knew nothing. He remained a man in hiding.

Someone opened the door and Carolyn stood up. A woman, crying, was holding a handkerchief to her face. "Carolyn?" she said uncertainly through the linen pressed to her mouth and then slumped down on one of the vanity stools; head sagged to limp arms, she began to sob as if her life had been destroyed. A moment later her purse, a small black satin bag with rhinestone studs along the edge, slipped to the floor, lipstick rolled under the far couch, a mirror broke, and Carolyn, not knowing what else to do, stooped and began to assemble coin purse, comb, perfume vial, some keys.

Then she stood up, laid the evening purse beside the bent head, and said uneasily, "Is there anything I can do?"

A violent shaking of the head was the answer; an instant later a tear-splotched face raised itself up and Ginny Mathewson said, "I've had too much to drink." But she didn't look drunk, Myers' wife. None of the signs were there and who, Carolyn thought, should know them better than I?

She must be very calm, she must keep control; above all else there could not be a scene in the ladies' room of the club. There might be a lot else, but there could not be that. She owed Ralph something, after Christmas Eve.

Coolly, Carolyn opened her purse and extracted cigarettes, held them out. Ginny did not want one. It was only a second later Carolyn remembered that Ginny did not smoke. They had been together enough so that she should have remembered.

While she lighted her own, Carolyn ran through the alternatives —flight, brazening it out, stalling for time. She chose the last because she could not make up her mind which was the least dangerous. Anything, it occurred to her, looking at the distraught face in front of her, might be dangerous if Ginny *knew*.

"You want an aspirin or something?" Carolyn said into the silence that was like a growing thing between them, seeming even to have a color, green, on which her eyes froze, the color of Ginny's gown, high-necked, long-sleeved, the sort of dress you bought to wear year after year and changed with a belt, a clip, a new pin.

Myers' wife shook her head, adamant. "I—" She bit a wet lip, struggled, blinked back tears, raised the sodden handkerchief, sniffled, blew, bit her lip again, looked down, derelict, bereft, a woman without pride, without—*areté,* the word Lois had used.

"I—I—oh Carolyn, what am I going to do? He's gone off again. He goes off with any woman who'll go with him, and everyone knows. Everyone. It's so—so humiliating. I mean, I try to pretend, but—on the dance floor—just now—did you see? With that Walters woman? I've never been so ashamed in my life. Everyone was watching. Everyone."

She doesn't know, Carolyn thought disbelievingly, while she watched Myers' wife blow her nose, wipe at her eyes.

"I'm sorry—I'm so sorry—but you don't know, you have no idea what it's like—always waiting, always watching, knowing it's just a matter of time—"

It was as if Carolyn were listening to Ralph; Ralph was being repeated, here in this room. Perhaps that's what pain was, a repetition: anguish had to be renewed, got through, all over again each day, and part of pain was the refusal to believe what was. We all tell lies to ourselves to go on, she thought.

"—and then you think after a while you'll get used to it, but you never do. Never. It's just as painful the twentieth time as it was the first and—and I just can't take it any more, I've come to the end of my patience, it's just too much to expect me to go through. I can't, it's gone on for so long I've even forgotten what it was like to laugh and have a good time, look forward to something. Now I just get through, I just go on from day to day, as if it were an ordeal—it is an ordeal—I wish sometimes I were dead. I'd be better off than being like this, just—just *pitied* and laughed at all the time." The tears ran down her face, her mouth quivered and grimaced.

"You don't know what it's like. You have absolutely no idea what it's like to be married to a man you can never count on. Ralph, he—" Ginny Mathewson brought the crumpled handerchief to her eyes. "Oh, I'm so miserable," she cried, "I'm so unhappy. Perky Walters—that's just the last straw."

In back of Carolyn, the dripping faucet seemed to pick up pace, the fan suddenly turned on high. With great effort she lifted one arm and put another cigarette between her lips. The paper came away and she felt a little flicker of pain. Striking a match, she held it up and inhaled, watching the fire dance up, die.

"I've never liked her—never. That's why he did it, because he knows I can't stand her. He's trying to get back at me because—because—Carolyn," she cried, her head dropping onto her arms again, "I'm going to have another baby. I thought I was all over that—and I'm going to have another child. Isn't that awful, at my age?"

Carolyn stared.

"I've got—I've just got to pull myself together. I'm so sorry, Carolyn, I just can't help it. Perky Walters. I don't know what to do—at my age, oh it's too ridiculous."

"You're not that old," Carolyn said mechanically.

"I'm over forty, I've got a girl in high school. Timmy's twelve. How will it look?"

Carolyn had no answer. She really didn't know.

"So you see—" Her voice trailed off. "Why did he have to do it? Tonight of all nights? We had such a nice Christmas, everything was going so well, I'd told him—you know—about being that way—and he seemed—I thought—why did he do it? Oh, why did he do it, tonight of all nights?"

It was the question women always seemed to be asking of their men or men of their women, Carolyn thought.

"I've got to do something about my face, I'm just a mess. My eyes look awful. And my head's splitting, just splitting. I don't suppose we'll go home for hours. You know how he always likes to put the party to bed." She went into the other room, where the washbasins, the toilets, were. Carolyn heard water running.

She and Ralph hadn't slept together in months. There had seemed to Carolyn something immoral about making love with Ralph when it was Myers she cared about, Myers to whom her body had committed itself. Yet all the time Myers—

All the times he had held her in his arms, all the times he had been inside her, it had all been a lie. And suddenly, as if this moment had been waiting to come to her, she had an image of all the times he had taken her hand and pressed it against him. "You want it? You want it—say so!" The memory shamed her because it brought back forcefully their whole private language of love, those odd phrases with which he had taken her, cupping hot hands over her loosened breasts and whispering, "How are your bazookers— they lonely?" and then running his hand down her belly, over her flanks, "And your pussycat, that lonely, too? You want a little screwing? You want a little of the business?" while under his hands her body turned, bedclothes tumbled all about, heaving, they lifted themselves on one another, their flesh wet and sticky and making sucking noises.

Ginny Mathewson stood in the doorway, her face stripped of make-up. She looked old and half sick. "Have you got any lipstick, Carolyn? I seem to have lost mine."

"It rolled under the couch."

Down on her hands and knees, her dress in the dust, Myers' wife groped. "Oh, here it is." She straightened up. "I'm—I'm so sorry, Carolyn, so terribly sorry I—"

"It's all right."

Ginny Mathewson spread out a tissue, laid down a powder case, eyebrow pencil, mascara, the lipstick on top; in a moment she was maneuvering make-up over her face, covering pores, working with reddened eyes, drawing on a happy red mouth. When she laid the lipstick down, she spread her blood-colored nails out and looked at them. "I'd leave him," she said in a voice so low that Carolyn had to strain forward to hear, "if I had any place to go. But the truth is, with the kids and all—I—we're up to our ears in debt. Maybe that's what keeps us together, the debts. He owes everybody," she said. "He's going to be posted here at the club if he doesn't do something, but what does he care? Does it bother him I have to go from store to store sometimes and plead for a little more credit? No, he's just out opening new accounts."

Across the bleakness of her face, an expression flickered. "And yet—you know, Carolyn, he can be so—so nice. Why does he have to ruin all our lives when he could—you know—be like other husbands? But he can't," she said. "He isn't made that way."

Carolyn stood at the door, one hand on the knob. She felt it was impossible to listen any longer. Ginny Mathewson was looking at her and gratitude shone from her eyes, a weak smile fastened itself to her face. "I can't tell you, Carolyn, how much I appreciate your just listening to me. If it had been anyone else—but, I don't know, you always seem so—so remote from the others, the way they talk. You don't gossip. I always think of you," Ginny Mathewson said with a catch in her voice, "as a good person."

Choked, blinded, deafened, Carolyn opened the door. She had gone as far down as she could go. No matter what happened to her after this she would never be able to forget—or face—that simple sentence. At the last, after every excuse, it would still be there to smite her. God might not listen in the kitchen but somewhere He was always waiting, no matter what name you called Him, even the self which had to tally up its own accounts, and what was God but a calling to account? Somewhere He always waited, as the reckoning.

For the first time Carolyn was conscious of Christ as a real figure, someone who had suffered, who had actually hung, suspended from nails, hour after hour, a man in torment, deserted, despairing, dying under an uncaring sky. He had suffered. It was the first time those words had meant anything to her. Like the rest of them He had suffered, and because of that she was able to feel close to Him, to understand, however little, what the pageant meant—the life and death of a man with a tongue that could make them have meaning. It was an individual to whom she paid tribute now, someone who, from fragmented episodes and meaningless phenomena, had fashioned a whole history, a purposeful pattern, an end for all of them, and lifted it from simple suffering and sacrifice to an act that meant more than its component parts, who had given to the suffering meaning.

Ultimately, Carolyn thought, it was not man who should ask *why?* but life that should ask that question of each individual. Each man on his own should respond, as best he could, so that in the end it was not man who questioned life but life that questioned man.

And what would you answer, what would you say when life asked, *To what purpose?* Something inside said, To be responsible, that is the essence of what we should all be, responsible.

It seemed to her that to be responsible you had to confront your fears and name them—love, alcohol, unworthiness—whatever they were, and they were legion, ask anyone. But only after you labeled them were you able to live with them, to act against them.

"My wife in there?" He had been drinking heavily and his face was flushed, the lines around his eyes pronounced, the mouth slightly open, sensual, moist. He took hold of her shoulders, bringing her closer to him repeating, "My wife in there?" holding her imprisoned under firm fingers, and she waited for her flesh to respond to his touch, as it always did, almost as if the whole of her poured toward him when he touched her. He might at any moment bend over and whisper, "I've been looking everywhere for you, where have you been?" so that she was not surprised when his head came close to hers and he said in a low, hoarse voice, "Christ, you look beautiful in that dress."

She closed her eyes and stepped back, swaying slightly. "She's— inside. Ginny's in there," she heard herself say in almost a whisper as the odor of liquor assaulted her, his hands came up and pulled at her arm and he pushed her through a half-open door across the hall and kicked it closed; he was holding her against him in an angry embrace, teeth cutting into her lips, tongue tasting of alcohol, the whole of his mouth rank with tobacco, whisky, other women's mouths.

"You are an evil person," she said against his open mouth, "an evil, evil person. Let me go."

Ralph was having trouble getting the car started. It was the cold, he said. The engine coughed and sputtered, seemed for a moment ready to catch, then died with a complaining whine, while Ralph pumped up and down on the accelerator, pulled out the choke, muttered under his breath.

A small sprinkling of snow had started, a few flakes falling here and there through the dark ruff of night. Moonless, the night lay around them like something solid. Ralph, ramming at the motor, suddenly paused and looked out. "Lot of snow this year," he said, and then after a pause, "God, it's cold out here."

"Three o'clock in the morning coldness."

"What?"

"Fitzgerald—there are times it seems as if it will be three o'clock in the morning forever."

"Oh."

He began working with the starter again.

She wondered when—or if—he was going to say something about the evening. Since Christmas Eve, something had been settled. But it was hard to put into words just what. Not like the hands Myers had put around her, which were implacable in a basic indifference born of some kind of perverse politeness that prompted him to parody passion, as if it was his duty as a gentleman to make a pass at her—while his wife cried in the ladies' room and pressed palms over the parturient abdomen. But Carolyn in all her shame knew that nothing could ever redress those public tears; what was worse, there had been no redemptive payment demanded of her. She had got off scot-free; her husband still loved her, the big house rose round protecting her, her children were well and strong and reasonably brilliant—they would go to the best colleges; even the face reflected in the windshield in front of her did not look its age; she was still a striking woman, one men would turn to gaze after, one who inspired desire. Lucky, lucky Carolyn Ashwell—Tryson.

"It won't go," he said at last.

"Let it rest. Maybe it's flooded."

"All right, but aren't you cold? I can't remember when it's been this cold." When he spoke, his breath made steam. Between them it faded, vanishing forever.

"I'll survive."

"Maybe we should call a cab." Politely he reached over and offered her a cigarette; she might have been someone else's wife, the way he was behaving. "You have a good time?" he asked. "I thought it was—I don't know, more out of bounds than usual. You weren't drinking at all," he said after a pause.

"No."

After a silence, he said, "It makes it—easier."

"Yes, I guess it does."

"I was surprised," he said after a moment.

"I know—I know it isn't easy for you—when I've been drinking —that *nothing's* been easy for you, Ralph."

"No, it hasn't. I love you, Cat. I've always loved you. Sometimes I don't want to but I always have, I always will."

"I'm sorry, Ralph, I wish—I wish, I really wish, I'd made you happier. It isn't because I didn't want to."

"Maybe I'm not—not enough for you. I thought, back when we got rid of the other house, I thought we might work something out, and for a time I thought it was possible to start over, change things, and we did, for a while, and then it all changed, all slid back to where it was. Now sometimes I think we're worse off than we were —before."

"Ralph," she said slowly, "I want you to give me a divorce. I want to give you a chance, another chance, to start over. You could still make another life for yourself—"

"What do you mean 'make another life for myself?' You're my life."

"But the life you've made with me isn't a good one. You know that yourself."

"Don't talk like that," he said sharply.

"I feel—I feel the only way I can make up for what I've done— don't you see, Ralph," she pleaded. "If you were to start over, find someone else—" He shook his head impatiently. "Yes, you could. You could find someone else if you looked and—"

"I don't want anyone else."

"But how can you keep on with someone—someone who's hurt you so?"

"I'm not like you. I'm slow and when I make up my mind, it stays made up. And when I feel something I can't just turn it off and on. I didn't marry you for as long as I thought it would go well, I married you for the rest of my life and—" He had his arms around her and she felt herself pull back. "Don't, Carolyn, please don't. I can't stand it when you're like this."

"I can't help it. You're so good and I—"

"Please don't. Please—let—me—touch you."

"Ralph, I—I *can't.*"

"*Can't?*"

"It's something I can't control. I want to—I want to be close to you, you'll never know how much I want to, but—we've never—never made love as if it mattered—not for years and years—and there's nothing left now—there's nothing left there, it isn't that kind of love any more—and that kind of love, that's the beginning, what everything else is built on. We don't feel that way about each other any more—we haven't, not in years—and that's—that's important to me. I want someone who wants me, really wants me, someone who makes love as if it matters—we"—she faltered—"we don't *feel* alike," she said. "We don't react to things the same way, our whole way of seeing things is different. Our whole way of feeling things is different."

"And you think if you got a divorce, you'd be better off?"

"I think *we*'d be better off. You'd—"

"Carolyn, don't you care for me at all? Haven't all these years made any difference?"

"I feel," she said slowly, "that I've done a bad thing, a very bad thing, and I should pay for it. It's like one of the children, the way I love them, that's the way I feel about you, Ralph, and that's—"

"That's not enough," he finished for her.

"No, that's not enough."

"And you don't think it will ever be any more."

"No," she said. "We've had years and years—and it's always been the same, something was missing, and no matter how we tried we could never fill up what wasn't there, we always had an emptiness in our lives, where that something should have been; and I know part of what was missing was my fault—because I wanted so much, *too* much, and I didn't give enough myself, but that was because there was something missing in me, too, and as time went by I couldn't seem to find myself, something was lost somewhere, and I didn't know where, I didn't even know *what,* just that there was an important part missing and I had to find it."

"And you think divorcing me will help you find it?"

"I've gone on for such a long time letting things happen, shaping my life by what's happening *outside,* but what's inside, the things—

the decisions—I should be making myself, the substance that should be inside, that's just a blank."

"Supposing you were to go away for a little while?" he asked. "Say you went for a little while some place, by yourself, do you think that might make a difference?"

"I don't know—it might."

"Would you give it a try?" He stepped on the starter. The motor suddenly caught. "Will you think it over, Carolyn, give us a little time to work something out?"

"A little time to work something out?"

"I know I've disappointed you, Carolyn. You wanted so much and I just couldn't give it to you. I wanted to, but I couldn't. It wasn't there to give. But, Carolyn, Cat—oh Cat, I wanted to be what you wanted, but sometimes I didn't know what it was, sometimes I wasn't sure even you knew, and now—don't tell me it's too late. You know there's a lot of real hurt in love, you can't help the hurt. I know this has been hard, there's one thing I've told myself I'd never ask, but it's something I've got to know. Are you leaving me because of *him*? Is that why you're going—because you want to go to him? Because you love him, the way you can't love me?"

"No," she said slowly and with finality. "I don't love him—I don't think I ever did. It was something else. And it's over now. I saw that tonight. Maybe I knew before, Christmas Eve, but I didn't really realize it because I was in a kind of shock, I was numb, frightened, I couldn't see anything the way it really was. And I was drinking, that was a part of it, everything was distorted in the alcohol, I felt unreal, everything was out of focus, I was going through whole days without realizing what was happening."

He reached around her and flicked on the heater. The sound of forced air filled the car. Over his shoulder she saw the snow falling faster now, the world outside was white. She had loved him—she had hated him—more, she thought, than anyone in her life. And now? Even the hate was gone, all that endless engulfing hate she had felt only a week before—repetition had enfeebled it. Daily it had devoured itself until there was almost nothing left. Impatience —that was what she supposed she felt. Perhaps even a little pity. But mostly nothingness. You could not will love, any more than you could sustain hate, though it was easier to prolong anger than ardor. She did not love him. That was all there was to it. She did not love him and all the best intentions in the world would never lead her to it. But, in the pity she held for him, she could not say it. She just wanted to be away—*rid of him.*

"Cat, oh Cat, I love you so much. Let me make love to you so that it matters . . . please let me try . . . at least let me try . . . give me that much of a chance."

He had his hands hard on her shoulders. Did he mean to make love to her here? In an automobile? In the parking lot of the country club?

"Cat . . . oh Cat . . ." he said, his voice urgent, his hands at her breasts. "Don't . . . oh, don't . . . don't push me away . . . let me show you . . . oh, just let me show you . . . here . . ."

He had hold of her hand, he was trying to make her feel through the cloth of his pant leg the swollen center of his love. "Carolyn . . . oh Cat . . . Cat . . ."

"Don't, Ralph, please. Please don't . . . *stop it!*"

Then he was slumped behind the car wheel. "You really don't want me, do you?" Ruthless to himself, with or without statistics, he would always be. But she had been brought up in the wrong traditions so that somewhere deep down she still believed in the old untruthful laws of conduct. It was beyond her to tell him the truth: that she could not stand to have him touch her.

In the silence snow fell; they were shut in as if by falling ash: found entombed thousands of years from now—who would know what cruelties had just passed? A couple in a car. Well-dressed. Comfortable. Caught at the moment of going home after a dance. Her rings artifacts for some modest museum. Their bones a mildly interesting reconstruction of man, twentieth century, Americanus; would they also differentiate Middle West? No one would know that at this instant for both of them something was irrevocably ended. Time . . . or the heart . . . or a whole illusion about life . . . that love was worth all the words written about it . . .

"I'll get out tomorrow."

"Yes," she said, "I guess that would be best."

But what struck her was that even at the end he was the one who had to pay, who suffered most. She was to be left in the nice house with the children.

But then perhaps even this wasn't true. Humbled though he seemed, there behind the steering wheel, there was still something perfect, intact, an indestructible self. It occurred to her that his bones, uncovered thousands of years from now, should have solidified into some kind of statistic capable of being assembled, numbered, and made into a whole, the large scale of his life reduced to something small enough to make meaning and the men who worked over his remains would feel the chill faint dead breath of another man, someone like themselves capable of the quick, indefinable transition between joy and grief, at one moment filled with a sense of his own being, and the next plunged down into feeling that he had no excuse for ever feeling happy again. In Ralph's remains there would be meaning, whereas her own would have been ground down into fine silt around the hard uncrushable stones of her fingers and the bright glittering gold fillings of her teeth. Those who came on her would pass by as if she had never been. Perhaps that was her punishment—it was she who cared to be remembered, he only lived as best he could.

Chapter 13

CAROLYN PUSHED past Lois and looked at the bed where the ice-blue dress lay puffed out with tissue paper to keep the sleeves and bodice in place. It was a lovely dress, but all those buttons—it closed in back with a long row of buttons covered in the same silk as the gown, with hand-stitched loops that took forever to fasten. There must have been thirty-five or forty of those tiny little buttons—but Lois had wanted a dress that would look nice in back when she stood at the "altar." Now all Carolyn could think was how long it would take to do those buttons up. "Hurry, oh please hurry," she heard herself implore in a voice almost like her mother's. "I mean, there's so little time and—"

Lois was tissuing the cold cream off. "It won't take me long," she promised. "My hair's all done. All I have to do is put on make-up, the dress."

Carolyn sat on the bed and watched as Lois applied powder to her face. Her heavy hair was in two dark wings that made a frame around the heart-shaped face. It was a plain style, but very beautiful on Lois, showing up the clean, classic planes of her cheeks. She looked like a Cycladic idol, cut down to the bone in brutal blazing beauty, the mystery of the ages and of the female chiseled in her forehead and the smooth slope of her nose, that pure, straight, beautiful nose.

She was far more lovely in the severity of her style than Carolyn could ever be with her own modish—but, it now seemed to her, fussy—bouffant, so carefully combed out by Opal that morning. Carolyn thought of good-natured Opal, laughing, her wine-colored nails massaging Carolyn's scalp, her hands moving with deft precision teasing the hair, her teeth openly displayed in good nature.

Carolyn looked down at the polish on her own nails. She had taken the cigarettes and matches from the dresser a moment before; perhaps that was what had reminded her of Opal. But what gave her pause now was the torn match case she held in her hand. Myers always tore a used matchbook in two, an unconscious habit by which now she had tried at a distance to align herself with him, the magic motion of affixing herself by recreating one of his individual actions.

She had not, no matter what she told herself, stopped caring.

"I guess I'm ready for the buttons."

Carolyn stood up, feeling pierced suddenly and painfully by the memory of that moment in the kitchen when she had felt she couldn't go on, when she had prayed, supplicating a god who hadn't come. How could He come when *she* had lost Him? I knew it all right then, she thought, looking down at the torn match folder. But I couldn't root him out of my heart. I still haven't.

Her hands began to fumble with the beautiful blue buttons.

He had that same hideous ill-fitting suit on, but the face was no longer hangdog. What was Pete doing in the hall anyway? It was almost time for the ceremony to begin; Carolyn had just come out of Lois's room to check that everything was in order.

Embarrassed, but determined, he stood at the top of the stairs, obviously waiting for her. Well, Carolyn thought, there's no point in trying to avoid him, I might as well get it over with; and widening her mouth into what she hoped was a smile, she came abreast of him and put her hand lightly on his arm, said, "How are you, Pete? How's come you're not downstairs? We're just about ready to start."

He flushed, fished about in his pockets so that automatically Carolyn started to open her purse for cigarettes; then she remembered how little time there was.

"I guess—I mean—when I came out to your house that time—"

"Forget it."

"No, I—"

"Forget it, I have."

"I mean—I guess I said some things I shouldn't." Nervously he moved from one foot to another. "I had no right to say—what I did. You and Ralph, you've both been more than decent—I was pretty far along or I wouldn't have said anything. You know that, don't you, Carolyn?"

"It's all right. Forget it."

"You—you didn't say anything—to Ralph?"

"No."

"I mean, I mean—I wouldn't have blamed you if—you know— you'd been, well, mad enough to—to say something."

"I considered it from *your* point of view."

He gaped at her.

"Looked at objectively, I probably am no fucking good."

His eyes bulged, he seemed unable to speak.

"I mean, what have I got to show for what, such as it is, I am—it's all, as you so precisely put it, because of a rich husband; that hardly says anything for *me,* does it? It's more like it's the other way round: I'm something Ralph has to show for what he's earned out of life. Ralph's wife—and if you look at Ralph's wife, look at her close, what do you think? You think, poor Ralph. He's got that bitchy wife and he's such a nice man; wouldn't you think he deserved better?"

"Frances is wearing a beetle," her mother announced, appearing from behind the balustrade. "You'll have to speak to her. We can't have *bugs*—I don't care what South American country they came from—at Lois's nuptials." She grabbed Carolyn's arm. "There's time, there's still time." She began to drag Carolyn down the stairs. "Wouldn't you think just once in her life she could stop trying to steal the spotlight—my own sister, my own sister trying to upstage me in the only wedding I'm ever going to have—"

She was jealous of Frances, always had been. "She won't be standing up front—" Carolyn began.

"She'll elbow and push her way in, you'll see. And she's got that awful bug crawling all over her—I've lost my flower, Carolyn, someone's hidden it—for spite."

Carolyn stopped a man fleeing past with a white lily. It was one of those waxen things they sell at Easter in commemoration of the Passion, hideous beyond description. "Have you seen an orchid—"

"A *white* orchid," her mother said.

"I'm in charge of the potted plants, you'll have to ask Gregory about the cut flowers." And he vanished.

"She's got it," her mother shrieked. "She's holding it right in her hands." With a bound she went by Carolyn. "Frances Timble, that's *my* orchid."

"Of course it's your orchid. Whose else did you think it was—"

"You were going to take my orchid. Oh, how could you? *How could you,* Frances, when you knew—"

"Iris, you left it on the back porch. It'll freeze in this weather. I just brought it in so that—"

"I've never had a white orchid in my life and—*on the back porch?* Who put it there? Here, let me have it. Is it hurt? It didn't— oh, if it's been affected, I don't think I can stand it."

"It's all right, Iris. Nothing's the matter with it, it's just a little frosty around the folds." A black insect the size of a half-dollar was slowly making its way over Frances's shoulder, restrained only by a slender silver chain fastened with an ornamental silver safety pin to her dress. Its long hairy legs contrasted strangely with the bright fake stones glued on its beige back; the thin weasel-like head was rooting at the cloth of Frances's dress. Angelina, Frances's Mexican termite, smuggled in by handbag, was searching for her water-soaked wood, which, according to Frances, was all that was needed to keep her alive the next two or three hundred years. Carolyn felt vaguely sorry for the insect; when its value as a conversation piece ran out, so, she was sure, would its water-soaked wood.

"DON'T YOU DARE PUT THAT LILY THERE," Frances shouted into the other room. "My god, who ordered those? Did you order those, Iris? Well, they'll just have to go. Take them away," she commanded, advancing as if in full armor. "We are NOT having lilies, I don't care who ordered them. Haven't you got any gay little tulips and nice young daffs?" She lifted the offending pot. "Look at that disgusting thing, it's pollinated all over itself." She shook the pot and ripe yellow loosened from the stamen seeded itself over the waxen petals. The beetle clawed and clung to her shoulder.

"But, Frances, they—"

"No lilies, Iris."

"But, Frances—"

"I'll let it drop." She held the pot up menacingly. Angelina hung on.

"All right, all right," Iris agreed hastily. "Leave out the lilies," she advised the young man. "Just bring in the chrysanthemums and glads."

"*Glads?*"

"What's the matter with glads?" Iris asked innocently.

"What's the matter with glads?" Frances asked the world at large. "Nothing," she said bitterly, "except that they're impossible, that's all. They're for funerals, Iris, that's all they're good for, *burying people*. We are not burying Lois. This isn't a funeral. We had the funeral last fall. You remember Ada—you should, the way you boondozzled that poor old boob of a priest into getting her buried from the church. Listen, Iris, how'd you'd like me to post a couple of anonymous letters about how you finagled that? Excommunication, Iris, *excommunication*. Out go the lilies AND the glads."

"Well, if you really think—"

"I not only think, I know. And I've got to do something about that hat. I'd just like to get my hands on the salesgirl who sold you that hat. Jules is out with Erwin," she said to Carolyn. "He's mad as a wet hen about the car. That rather fits him as a description, don't you think? A wet hen. Something's the matter with the coils. When it isn't stopping, it's sputtering. Oh, here you are, lover," Frances said to her husband stamping into the front hall. "Is that big bad old car being good now?"

Jules snorted. "The son of a bitch—I beg your pardon, Iris— had a mechanical seizure on Ninth," he said to Carolyn through clenched teeth. "Right in front of the bloody Capitol, the coil or some such dastardly apparatus took it into its head to go on the fritz. *I had to be pushed*," he said in an outrage so intense it seemed apoplectic.

"Now, lover," Frances said soothingly.

"Don't lover me," Jules said, the only time Carolyn had ever seen him angry. There was something magnificent and wonderful in the way Jules finally turned on them all and, as Stu would have said, cut the crap. "I paid eighty-five hundred smackeroos for that motorcar and it wasn't to be made a jackass of in the midst of a hick town like this. Roots," he said, unable to control himself. "I must have been out of my mind. And you can quote me in any forum of the world—*Francesca*."

For once in her life Francesca was speechless.

"When it came into my cranium to make the purchase of that machine, THAT MAN told me it had the finest automotive engine in the world. You remember what he said about all those lubricated parts and the air-cooled engine?" Jules demanded of his wife. "How there were all those precision parts and microscopic adjustments? Well, what I want to know is what happened to this supersonic wonder when it expired under that excrescence they call the Capitol building, that's what I want to know."

"Never mind, dear heart, we can always go back to the Caddie."

"Go back to the Cadillac? I'll never be seen dead in that car again. It's as old hat as a Packard. We're going to get a Mercedes—a Mercedes *Three Hundred*," he said. "None of that tinny Two-twenty stuff for me."

He turned his attention for a moment solely on Carolyn. "I respect and love my wife," he said. "But do you know what she did? I'll tell you what she did—she got out of the car right there in the center of Ninth and started waving cars down, that's what she did. I've never been so humiliated in my life. I paid two hundred and forty-five dollars for that dress—I can show you the bill—and she treats it like a uniform." Abruptly he sat down on one of Iris's mohair chairs; it sent up a scream and he shot up, startled. "Oh, the furniture," he said after a moment. "It seems we all suffer, even inanimate objects. I won't drive home. They can come and *tow* it away. Dear girl, forgive my intemperate outburst. In my younger years I would have been tempted to turn to the coward's courage, but as it is I think I will avail myself of Iris's downstairs facilities and soothe my soul in the Eastern manner."

They watched him go, a poor crumpled thing. Maybe it was the jacket that made him look so old, one of those "youthful" plaids.

"He's never going to last out the winter," Carolyn heard Frances say in an awed tone. "I feel it. Right here in my bones. Just like Ada. I should have known last week, when he decided not to go bowling. With Ada it was the cards—oh christ, not more bad flowers. Don't bring those things in here, Esther—"

There Esther stood—battered hat, worn coat, flowers, galoshes and—Harold. God help them, she was in some kind of habit. Ready for the vows Carolyn supposed.

"They're for Lois, I brought them for Lois. Frances, what's *that* on your dress?"

"Lois isn't—"

"Frances, you've got some kind of insect *crawling*—"

"Stop that screeching, it's only Angelina. Why didn't I stay in Acapulco and tend my tan? Because someone has to watch out for

Iris's hats," she answered herself, "And Esther prowling round the halls with posies." Then she disappeared down the corridor, leaving Carolyn stranded between Esther and the Grand Master. The master stood, cock of the walk in basic black, and in her mother's teak hallway he had the nerve—*the nerve*—to hand her his hat. Carolyn handed it right back.

"Carolyn," Esther said in that hoarse, excited way she had. "Have you met the Reverend Cameron? I don't think you have. Harold, this is my niece, Carolyn, the one with the big house . . ."

Harold hardly pretended to listen. He stood for a moment looking at Carolyn as if he could see right inside her and he took it all in—excessive drinking, carnal lust, irresponsibility, adultery, the whole thing; then he appeared to grow bored with even this. Abruptly he looked away, gazing up at the ceiling, his fine dark eyes rolled back, his mouth quivering slightly. He had his hands tucked in in front of him as if in prayer.

Like something fated, it seemed to Carolyn she could read, like Madame Zolar, right into the future. Esther would leave him all her money. The Instrument would be toted around the countryside and played for the benefit of small, "appreciative" audiences, Harold ending his days somewhere in Vermont on one of those nice, inbred mountainsides. The money all used up, but not quite all the charm. A great sense of relief swept over her. They would be over and done with arguing about Aunt Clara's money once and for all. They would be spared the squabbles that came with the dividing of the spoils. They might even be forced out into the world to make it for themselves.

Harold had closed his eyes; a far-away, dreamy look crept over his face.

"Is it coming?" Esther asked.

"It's coming," he said.

His voice died away; he seemed in some kind of trance; he had blinded himself, his eyes closed. Then he began to sway. He rocked back and forth, his hands folded in front of him.

"You ever get your visa?" Carolyn asked, trying to stop him, trying to be polite.

Harold answered, eyes closed. "They—ah—are—ah—working

—on—it." Without opening his eyes, still swaying, he said slowly, "Have—they—ah—begun—ah—the ceremony—ah—yet?"

"No, it's just about to begin. Ten minutes at the most. I've got to—"

"I haven't—ah—much—ah—time. It's—it's coming on—*It's coming on*—is she here?"

"Lois, *Lois!*" Esther shrieked at the top of her voice.

"It's coming—it's coming—"

"Lois, oh Lois, LOIS, come quick," Esther screamed at the top of her lungs.

"Merciful god in heaven, don't yell like that," Iris pleaded, bobbing up from behind the bedroom door, caramels, Carolyn noted, in hand. "What will people think—good heavens, what's the matter with that man? Is he *sick?*"

"It's coming—it's coming—"

"And what are THOSE? Oh, Esther, not flowers AGAIN!"

"It's come." Harold opened his eyes. "She has missed her opportunity for the emanations. They never come twice in the same day. What a shame the bride couldn't have made her vows while one of my apostolic moods was on."

In a few moments now the music would begin. Carolyn could picture Jules at the record-player holding the disk carefully in his immaculately manicured hands; when her mother gave the signal, he was to drop it gently onto the cradle, turn the switch; at the sound of the first strains Carolyn would start down the stairs, Lois after. Erwin would step forward, Lois would take his arm, the three of them would pass into the living room where at the "altar" Stu and Neal waited. There was no need to be nervous, they had practiced it very carefully the day before. Even Erwin understood his part. And he was so proud of giving her away.

As soon as the whole wedding party was at the altar, Iris would give another signal and Jules would shut off the machine. The service would begin. Carolyn wondered if the Justice of the Peace would use the word *obey*.

Lois came out quietly. Her face was drawn, tightened until it looked like a mask, but her hands in the long white gloves were still.

She would not remove those gloves. The ring finger had been unstitched; Neal would open it up, slip it back, and put the ring on.

Carolyn's dress was darker but close in pattern to Lois's. She wore gloves too; their shoes had been dyed to match the color of the cloth of their gowns.

In the deserted upstairs hall Lois hesitated, perhaps conscious, like Carolyn, that below them in the living room everyone waited; there were sounds from downstairs, the rustle of people taking their places, whispers of last-minute snatches of conversation, a cough that seemed close to a signal, the heavy sound of steps, a man's— whose? There were so few men left in the family. But now there would be a new one. A nice new one, Carolyn thought, remembering the moment three days before when she and Lois had gone to the airport and she had first seen the man Lois was going to marry. He was a miracle of seeming immobility in the midst of all that motion. Even Lois seemed to be coming apart with all the detail—blood tests, licenses, wedding crises. He was not what Carolyn had expected (she was not quite sure what she had expected), but he had something basic she admired. Nerves of steel, she had said to herself, watching him meet her mother for the first time. Iris had rushed up to them like an umbrella ready to unfold: without waiting for an introduction, without even saying hello, she had burst open. "We can't have a *Jewish* ceremony," she had said, "I'm sorry, but this is a Catholic household, my mother . . ."

"Mrs. Ashwell," he said very quietly, "we couldn't possibly be married by a rabbi. Lois isn't a convert."

"A convert?" Iris's bumbershoot went bust. It was clear the idea had never occurred to her, but now that it had—

"Anyway I'm sure that anything you've arranged will be all right. Look at these floors," he said, bending down. "They can't be real teak, can they? And they're in beautiful condition. You must work awfully hard to keep them like that." Carolyn could have kissed him.

In five minutes now Lois's whole life would be altered, and it came to Carolyn that Lois was frightened still; yet she managed a small smile. "I want to stop and see your father," she said. "There's still time."

Side by side they moved down the hall. The door to her father's room was open and Carolyn could hear him breathing unevenly; only a spark somewhere deep within his body kept him alive, held together by some force of the spirit of which he knew nothing, sick so long that all the hair on his body had been rubbed away, yet the eyes that greeted them were bright. Carolyn watched as her father smiled and lifted a frail hand. He seemed surer of himself than he had been in months and he looked—happy, that was the only word. He had his teeth in—and his fancy maroon bathrobe on. Dressed for the wedding. Doing his best. She wanted to cry.

Lois bent over and kissed him quickly; then she stood up and turned slowly around so that he could see the buttons at the back of her dress.

The room smelled of wasted flesh and half-functioning apertures; the head resting on the pillow looked more dead than alive, but for an instant, as Lois pirouetted before him, the inevitability of death did not seem so bitter to concede. The cold purity of Lois's blue dress was like a blaze, her father's smile a small spark of fire, and Carolyn herself a kind of flame of forgiveness, as if she had seen in her mind all the episodes and scenes that constituted her father's —and her own—shame and was able to view them at last with an objectivity that came close to pity. She was no longer blaming him, no longer holding him responsible for the checkered childhood which she once felt had contributed so much to her own inability to bring to adult life the values by which it could be successfully lived. Childhood errors, she felt, were simply that, mistakes made a long time ago: but it seemed to Carolyn that what was *childish* was in persisting to point to them as excuses. So what if she had been ashamed of the boarding house and humiliated by her father's not having a job the way other children's fathers did, so what if it was true she had grown up feeling stunted by an atmosphere of wrangling, accusations, bitter denunciations, was that any reason to excuse her own *knowing* licenses?

"Pretty," her father said through lips whose skin was so thin that it seemed like palimpsest, the wrinkles like the written history of his life over which on thin parchment the final summation had at last been written: he was a man like any other and he must die. His eyes knew it; the faintly running machine that was his body knew it; the frail, foliated hands, like paper flowers, attested to it; but the lips that had given their verdict for the future in that tribute, *pretty*, asked only that for today they might all forget it.

Carolyn bent and kissed him.

"You, too," he said with effort, "pretty."

She read, in the gentle flutter of his eyelids, then in their tired closing, how much these efforts had exhausted him. As she and Lois backed from the room, she would have liked to hold out her pity to him, and her compassion, the only offerings she had that might matter now.

Breathless, wild-eyed, her orchid palpitating up and down upon her panting breast, Iris met them at the top of the stairs. "Oh, my god, she's gone and done it again," she cried, flapping a paper-protected coronet of flowers in their faces. "Only this time she must have *bought* them because nobody's got one blossom in his back yard this time of year. Whatever are we going to do with them, she wants you to carry them, Lois. It's Esther—Esther, Lois—she wants you to carry these awful flowers and, oh, you know how Mrs. Post feels about bridal bouquets when it's—it's a *second* marriage."

"An offer of forgiveness, you're reinstated?" Carolyn turned and asked.

"No, I don't think so," Lois said. "I think—maybe she wants in her own way to make some amends, too. But keep the money of course," Lois said, smiling.

"It's this religious phase," Iris cried. "That man in the funny suit has got her going on all this charity stuff. I mean, I think it's nice she wants to help the poor, that's good of her, but—but these flowers —Lois can't carry these awful *red* flowers. It wouldn't look right. I tell you, sometimes I think it was a whole lot easier when Esther just made our lives miserable—you know—getting into trouble in those stores."

"Give them to the caterer," Carolyn said firmly, "and tell him to put them on the table, in a prominent place—it'll be all right, you'll see."

"But she specifically said she wanted Lois to carry them."

"She can't—"

"I know that, Carolyn. You know I know that, but does Esther know that?"

"Mother, it's time to start. Go down and give Jules—"

"He's been impossible, just impossible about that car. Do you know what he said to me? No, I won't tell you. I won't spoil your day. Impossible, just impossible—all of them. *Frances has been in the champagne.* You look lovely, Lois, just lovely, and you smell so nice. You didn't put perfume on your hair, did you? Oh, never put perfume on your hair, honey, it turns it gray. Oh, Carolyn, I don't know what I'd do without you, I really don't. If only you'd make it up to Ralph—that wonderful man—if only—you'll regret it every day of your life if you make this break permanent. Mark my words: when they made him, they broke the mold."

They stood at the top of the stairs as if suspended over a void. From downstairs, silence; here in the hall, silence; outside the very air held still, the sun fell noiselessly in that late-afternoon hush that was four o'clock. Lois, motionless, waited at the top of the stairs; nothing moved in her, not even the working of her breath, save her eyes, which were a thick, dark color, as if she had been overcome by an uncontrollable impulse to know at all costs what lay ahead. She seemed nothing but an act of will, less alive at this moment than that dying man down the hall; all her energy burned on some message she saw inside.

A fear seized hold of Carolyn which had nothing to do with the unnatural stillness, the fathomless color of Lois's eyes, the faint scratching sound, suddenly rushing to fill the void of that quiet, which Carolyn identified as her father in one of his battles for breath. She heard him cry once faintly, frightened, "Mother." Then he must have remembered and silenced himself; that pale, waxen hush fell again.

With an immense effort Carolyn tried to put from her mind the warning that had sounded inside.

If I were superstitious, she thought—and did not finish the thought.

If the car had been working properly, she thought instead, the whole thing would never have happened. She had had some shopping to do and she had been overcome by one of those uncontrollable impulses to go, regardless of whether the car ran or not. It was a gray day, unprepossessing; rain was imminent, but she set off anyway.

The dirt road in to the house had two deep tracks in the mud; even by walking carefully on the side, she saw her shoes were going to be a sorry sight by the time she reached the highway and finished the quarter of a mile to the bus stop. Still she persisted. There were some books she wanted to order, some things to talk over at the travel bureau. Not England, not Germany, certainly not Greece— the south of France and Italy . . . April and May, in Europe—if that woman were wrong.

Of course she was wrong.

Ralph would take care of the children. He was impatient to be back in the house. Did he think that when she came back—of course he did. She remembered what he had said to her on the phone. "I think it's a good idea you're going, Carolyn. I don't know—maybe —but don't worry about the children. You go ahead and make your arrangements, stay as long as you like, and don't worry about money, and then—then—Cat," he said in an imploring voice, "maybe when you get back—do you think there's a chance? Don't answer now," he went on hastily. "But think about it, just think about it."

What belongs to the body and what belongs to the soul? My Catholic childhood—the crows, she thought, seeing a flock of nuns in her mind, whose shrill calls echoed even yet inside her head. Even when I lay in Myers' arms, I did not forget. You never forget.

Unless you substitute one superstition for another.

That woman on the bus . . .

> *this card,*
> *which is blank, is something he carries on his back,*
> *which I am forbidden to see . . .*

My dear—the lady on the bus leaned over, touching tentatively the basic book of French that lay on Carolyn's lap—you are thinking of going abroad?

She was about my age, very attractive, with the refined finish of good schooling, good grooming, on her lap a small black expensive kid bag.

All my life, Carolyn thought, I've had an antipathy toward speaking to strangers, but that day on the bus I stepped out of character. "Yes," I said, "sometime next month—it's my first trip abroad."

The woman looked at her for a moment, removed her hand, rose, pulled the cord for the buzzer, and, as she passed toward the rear door, paused for an instant, standing in the aisle, a small smile making her mouth into a curve, the expensively-gloved hand on the back of the scarred bus seat. "I hate to tell you this," she said, "but it's something I think you ought to know. You aren't going to live to see France," she said and passed, perfectly groomed, down the aisle and onto the back exit steps. When the bus stopped she alighted, then turned, that small smile still on her face, and waved.

And if it were true? If it were true?

I shall face even that, Carolyn thought.

Be happy, Lois, Carolyn wanted to cry out, and turned instead and pressed Lois's hand, receiving in return a smile from which, at that moment, it was possible to imagine all trace of doubt had fled.

Chapter 14

FISHING about in his pocket, the best man experienced a moment of cold and clear certainty that the ring had vanished. Stu's heart contracted; for a moment he even thought he might faint, his heart was jerking about inside so crazily; then the shocks stopped, he felt himself begin to steady, his fingers closed round the small circle. He could have cried in relief.

Next to him, Neal, nervously grating his hands together, looked as if he were going into shock. What did the best man do when the groom fell over? Damned if Stu knew—but something would be expected of him. Something always was.

With this ring . . .

If Stu could have bestowed upon Lois the gift above all others, it would have been that she take her vows in all the solemnity and joy she wished—and to which he felt she was entitled.

But it was something she would have to give to herself: married not by a priest or by a rabbi under one of those canopies or however it was the Hebrew service went, but plainly and simply by a Justice of the Peace. A Justice of the Peace and champagne; it was something for his mother to swallow.

"Not here, not in my house, not after one of the sacred sacraments," his mother had cried, "no alcohol."

"No champagne, no ceremony," Lois had said. "I'm quite in favor of something non-alcoholic for those that don't want to drink, but on the day I marry Neal *I*'m having champagne."

The choice was clear and for a moment Stu felt sorry for his mother. She was caught on the one hand by the courage of her convictions and on the other by the depth of her desire. She wanted her wedding. And if she was going to get her wedding, his mother was determined, like God in the act of ordering His universe, to run it right, even if it was a second-time-round affair. She had worried, for instance, more about Lois's dress than Lois herself had, stopping Lois in the hall for the hundredth time to remonstrate with her because she wouldn't wear white. Mrs. Post—propriety would never permit his mother to call her familiarly Emily—was quite firm on the fact Lois could not wear a bridal veil or carry orange blossoms, but oddly enough she could wear the color of virginity. To his mother's great disappointment, however, Mrs. Post took a strong position against the inclusion of bridesmaids in a second ceremony. For his mother to be completely happy, every member of the family should have had a function; being a guest, though guests were in obvious demand since Lois had no friends here any more, did not satisfy her. She wanted them all to (her word) *participate*. Whenever she said the word, Stu had a picture of Eileen

dancing down the aisle as flower girl, scattering rose petals right
and left, of Pete and Peggy paired off as young blushing bridesmaid
and arduous usher for the affair. His mother simply could not get
it through her head that *age* ought to have anything to do with the
proceeding; in her eternal way of overcompensating for everything,
she saw all of them, most of all herself, as youthful and in full flower.
That the bride was well into her thirties, had been married before,
and had a child who would be present at the ceremony, seemingly
stopped her not. Since she had discovered that Mrs. Post had de-
creed Lois could wear white (if she could only be persuaded to
abandon the blue she had brought with her from New York), his
mother's imagination had run away with her. She had even wanted
to order those silver-and-white monogrammed boxes for the wedding cake she had seen illustrated in the blue bible of her *Etiquette,*
and it had taken all Lois's and Carolyn's persuasive abilities to
make her accept the unseemliness of such a thing; for a fact, on
their own they would probably never have dissuaded her, but page
249 of the old edition of Mrs. Post had put Iris to some perplexity.

*A wedding in very best taste for a widow is held in a small church
or chapel, a few flowers or palms in the chancel the only decoration.
There would be two ushers or quite possibly none. There are no
ribboned-off seats, as only very intimate friends are invited. Usually
the bride wears an afternoon street dress and hat—which may be of
color or equally well be white. There may be a family dinner after-
wards, or the simplest afternoon tea . . .*

"It doesn't say anything about a cake—or boxes," his mother had
insisted. After a moment she had said, puzzled, "But that's for a
widow, you're not a widow, Lois—not a real widow. Isn't there anything about—about *divorced* people?"

The only thing they could find was under invitations and it didn't
sound very encouraging.

"Well," Iris had conceded, but reluctantly, "that does sound as
if—as if we should do it—*subdued*—but I'm going to have a pretty
buffet, with flowers and ribbons and all the good things and—"

"And champagne," Lois had finished firmly and that was when
the fireworks had started.

It was to his mother's credit, however, that she hesitated. With the dream so close at hand, some would have snatched; it was characteristic of his mother, too, however, that before she did grab, she gabbed.

The champagne was in the kitchen now. A kind of sign perhaps. Girls did not take their proper positions in life until the women ahead of them had laid down the grinding stones and moved back from the principal place by the fire.

If only his mother could have felt some of the renewed sense of life that was going on around her—Lois getting married, beginning, in a way, all over again, he starting out all over, Carolyn—well, perhaps it was better not to dwell on Carolyn. His mother would never see that some bad endings were often necessary before you got good new starts. And, much as he liked Ralph—and was sorry for him at this moment—in his heart Stu felt that what Carolyn was doing was right. She didn't love Ralph, Stu had known that all along: she had been thrown into an affair by the evidence of her own empty life in an attempt to erase the sense of hollowness, uselessness, inside, and, like all affairs based on desperation, this one had brought nothing but more despair. You could not go looking for love, trying to ambush it; you could not decide on love, it was not an emotion the mind was ever successful at simulating; you could not even substitute ardor for admiration, much as you might hope to. What happened was always entwined with the unexpected; one of the main elements of attraction was how unprepared you were when emotion overtook you.

Christ, he ought to know. Standing in the middle of a hardware store going bankrupt all around him when Betty walks in, wants to buy some paint, doesn't know the goddam difference between a rubber base and a plastic one. That was how you got to the Alaskan wilderness with an old car, very little money, and high hopes.

He acknowledged the fault of an unconditioned and undisciplined mind, one that wanted too much—all right, he might never amount to much; all right, he had made a mess of his life; all right, he had a wife he didn't want and a kid he'd never knowingly have brought into the world; all right, lots of things, but they weren't going to beat him.

To hell with them. To hell with all of them, Stu thought, I'm not going to end up like the rest of them, he told himself, looking into his brother Pete's face, thinking, The poor bastard, he's really had it, he'll never break out.

Of all the worries in the world the meanest and most relentless was one of money.

Why couldn't Esther leave her money to Pete? He was the one who needed it. And who, he asked himself, ever led you to believe that because a man is in need he shall be given? Is not the saying, Those that have shall get?

A very wealthy woman: *what if she left me her money?*

I'd be free. Free. Buy my way out.

Cut that out, he said to himself sharply, can it.

Make it yourself or break it yourself, but don't look for external solutions. Anything that counts has to come from inside.

Being a man was fighting back. Somewhere, in each man's life, he felt, there was some small thing which made it have its own meaning.

He had been saved, he supposed, by his son.

The boy had not completely sundered the circle of doubt which was drawn about him, but an opening had been made, and since that night when he had waited hour after hour in the hospital for the coming of his child he had been trying to slip out. Sometimes he felt escape had finally come, but he had been too quick to seize on small signs; he had gone to the outer edge only to be thrust back, imprisoned once again in his doubts and despair; failures had unmanned him for a time, frustration had dogged him, defaults had frightened him. But somehow, through it all, he had managed to hang onto one thing: I have the boy, I won't give up.

And now what he was doing was—no matter how he tried to rationalize it—abandoning his son.

But, with more than half his life gone, he must make a break, must try a last desperate assault against the boundaries of that encompassing circle. If he did not break out this time, he would have to reconcile himself to the invincibility of those walls. Who wanted a lifetime of watching the clock turn 300 rotations a minute, 18,000 an hour, 432,000 a day, conscious each day and every moment that passed

passed only to repeat the incessant chant? How much longer do I have to wait until I get out—for good?

A failure.

Like his father, the constant crisis of his life to know who he was.

And now he lay upstairs husked of himself, a sick man upon a bed, who looked up at them with empty eyes. He had been seized by sickness, pinned down by old age; the very identifications he had once made with his body had been taken away and the mind—that trembling, uncertain reed upon which he had cast himself with desperate, imploring cries—had bent. Broken now, it lay no longer able to assist even the smallest call for help; while all around his father the family rustled, yet not one of them could be relied upon, strangers who had witnessed the agonized transformation from what had been, a body they all knew, to what was, the thin skin that covered the unknown skeleton, the wasted, weak frame upon which no label of love might be fastened, no tag of identity appended.

Failure had stripped his father of his actuality, had made him homeless in his own house, faceless and formless before his own mirror, unreal to his own bone and flesh, the three children—Stu, Carolyn, Pete—who had flowed from his loins. He would never know what he had been. Worse, he did not now care. Sickness had robbed him of all.

God, he wanted a drink. He must get hold of himself.

A drink.

None of that bad business since Betty.

Months and months.

The desire was one he could chart, no pressure from his mind, but a direct demand by the body, a concrete, physical thing he had to fight.

Shaking, perspiring, horribly thirsty—even his soul shook with thirst—he felt flooded with cold.

Just don't let the others notice, he thought.

The worst times were when the violence started coming out, when he got into a fight and—

I can't get drunk. No matter how much I want to, he said to himself. You hear? No getting drunk.

It was little enough to offer but it was all he could give to this day. To tomorrow he would try to bring better. It was the only code in which he could believe for a world where there were no rules.

The only person he'd ever really been able to tell he cared was Betty. "I want you to know one thing, I love you": he was always saying it. Could you say it too often? Did women ever get tired of hearing you say you loved them? He bet they did. Especially when what you were really saying was you needed—you wanted—something from them, an indirect demand for more of their time and attention, their understanding, that was what saying *I love you* so often meant.

The truth was he asked too much from her: he *expected* too much. Like not being upset, like understanding why she hadn't been asked to the wedding. "No, of course I don't mind," Betty had said. But Stu could tell she did. She minded like hell but she was going to be a good sport about it. What else, he wondered, could she do?

He sat stirring his coffee, not saying anything. The scene was far from over. If he knew women at all, she was just getting warmed up.

"I mean," she said, plunging her hands into the bowl wrist-high in flour. For some unearthly reason she had gone crazy on making bread. Ever since he'd said "Alaska" he'd come in to find her messing about with yeast and flour. He was always stumbling over bowls left over the hot-air registers so that the dough could rise—and trying to comfort her when the damn thing didn't do what it was supposed to. Betty's bread always had big holes in it or came out so heavy it made him think of some of the stuff he'd had in the Army.

"I don't blame *Lois*." Ah, now he saw. His mother was in the line of fire. "She can't do what she wants. It isn't *her* house." Since there was no denying that, Stu agreed as how no, it wasn't Lois's house. "And I know how your mother—"

"—makes life impossible for everyone," he finished for her. "So you see she didn't single you out, honey, she's impartial in her impossibility. We all suffer equally."

Betty stopped kneading and stared at him. "Very funny," she said and he had sense enough to keep still.

"And of course I can understand how it might be awkward," she went on, but she didn't sound as if she understood at all, she sounded as if she were being sarcastic, and she was, for a moment later she said, slapping a ball of dough on the table where he knew from past experience she would let it rest for ten minutes until she took to slapping it around again until it was what the book described as "smooth and elastic," wondering if after all he wouldn't come out maybe knowing more about baking bread than she would since she always forgot what step she was at and asked him to read her the directions, her hands were all covered in flour, it was amazing what a man got to know being around an enterprising woman, he had begun to believe the wilds wouldn't faze her at all, she'd just push the trees apart and plow her way through until she found a spot where she thought her bulbs would take hold. Christ, women—she was planning to cart a lot of crocuses out to Anchorage, there was absolutely no deterring her. She had said they needed a touch of civilization wherever they went and crocus bulbs were small and would split. If she took five hundred—*five hundred*—in a few years they'd have a whole field of flowers in the spring. Must have got it from her mother who, he remembered, always set a small portion of her weekly wages aside for seeds. "We had lovely zinnias," Betty had said proudly, though Stu himself considered them a punk flower, they had that funny smell. Now she looked at him with the calculating gaze of an artillery captain aiming to blow the enemy higher than hell. "I can understand the *problems*," she said, "but I can't understand your mother's *attitude,* why she won't even *meet* me."

"It's probably in Mrs. Post," he said wearily. "Something about your not introducing the second wife to your mother until you've gotten rid of the first. Old Emily's long on that kind of thing, how to meet who when and in what gloves."

"I suppose you think *that's* funny."

"I don't know. I just threw it out. How did it land? You find it funny, it amuse you at all?"

She gave him a measuring look. "A pet lamb makes a cross ram, my mother always used to say."

"Well, there you are, you can't score all the time."

"*You* don't think it's funny she won't even come over and meet me?"

"She's got a lot on her mind, honey—Lois getting married, the old man getting ready to pull out. When she comes onto a scene, she likes to give it her undivided attention. If she came over here now, she'd be at a disadvantage, all this other stuff on her mind. You might get the wrong impression, might even feel she was a nice, normal old lady ready to accept what was, and that wouldn't be fair to you, because of course the preplanned counterattack is her specialty."

"You shouldn't talk about your mother like that, Stu."

"Don't say it so automatically. Try to put a little feeling into it. *Don't* talk about your mother like that, Stu. *Don't talk about your mother like that, Stu.* DON'T TALK ABOUT YOUR MOTHER LIKE THAT, STU."

She flung the dough into the air, slapped it in the bowl, held a dishcloth under the faucet to dampen it, then covered the bowl and carried it into the front room and set it over the ventilator by the couch. He made a mental note to be on guard in that area of the room. He had followed her as far as the door and stood directly under the lintel, gazing at the bright eyes and outraged mouth that met his glance. She was in no mood to be fooled with, he could see, and yet he couldn't control the urge to lighten the heaviness that had come between them recently—the tension, he recognized, that had built up while she waited for him to decamp for the north. He warned himself to go easy and, smiling to show he had both their best interests at heart, he crossed the room and laid his hands lightly on her shoulders. She smelled of yeast and there was a scar of powder along one cheek. He felt an ambush of emotion overtake him and without realizing it his hands tightened, he drew her closer, wondering how it was possible a man could care so much for a woman and still not resist the impulse to hurt her. Even animals answered for the cruelties of their mating. What strange change along the line accounted for a man's ability to turn his face away from pain and say, I am not moved?

He smelled the soft shy odor of shampoo on her hair; he felt under his hands the thin skin stretching over the blood and bone he would never know but which he held now imprisoned in his arms, a strange and mysterious way the world worked, to show only the outside of things, when what went on hidden, inside, was what counted.

The dream—always the feckless dream. A man had to have it to keep going. If he gave up his dream, he went dead—unless he had sense enough to substitute another. Once he looked—really looked—at life, only a fool or madman could convince himself to go on. Unless he had a dream. Every single thing a man tried to hold to broke or rotted or wasn't strong enough to bear his weight. For what was there in the clear light of life as it really was? Failures from inadequacies, repeated disappointments, love based on false hopes and ambitions on insufficient talents, senseless sufferings, empty deaths, and worst of all the unescapable flash of *seeing* how one had deluded oneself in all one wanted—in the person one loved, the work one hoped to do, the structure one tried to make of one's life. Even to the god one wanted to believe in. With the best intentions in the world, with all the high hopes a heart was capable of, a man started on his way, dazzled by his vision, confident in his body, strong in the determination of his dream, only to find, a few steps on, how easily he stumbled, how quickly the images he had in his mind blurred, how readily his own body failed him, his own weaknesses undermined him, his own illusions betrayed him—to say nothing of how the world waited to fall upon him.

And if we find, Stu thought, we cannot trust ourselves, we always fall into the trap of believing two can never be as lonely and frightened as one. We make love the final mercy on which we throw ourselves.

Dreamer, *romantic,* he spat in disgust to himself.

Still, it wasn't just the crazy romantic in him. Knowing when to recognize what was real and accept it and when to recognize it but fight against it was one of the major problems of a man's life. The question was when to submit and when to rebel. And that took a kind of special insight, a different kind of knowledge from just seeing what was around you for what it was, you had to interpret it so that you came out with what was unalterable and what was able to be changed. Maybe a good part of a man's whole life was spent in recognizing when he was right to be romantic and when he had to bow to the unalterable.

A farm, he thought, a little square of earth of my own. I'd fence it off. Carolyn had a thing she said about how all life was the building of fences. Something she'd read in one of her books no doubt, but maybe she was right: maybe for anything to have meaning you had to narrow it down, to give your energy a place of focus, work where your work came to something, where it *showed*.

Get himself a hundred and sixty acres all his own, go slow at first, not try too much. Go up by himself, take a good strong tent, look over the land, go around day after day studying, planning—here's where it'd be easiest to clear and start the first sowing, and here a good place for the house, near a stream, he thought, we wouldn't even have a well, have to carry water, christ, he thought, think of that in the winter, those long winters, the stream frozen, how could you get water? Snow, he told himself, melt the snow. No electricity either, lamps—a wood stove. Awfully primitive. How could a girl like Betty do it? Break her, he thought. Probably me, too.

Go up there with a tent—start soon, say March, get up there for spring, the flowers—the mosquitoes, he reminded himself—camp out, take my time, start clearing, use the wood for a cabin, nothing fancy, one big room, that's all we'd need at first.

Christ, could he do it?

I'm forty-four, he thought, I've never had what you'd call a hard life. That's a good one, he thought. It's been hard enough. It just hasn't been—what was the word?—active.

My body's gone back on me, soft, an old man's apparatus.

He felt exploringly along the loosened flesh—the rubbery middle, the pouched hips, the fatty chest. He knew with a kind of final, unappealable sentence that it wasn't the kind of body you should take pioneering.

All you had to do was look at the figures to predict how close to the margin of failure you always were out there—almost three hundred and thirty thousand acres had been patented for homesteading, but only a little over twenty thousand were still being tilled for farming. Or like the guy said, "You should not arrive in Alaska to farm without a return ticket and a home to go back to."

A home to go back to. That was a rich one.

At each major step to his goal, he was faced all over again with the abandonment, the betrayal, of someone—his mother, his wife, his son.

How, Stu asked himself, could you explain to a nine-year-old boy that, though you loved him more than anyone else in the world, his coming had been an accident? And yet Stu had loved him, though he had never meant to have him in the first place. How could he explain to his boy that it was also possible, in love, to want to make a child, to show you had belief, that you wanted to proclaim your stake in the world about you, the world that had once seemed so worthless, that because you loved, you wanted a part of you to go on, you wanted something that served as a pledge in the world long after you and the children you had brought into it were gone—that that was precisely what you did believe, that it was a world that would go on.

How could he ever explain to his boy that it was with a woman other than his mother he wanted to make that commitment? How could any child understand?

But one of the things Stu believed in was telling the truth. Even to children. Perhaps most to children. They were the ones who might be helped by it. For the others, perhaps it was too late.

"Tom," Stu had said, bending over him, "listen to me. Your mother and I can't make it together. We've tried and we can't." Even to his own ears, his words had sounded of sophistry, and goddammit, he did believe in the truth and he would tell it, whether the boy wanted to listen or not. He would not fumble through those frail apologies his own father had used. He would tell the truth and be damned with it. "I'm going because I have to go. I've got to get out because if I don't something bad will happen. And none of us —none of us—will be able to help it."

For the first time the boy showed signs of listening.

"If I go there's a chance we all can pull out of this and organize some kind of lives for ourselves—most of all you. If I don't go, we'll all just stay stuck in the same mess. And we'll deserve what we get, which is nothing—worse than nothing. If something's wrong and we haven't the courage to change it, then we shouldn't blame anyone but ourselves. I hope you understand but if you don't, you don't. There are times," Stewart had said, "when I feel adults don't have to explain to kids. And you're still a kid, a big kid, but not big enough to see all of this. And in a way I hope you never are. I'll be going," he said, watching his son's face, "but it isn't permanent, Tom. You'll be living with your mother winters, to go to school, but summers, I hope you'll be with me. I'll want you to come and I hope you'll want to come. Alaska, maybe," he brought out at last. "I know it's pretty far away and all—that it'd be—well—way away, way out, in the woods. Wild. Nobody around. But you could come visit, summers. We'd figure out a way to get you in, I promise you that, and summers you'd come and be out there, learn to hunt and fish, there'd be plenty of hunting and fishing, a wild place like that, lots for a boy to do—what I mean is, Tom, I wouldn't want you to think I was—leaving you, you know, going that far away, to feel there was no place waiting for you there, too. In the summer. In the woods that way, hunting and fishing—you think you might like that?" he had asked anxiously.

"Sure. I guess so. I don't know. I'm not much good at using a gun, fishing—"

"But you could learn," Stu said eagerly to the son who had always liked to stay inside buried in a book. "Out there it would be natural—easier. Not forced, the way it seems to you here. You'd like it, I know you would. And you could bring books along, read, there'd be plenty of time to read—"

The boy stood up so that Stewart was forced to face him. "You're never—coming back—here?"

"No, son, I'm not. I thought you understood that—that it was all over between your mother and me." He stood up too, bringing his hand down on the boy's shoulder. "Damn it, son, I care about you. You know that. But I care about myself, too. I've got a responsibility to myself, too."

His son was quiet; his son never said much about how he felt, but Stewart saw something in his eyes. No matter what came after, what pretenses, what protestations, he had lost the boy. That night he had lost his son.

He had climbed the stairs wearily, knowing that ahead lay another scene with Ethel, the packing of a bag, going out into the

"I feel—I only feel terribly sorry I don't feel for you—the way you want."

"There's nothing can be done." It was not a question but a statement of fact: there was nothing that could be done, and there was no way he saw to answer. She turned. She looked on his face for his answer and saw, he knew, the end to any hope she might have had.

She did not weep; for a moment she made no movement at all, just stood there—stiff and hurt. It was all over, at last. Whatever was said and done between a man and woman had taken place between them; now all that remained was to part from each other forever. But wasn't that part of the pattern, too?

Coming down the stairs with his suitcase, he saw his son waiting for him at the bottom. Tom was standing there, still, patient, but there was something about the hunch of his shoulders that seemed to Stewart a warning. When Stu got to the bottom step, he put down his bag. "I wish you could come with me," Stu said. "I'd like to have you with me."

"Sure."

"I mean it, Tom."

"Yeah, you mean it, but you'll go and I'll—I'll be left *here*."

"But, son, even if you could come, even if there was a way for you to get to school up there, you—you couldn't just leave your mother."

"*You* are." The boy turned away. "It's all right," he said bitterly, "for *you* to talk about how you have to get out, it's all right for you to say you have a right to your life, you're older, you can do what you want, but kids—kids, they haven't got any rights, they just have to go along with what their parents tell them. Sure, I'd like to get away from here, go some place else, be different, but you can't take me, and Mom—she isn't going to go anywhere—"

Stewart took hold of the boy's shoulder. Tom struggled and pulled free, standing back with anger all over his face. "What you want is all right because *you* want it and what she wants is all right because *she* wants it, but who cares what *I* want? Who ever even asks? It wouldn't hurt none—"

"Any."

night—reminiscent of other arguments a long time back when they used to quarrel and he ran out into the night, headed into the first bar, picked a fight, landed up back home battered and beaten, and she took him back, always she took him back except for once, after the war, when she had shacked up with another man, before her legs and looks had gone and she had started to go downhill at that dizzying rate of speed; why had she always taken him back? She didn't love him, they were just, he supposed, bound to each other by so many years of inertia and the lack of any effort to make the break. Anyway, a break for what? He had something now but she had nothing.

Nothing, he thought as he stood in the door and looked at Ethel, a large German girl gone blowsy, her face so misshapen in the mix-up of her emotions that it was hard to recognize her as the girl he had once desired above all else. "What is it now?" she asked suspiciously. "What you want now?"

He tried to think how to phrase it.

"The least you can do is answer when someone talks to you, that's only common decency, anybody knows that, someone talks to you, you answer back."

He waited and then saw that his patience, his indifference, his tiredness, were only inciting her to anger. In order to shorten the scene, he would have to pretend he was angry, too. He tried to sound so as he said, "Oh, for god's sake, let it go, I'm all tired out. Let's just call it quits without the dramatics and save ourselves a lot of trouble and turmoil." But even to him his voice seemed weak and unconvincing. One trouble all his life had been his inability to feel the angers he should feel and falling into the ones he shouldn't.

"I'll bet you're tired. Oh, I'll just bet you're tired, out screwing around—"

"Let it go," he said wearily. "I wasn't out screwing around, if that's what's eating you."

"You expect me to believe that? You expect me to swallow a bunch of crap like that?"

"I don't care what you do, Ethel, and that's the honest-to-god truth. I have no interest at all in what you do. Now let me past."

"You may not care—you never cared—never—if you'd cared—"

She was moving rapidly from outrage to self-pity. "Look at me," she cried, and involuntarily he found his eyes riveted to that aged, atrophied face, as if all her features had alchemized into iron.

"Don't," he said, feeling distaste as a physical thing, like something rotten inside his mouth.

"I'm your wife, why shouldn't you look at me?" She had moved close to him, her eyes wild, her breasts bobbing up and down under the sleazy housecoat only half pulled around her. He had a moment of absolute horror when he thought she might throw back her robe and expose all her aging flesh to his eyes, hopeful of moving to something she could understand, sensuality, but it was something else she had in mind. Fear, he saw, had made her eyes that bright.

"You want someone young. You've worn me out and now you don't want me no more, you want someone young and pretty. But what about me? What's going to happen to me?"

He cursed her, he cursed himself because he couldn't stop himself from being sorry.

"Ethel," he said gently, "it's not going to do any good, no matter what you say. I wish it would, but it's not. I don't love you any more, I can't help it, but I don't. What you've got to try to understand is I won't, no matter what you do or say, I never will. I'm sorry but I just won't, I *can't*." But he saw he still hadn't got through to her. "It's all over, Ethel. I'm sorry but I can't help it."

"You don't care nothing at all?"

He shook his head.

"Nothing?"

"I'm sorry, Ethel."

"You got no right," she said, turning away, leaving the way open for his escape, but he had to stay, he had to finish it once and for all. "No, it's like *I* got no rights, no rights at all."

"But you don't love me, Ethel. You haven't for years."

"I'm used to you and—*anyway I haven't anybody else.*"

He saw that was the worst of it: she didn't want him but he was better than no one. No one couldn't break the quiet of too still a house. No one could not make it possible to pretend things might get better. No one could not give you the illusion you were living

life the same as everyone else. She needed someo one did. But in this world it was everyone for hin the reconnaissance for love. And as with everyth wars, you needed a lot of luck to come out whole.

Trapped behind the lines of love, you lost all h one could come save you, you had to crawl out on said that to Ethel, she wouldn't know what he wa but he owed her at least the duty of trying to explai

"I did try," he said, and watched that body, as if it wounded, move slightly—automatically—away from words inflicted. "You remember," he amended, "I tried." She was still, listening. "I know you tried, E that. But it just wasn't there." He asked for help. Bes lently in his heart, with his mind, calling upon some fo not even identify to give pity where pity was due, to le for this instant the tongue that would tell her the things to know, those things that would help her go on. He ask this instant to be made a gentle man.

"Ethel, I've done a lot of wrong things. I've *wronged* yo know it, and if it's any help, in my heart I'm truly so ashamed. But the wrongs didn't come because I hated you— hate you. They came because I didn't love you. And that's that's something I can't help. We can't help whom we love the terrible predicament we're all in: we seem to have no over the people to whom we give the most important thing w —the—the—" Stu searched for the word—"the commitm ourselves. I never made that to you—I tried, but it's not som that comes consciously, it's not an act you make with your i it's something that happens deep inside, over which you hav control, and that's what makes it so terrible, it all seems some —somehow—like chance. Whether you get it or you have it so times and then you lose it and you haven't got it any more, you don't see what you did to deserve it, or not deserve it. It j comes and goes."

He had done his best; he waited.

With her back to him, she said in a barely distinguishable voice "You don't feel nothing for me?"

"—*none* to at least ask, but you don't even do that. You just come and make speeches and do what you want. You don't care about anybody but yourself, no matter what you say. It's easy enough to *say* you care but—" Pulling up inside himself with a hunched movement, abruptly he turned his back on his father and flounced from the room. Stu heard him bang the back door.

Help me to be a better man.

The thought had come unexpectedly and he looked at it for a moment without taking it in, disowning it. A man liked to think he had been as good as he could. But the truth called him out on this. So that he answered instead, I have fulfilled, to the best of my abilities, my obligations to the past; failures, such as they are, I have put aside since I have acted upon them and have now come to the moment when I must leave them behind. A time has come to put away the past and to try myself against the future, and if I break upon that, it will be a better thing, an effort well spent. A man, for all his limitations, ought to live ahead. One day the boy would understand.

Beware, I come, his heart called out.

. . . *pronounce that they are Man and Wife* . . .

Stu stiffened and attached a smile to his face. Shining, her eyes held to his, she came toward him. It was the look in Peggy's eyes that alarmed him more than anything else. "It's—it's just wonderful, that's what I think it is, just wonderful, going to a whole new country—"

"It's a state now—"

"Well, yes, I understand *that*," she said, looking vague and distressed. "But it seems like another country, doesn't it? I mean, going through Canada all that way—" She paused, her eyes searching his. "You know, I never knew there was any place you could do that any more, go pioneering. It's just wonderful there are some places left you can do that, isn't it?"

She'd never know.

"But what I mean is, after you get there—after you—what do they call it?"

"Get staked out?"

"—get staked out, then—I mean—" She was hanging onto him like she'd never let go. He tried to shake her off, but she was glued to him. "Stu," she said in an imploring voice while he thought, Here it comes, "Stu, take me with you. Take me with you, Stu, it's the last chance I have—"

Holy christ, she was going to cry.

"Please don't leave me here, I don't want to stay here, Stu. Don't leave me here, please don't leave me here—"

He looked down on her, half hating her. He had never given her any encouragement, but goddammit she hadn't needed any, stuck out there with the unending boredom of housework and the dreary monotony of never having money enough to escape into illusion every once in a while. If Pete had been able to buy her a fur coat and take her to Bermuda this might never have come up. She could have fed her imagination on other fodder.

My god, what he wouldn't give for a drink.

Back there again, he thought.

He was afraid to touch her. If he touched her she might go completely to pieces, disintegrate right before his eyes. And why not? All kinds of sins against the heart were committed that must be recorded there unseen; could not a time come when that frail vessel —pumper, purifier, preserver of life—refused to do its duty any longer?

She looked terribly white, her dark eyes dilated, one hand in a fist over the trembling of her mouth. In the woods, something Lois had said in the woods—*the only way we can start over is with truth, no matter how much it hurts.*

"I'm sorry, Peggy, I can't do it. You know that."

She shook her head. No, she did not know. "You mean you won't."

He let her read the answer in his eyes.

She refused to accept the verdict. "I won't stay," she said stubbornly, but she really didn't mean it. He could tell even she didn't hold any conviction of what she was saying.

What chance, he wondered, did the weak really have? When they couldn't even convince themselves of their delusions.

Why was it he always had to see such things so clearly? That was the thing that paralyzed all constructive action: he had commitments to the past that would not permit him to go ahead but seemed to keep him, with that perverse set of notions he had that he regarded as values, forever transfixed in an impossible, unmoving present.

At forty and after six kids she wanted to go back and start all over again. The worst part was that he couldn't blame her. Wasn't that what he was trying to do himself?

"I won't stay . . ." she repeated, standing there with the tears streaming down her face. What confounded and confused him most was the sense of boredom he was experiencing. It was all so predictable and so inevitable. He had the feeling he'd gone through it before, and often. Women were always clutching at you, asking you to mend their broken hearts or patch up their ruptured bank accounts. The tears did not move him; he was not, to be truthful, even interested. And it was this indifference more than anything else that inspired in him a feeling of his own accountability for her unhappiness. If he could not identify with pain—as, it seemed to him at this moment, he could not—how in god's green, bountiful, beautiful, and empty world could he expect to become better than he was? What was the use of running to Alaska to try to be a better man when all he would carry along would be the same old inadequacies that had hampered him in Springfield? Yet, at that moment, in the midst of Peggy's tears, her heartbreak, what was raging through him was a great greed to live, to do many things quickly, to grab hold of the essence of life and squeeze it dry. He felt that risk was somehow in proportion to the passion one extracted from events. The man who took a chance, plunged in over his head, understood the therapy of excitement; perhaps that was why Stu was going for the long shot. To the timid belonged the quiet hearth, the quiet heart, but to the restless and disaffiliated . . .

One of the troublemakers, he told himself, always have been, one of those who bring about their own ruin and—worse—the ruin of others: Betty baking bread and lugging a lot of bulbs out to the wilderness. Absurd, absurd!

Yet his heart yearned for such strange and irrational scenes.

To have hope, Stu believed, was a good thing.

Could he not give this poor creature in front of him a little of that? Why couldn't some man take the trouble to make her happy, that was all Peggy wanted out of life.

All?

The most difficult thing to find, he knew, is the love we think we deserve. No wonder eighty per cent of crimes of passion were committed against family or friends.

"Peggy—"

She looked up.

He tried smiling.

She looked away angrily.

Betty (thank god) would never act like this.

They all do at one time or another, his reason argued with him.

Still there was strong stuff in Betty. She was the kind of woman who should always have been holding in her arms an animal or a child, and though life had denied her both, she didn't blame anyone, he knew, but herself. He liked that in her, that sense of responsibility to what was right; but what he loved in her was the ability to believe the bad things might be of use, the wrongs of the past lessons from which her future might profit. And she had taught him that, too, bless her.

Life *is* unfair, he thought, but we must get on with it.

He took hold of the girl in front of him and held her firmly, forcing her to look up at him. "I can't find your way out for you," he said. "You know that, don't you?"

No, she knew no such thing, her eyes said.

There was nothing, he knew, he could do for her. She had asked of him what he couldn't give, as people asked of one another time and again things they could not, or would not, give. An impasse beyond bridging; forever after he would be an enemy to her.

So be it, he said to himself. There are enemies all about. Let the evening and the enemies in, he thought, I am ready for them.

Chapter 15

THE PANIC had passed, that moment of extreme misgiving Lois had experienced for an instant upstairs just as Carolyn finished fastening the last recalcitrant button. "I don't think I can go through with it, Carolyn," she had said. "I think I've—I don't know what's the matter with me, I'm just scared to death."

"Is there any liquor in here? Anywhere around?"

"I don't know. There's champagne, downstairs—but whisky, I don't think so. I feel as if I'm coming all apart, everything's breaking up in pieces I'll never be able to put back together."

"Lois, everyone gets cold feet at the last moment like this. Here give me that," Carolyn said, taking a cigarette Lois was playing with but had not lighted. Carolyn put it on the edge of a clear glass ashtray with yellow printing. INTERIORS BY ELONG, FURNITURE AND OFFICE EQUIPMENT, it said. There wasn't an ash on it. "Haven't you been smoking all day?" Carolyn asked curiously.

"No," Lois said. "I didn't feel I could. Not the way I am."

"I'll get you one of those Miltowns—"

Lois shook her head. "I've had two already. They just made me feel—kind of sick." Her hands, held out in front of her for observation, were trembling. "I'm like that all over," she said.

"In another hour you'll laugh about it."

Lois looked at her.

"You love him, don't you?"

Lois didn't say anything.

"And you wanted to get married, didn't you? You've never thought of anything else these last couple of weeks—"

A knock sounded loud and imperative on the door. "Lois, you

ready?" It was Iris. "It's almost time. You know you don't have a lot of time—"

"I know, I'll hurry."

Carolyn stood up. "If you really have doubts—" she began.

"I feel this is the only chance for happiness I have—maybe the last chance—and I want some happiness, Carolyn. I know that's selfish—but I can't help it, just some, not a lot, but enough to get back where I can feel the future really holds something. And maybe that's what I'm afraid of, that I'm asking too much, that I have no right to happiness, nobody does; it isn't one of the conditions laid down about living."

Her legs as she came down the stairs had been unsteady, her hands shaky, but when Lois reached the bottom and Erwin held out his arm, a sudden strength had come over her. He was smiling, everyone looking at her was smiling, even Esther, who, as if on principle, never smiled, was smiling.

Around her they were all gathered, people who were part of herself, sharers in experiences that had shaped them all before they had started their solitary journeys toward the self. She loved them —some more, some less than others, but for all of them she cared as one cares for what one has been given that cannot be denied, the body one uses to implement the mind, the family one finds as a focus for what must come to be called discipline, those who serve the filial tyranny and those whom the heart finds for its own. The child. And now. Neal.

You mustn't be afraid, she told herself.

I have always been afraid, she thought.

I will neither yield to the song of the siren, nor the voice of the hyena, the tears of the crocodile, nor the howling of the wolf.

I believe in Neal, Lois thought. I believe in myself.

We have come together to be better.

Even Esther had her own notion of salvation. Esther had her flowers. The link between the living and the dead—flowers, earth, her mother's earth, the lovely earth which, when her mother turned her back on it, came to reclaim her, to take her back where she belonged, but the price it claimed for her defection was final, to show perhaps how fatal that rejection had been.

And, as if in benediction, just before they started toward the improvised altar, she felt at last she understood in some way why her mother had abandoned life.

Instruct us in that hardest lesson of all, how to learn to love, she cried out to the gods in which she had no belief, how not to be afraid of life.

Tears bubbled over Iris's eyes. Her mouth quivered, her hands were cradled protectively about the orchid driven into her bosom with a pink plastic pin. Even the fake flowers on her hat trembled in trepidation. "It was so lovely," she exclaimed, throwing herself against Lois, "and now it's all over."

Lois tried to put her arms around her but Iris pulled free, flung herself back, hands clawing to keep from falling. Clutching Lois, she cried, "I only wish your mother—your poor poor mother could have been here. Oh, honey, you were a lovely bride." Then, unbelievably, the face cleared. "Come with me," Iris said briskly. "There's something I want you to have."

At the foot of the stairs, she paused for a moment, looking over her hall. The floors were scuffed and streaked, water-stained from Christmas. "That machine never did any good, not a bit of good at all. You have to get down on your hands and knees to make any real impression, you have to use elbow grease. I should have known that machine was too easy. You don't get anything you want that easily."

But instead of going up the stairs, she turned. It was to the back bedroom, the old sewing room, that she led Lois.

Iris bent down before the dresser and began a tug-of-war with the bottom drawer.

"Here, let me get that for you," Lois said quickly.

"It's a little blue box I'm after," Iris said. "Enamel. On the right side."

But the drawer would not give.

Lois forced her full weight against one side and shoved; she heard wood splintering, a grating, menacing sound, but when she tried to slide the drawer forward, it resisted; then, an instant later, it came free, she was looking down on old frayed but once elegant underwear. "From my trousseau," Iris said sadly. "They come to pieces if you put them on, but I've never been able to bring myself to throw them away." Her fingers fell lightly on an embroidered slip. "Mama did that," she said, and then an instant later, "or maybe Ella—I don't remember now. They were both lovely, lovely sewers. Of course Mama had trouble with her finger—you know she pierced it on the sewing machine, and it went stiff on her. It seems like yesterday. And it was forty years ago at least. Time is such a funny thing."

She reached to the end of the drawer and took up a small blue enameled chest. "My jewel box," she said. "You know there used to be some nice stones in Stewart's family. Nothing's left now—except this." Iris opened the top and took out a small chain with an elongated crystal teardrop at the end, a floating opal.

"I want you to have it, Lois. I was going to give it to Carolyn or Peggy, but I never did. I don't know why, the time just never seemed right. I want you to have it, honey." To the look on Lois's face, she said, "Because I love you, honey, just like you were one of my own, and because you gave me my wedding, I got my wedding at Sans Souci, it almost makes up for everything, and because—

"Because your Mama would have wanted you to have something to pass on, you know, to your own."

When Lois came upon her, Peggy was alone, slumped against the old Morris couch in the second parlor, the "family" room, eyes averted, hands joined, looking as unwanted and ugly as a discarded Kleenex. Elated, ebullient, almost effervescent (the champagne consumed, especially by Frances, with such relish), Lois was unable for a moment to understand; then apprehension, pure, simple, and without need of analysis, took hold of her.

"I hope you'll be very happy," Peggy said. "A long life, a long and happy life." She looked away. The head lifted itself, a pale thing with almost sightless eyes. "It was a lovely wedding, it really was," she said in a glazed, recitative voice. "And of course Mother Ashwell, she always hoped, you know—"

Heels clattered overhead on the stairs. Voices—happy, wine-tipped voices—touched the air. A door banged, footsteps shook the hall, all around laughter rose and fell, voices moved and soared, the world seemed to be opening out, but Peggy gave no sign of having heard.

"Mother Ashwell," she said, "she used to drive me crazy and now I hear her but it doesn't really get through to me. Not the way it did. So maybe I've changed, too. Maybe we've all changed." She looked down at her thin, red, ugly hands. Impatiently she raised one and pushed back the hair that had slipped over her forehead. "I used to envy Carolyn so. I'd look at her pretty clothes and her lovely house—Ralph was so considerate, she could have anything she wanted, and now it seems like she's no better off than I am. You could have knocked me over with a feather when I found out they were breaking up. I just couldn't believe it, but maybe it just goes to show— And you, I hope you don't mind my saying it, but you know I always thought you'd—well, find someone that was— right. Erwin, you, Carolyn, Stu, why can't any of us be happy? But of course you'll be happy now," she said as if in afterthought and in a voice so dead no one would have believed her.

"You want to know something, something awful, something I've never told anyone else?" She didn't wait for Lois to answer. "Well, all this time, for years and years, I used to think Stu and I—" She began to wring her hands, teeth pulling at her lip. "I mean, I used to think about him the way you shouldn't. I used to think he was going to come back to Springfield, this was a long time ago when he was still away, and, I don't know, something would be changed. And then he came back and Ethel was with him, she was going to have a baby, and then I was going to have Stevie, and everything was just gone out of me, so I just sort of went on, year after year just going on. I kept going, what else could I do, getting up every morning to the same things, all the awful washing and ironing and doing dishes and cleaning that I hate, and Pete coming home, it was worse when he was in the house, sometimes I wished he'd *never* come back, but I kept going on, I still had a little hope left, I think, not much but a little, and then Mother Ashwell, she called up and she said, you know, that Stu and Ethel were going to split up, and it's silly, I see that now," she said, clutching her hands in front of her, "but I thought—*would you believe it, Lois, I thought it might be because of me,* that Stu might have felt the same way, and then the day before Christmas Pete didn't go to work, he went out and got drunk and I thought, this is the last straw, the absolute last straw, so I decided—I know it sounds crazy, but it didn't seem that way at the time, it seemed like what I *should* do—anyway I decided to say something to Stu, and you know what, Lois, all these years, all this time I had thought there was something there, there was nothing, nothing at all, he wasn't leaving Ethel because of something he felt for me. I don't think he even knew what I was talking about, I think he was just—just *embarrassed.*

"It's as if—as if I *can't* go on, there's nothing to go on for, not one single solitary thing in the future I can see to go on for. I shouldn't be saying this to you," she said breathlessly, "not today. But I've got to talk to somebody, I've just got to. Lois, oh Lois, be happy, will you? I want someone to be happy. Oh, Lois, what's going to become of me, why did this all have to happen to me? I never wanted my life to be like this, I never wanted to end up like this. Just tell me this: what's the point of all this unhappiness—of all *this*—"

Before Lois could try to frame an answer, any answer, she said all in one breath, "I do hope you're happy, I really do. And I mean, talking like this on your wedding day—"

The blue bridal dress, the blue bridal shoes, blazed up at Lois. What could she say?

"How will I ever get over this?" Peggy asked. Her head dropped, her hands dropped, nothing about her seemed alive.

There was no answer, unless, Lois thought, you had it, inside, where it might have come from from the start, or where, God, or whoever it was, willing, you were let learn it.

In the silence Lois unclasped the chain around her neck. "Take it," she said, holding out the opal, which was, after all, perhaps Peggy's anyway. "I don't know how I can help but I want you to have this. Iris gave it to me—" Peggy looked pained. "She gave it to pass on, as she said, 'to one of my own.' " Giving Peggy an opal when she was asking for a new life—trying to make her think they were alike, they were all alike, all of them 'one of my own'—oh the cheapness of it, the cheapness of it.

But I meant well, Lois wanted to cry out. But if you do not believe in God, from whom do you ask forgiveness? To whom do you pray? Surely not to the cold, uncaring stars.

Nevertheless, she thought, you sent out messages. Perhaps in the small infinitesmal hope that there was something somewhere to hear and to answer, to hold out hope.

And who knew? From all those gaseous unexplored masses, who knew? Another solar system, another sun, another planet like this one, another pale promising Christ to come and make it all have meaning.

For surely somewhere there had to be an answer.

Otherwise what good were the rituals? What good were any of their efforts? Their passages? What good were even they themselves?

So that it was she, not Peggy, who began to cry. For she had seen that you can never idealize the world into what you want it to be. Not even on your wedding day. And certainly not with a few words, a small gift, and the notion that compassion was enough to heal the weak's wounds.

But Peggy did not cry.

She held up her shining stone, she turned it slowly in her hands, the milky fluid in the stone catching the light, the stone itself radiating its soft sweet hues, as if perhaps in some far off universe the dead's hearts were extracted, hung on trees, and dried to turn to semi-precious stone, in that land where diamonds glitter on the ground and the bushes bear human heads, where the sun rises and sets to the cry, "Glory be to the Forgotten King!" and life has at least half a chance of lasting long enough to form for itself a meaning, to find for itself some value, to be set at least in semi-precious stone.

For though at this moment Lois's eyes saw no meaning, no purpose, her heart rebelled at such a simple intellectual exercise. It refuted the obtuse simplicity with which at this moment the world had presented itself as nothing more than matter, an endless procession of events which added up to nothing.

What her heart told her was something in no way so simple, something not so easily understood, but something unperceived yet in the air, like an echo from that ancient music of the orphic lyre by which minds were moved, soothed, purified, and immersed in a god of their own invention. That was what life seemed: each man endowing god again and again in his own image. So that life might go on, and each man have his own peculiar cry of salvation: having lived, I have given, such as I could; and having given, I have been worth while, such as I am. I myself have made my own meanings, such as they are.

And this marriage, Lois told herself, is of much meaning. For me.

Outside the sitting room, it was growing dark rapidly, a silver sheen, stars, working their way through the velvet sky; all around, shadows were falling in stiff, straight flight through the branches of the trees. The tall tree in front of Sans Souci sent softly some offering to earth; it fell, with a small thud, upon the silvered ground; out in the darkening night a bird started to call with a strong, insistent voice, as if issuing a warning. The cry hung in the dark tangled trees and the thick bushes under which the past lay, shrineless, effaced, forever out of sight.

"I'm afraid of love," Neal had said in the midst of that act Christmas night, "because I know the terrible things that can be done in its name. I want you, I want you more than I've wanted anything in my whole life. Lois—oh Lois, look at me, it's going to be all right. I'm not afraid of what I am any more—do you understand? I can accept what I am. All of it. And part of that is because of you. Because you—I don't know how to say it—because *we* are what we are, and we can change some of it, but the rest, we couldn't change that and still be ourselves. I wouldn't want to change you—even the fears the good Jesuit fathers put in you, so why should I—why should I want to change what I belong to? Hold me," he said. "Put yours arms around me and hold me. I need you," he said. "Oh god, how I need you."

Out in the twilight it was very quiet and peaceful. Now dies the day, she thought, the birds are still, the woods at rest, and for a moment not one lamp is lighted.

What we have learned, she said to herself, is not to count alone on words, or even on images, but on what has happened to us, what has passed inside. When we feel the worst has happened, then we can love again since there is nothing to lose or fear any more: that lesson which, put simply, is to give back what we should like to receive, whether we'll ever receive it or not. All love is an act of generosity—even the falling of leaves and the coming of darkness. Those who have traveled far respect stillness. And self-respect.

Blind poet, take me into your all-seeing heart and reveal the eternal mysteries; sing of all I am and can become.